dominique

NEVER SHALL I LEAVE YOU SERIES

dominique

robert holliday

Trilogy Christian Publishers

A Wholly Owned Subsidiary of Trinity Broadcasting Network

2442 Michelle Drive

Tustin, CA 92780

Copyright © 2024 by Robert Holliday

Scripture quotations marked ESV are taken from the ESV® Bible (The Holy Bible, English Standard Version®), copyright © 2001 by Crossway Bibles, a publishing ministry of Good News Publishers. Used by permission. All rights reserved. Scripture quotations marked NIV are taken from the Holy Bible, New International Version®, NIV®. Copyright © 1973, 1978, 1984, 2011 by Biblica, Inc.TM Used by permission of Zondervan. All rights reserved worldwide. www.zondervan.com. The "NIV" and "New International Version" are trademarks registered in the United States Patent and Trademark Office by Biblica, Inc.TM Scripture quotations marked NKJV are taken from the New King James Version®. Copyright © 1982 by Thomas Nelson. Used by permission. All rights reserved. Scripture quotations marked KJV are taken from the King James Version of the Bible. Public domain.

All rights reserved, including the right to reproduce this book or portions thereof in any form whatsoever.

For information, address Trilogy Christian Publishing

Rights Department, 2442 Michelle Drive, Tustin, Ca 92780.

Trilogy Christian Publishing/ TBN and colophon are trademarks of Trinity Broadcasting Network.

For information about special discounts for bulk purchases, please contact Trilogy Christian Publishing.

Trilogy Disclaimer: The views and content expressed in this book are those of the author and may not necessarily reflect the views and doctrine of Trilogy Christian Publishing or the Trinity Broadcasting Network.

10 9 8 7 6 5 4 3 2 1

Library of Congress Cataloging-in-Publication Data is available.

ISBN 979-8-89333-366-4

ISBN 979-8-89333-367-1 (ebook)

TABLE OF CONTENTS

Foreword 7

Preface 9

Chapter 1 11

Chapter 2 19

Chapter 3 25

Chapter 4 29

Chapter 5 37

Chapter 6 47

Chapter 7 53

Chapter 8 61

Chapter 9 67

Chapter 10 73

Chapter 11 81

Chapter 12 89

Chapter 13 93

Chapter 14 99

Chapter 15 103

Chapter 16 107

Chapter 17 115

Chapter 18 123

Chapter 19 131

Chapter 20 139

Chapter 21 147

Chapter 22 155

Chapter 23 163

Chapter 24 167

Chapter 25	175
Chapter 26	183
Chapter 27	189
Chapter 28	197
Chapter 29	203
Chapter 30	211
Chapter 31	219
Chapter 32	227
Chapter 33	235
Chapter 34	239
Chapter 35	249
Chapter 36	255
Chapter 37	259
Chapter 38	265
Chapter 39	271
Chapter 40	279
Chapter 41	283
Chapter 42	291
Chapter 43	297
Chapter 44	301
Chapter 45	305
Chapter 46	309
Chapter 47	315
About the Author	321
Endnotes	323

FOREWORD

Dominique portrays a captivating picture of the delicate struggle that unfolds in the lives of people who search for a lifestyle of pure authenticity while encountering a more common routine of duplicity. Sometimes, the conflicts are glaring; other times, these conflicts are much more subtle—either way, they are universally present in the imperfect world that desperately needs forgiveness to be more prevalent and persistent.

The author, Bob Holliday, crafts a tender story that combines biblical wisdom with experiences that most people encounter, pursuing the heart of a heavenly God while wrestling with challenges of living in a troubled world with personal weaknesses, limitations, and corrupted influences. These words of King Solomon whisper through the story: "Truly, this only I have found: That God made man upright, but they have sought out many schemes" (Ecclesiastes 7:29, NKJV).

I have known Bob for many years, and I have witnessed his humility as he lives out his desire to one day be made perfect and complete and completely purified by the saving grace of a forgiving and just God. He models long-suffering, mercy, and humility as he engages individuals in a culture whose hungry tentacles seem to drag and pull individuals from their desires for purity, unselfishness, and truly joyous living. With many years as a hospice chaplain, as an educator, and as a servant-hearted leader, Bob personally embraces these struggles with the truths of a just and merciful God to guide him. His friendship and personal counsel always deliver a keen understanding of the tension between living with earthly restrictions while pursuing heavenly callings. I believe that Bob's intimate portrayal of individuals in *Dominique* will draw the reader to a mirror that challenges them to see themselves and others around them with more understanding. Most of all, to see that authentically walking clothed continuously with forgiveness is truly living and is truly what our world needs as well!

Todd Fonda

Community Outreach Coordinator

Auburn Crest Hospice

PREFACE

Prior to turning to chapter 1, please allow me a short moment together with you. My name is Robert Holliday. With this time, I am hoping to briefly explain why I wrote *Dominique*. Years ago, a depressing statistic was made known to me.

In 2019, two studies, Barna Group and *USA Today*, "found that nearly 75 percent of Christian young people fall away from the faith and leave the church." Three out of four of our children are led to believe the culture, not Jesus, has the answers they seek.

I have worn many hats. Here are a few of those hats. I have been a business owner, a Christian school teacher and principal, and finally, a hospice chaplain. The wearing of these varying hats has come to be a testimony to God and His amazing grace in my life, and I am thankful for those who came alongside me when at my worst.

I have stumbled in so many ways, but His grace is my life. By His grace, I have learned to apply that same grace liberally to fellow sojourners, not perfectly, but a Good Samaritan I need to be. I have found that this is how lives are changed and souls are won for the kingdom.

In 1 John 3:18 (NIV), Jesus said, "Let us not love in word, or in tongue, but in deed and in truth." It is hard for the lost to believe He exists unless they see His existence in the life of someone else. Only then can they receive and live by God's grand promise: "Never will I leave you; never will I forsake you" (Hebrews 13:5, NIV).

This verse is the recurring theme of the book. The hope in this book relies on the character of God. He either means what He says, or He is a liar. His clear proclamation in Scripture contends, "Never will I leave you; never will I forsake you." The faithful, those who believe that He exists, see unseen things and are willing even to die rather than deny their faith. That is the power of God in the believer and the testimony of God's care.

Hebrews 11:6 (NIV) says, "And without faith it is impossible to please God, because anyone who comes to him must believe that he exists and that he rewards those who earnestly seek him."

Dominique came to life on a rainy spring afternoon. I found her while driving, content in the splendor of the day, on the most beautiful mountain road. Coming to a sharp curve in the road, there in the drainage ditch, which ran along the roadside, were three teenage girls. They were dressed in uniforms, and it appeared as if they were distraught, marching as it were, face down, focused on their destination. Their destination, just a short distance away, a large Christian school, awaited their return.

It appeared to me something was amiss, as if their countenance had fallen. The Hebrew word for "countenance" is not just the look on your face; it speaks to the body, mind, and heart. Their whole outlook was negative. How many of these lost and lonely people cross our path daily?

Maybe living in that environment had something to do with these girls' downcast expressions; I do not know, but I do know God can turn the calamity of any environment, using just one broken and burdened soul to draw to Him, a world of people. That day on the road, in that environment, *Dominique* came to be. I saw her come to life.

Background: Dominique grows up in a wealthy family, where, along with a plethora of other worldly enticements, God fits neatly among the rest of their compartmentalized lives. This story takes you on her journey of suffering and the many failed endeavors she tries to find peace.

CHAPTER 1

Balance was impossible as they descended from the rain-soaked forest. They had lost the trail some time ago and were now woefully disoriented. Scrambling on the wet grass, they slid down the steep hillside until, finally, they saw the road below them. Struggling aimlessly to stay aright, they hoped to reach the road without a headlong spill into the waiting drainage ditch.

This drainage ditch not only funneled the water away to its destination but also doubled as a pathway that ran alongside the road, which led the traversing trio home.

You would think teenage girls would be more excited about an outdoor trek, but no, there was no playful screaming, no laughing. This roller coaster-like experience on the hillside was just a matter of fact, menial wrestling with the elements and gravity.

Frustration etched their faces; it was evident they hated this excursion. Dominique landed first in the ditch but did not even glance back to see how her two companions fared. Red-faced, forgetting the team idea, she just set her sights and strode off toward the finish line.

Since it had rained all day, the ditch was slippery as well. Dominique looked frazzled in her uniform. She was hot from the long hike and perspiring. Her scarf was off her head and loose around her shoulders. Her dark hair, pulled back in a ponytail, was soaked. Soaked, too, was her heavy wool coat, which weighed twice what it did when they left on what she considered a march through purgatory. Her ankle-length skirt, drenched and clinging to her, coupled with wearing knee-high rubber boots and the lack of footing in the ditch, just enhanced this endless nightmare. Stumbling, she cried out, "I don't belong here."

Just seconds later, holding hands, Sarah and Rachel sprawled into the ditch together; both, like Dominique, were exhausted and soggy. Frustrated by this degrading expedition, they looked at each other and then at Dominique striding away. Sarah, needing wipers to see Rachel through her dark-rimmed glasses, said, "There is no way we will catch up with her; let's just let her go."

Rachel disagreed, saying, "If we don't hurry and catch her before she gets back, she will tell Mrs. Martsen some desperate story about how we held her back and how she had to go on without us."

Sarah countered, "Let her go; she knows we are not supposed to separate."

"Stay in threes, ladies," that's what Mrs. Martsen said, reminding the entire group before they departed. "Stay in your group and finish with your group."

Sarah continued, saying, "This is just Dominique making trouble. This is what she always does; she only cares about herself."

***

Actually, this was a very normal Saturday morning, a picturesque opportunity for local drivers out early on this wet but beautiful winding mountain road. You would expect to see three girls walking on this damp spring day, for just down the road is their destination: a private Christian school for girls.

A sports car with two teenage girls sped by, passing the threesome plodding along in the ditch. The ditch dwellers looked in such disarray to the car dwellers. The girls in the car couldn't help but find it amusing. As if rehearsing lines from a daytime soap opera, the passenger chuckled indifferently, "Those poor unkept William James girls, how deplorable they are; they have no place to hide from the radiance of their plainness."

The driver mockingly replied, "How sad, and don't they know there are other hairstyles; ponytails every day, my god, how sanitary."

Then she continued, "I can't imagine what would force someone to attend a private Christian school. Makes you wonder, what is going on each night in a place that is full of teenage girls?" Laughing together, they continued on down the road.

From the ditch, Dominique saw the girls in the car laughing and pointing as they drove by. "Nothing new," she told herself. "What do they know?" But her pace quickened, and her temper flared. Being reminded once again of the searing pain that was her life, she set her jaw and plodded on, pondering the memory of delightful days when she was the one in the sports car, laughing at the deplorable on the road of life.

* * *

Williams James is a private Christian school for girls. The William James campus sits on a large parcel of land settled in upstate New York, north on Highway 87 between Kingston and Albany, 125 miles from the city and West of the Hudson River.

The school uses the Eupheus method for learning. In Greek, "Eupheus" refers to the "active seeking of knowledge," and it is the willingness to keep learning that makes all the difference. The campus is self-contained, with several dorm rooms, three large classroom buildings, administrative offices, a dining facility, and a dispensary.

Most of the land is wooded, with many hiking trails and campfire sites. On the back side of the dorms, there is an outdoor pavilion for special events. Adjacent to the office area, settled neatly in the woods, are three large decorative classroom buildings, the crown jewels of the William James campus.

A total of twenty-one classrooms, and between each of the three buildings are two large, screened walk-through areas. Each breezeway contains comfortable chairs and tables, and when weather permits, they hold outside classes there.

Passing through the ornate gated entrance to the campus and traveling up the winding brick driveway, at first glance, is mesmerizing, a delight to the eyes. The classroom complex blends wonderfully into its wooded backdrop, and the portico, which attaches to all three buildings, juts stunningly, upward and outward.

Created with large red fir beams and constructed without metal anchors, this portico is elaborate, to say the least. There is room to park fifty cars comfortably under its extensive canopy. Waterfalls, ornate trees, and statues abound everywhere.

Architecturally, there is no school like it. This school speaks to a prestige and nobility beyond what most schools would find a need for, and yet, this is intentional.

Not to be outdone by the structures, the school also boasts an unsurpassed teaching staff. A renowned and highly credentialed academic staff conjoined with this magnificent campus, William James is an educational opportunity second to none.

For twenty-five years, this institution has been the elite destination for those desiring excellence in high school education. This bulwark for defending critical thinking is attributed to none other than its founder, the visionary who dreamed William James into being—the pillar on which it is all sustained is the acclaimed scholar—Dr. William B. James DRS. Wesleyan School of Divinity Quebec, Canada.

As shepherd and overseer, Dr. James's vision has propelled William James to be recognized as "the" high school in the nation, the institution where parents can invest and partner with an exemplary staff to raise leaders equipped to impact an ever-changing world.

Tuition is pricy—only a select group of families can afford to enroll their children at William James, but with that financial commitment comes the promise of a stellar environment, with an emphasis on excellence in education, coupled with a biblical emphasis and a strict model of discipline; it is a sound investment. Students are equipped to make a difference in their culture and are assured of top university placement after graduation.

* * *

Nearly running now, Dominique was drenched and drained of strength. She would be this year's first competitor to complete the course. Each year in April, the senior class orchestrates a fundraiser, and the funds are distributed to local charities.

William James senior girls solicit friends and family to sponsor them—so many dollars for every mile covered on designated campus property. This fundraiser happens every spring, and with many wealthy families supporting the school, generous contributions are the norm.

With the fundraiser comes great excitement. Family members are visiting, getting together with their students, and the campus is buzzing. The school's mission is to raise dedicated, strong, passionate women for the kingdom of God. Giving to the needy helps the girls realize the blessing of "considering others better than themselves."

Today, the gathered school family is chattering and moving about, trying to see down the driveway and find their champion coming to the finish line. The assistant to Dr. James, Mrs. Janet Martsen, was also expectantly peering down the road as well; it was time to start receiving the girls back from their adventure.

* * *

Coming to the finish line, exhausted and infuriated, Dominique began to devise a plan to thwart the discipline that would be exacted by Mrs. Martsen. Not following the directive "to stay in groups of three and complete the challenge together" will surely have consequences.

Mrs. Martsen is well aware of Dominique's ability to malign the rules and blame others for her failings. The first thing Dominique noticed as she passed through the campus gate was that Mom and

Dad's Bentley was not in the parking lot; they rarely attended school functions. Their absence would make things easier for her to manage Mrs. Martsen.

Dominique decided to use the crowd of visitors to her advantage. She thought, *With all these families anxiously awaiting their girls to finish the course, how could Mrs. Martsen chew me out for being all alone?* As Dominique was coming up the driveway into campus, she and Mrs. Martsen's eyes met. Dominique, keen at evaluating Mrs. Martsen's mood by just looking at her, said to herself, "Since I am unattended by Rachel and Sarah, clearly, this body language was Mrs. Martsen's, 'don't mess with me' love language."

Ready to set her drama into action, Dominique viewed the onlookers as the audience of her play. Having practiced so skillfully with her parents, she was getting quite good at battling adults.

Looking so motley and struggling to stay on her feet, the school family began cheering. They shouted encouragement to Dominique—their heroine, looking saintly, bearing the elements, to finish the journey. Looking like anything but a shyster to the waiting crowd, Dominique fell at Mrs. Martsen's feet, crying out, "Please, somebody help me." Woefully, she rolled back and forth several times on the driveway. Whimpering, she uttered, "I have never been so sick in my entire life."

Of course, Mrs. Martsen did not buy into Dominique's pitiful spectacle, but with so many parents showing deep concern, coupled with her drenched and feeble condition, Mrs. Martsen knew Dominique had won this battle, so she called staff for help.

In the dispensary, after physical checkup, shower, and clean clothes, Dominique, knowing her situation was not over with Mrs. Martsen, was deep in thought on how to muddle the tale that Sarah and Rachel would tell.

Mrs. Martsen and Dominique have had many go-rounds. There were so many that Dominique was expelled in her first year at school. Her dad and Dr. James have been friends for years. They grew up on the same streets of Manhattan. Dominique had no special academic prowess and was in trouble constantly in public school. It was her father's relationship with Dr. James that opened the door for her enrollment at this school. With promises of improved behavior and a sizeable monetary gift to the school, Dominique was enrolled once again.

Mrs. Martsen is legalistic in her approach. She believes rules were meant to be followed, not ignored. She is not known for her compassion, but she is fair with all the girls; Mrs. Martsen affords no special treatment to students. She also believes that enabling and spoon-feeding children was to their detriment.

To Dominique, the chance of her transforming into the model student at this school was like making a square peg fit into a round hole: impossible. This school was a contradiction of everything she believed. Though only sixteen, when she arrived, she quickly came to the conclusion this place was out of context with everything happening in the real world.

She often thought, *I will die if I have to stay here.* She dreamed of how to get away from William James and Mom and Dad. *But how can I get away? They would eventually find this fugitive and forcefully remand me back to my fate.*

***

Tensions between Mrs. Martsen and Dominique started in the early days of her enrollment, but long before Dominique arrived at William James, she was already living as a prisoner, trapped, mostly of her own making, in a house of severe tension—her home.

The family of Dominique's father, Thomas Meunier, has a very rich French heritage; due to religious persecution in the early 1800s, they were forced to exile, migrating to Quebec (New France), Canada.

Most of his ancestors were clergy. Many were persecuted and died for their faith in France. After World War II, Thomas's father married Thomas's mother in Quebec. Wishing to start life anew in America, they applied for citizenship. Dominique's grandfather was ostracized by his family for leaving French Canada, which his church family considered the new homeland. There was such bitter railing and religious hostility on both sides that it ended in a formal excommunication for Thomas's parents.

They settled in New York City and began making a home. Thomas's dad became a pastor, and they started a family. Thomas was the firstborn, and his dad had high hopes for him to follow in his pastoral footsteps. Thomas had ideas of his own that would not be his legacy. It was not that church and faith were not important, but the love of God, which his dad preached incessantly, was nowhere to be found in his ubiquitous and hypocritical father. He thought, *If my father is the example of fatherhood, who needs a father, heavenly or otherwise?* He left home at fifteen and started working the streets of New York.

Money became Thomas's god. He worked two or three jobs at a time on the Lower West Side, where he rose financially to prominence in the community. There, on the West Side, he met his wife-to-be, Marie. His savvy on the street led him to purchasing several unique pieces of real estate, one of which he sold where the World Trade Center is located.

Money was never difficult for Thomas to procure, and without financial difficulty, it was time for Thomas and Marie to settle into beginning a family. As children came, Thomas and Marie were united in their desire for their kids to be in church. Church, for Thomas, was more about how to use God to your advantage than to know Him personally.

He quickly figured that out, doing business deals in Downtown Manhattan. Using God was good for business, so church became a weekly ritual. Church was not about commitment to God but more about status among the elite in the neighborhood.

Four children were born to Thomas and Marie Meunier, the last being a girl. They were so looking forward to having a baby girl that they actually prayed to God for a girl. They were sure of God's blessing when she was born.

Feeling so blessed by God's gift, they thought she should have a good French name with religious distinction, so they named her Dominique. Dominique is the French name of Latin origin that means "of the Lord." The only girl and the delight of her father's eyes, it wasn't long before she had her dad, as they say, "wrapped around her little finger."

Her brothers were all older; she was born four years after their last boy was born. The two elder boys were very outgoing, and because they were so much older, as she grew up, they were rarely around.

Thomas was a strict disciplinarian, and the children did not want to disappoint their father. Though Marie believed in discipline, she was different than Thomas; she believed behavior problems with the children led to positive outcomes and character building. She believed that good came from the trial endured, and she would take pride in her children as character was developed through their difficulty.

Her sacrificing love for her children made them feel safe in their home and endeared them to their mother. Still, it was a balancing act in parenting to keep the family dynamic solvent. Being overly protected by three brothers and a doting dad, Dominique was gullible and spoiled, a bad combination.

At first, she loved the church and the Sunday school teachers, and she felt safe there, but being so indulged at home, she was unable to apply biblical insight to real-life situations. Her circumstances, playing havoc on her emotions, left her woefully weak in discipline. As she aged, life challenges demanded maturity, but she had little to draw upon. This frustrated Thomas; he loved Dominique so much but mourned that she made such poor decisions.

The last opportunity for Dominique to embrace critical thinking from a biblical perspective was lost when she concluded that church was boring, unimportant, and hypocritical. Mom and Dad just seemed religious to Dominique. From her point of view, her parents were about shady deals and worldly pleasures; a real God became a phantom to her. She believed her family thought "God was best kept in a box." When some difficulty came their way, she would mockingly quip, saying, "Here we are in trouble again; we better pull the old man out and dust Him off."

Dominique developed her own worldview; she loved thinking for herself, and she began to manipulate her parents. She feigned religious platitudes for her parents' sake, but for all points and purposes, she was apostate.

Once, when she had just started high school, Dominique told her mom and dad she wanted to spend the night with a girlfriend. Their daughter not being in the home for a night—this would be a first for the Meuniers. They knew the other family well, and with stipulations, Thomas and Marie begrudgingly agreed to the sleepover.

The two girls' plans were dubious from the get-go. With several of their other church friends, they orchestrated a breakaway in the middle of the night. As evening continued, not long after the Meuniers were settling in for the night, they received a call from the host family, where the overnight was happening.

Frantic on the other end of the line, this father shared with Thomas that the girls were not at their home. Panic gripped Thomas and Marie, and they called the police. The police found the girls in sleeping bags, with food and booze, at a park in the city.

Dominique was grounded for life, and she knew she had lost her father's trust, but she thought the punishment did not fit the crime. She told her parents, "I am not a child; I am fifteen years old, and you are making way too big a deal of this. The parents of my friends at school are much more understanding than you."

Initially, her complaint did little to help her cause. Thomas looked sternly at his daughter and said, "Listen, young lady, we have rules in this house, and you will abide by them." Dominique rushed out of the room, sobbing. Thomas and Marie looked at each other and shrugged as if lost at what to do with this girl.

Over time, slowly and inevitably, Dominique once again attained to her old status as ruler of the household. Thomas and Marie began to wonder, "What have we done to raise a daughter such as this?" Their marriage began to suffer.

Thomas began to blame Marie, saying, "You are too soft on her; you never support the discipline I put in place."

Marie just laughed at Thomas and said, "Me? You give her everything she wants. You think she will love you because you lavish her with gifts; she has you fooled, and you cannot blame this on me."

CHAPTER 2

For Dominique, trouble was her constant companion. The battle with her parents was unending. Thomas and Marie were out of ideas and options. One day, Marie said to Thomas, "Maybe she needs a change of scenery?"

"What do you mean?" Thomas asked.

For some time, Marie had been thinking to herself, *What can be done with our daughter?* Marie explained to Thomas, "Dominique is making us all miserable. She is rarely not in trouble at school or at home; her brothers are ready to kill her, and if she is this wild and unreasonable at sixteen, what will she be like at eighteen?"

Thomas had no idea his bride was this upset with her daughter. Shocked, he said, "You sound like you have had it with Dominique. Is that what I am hearing?"

Marie countered, "No, I have not had it with her. I love her more than ever, but we are not helping her grow up. Maybe loving her best is to do what is best for her."

Thomas's frustration was getting the best of him; his gift was not conflict resolution, and he raised his voice and said, "What, what do you want to do?"

Marie, not sure how to broach this topic, began carefully, "Thomas," she said, "when was the last time we had peace in this house? You stay away at work longer now because you do not want to fight with your daughter when you do get home. After I have been stuck here with her all day long, trying to put out fires, I need your support, but what do you do? You support Dominique.

"I know you love her as much and maybe more than I do, but we cannot go on like this—change, something different is critical now." Fearing Thomas's love for Dominique would blind his ability to do what is best for her, Marie came up close to Thomas, put her hands on his shoulders, looked firmly into his deep blue eyes, and said, "We might have to send her to a private Christian school."

Thomas stepped back, pulling away from Marie, not sure what he heard. He instantly envisioned Dominique with strangers, no friends, at a new school alone for hours each day. Thomas always believed his children should attend public school; he believed they needed that dynamic to toughen them up for real life, and due to his upbringing, he was suspect of anything religious.

Now, staring with dismay at Marie and shaking his head, he said, "What about the cost?" He blinked his eyes, stood up straight, and looked at his wife as if she was crazy. With disbelief in his voice, he said," Marie, how will a private school change anything? She will still be out of control, but now we will have to pay for the abuse."

Knowing Thomas did not handle family crisis well, Marie moved in close again and said, "Thomas, I am talking about 'in-house' schooling—she would live on campus."

That was all Thomas could bear; he had heard enough. He threw his hands up in the air and walked out of the room. Marie began to reach out to stop him, but knowing Thomas needed time and space to digest this new information, she just watched him walk away; she bowed her head and stood there alone.

Later that evening, after calming down, Thomas started to realize that Marie was right; Dominique had them over a barrel. Though boarding school was out of the question for Thomas, he thought maybe the change of scenery would make a difference in their home.

He put a plan in place. He and his brother were business partners. They had several business opportunities in the city already on the books: one deal closing soon. He calculated, what if his brother and his brother's son, who is the same age as Dominique, could come and spend part of the summer with their family? Their house was more than ample to accommodate two guests, and he and his brother could do business, while at the same time, a different family dynamic might snap Dominique out of being so self-absorbed.

He thought to himself, *This is a good plan.* He began searching for Marie to discuss this option. When he found her reading in the drawing room, he gently moved alongside her on the sofa and put his arm around her. "Marie," he said softly, "I am sorry for walking out on you—you are right, something must be done, but can we not explore other options and make sending our daughter away our last resort?" Marie closed her book and turned to Thomas, knowing he would do anything before sending Dominique off to boarding school; skeptically, she looked up into his face, waiting to hear his proposal.

***

So, in the summer before her junior year in high school, Dominique and her folks welcomed her cousin Durand and his dad, Dumas, into their home. They had come to New York to stay with them for the month of July and, after that, return to Quebec. Durand was also headed into his junior year of high school.

Dominique knew that her uncle, Dumas, had many businesses dealing with her dad, but they rarely met in New York, and she hadn't seen her cousin Durand since grade school.

Thomas and his brother, Dumas, were a year apart, and both left home to get away from Dominique's grandfather. They were much alike physically, but Dumas had a quick smile and a timely joke for everything, whereas her dad was much more somber.

Dominique was surprised at how much Durand had grown up. After a brief reacquaintance with family small talk, Durand, not knowing what to say, shared with Dominique that he had just passed his driver's license test and was looking forward to taking her into the city. Dominique chuckled and thought, *Boys, always trying to impress, but it is a start at getting to know each other again.*

Dominique didn't have many friends who were boys; they were boring to her. She and Durand were just children the last time they saw each other. *Maybe this will be fun*, she thought, a change from her normal sedate and boring summer life.

After settling in, Durand came down from his room to find Dominique snacking in the kitchen. As he entered, she asked, "You want some chips?"

Durand said, "Sure." As they were munching chips, Durand said to Dominique, "What is so great about New York City?"

Dominique parried sarcastically, saying, "This is the center of the universe, and we have everything."

They sat and discussed the possibilities of an outing together. Rarely attracted to guys, Dominique tried to play it cool, but looking like a model poster, Durand was hot. Thinking he looked so much like his mom, Dominique posited the thought in her mind, saying, "He looks like Adele, blonde and beautiful." Except for her looks, Dominique barely remembered Adele.

With each day, Dominique was drawn closer to her cousin. He was tall, muscular, and endowed with the most beguiling smile. Whenever they were close together, Durand would seem to lean in, his curly hair nearly touching Dominique's face, as if he was trying to get a whiff of her scent. At first, Dominique thought this was weird but soon found it alluring. There were many boys at school who vied for her attention, and for a good reason—she was thin but beautiful: alabaster skin, long black hair, and dark black almond eyes, like her mom's, with eyelashes that looked like paint brushes.

Dominique felt that the boys at school were terribly immature. Durand seemed much older, and his French accent was more than cute. Though, like the rest of the family, Dominique spoke fluent French, she was Americanized and had no accent.

After several chaperoned visits to the city, Dominique asked her dad if she and Durand could go to the city on their own. Her dad said, "Absolutely not," but Dumas, with his thick French accent, rebuffed his brother and said, "Are you never going to let this child out of your sight? How will she ever learn to be responsible without taking on responsibility?" Besides, he said, "She will be with Durand; he will protect her."

Still remembering her betrayal from last year's sleepover, Thomas reluctantly consented to the excursion. "There," said Dumas, "your uncle has rescued you from the dungeon."

Dominique winked and said, "Thanks, Uncle, you truly are my knight in shining armor."

Early the next morning, they excitedly departed for the city. Thomas allowed Durand to drive, and they sped off to what they hoped would be a blissful day. Rather than plodding around viewing the woeful and limited tourist traps, Dominique wanted to give Durand the grand tour, helping him understand the great history of New York City.

Durand made the day more than just an outing; it was almost romantic. Indiscriminately, he would gently touch her hand, and occasionally, while staring at some building erected a hundred years ago, he would put his arm around her shoulder.

It was a blistering July day in the city, so Durand bought each of them an ice cream cone. Dominique thanked him. As Durand started to take his first lick of the ice cream cone, Dominique thought it would be funny to smash the cone into his face, so she did.

With ice cream all over Durand's face, she laughed, then screamed in panic, trying to run away from him. Durand chased her, quickly caught up with her, grabbed her by the waist, and, with ease, swept her off the ground, threatening to put what remained of the crumbled ice cream down her blouse.

They laughed together, and as Durand slowly settled Dominique to the ground, their eyes met. For Dominique, it was embarrassing and wonderful all at the same time. Looking quickly away, Dominique felt awkward and unsure. *What is happening?* she asked herself, but Durand never took his eyes off her. They were so close; she felt the heat of his body touching hers. *This is my cousin.* She recoiled at the thought and pushed herself away, unable to make eye contact.

After cleaning up the ice cream mess, Dominique felt uncomfortable being together, and she was no longer excited about the history lesson. She told Durand, "Maybe we should be heading back." Durand, being very casual and unaffected by what took place, agreed, and they headed home.

* * *

That night in bed, Dominique found herself perplexed. She thought, *Am I falling for my cousin? It cannot be*, she mused. *Maybe to the French, this is normal*, she assured herself. *Here, this is incest.*

After that strange day, it became harder for Dominique to spend time with Durand. For the next two weeks, they spoke, but only small talk. She could tell it was frustrating for him since they lived in the same house, but she still felt weird.

One day, Durand went for a walk by himself. He appeared to be aloof, and Dominique believed he was angry about them not spending time together. Uncle Dumas walked outside onto the patio, where Dominique was watching Durand walk away. He smiled and sipped on his coffee. "You two have problems?" he quipped.

She turned to see him; he reminded her so much of her father. Remorsefully, she replied, "We used to have such fun, and now it seems like we are barely friends."

"What is it?" Dumas questioned.

Embarrassed to go into detail, Dominique just shrugged and said, "I don't know."

Dumas, hoping to help, told her, "You are just young and need time to grow up. At sixteen years old, life should not be this hard; don't you forget that."

Dominique thought to herself, *If only you knew how hard this was...* Dominique knew the days would fly by, and soon, it would be time for Dumas and Durand to head back to Quebec. She decided she needed to talk with Durand before he left.

* * *

Staying on the patio, Dominique hoped to catch Durand when he returned from his walk. Finally, she caught a glimpse of him, hands in his pockets, with his head down, slowly moving along. When Durand looked up and saw Dominique looking at him, he sped up his pace and veered to avoid her. She ran off the patio and onto the extensive lawn toward him. "Durand," she called. He put his head down and walked away faster. "Durand, please," she begged. He slowed, finally stopping with his back to her.

Knowing she was the one who caused Durand's pain, Dominique nervously, slowly, walked up to him. She didn't have a clue how to begin to explain the situation. She stopped a few feet away from him and said, "Durand, can we talk?"

He didn't turn around and said nothing. Finally, after what seemed forever, his shoulders rolled forward, and he slumped. He let out a little sigh and then turned sideways. However, not facing her or looking up at her, he said begrudgingly, "What do you want?"

Moving closer, Dominique stepped out where she could face him. Seeing him so sad and angry hurt her. Though she was fond of Durand, Dominique knew there was no romantic possibility for them.

She began to explain, "Durand, I am so sorry for this last couple of weeks of ignoring you. I have treated my cousin badly." She used the word "cousin" in hopes Durand would catch her drift.

She continued, "I am not sure how to start, but I was afraid after what happened in the city, you know, after the ice cream deal. It scared me because I was becoming emotionally attracted to you, and something inside me wanted that. When you lifted me down, and our eyes met, I was hoping you would hold me and kiss me."

At this point, Durand slowly raised his head and made eye contact with Dominique. That flustered her, and she did not know how to proceed. They stared at each other for a few seconds, and then Dominique looked down, but Durand's eyes never left her face. She stood there looking down, not knowing how to go on. Durand just continued to stare at her.

The silence was deafening, and Dominique reluctantly looked back up into Durand's eyes. His expression had not changed at all. Dominique anxiously asked him, "Do you have nothing to say?" Durand started to open his mouth but then said nothing. Dominique folded her arms and stood up straight as if body language would force a response. She was becoming frustrated with Durand's silence.

Waiting no longer, she spun to turn and go, but as she did, Durand gently grabbed her arm and pulled her back to face him. He delicately took hold of her shoulders and drew her in close, his eyes never leaving hers. He paused, staring at her, then leaning down, moving closer to her. Dominique was captivated by his gentleness. Durand closed his eyes, and just before their lips touched, Dominique recoiled again, breaking loose from Durand's embrace; frightened once again by him, she cried out, "What is wrong with you?"

Perplexed and blushing, she stepped back to keep Durand at a distance. She just stared at him, hoping for a reply. Durand's face became red; he stood up straight and, for what seemed like a lifetime, stared at her; his eyes appeared to be protruding from their sockets; then abruptly, he turned and stomped away, never saying a word.

* * *

Later on, that night in her room, Dominique could not get hold of her feelings. She was numb and was lost for understanding. *How did I get to where I am?* She asked herself, saying, "What actually took place out in the yard?" She kept going over it again and again. *What have I said? How did I explain things? What did he hear me say? His response was nuts?*

At supper, Dominique couldn't believe how crazy things went. It was beyond strange. Durand would not make eye contact. Her mom and dad asked him questions. His dad tried to engage him—he would offer only glib, monotone responses as if to say, "None of your business." And when he made those glib responses, Mom, Dad, and Dumas would look at Dominique as if she had some answer for why Durand was acting so strange. All she could do was shake her head and roll her eyes.

That night in bed, Dominique could not fall asleep; everything was so bizarre and blurred. She kept thinking, *I didn't really tell him anything; I just explained to him about us being cousins.* She kept going over in her mind, *Maybe he thought, from what I was saying, that I was romantically inclined and wanted him to kiss me.*

That is it; that is why Durand was just responding to my perceived desire to be held and kissed. Then she thought, *Wait a minute, is he that stupid? Does he not know that first cousins are family and off-limits?* Going back over things again, she queried, *How is this my fault?* Just before dosing off, she decided to give her and Durand one more chance to reconcile.

At the beginning of the year, Thomas and Marie had scheduled a business meeting for the end of July. Dumas knew of this meeting prior to him and Durand coming—in fact, it was this business opportunity that he and Thomas were engaged in that brought him and Durand to New York. It also offered a great opportunity for family time in the city.

The plan was that Thomas and Marie would fly out to meet with friends on the 28th, and then Dumas and Durand would meet them in Philadelphia on July 29th, where they would sign the documents and then continue on to Quebec. Marie's sister, Colleen, would be coming over to stay with Dominique, but she couldn't arrive until the morning of the 29th, so Dumas and Durand would stay with Dominique until Aunt Colleen arrived. Colleen would stay with Dominique until her parents came back on August 2nd.

CHAPTER 3

Dominique's aunt, Colleen, was her favorite person in the entire world. Dominique was always lonely for her aunt, Colleen, and saddened that she did not come to visit more often. Dominique could not put her finger on exactly what it was that made Aunt Colleen so special, but to Dominique, she was the real deal.

Being incapable of knowing her own frailties, nor having the motivation to even acknowledge them, Dominique had no way of knowing just how vain she really was. Naturally, then, it was easy for her to find most people, beginning with her parents, flagrantly superficial. In fact, Dominique was sure she had a gift. She prided herself on the ability that, within minutes of starting a conversation, she could identify a phony person; at least, that is what she told herself. Due to this gift, most of her friends liked her from a distance, but because her parents had money, they would tolerate her.

Dominique knew Aunt Colleen saw her for who she really was but, strangely, loved her anyway. If anyone else tried to hold Dominique accountable for her actions, she would ditch them in a hurry, but Aunt Collen was nearly magical; she had a way of making sense of everything, and from Dominique's perspective, her greatest gift was she did not judge people.

Aunt Colleen's husband left her years ago for another woman. They divorced soon after that; it was a devasting blow. They had no children, and Colleen could not see herself trying marriage again. So, she quit trying to find love and nearly lost the ability to love at all, but Colleen found a place to love and be loved when Thomas and Marie invited her to move in with them. At the time, with Marie pregnant with Dominique and bedridden, Colleen was a God-send to the family.

Marie cherished her big sister because she was her rock, the one who was always there to help Marie cope with a growing family and a vacant husband. Thomas and Colleen had their issues, but knowing he could not be home nursing and running the business, too, he wholeheartedly agreed to Colleen moving in with them. Not that Thomas wasn't excited about this little girl coming into their lives, but because everyone knew the business was his first love.

***

After Dominique was born, Marie remained weak and could hardly get out of bed on her own. So, Colleen was called upon to take care of Marie and Dominique, along with all the other needs of home. With the two older boys in college, there was only Chase, their four-year-old son, left to care for, so Colleen began playing the role of a second mom to two children.

Marie ended up bed-bound for about a year after the birth. Thomas spent as much time as he could with her, but in Colleen's eyes, he had very little empathy for Marie. She could see that his main concern was the business, which frustrated Colleen.

Colleen and Thomas would clash over family dynamics, and this became a bone of contention. Colleen would talk to Marie about how she saw things, and Thomas would share with Marie how he saw things. That left Marie in the middle, trying to do a balancing act, and she really did not have the strength for it.

She would encourage them both to work things out, but she could see how hard this was becoming. Thomas was getting agitated and feeling managed by Colleen. Colleen, on the other hand, viewed Thomas as selfish and unattached to his family.

* * *

Thomas remained committed to church and showed up every Sunday. Thomas and Chase would go to church, and since Marie and Dominique could neither attend, Colleen would stay home with them. Colleen felt Thomas's excuse for going to church was bogus. She believed he didn't go to church to get in touch with God but to get away from the responsibility of meeting Marie's needs, and it was convenient because, while Chase was in Sunday school, Thomas got to go hang with all his business buddies.

One Sunday, Colleen had just taken care of Marie's needs and was holding Dominique in the family room, feeding her a bottle. She looked into Dominique's dark black eyes; those eyes never failed to captivate Colleen. She was mesmerized by the beauty of her tiny niece. Her emotions were always in high gear whenever she held Dominique.

As her stare continued fixed on this almost angelic creature she was holding, worried due to the family dysfunction, she said to herself, "What is going to become of you, my love?" Tears began to swell in her eyes, and she promised Dominique, saying, "No matter what, I will never leave you." It seemed like Dominique understood; she stopped suckling for just a second, looked into Colleen's eyes, and with the bottle nipple still embedded around her lips, she smiled the most beautiful smile as if to say, "I know." With tears falling down her cheeks, Colleen smiled back and said out loud, "I am so blessed to be your aunt."

After her bottle, Dominique fell asleep, and for the first time, Colleen was able to take her eyes off the bundle of love she was holding. She looked up to view her surroundings. Colleen was finally finding comfort in her life, but she paused to ponder the question, and she thought to herself, *When will I know peace?* Colleen did not know how to get along with Thomas, but she knew that for Marie and Dominique's sake, she must, or there would be no peace in the home.

She looked at the end table next to her chair, and lying there open was a Bible. Colleen and Marie rarely talked about spiritual things; there didn't seem to be a need. She remembered when God seemed important, but she was just a young girl then. She wondered why the Bible was even there and who would be reading it.

Not knowing why, something drew her to the book on the end table. Putting Dominique down in her cradle, Colleen moved toward the table. Having arrived, she positioned the Bible so she could read it. Someone had underlined a passage in red ink. Leaning over so she could see it better, Colleen read the underlined verse, which said, "Never will I leave you; never will I forsake you."[1]

Leaning back, Colleen was somewhat shocked at what she just read. She leaned back in again to reread the verse. She noticed she was reading from the book of Hebrews, and the verse was 5, chapter 13.

Looking for some context in what she was reading, she read the words prior to the red ink section, and they said, "And be content with what you have, because God has said…" Then, she read the underlined passage again: "Never will I leave you; never will I forsake you." She paused, moved back into the chair again, looked down, and realized those were the very words she had just spoken to Dominique, which made the baby smile.

The word in the verse that jammed into her thoughts and wouldn't leave was the word "content." This word had a double effect on Colleen. One, it troubled her, and she skeptically said to herself, "Is there such a thing as 'contentment'?" And secondly, it gave her hope, which scared her. Could she dare to hope there is really a way to find true contentment?

Deep in thought, rolling the verse she just read around in her head, Colleen decided to see how Marie was faring. Feeling melancholy, trying to discern why this Bible verse was haunting her, she moved from the baby's room to Marie's room. Her last thought before entering Marie's room was, *Who really has contentment? I don't know anyone who is truly content.*

Those thoughts trailed off as she entered the room. Marie looked up with a welcoming smile. Colleen was so worried about her sister's health that, though smiling, Marie still looked very frail to Colleen, and she wondered when and if she would get well again. Colleen smiled back, moved over to the edge of the bed, and reached out to hold Marie's hand.

"How are you today, my dear?" Colleen asked. Marie attempted to muster a strong response, but to no avail; it was evident to Colleen that her baby sister was still very weak. Maire asked how Dominique was, and they settled into small talk.

After some time, Colleen couldn't keep it in any longer. She had to ask Marie the question that was burning in her mind, so she said, "Who is reading the Bible out in the family room?"

Seeming surprised and somewhat embarrassed by the question, Marie sheepishly responded, "Oh, I am."

Colleen didn't respond, but by the look on her face, Marie knew she wanted to know more. Marie seemed kind of sheepish about the revelation and appeared to struggle with explaining why she was reading the Bible.

Marie began to explain how family and her health were taking its toll. She explained how she was just out of answers, and no matter where she turned or who she talked to, no one could help.

Marie continued to explain that Thomas was full of good intentions but had no way to follow through with anything, and with her being ill, she could not help much at home. Couple that with Chase falling through the cracks, not to mention being pregnant and fearing for the baby's health. She finished by saying, "I was at the end of my rope, and you were not here yet, so I turned to the Bible in hopes it would be my help."

Colleen's first internal reaction to Marie's answer was, *She must have been so desperate, and I must not have been sensitive enough to know her desperation.* Thinking to herself, Colleen said, "Desperation leads to desperate choices." Colleen had no idea that Marie would even think of turning to God. So, she said to Marie, "Did it help?"

Marie cast her gaze down and then looked away. Then, she lifted her eyes and looked straight up into Colleen's eyes and said, "I read the Bible and underlined verses that seemed to offer hope. I prayed and prayed, and I heard nothing. I waited and waited and received nothing. As before in my life, when you need Him, He remains an unavailable savior."

The hostility in Marie's voice was obvious. Attempting to confer empathy, Colleen said softly, "I am so sorry, honey."

Marie shrugged her shoulders and lifted her hands as if to say, "Why should God surprise me with help?" Then Marie surprised Colleen by saying, "Hey, look who showed up to help me?" Pointing at Colleen, she praised her and said, "You are my savior, and I have all I need now." That statement seemed to lighten the moment, but Colleen was not convinced.

As Colleen left Marie's side to check on Dominique, she felt a tinge of remorse in her soul. She wasn't mad but was essentially grieving the conversation and the outcome of Maire's story. She thought to herself, *If God chooses not to be, who is going to be my savior? Will I ever know peace?*

As she walked toward the baby's room, she glanced at the open Bible on the end table, and her thoughts went back to the verse: "Never will I leave you; never will I forsake you." She thought to herself, *If God is who He says He is, then where is He?*

Remembering her grandma's words and strong faith, Colleen recalled one of Grandma's stories, and it ran through her thoughts, saying, "God spoke the universe into existence…" *And if He really loves people, like He says He does, could real contentment come from any other source?* She thought to herself as she headed into the kitchen to begin supper, *This is a mystery.*

CHAPTER 4

With the calendar running out of days and the closing in of the time for Thomas and Durand to depart, Dominique knew time was of the essence, and now was the time to patch things up with Durand. She decided to wait until her parents left for Philadelphia.

Meanwhile, Durand's demeanor remained unchanged. The family knew something was wrong, but he would not open up. Dumas tried several times prior to Thomas and Marie's departure but to no avail. Finally, the night before Thomas and Marie left, Dumas made some headway. He walked into Durand's room and nonchalantly moved close. Durand acted as if he didn't notice, and then Dumas jumped onto the bed, grabbing Durand in a bear hug.

At first, Durand fought the invasion but then realized Dad just wanted to spend time with his son. They wrestled, laughing until the moment subsided. Together, they sat up on the bed; Dumas ruffled Durand's curly hair—they were looking at each other. Dumas said, "There's my son." Durand lowered his eyes but said nothing.

Dumas continued, "Are you about ready to go home, Son?" Durand shook his head to affirm he was ready. "Have you enjoyed our visit?" Dumas asked.

Durand finally said something, "Yes, Dad, it was fun at first."

Dumas saw an opening and decided to push on, saying, "We all have noticed a change recently. At first, you seemed very happy, but in the last few weeks, it seems you have been very sad. What happened?"

Dumas could see by Durand's demeanor that this was a difficult topic to discuss. With some trepidation, Dumas said, "Come on, Son, talk to me. What's up?"

Durand rarely confided in his dad; he and Dumas were more at odds than Dumas knew. But Durand was frustrated and needed a place to vent. He sat up; it was evident he was angered because his face started to flush.

"Okay, Dad," he began. "It was great to see Uncle Thomas and Aunt Marie; I missed them. I was not prepared for seeing Dominique." He became more animated and went on, "The last time I saw Dominique, all I remember is a spoiled little brat who did her best to keep me in trouble. When we arrived and I first saw her, I could not believe how she had changed, had grown up."

Remaining silent, Dumas waited for Durand to continue, but it seemed Durand was stuck and could not go on. So, Dumas whispered an elongated "*annnnnd*."

Durand looked up again, answering, "Well, she turned into a woman, and as I watched her interact with our family and some of her friends…" He paused. "You know, I actually thought prior to our visit that she hated me, but though still spoiled, she seems to care about me now."

Pausing again and then trailing off, he said, "At least until recently."

Dumas knew something had happened, and it was very hard for Durand to talk about, but Dumas continued to push, saying, "What happened recently?"

Durand just blurted it out, "She is a flirt, Dad."

Dumas was shocked to hear his son use that descriptor for his niece. He had always treasured Dominique. "Please explain," Dumas insisted.

Durand tried to brush it off by saying, "You wouldn't understand."

"Try me," said his dad.

"You won't like this," said his son. Dumas motioned him to proceed. Durand began to explain, "Do you remember the day I took Dominique to the city?"

Dumas nodded as to say yes. He was dying inside, wondering where this was going. Durand continued to tell the story just as it happened that day. He described the casual touching, the ice cream incident, him grabbing her and playfully lifting her up, the meeting of their eyes, and the way she looked at him as he put her back on the ground.

"Durand," Dumas interjected, "is this what has been eating on you? These things are normal and part of growing up—"

Durand interrupted, "Dad, I am not a little boy; I know about girls and attraction." He looked calmly at his dad and said, "No, that is not what is eating on me…" He continued, "For days after the incident in the city, Dominique would not look at me or talk to me. I thought she had a good time; I know I did. She was amazing to be with. So, the silent treatment was a bummer. When I approached her, as I have since arriving, she would act busy or uninterested with me being around. That hurt, and after many tries to engage her, I just gave up; I was angry."

"Son, you are blowing this out of proportion," Dumas said, trying to show he understood, and began again to explain the simplicity of their encounter.

Durand was getting frustrated with his dad. He looked at him and said, "Dad, there is more…"

Now, Dumas was nervous, seeking to know what else there could be. He asked, "What?"

Durand started again, "Dad, do you remember the day I went for a walk: you were having coffee in the kitchen, and Dominique was there looking out onto the patio?"

Dumas nodded and said, "Yes, in fact, as you left, I asked Dominique if you two were okay."

Durand went on to tell his dad how the walk was miserable and just made him more frustrated. He continued, sharing how Dominique came out to meet him and begged him to listen to her. Dumas's eyes kind of widened as Durand related how she was confused and unsure about the physical interaction they had.

Durand went on to tell his dad that Dominique basically told him she was attracted to him and had spent some time thinking about him holding her and kissing her. Continuing, Durand said, "So I grabbed her gently, leaned down to kiss her, and she freaked out. She pushed me away and yelled, 'What is wrong with you?'"

Dumas stopped Durand and said, "Son, this is your cousin!" Durand wasn't sure of the point his dad was trying to make and just shrugged his shoulders. Dumas raised his hands, shook his head, and said, "Son, you are related; she is your family." Durand still didn't see this as an issue, or at least he didn't care to contemplate it. Dumas said, "Do Marie and Thomas know about this?"

Durand stuttered, "I-I don't know; Dominique may have told them, I don't know."

Now that Dumas was involved, he wished he wasn't. He was dumbfounded, and he called out, saying, "Durand, you cannot marry your cousin."

With that, Durand whimsically mused, "Who is talking about marriage?"

Dumas knew it was time to stop and rethink what he was learning. He thought he knew his son better; Dumas felt guilty for Durand's lack of understanding of life. "Son," he said, "let's discuss this more at another time."

Durand just flippantly replied, "What's the point?"

That night, both Dumas and Durand struggled to fall asleep. Dumas remained awake, worried about how much Thomas and Marie knew of this disclosure. Durand had other problems; he was remembering back to the days when Dominique would play tricks on him and humiliate him. It appeared to him she was just up to her old ways. He was contemplating how he might get back at her.

***

It was a busy morning as Thomas and Marie prepared for their trip. Marie loved Philadelphia and was rambling on to Thomas about what all they would do, what she would wear, and how excited she was to spend some time in Philadelphia.

Not really listening, Thomas was deep in thought, mulling over the prospects of this new deal Dumas and he had negotiated. He kept going over all the planning details and the work that went into making this day happen. Neither Thomas nor Marie were conscious of the turmoil whirling around their domain.

As was her norm, Dominique was sullen, but Marie saw this as a normal extension of her daughter's inner psyche. Thomas noticed that Dumas seemed kind of nervous. Thomas decided his brother was nervous about this new business deal. Little did Thomas know of his angst. Marie was concerned about Durand, but he was still being his sour self, and she thought, *I don't have time today to worry about him; he is as moody as Dominique.* "Sixteen-year-olds," she said under her breath.

Thomas brought them all together, and they went over the itinerary for the days ahead. Thomas reminded Dumas of what was necessary for Dominique since he would be watching her until Colleen arrived the day he and Durand were scheduled to leave.

When the car pulled up front to take them to the airport, they shared hugs and goodbyes. Thomas and Marie jumped into the back seat; the driver loaded the luggage, closed the car door, and down the driveway through the gate they went.

Thomas, Durand, and Dominique stood on the porch and waved goodbye. As the car disappeared down the street, the three on the porch disappeared as well. Without saying a word, they scattered, heads down, all going in different directions: Dominique went to her room, Thomas to the kitchen, and Durand outside, rambling around the grounds.

***

Today was the only day left for Dominique to clear things up with Durand. *There is no easy way to do this*, she surmised. *I may as well just make this happen.* She left her room and headed to find Durand.

Dumas could not figure out why he was in the kitchen; his head was swirling. Knowing he was leaving tomorrow, he felt he owed it to Dominique and Durand to try to help smooth things over. He couldn't get past how unconcerned Durand was about having romantic feelings for his cousin. Gathering his thoughts, he was led back to that devastating day when Durand lost his mother and he lost his Adele. *Has it been three years already?*

Adele was the glue for the family. Adele always knew what to do. She was the calm in their storms, the peacemaker in conflict, and she was for Dumas, the joy he had lost years ago, trying to please God and his dad.

Reflecting back, it was becoming clear Durand had not been the same since he lost his mother. Guilt started to sink in again, and it hurt to put things into proper perspective. He said to himself, "I have been a terrible father."

Without Adele, Dumas was lost. He had become inward, and the business took all his time. There was little time to be dad, so he gave Durand a lifestyle without problems, filling up his life with all the things money could buy. "What a fool," he chastised himself.

Yes, there were times when they would do things together, go to events, and eat out. They would even talk about girls and dating. Dumas had fooled himself into believing that Durand could tell him anything, that he was his confidant. He had been so blind he really didn't know his son, and now that the blinders were off, it was terrifying, and the reality was that he had abandoned his only child. And now Durand was so confused that he agonized, "And how can I begin to help him?"

He knew he would have to start by trying to make sense of Durand and Dominique. He didn't know what to think about Durand's side of the story but knew to get the full picture, he would have to get it from the horse's mouth, so he headed up to Dominique's room to have her explain things.

***

Durand was most ready to get out of New York and back to Quebec and his friends. Durand felt his dad had coerced him to make the trip to New York. Dumas didn't really care for most of his son's friends. Durand was surprised when he arrived at his uncle's home. Dominique was so different, exciting, and beautiful from what he remembered. He was attracted to her instantly.

Dumas didn't know the darker side of his son. Durand had been hooked on porn since he was twelve years old. Dad had no idea, but because Durand spent all his time on social media, Dumas had planned several times to take all his son's devices away. Dumas had no idea it was more than just friends and video games that captivated his son.

***

Still angry with Dominique, Durand decided to stay away from her until they left the next day. That would be hard because his dad loved to cook, and he would call them together to have one last supper prior to them leaving. He thought, *I will just hang outside till Dad calls for dinner.*

Just then, Dominique walked outside and started coming toward Durand. She was at a loss as to how to fix things, but the first step was finding Durand. Seeing her coming, Durand started around to the front of the house. Dominique thought, *You can run, but you can't hide.* She followed him. Durand picked up his pace, thinking, *If I can get to my room...* Dominique stayed on his trail. When she saw him go in the front door, she smiled, thinking, *I've got you now.*

As Durand went into the foyer, he saw Dominique coming to the front door, and he burst up the stairs as fast as he could. As Dominique came through the front entrance to the house, she heard Durand's bedroom door slam shut. She calmly walked up toward Durand's door, hoping to muster the courage and contemplating the words she needed to say. Finally, as she stood before his bedroom door, she thought, *This is it.* She paused for just an instant and knocked on his door.

* * *

Not knowing that Dominique had left her room to find Durand, Dumas was slowly heading up to Dominique's room to begin what he hoped was a healing for these kids. He loved Dominique so much; she had always been his favorite. He knew he was no good at these things. He tried to think back, *How would Adele do this?* Arriving at the top of the stairs, he started to get cold feet, so he leaned against the handrail and shook his head as if to clear his thoughts.

When it came to things being hard, Dumas knew he was a coward. His default was humor: just tell a joke or do something dumb to take the heat off. He couldn't imagine how that would help now, and he was not a counselor. Terrified, he concluded, "I have nothing to offer."

Just before he turned and ran, something came over him. He knew that Dominique loved him. Uncle Dumas was her "knight in shining armor." He shook his head and said, "No, no more weakness." That statement to himself affirmed the fact he knew: "I love her too much to do nothing." With new confidence, he walked straight to the door and knocked. He waited a while; there was no answer, so he knocked again, but there was still no answer. So, he called out, "Dominique, it's Uncle Dumas. Can I come in?"

He turned the doorknob and peeked in, saying, "Dominique." He opened the door completely, which revealed she was not there. *Strange,* he thought, *I saw her go upstairs just a few minutes ago. Maybe she went to look for Durand; he is out in the backyard.* Then, he quipped, "I probably need to be there as a referee." So, he quickly descended the stairs, heading through the kitchen and out to the backyard.

When Dumas came off the patio, he could find neither one of them. His first thought was, *They are not in the house, and they are not in the backyard.* That scared him. He hurried around to the front of the house and looked down the driveway, and they were not there either. *Maybe they had decided to walk over to the park?* He hoped so. Not wanting them to have another blowout, he thought, *I need to be there.* So, he quickly headed over to the park, which was only ten minutes away.

* * *

Not knowing that Dumas was on his way to the park looking for her and Durand and having already knocked on Durand's door, Dominique was still waiting for him to respond.

She knew he was mad and may not let her in; she said to herself, "I am not going away." Then, Dominique thought to herself, *Why am I so concerned about fixing this mess? Why am I so emotional? This is not like me.* She knocked again—silence. "Durand," she called, "please let me in. I want to talk to you."

This was Durand's worst nightmare. He yelled, "Go away!"

Dominique responded, "Durand, I want to apologize for how I hurt you."

Durand was thinking to himself, *Yes, you did hurt me, and now I will hurt you; you can stand out there all night.*

"Please, Durand," she tried again. "Let me in; won't you give me a chance to make things right?" This was all so overwhelming, and she had no idea how to make Durand understand. Her heart was aching, and she began to cry. Durand had pretty much decided to have nothing more to do with this fickle cousin, but when she began to cry, something in him changed.

Dominique continued to weep at the door, and he walked over to listen. "Please," she whispered. Durand slowly unlocked the door. Dominique was surprised but excited; she wanted more than anything to patch up their relationship. Durand quickly opened the door, which startled Dominique.

There he stood with his head tilted down. He glared at her, and his face was red like before. "What?" he barked. "Do you want to tease me some more? Haven't you had enough fun at my expense?"

So Uncle Dumas would not hear, Dominique walked around Durand and closed the door. She wiped the tears from her eyes and agreed with Durand, "Yes, I have been cruel, and I am sorry; please forgive me." Durand turned, walked over toward the bed, and stood there with his back to her.

Nearly begging, Dominique said, "Please, let me explain my strange actions to you. When you arrived, I was so excited to see you again. You had grown up, and I saw this young man, not the little boy I remembered. You seemed so mature and, to be honest, very handsome." She stopped to gather strength and direction. "I am sorry, but I became infatuated with you. I liked it when you touched me and were close to me. I am embarrassed of how I acted and led you on. When you wanted to kiss me, it became very evident that I was wrong in leading you on this way."

Dominique had to pause again; Durand had not moved. She slowly moved toward him and said, "Won't you look at me?" Durand remained stiff, unmoving. Starting again, Dominique said, "That day in the city, when you tried to kiss me, I should have said, 'Durand, you are my cousin,' and the reason we are at this hard place is because I haven't been mature enough to handle it." She took a deep breath and continued, "I should have said, please forgive me for leading you on. We cannot be romantic toward each other because we are family; we are related."

Durand remained frozen where he stopped; Dominique wanted him to respond, to say something. He seemed to be breathing harder, so she stepped closer and reached out to touch his shoulder. As she did, Durand whirled with fire in his eyes; he fiercely grabbed her arm and pulled her toward him. Screaming, he said, "You want me to forgive you, you who have teased me your whole life?" He pulled her hard up close to his face.

Dominique was horrified; he was gritting his teeth, and she could smell the heat of his breath. She said, "Durand, you are hurting me."

"Like you hurt me, right?" Durand scowled.

He looked possessed to Dominique. She screamed and tried to run, but he brutally flung her around, and at the same time, like a boxer hitting a punching bag, with all his might, with a fierce uppercut, he punched Dominique in the stomach. The pain of that blow was so searing Dominique nearly lost consciousness; she could not breathe, she could not get any air, and try as she may, she could not scream.

This strike bent her over; her eyes were bulging, and the blood was running to her head. In the midst of this searing pain, the like she had never known, she began to panic. Due to the horror of what was happening to her, she thought her heart was going to explode. Durand grabbed two handfuls of her hair and threw her onto his bed. She still could not breathe; she could not move, even as he started ripping her clothes off.

* * *

This wasn't the first time Durand had sexually assaulted a girl. This mastery over women made him feel powerful, and it brought him great satisfaction knowing that the complete humiliation of Dominique was his doing, payback for what he had so long endured from her. Finished, he was disgusted with her; he pushed her off the bed with his foot and told her, "Get out, tramp."

Barely aware of her surroundings and sobbing uncontrollably, Dominique stumbled awkwardly around, looking for her belongings, and fell to the floor. As she fell, Durand screamed at her again, "I said 'get out'!" He jumped from the bed, roughly pulled her up off the floor, stuffed her clothes into her arms, took her by the back of the neck, and shoved her out the door. Dominique turned to say something, but Durand slammed the door in her face.

She felt nauseous, and she could hardly walk. Lost in the trauma of what just happened to her, Dominique stood naked in the hallway and unembarrassed. Looking down the hall, Dominique began moving slowly to her room. Once inside, she shut the door, leaning against it; she slowly slid to the floor, crying bitterly.

CHAPTER 5

Dumas was getting nervous; he could not find these kids anywhere. The park was a bust, so he headed back to the house. Becoming frantic, he hurried back; he was starting to become angry and said to himself, "Why is this happening to me?"

Meanwhile, Durand was so pleased with himself that he dressed and headed downstairs to get something to eat; he was famished. Just as Durand entered the kitchen, Dumas entered simultaneously and said, "Where have you been, Son? I have searched everywhere for you."

Durand responded, "I was outside for a while and then went up to my room; I got hungry and just now came downstairs. Why are you looking for me?"

Dumas thought to himself, *I did not check Durand's room before I left.* "Well," he said, "I am really looking for Dominique, and I thought you two would be together; she wasn't in her room."

Scoffing flippantly, Durand dismissed his dad, saying, "Why would I want to spend time with Dominique? I cannot wait to get home and away from her."

Dumas was running out of time and patience with his son. He told him, "You know you have a part to play in this whole mess; for God's sake, you were trying to hit on your cousin, and once again, I am left to be the one to clean up your mess."

Durand just turned to the refrigerator and started scouring for food. With his head inside the door, he said, "Maybe she is in her room; I think I heard some noise up there before I came down to eat."

Regretfully, Dumas said under his breath, "My son is hopeless," and he headed again upstairs.

Climbing slowly back up the stairs to find Dominique, Dumas began to doubt Durand's story and what really happened between him and his cousin. Dumas recalled the warning the therapist gave concerning Durand's illness. The therapist explained to Thomas, "Durand suffers from cognitive distortions, which describe irrational, inflated thoughts or beliefs that distort a person's perception of reality. This disorder enhances his ability to not see things the way people around him do; a real liability when it comes to getting to truth." He cursed himself, saying, "I should have told Thomas and Marie about Durand's issues."

This woke Dumas up, and he thought, *Is my son really healing?* "Oh, Adele, I need you now," he whispered. Then, mocking himself, he said, "You old fool!" But he wished she could hear him. His next thought surprised him; he prayed, "God, will You help?" Then instantly, he countered, "How really foolish you are, Dumas? Why would God, after all these years of you running from Him, want to hear from you now?" Dumas resigned himself to being all alone on this one.

***

When Dominique heard Dumas at the door, her first thought was, *Uncle Dumas, my knight. Uncle Dumas loves me; I know he will help me.* She was completely shattered, brutally beaten, victimized, and needed a strong, loving shoulder to lean on, but in the midst of that fairy tale, the thought raced into her soul. She shuddered at the thought; with her mind racing, she said to herself, "I can't share this with Uncle Dumas." She knew she could never share this with anyone. She began to cry again silently. "I brought this on myself; who will believe my side of the story? I can't even tell Mom and Dad; I am all alone."

She pondered, *What do I do now?* Sheepishly looking heavenward, she contemplated a second, then brushed it off, saying, "What has God ever done for me? It isn't worth the effort; He's not there when you really need Him."

Abandoned and alone, holding back the tears, crumpled at the base of the door, she lied and told her uncle Dumas, "Sorry, I can't come to the door. I just got out of the shower; I'll see you at supper, okay?"

"Yeah, okay," Dumas said through the door. Dumas finally had to resign himself to the fact that it was 8:00 p.m. and dinner needed to be made; there would be no time to work through these difficulties before bedtime.

He finally concluded that he had tried, and the kids would just have to grow out of this thing. *They are young,* he thought, *and we are leaving tomorrow. They will face much tougher things than this. Life is hard, and they need to start learning that.*

Even as Thomas spoke to himself with such confidence, he was unsure of how anything he just said would help. "I know how hard being young is," he said, feeling sorry for himself. Terribly missing Adele and their life together, Dumas stared out the big window at the end of the hall. He sadly lowered his eyes for just a moment, then straightened himself and looked up; he lifted his eyes, and his countenance became brighter. He acknowledged to himself, saying, "God knows I tried to help."

Satisfied with his effort, he briskly began down the stairs. With all that behind him, Dumas was able to start contemplating how much had to be done before he and Durand left in the morning.

Arriving back at the kitchen again, he hollered at Durand, "So, before we leave New York, what do you want for your last supper?" Durand just shrugged, but still looking at his son, Dumas was stopped by the words he had just spoken: "Your last supper." For some reason, a Bible story his dad told him long ago came fresh back to materialize in his heart and mind.

The Last Supper story had haunted him since childhood. He remembered his dad's unrelenting wielding of that story to guilt him into settling into the church and ending his reckless lifestyle. His dad would remind Dumas that, like Judas, if he continued to betray his faith and his family, Jesus would not allow him to sit at God's table in heaven.

After years of a steady diet of judgment and condemnation from his dad, Dumas finally came to the conclusion that maybe his dad was right—he was like Judas. His heart had become callused to anything about God. He reasoned to himself, saying, "As Judas was to Jesus, I am as well." But something was happening; Dumas was caught up and captured in the memory of how he used to truly love Jesus so much.

With his dad's hypocritical portrayal of Jesus, Dumas described him only as an angry tyrant who didn't want his children to have fun. Having come to that fateful realization, Dumas bid Jesus and his family ado; he walked away, wishing never to return again. But now, for some unexplained reason, Dumas was wracked with conviction and anger as he thought back to the words he had just told himself upstairs outside of Dominique's door.

He recalled his smooth-talking excuse for caring when he said to himself, "God knows I tried to help." That statement echoed back into his mind and crashed into his soul. Dumas thought, *God knows better than anyone what a liar I am.* Powerful memories poured over him; he didn't know what to make of this onslaught of spiritual recollection. His mind went back to days when he had more answers and more hope, and life made more sense.

Remembering the words of the carpenter, he almost wished he were young again. Then, in his memory, he heard Jesus say, "I have longed to eat this last supper with you." Dumas also remembered his Sunday school teacher and the many times he had heard him talk about God's goodness and the promise of heaven: how God loved him, how He sent His Son to die to take away his sin.

Dumas was struck by an overwhelming emptiness and loneliness, and his heart was breaking. His mind was swirling with thoughts of Adele; he nearly cried out loud, "How I miss you!" It was all coming apart; Durand's problems pummeled his thoughts, and finally, the culmination of it all, his glib response to Dominique's need, only multiplied his sorry condition.

Feeling so out of control, Dumas' head dropped down, emotional fatigue overshadowed him, and he cried, "I am so lost, and I have no place to go." Then, as his vexed soul shuttered, he weakly mumbled, "I have run for so long; if only now there was still a setting for me near the host of that last supper, but for the Judas in me." Not wanting Durand to see him, Dumas quickly stepped out of the kitchen onto the patio and wept inconsolably.

***

At 9:00 a.m. the next morning, Aunt Colleen arrived. Dumas and Colleen were not close. She felt he was melancholy, never serious, and was always sucking up to someone. After ringing the doorbell, she waited for what seemed to be too long; then, Dumas opened the door.

She anticipated his normal, boisterous welcome and a big hug, which nearly always lifted her off the floor; it made her feel uncomfortable, but instead and rather sheepishly, Dumas made quick eye contact and looked away. "Hello," he said, gesturing for her to enter. Then, he added, "Welcome to our party."

Colleen was pleasantly surprised that she didn't receive the crushing hug, but she knew something was not right. She stepped in, and Dumas closed the door behind her. She turned to Dumas and said, "What's with you? Did you wake up somebody else today?"

Whenever Colleen and Dumas were together, they incessantly bantered back and forth. Dumas just sheepishly grinned and said, "No, I… I just didn't sleep well last night, but it's good to see you."

Colleen asked, "Where are Durand and Dominique?"

It had been a long time since she last saw her favorite niece, and she was anticipating Dominique to come running and jump into her arms, the big hug Colleen liked immensely. "Durand is always late," Dumas answered. "He is still packing upstairs, and Dominique got sick last night, and she didn't even come down for supper."

He went on to tell her of the evening circumstances. "She has been in her room since around eight last night. I went up to talk to her before supper, and she had just taken a shower and said, 'I will see you at supper.' I left but went up about an hour later, and she said she was sick and would not be coming down. Just before bed, I knocked on her door again, and she said she was still not feeling well and had gotten into bed. I asked if I could get her something. 'Thank you, no,' she said. This morning, I knocked again, and she said she was still awfully sick. I asked if I could help, and she just said, 'No, I will wait for Aunt Colleen.' I have been worried because she would not see me," he told Colleen. He finished his thoughts by saying, "I am glad you are here."

Not knowing what to say and just grasping at straws, he said, "Maybe it is that time of the month?" Colleen knew how weak Dumas was, and inside, she was angry with him for not making more of an effort to see Dominique. Dumas looked at his watch and realized it was time for them to go. He smiled at Colleen and said, "I need to grab Durand and get on the road."

Colleen said, "I understand; I will check on Dominique."

"Thank you," Dumas said and yelled up the stairs to Durand, "Son, we are out of time; let's go."

Durand came running down to the foyer with his suitcase; he appeared as he always did to Colleen, aloof and arrogant. He brushed by Colleen and said, "Hey."

Colleen nodded, and father and son headed out the door. As the door closed, Colleen felt uneasy about Dumas and Durand's demeanor. *Something is wrong*, she thought. Colleen turned, facing upstairs, worried; she grabbed her luggage and quickly ascended toward Dominique's room.

*　*　*

After Uncle Dumas left her door the first time, Dominique sobbed. She could not stop sobbing. She cried, wishing Mom and Dad were home. She cried due to the pain she was feeling. She cried for so long that it made her sick, but due to the pain, she could barely crawl to the bathroom. She didn't make it and threw up on the bathroom floor. Dominique was unable to move herself from the cold bathroom floor. Laying there in her own vomit, spent, she fell asleep.

When Uncle Dumas came back a little while later and wanted to know if Dominique was coming to supper, his knocking on the door woke her. She was confused with her surroundings and still in great pain, and when Dumas asked if she would come down for supper, Dominique raised her head to answer but could hardly get a word out; her head was pounding, and her throat was parched. She replied, "No, I am sick; I will just stay in bed."

After Dumas left, she spent some time lying there. She thought, *I really need to get to my bed*. So, rising slowly, she found her T-shirt and underwear on the bathroom floor and painfully adorned them. Dominique half crawled half slid to the vanity, where she struggled to pull herself up. As she rose, her head started to pound, and she became nauseous again.

Trying to stand upright, she caught her likeness in the mirror; she was aghast at the image that looked back at her. All over her head, her long black hair was strewn everywhere, fuzzy, matted together with vomit clumps. Her face was grotesquely too white and gaunt. Her bloodshot eyes were sunken and darker than she ever remembered. The deep redness around her puffy eyes jumped out from the pale reflection of her ashen face; she gasped at what appeared before her.

Forced to look away, she started moving over to the edge of the bed and sat down. The throbbing pain in her stomach made it difficult to lie down, but when she moved her head down toward her knees to relieve the pain, she became nauseous. Sitting up made her head feel like it was going to explode; she was forced to roll over onto her side. With her feet still on the floor, she put her head carefully on her pillow. Finally, some of the pain began to subside, which left her with something other than the physical pain to consider. Yes, an even greater pain was welling up, the pain of remembering her ordeal.

Dominique was finding it hard to grasp the depth of the evil she had just experienced. Fear began to turn into anger. Lost in her resentment, she forgot about time. She could only focus on the hatred she had for Durand. Growing weary from the strain of hate, she carefully lifted her legs up into bed, pulled her knees into the fetal position, and dozed off.

Around eleven o'clock, Dominique awoke again to Uncle Thomas knocking on her door. She knew he was worried, but she could not let him see her like this. She said again, "I am still sick; I will just stay here till morning when Aunt Colleen arrives. Thanks for checking on me." After Dumas left, she was no longer able to sleep. Dominique began to think about the difficulty of what was next. *What will I do?* she thought.

Visions in a loop played over and over as night rolled into early morning. Around seven o'clock, just as Dominique began to doze off, Uncle Dumas was at the door again. She thought, *I can't help but worry him; how could I confide in him?* As before, she told Dumas she was not improving and would wait for Aunt Colleen to help her.

As she listened to her uncle moving down the hall, a dreadful thought encroached upon her frailty; she thought, *How will I tell Aunt Colleen? She loves me deeply; she is my protector and confidant.* Then, a fearsome actuality gripped her, and tears welled up again in her eyes; it scared Dominique. She trembled and said to herself, "She has always been able to read me like a book. What will I tell my aunt, Colleen?"

* * *

Having just arrived in her Philadelphia hotel room, Marie was busy putting things in order. She always loved going to metropolitan areas. Many of their friends lived in Philadelphia, and these friends always had much to do and talk about. Marie was feeling sort of guilty for being relieved at not having Dominique around for a few days, but now that they had arrived, she decided she was going to relax and enjoy city life. *Besides*, she thought, *parents need breaks from their children. And I really need a break from this one and her cousin.*

Once they arrived, Thomas and Marie were always in two different worlds. Thomas was all business, and Marie was hungry for fellowship. Prior to leaving for Philly, Marie made plans to spend her first night with her best friend, Chloe.

Chloe and Marie first met when Thomas and Chloe's husband, Antoine, partnered in a business opportunity. Marie found Antoine too serious, kind of like Thomas, "all business," but Chloe was like a breath of fresh air. Chloe could light up a room by just entering. She engaged everyone she met, and Marie never heard Chloe say a bad word about anyone. She also dealt with calamity better than anyone Marie knew. There was something about Chloe, a confidence, a peace that was contagious, and for some reason, she made Marie, just by being around her, want to be a better person.

So, having this chance to be with Chloe was like medicine, like inner healing, and Marie was in dire need of refreshing. Contemplating in the car on the way to Chloe's home, Marie reminisced about those wonderful days past spent with Chloe. She thought to herself, *I need to spend more time with Chloe.*

She balanced that thought with how sometimes Chloe could be a matter of fact as it pertains to morality and right and wrong stuff, but for the most part, Chloe was one in a million, even if she was a little overzealous on religious matters.

Breaking into her thoughts, Marie remembered she had not called home yet to verify if Colleen had arrived and to let Dominique and Colleen know they landed safely in the city. Marie felt warm and serene as she placed the call. She also felt somewhat giddy and excited to see Chloe. Watching the city lights go by made her countenance almost glow. She smiled and thought, *This will be a great break from home.*

***

Still scrutinizing the oddity of her meeting with Dumas downstairs, Colleen had arrived at Dominique's bedroom door; she knocked lightly, saying, "Honey, it's Aunt Colleen." Putting her ear close to the door to hear a response, she grabbed the doorknob, but it was locked. She knocked again, fearful. Now she raised her voice and said, "Dominique, is everything all right?"

Knowing that if Aunt Colleen didn't get a response soon, she would break down the door, Dominique could be silent no more. Accepting the fact that there was no place for her to hide, Dominique answered, "Just a minute."

Trying to make her hair look presentable, she limped over to the door and unlocked it. Colleen was ready on the other side; as soon as she felt the door unlock, she wasted no time. She quickly turned the door handle and pushed the door open.

Standing there struggling not to bend over, Dominique forced a weak smile and said, "I am sorry I took so long, but I am very sick, and I don't want to give what I have to my aunt, Colleen."

Startled at what she saw, Colleen just stood there staring at her decimated niece. Then, she gasped, saying, "Dominique, what has happened to you?" Dominique explained that she had been sick for a couple of days and hadn't eaten or slept much.

Taking stalk of the whole situation, trying to factor in Dumas's explanation of the last couple of days, as well as Dominique's side of the story, Colleen questioned Dominique, saying, "You didn't ask for your uncle Dumas's help?"

Knowing that her aunt was the best at getting to the bottom of things, coupling that with knowing she was not easily duped, Dominique replied, "I didn't want to bother him, and I really didn't think there was much he could do."

Dominique went over in her mind how many times Aunt Colleen had helped her. *She is the best aunt anyone could want. So many times when I needed to talk, she was there.* Dominique remembered how Aunt Colleen defended her and took her side, but she also remembered how her aunt helped her through some of the disasters Dominique would get herself into. Aunt Colleen would reason with her and say, "Honey, this situation is of your making; what are you going to do to make it better?"

Dominique was straining to remain upright and hoping to get Aunt Colleen off the questioning mode. She told her aunt, "I need to lie down." Taking Dominique tenderly by the arm, Aunt Colleen led her over to the bed.

Dominique winced several times as her aunt tried to lay her back upon her pillow. With her eyes closed and trying not to reveal too much pain, Dominique said, "Thank you, that feels much better." Aunt Colleen put the back of her hand on Dominique's forehead, checking for a fever, and surmised Dominique was not feverish.

While brushing Dominique's hair away from her face, Colleen noticed a rather large bruise on Dominique's neck. Sitting on the edge of the bed and trying to make sense of the neck bruise, Colleen slowly lifted the left sleeve of the T-shirt Dominique had pulled on while on the bathroom floor. There on the back of her arm was another bruise, which looked like someone had roughly grabbed her. Colleen looked straight into Dominique's eyes and said, "How did you get these bruises? Dominique looked down, thinking, *How do I get around this?*

Embarrassed, Dominique looked up; she could not let her know what really happened, so she lied. She sheepishly began, "I was so sick and tried to get to the toilet but threw up on the bathroom floor. I ended up slipping in my vomit, striking my neck on the vanity, and as I fell, I landed hard on my arm. I lay there, unable to move, and fell asleep, lying in my mess. That is why my hair is so ratted, and I bet I stink terribly."

Colleen was having difficulty believing the story. Dominique did smell awful, but she knew Dominique was not telling the whole story. Seeing her so hurt, Colleen left the interrogation and asked Dominique, "Sweetheart, how can I help you right now?"

***

After getting Dominique comfortable, Colleen went downstairs to get some tea and crackers. Dominique was dehydrated and needed nourishment. While busy in the kitchen, Colleen's thoughts were racing. She knew Dominique too well. *Dominique lied to stay out of trouble; that is her MO, but why, suffering like she is, lie and hide the truth?*

Looking back, Colleen went over Dominique's story in her mind. Dominique never made eye contact. From past experience, that is a dead giveaway, she reminded herself, saying, "She never makes eye contact when not telling the truth."

Colleen kept searching her thoughts on how to help Dominique physically while wrestling with how to pull Dominique into a conversation about what really happened. Baffled but determined, her mind was swirling, and anger was beginning to set in; she reacted inwardly, saying, "What happened to my beautiful Dom?"

Just then, the teapot started to whistle, and at the same time, the phone began to ring. To kill the whistling teapot, Colleen raced over to turn off the stove so she could answer the phone. The phone had rung several times before she got to it. Somewhat out of breath from rushing around, she answered the call, "Hello."

It was Marie on the other end. "Oh, you are there. I'm so glad to hear your voice," Marie said.

Colleen, surprised by the call but glad to hear her sister, said, "Yes, and I am so happy to be here." Colleen couldn't help but sense the excitement in Marie's voice.

Marie continued, "I suppose Dumas and Durand are already on their way to Philly?"

"Yes, they are off," Colleen confirmed.

Marie continued, "And how was your reunion with Dominique? She was so excited that you were coming!" Pausing for just a minute, Colleen put her thoughts together, a little too long of a pause for Marie; Marie quickly asked, "Is everything okay?"

Colleen was contemplating how to tell her sister about Dominique's plight. Knowing each other as sisters do, Colleen realized she would have to come clean with what she found when she arrived. So, she said, "No, everything is not okay."

Marie gasped and said, "What?"

Colleen began to explain, saying, "Dumas told me when I arrived that Dominique had been sick for most of the last night and this morning."

Marie interrupted, "What is the matter?"

Colleen continued, "Let me tell you. Dumas went to her door to get her to come down for supper, and she told him she just got out of the shower and would see him in a little bit. She didn't show up for supper, so he went up again, and she told him she was not feeling well and would skip dinner. Dumas went up again later that night and asked if he could help. She said no. Again, this morning, he went back, and she told him she was no better and that she would just wait for Aunt Colleen. I think Dumas was concerned and tried to help, but Dumas is not one to really want to get involved." Colleen had to get that in.

Marie was starting to get nervous and said, "Colleen—"

Stopping her, Colleen said, "Let me go on." And she continued, "After the boys left, I went upstairs thinking about how weird Dumas seemed; he was not himself. When I arrived at Dom's door, it was locked; she didn't answer right away and was slowly getting to the door. When she opened the door, I was shocked at her appearance."

Marie kind of gasped again on the other end of the conversation and said, "Colleen, tell me what has happened."

Colleen went on, "Staring at Dominique was painful. Her face was sunken, her eyes swollen, and she looked ghostly white. She was dehydrated, and her hair was all over her head, matted and in disarray. I found a large bruise on the back of her neck and one on the back of her arm."

At this point, Marie let out a cry and said, "Oh my," and started to weep.

Colleen went on, "Dominique explained to me that she got sick and could not make it to the toilet and threw up on the floor, which she slipped in and hit her neck on the sink and hit her arm on the tile floor when she fell. She said she fell asleep in her own vomit on the floor."

Marie was starting to feel relieved at this point because this story made sense, and she said, "Is she better now? Thank God you are there."

Colleen paused again, which Marie picked up on instantly. Marie asked, "What aren't you telling me?"

Colleen began again, "I don't believe this story; I don't believe she is telling the truth."

Marie asked Colleen, "What do you mean 'she's not telling you the truth'?" Pausing again to gather her thoughts caused Marie to react, and she half yelled, "Colleen, what is happening?"

"Well," Colleen began, "Dom is hurt in ways that are not consistent with her story. Also, she would not look me in the eyes, and that is a dead giveaway: she is not telling the truth about her injuries."

Anguishing, Marie asked, "What do you think happened then?"

Replying carefully, Colleen said, "I don't know for sure, but I need to spend some time with Dom to evaluate if she is sick or if she is injured."

At that, Marie started to panic. She told Colleen, "I am coming home right now."

Colleen said, "Marie, it is pretty late notice to catch a flight, and with the traffic, you won't be home for several hours. Please talk it over with Thomas; there may be business issues that can't wait. Either way, I will not leave her side, and I hope after getting her settled, she will open up about what happened."

At this point, Marie decided she would not be spending the night in the city, and in frustration, she cried out to her sister, "I am not waiting another moment; I am coming home now." She ended the conversation by adding, "If Dominique is injured, how could Dumas not know?"

This thought put both sisters on the same wavelength.

CHAPTER 6

Marie hung up and called Thomas. He did not answer; that is the way it is when Thomas is doing business. Agitated, she screamed at her phone, "Why don't you ever answer your phone?" Marie told the driver to turn around and go back to the hotel. On the trip back to the hotel, Marie tried several times to reach Thomas but to no avail, which only angered her more.

Arriving at the hotel, she hurried up to their room and tried Thomas again. No answer. Having become beside herself, she cried out, "To hell with you, I am going home." Hurriedly, Marie began throwing clothes into a suitcase, but right in the middle of this, she remembered she needed to call Chloe.

Chloe picked up on the first ring, and having someone to share with, Marie burst into tears. Sobbing now, she tried to let Chloe know what happened and that she was sorry but would not be able to make it over.

Chloe was instantly alert, but Marie was not making sense. Chloe calmly said, "Marie, I know you are hurting; please slow down and tell me how I can help."

Marie took in a few deep breaths in between sobs and started over. Feeling comforted now, knowing Chloe was on the other end of the line. Beginning again, she said, "I just got off the phone with Colleen; Dominique is injured or sick, and she won't tell Colleen what happened. I must get home now, and I can't get hold of Thomas."

She continued, "Colleen was sketchy on details, and I am freaking out." Marie asked Chloe, "Would you try to contact Antoine to see where Thomas is?"

Chloe assured Marie she would track Thomas down as soon as they got off the phone. Chloe told Marie, "I am so sorry, Marie… Is there anything else I can do?"

Still holding back the tears, Marie said, "No, but I don't know what I would have done if you hadn't been available. Thank you! I love you."

Chloe responded calmly, "I love you too, but are you sure you can travel home alone?"

Marie assured Chloe she could. She said, "I have already asked the driver to keep the car running; he is ready to go."

"Before you hang up," Chloe interjected, "can I pray for you, Thomas, and Dominique?"

Marie was somewhat taken aback and said, "Do you mean on the phone?"

Chloe answered, "Yes…" She sounded so sure and sincere and said, "I believe God answers prayer, and He knows what you need right now."

Marie heard herself say yes but then thinking, *Why did I say yes?* She asked herself, *I don't know what to do. Do I bow my head and close my eyes?*

So, Marie sat there on the bed, uncomfortable and confused, thinking, *Does God really answer prayer?* And then Chloe began talking to God. Chloe spoke as if she knew Him; she poured out her heart for God to heal Dominique and bring peace to Marie's family. Chloe told God how much she loved Marie and that she knew that God loved her more than she ever could.

Marie could tell Chloe trusted God; it was evident by how she called upon Him with boldness and humility at the same time. Marie was fixed on the words of the prayer, and although she felt somewhat embarrassed, it took her to places she had never been before, and she could feel the comfort flowing out in Chloe's plea to God. When Chloe said, "In Jesus's name, I pray. Amen," it caught Marie by surprise, almost hoping it wouldn't end.

Marie was still contemplating what had just taken place when Chloe said, "Call me if you need anything. I will come to your home if you need me, and I will keep praying daily for you."

Marie said, "I know I can count on you, Chloe. Goodbye."

As Marie ended the call, everything began to move in a kind of slow motion. She was not frantic as before; Chloe's words subdued the pain and anxiety. Marie felt weird but, at the same time, comforted in Chloe's prayer. Marie grabbed her bags and headed for the door, but she was not running for the door, and somehow, she didn't feel the panic like before.

***

Somewhat bothered by the call, Antoine answered it, thinking, *Chloe, I know you know we are doing business.* Antoine said, "Hello."

Chloe calmly asked Antoine, "Is Thomas there?"

"Yes," Antoine replied, "but we are very busy here. What is it?"

Chloe told him, "Dominique is sick or injured. Marie isn't sure, but she has been trying to get hold of Thomas for about an hour with no luck, and she is heading home. He should call her."

Antoine's first thought was, *That girl is such a pain.* Then, he asked Chloe, "Is this so serious that the deal tomorrow can't happen first? Thomas and I are going over details for tomorrow right now."

Without missing a beat, Chloe said, "Thomas needs to call Marie. Dominique needs her parents; that is the message."

Finally, sensing the urgency in his wife's voice was all he needed to know. Antoine told Chloe, "I will go directly to him now and let him know."

Chloe hung up and began praying again.

***

Having the reputation for getting a little cranky prior to pulling off a big deal, Thomas was on edge. For Thomas, nothing is ever in the bag; even with the best due diligence, anything can go wrong. He and Antoine were going over all the variables with Dumas when Chloe called.

As Antoine came back into the room, Thomas asked, "Who was that?" After hearing Antoine's answer, Thomas could not believe his ears. "How can this happen tonight?" He grimaced. "Maybe Marie is right; maybe we do need to put Dominique into a boarding school. We can't leave for a day without her drama overtaking us."

Antoine just shrugged his shoulders and said, "What are you going to do?"

"Well, first," he said, "I'd better call and calm Marie down." He hated these confrontations involving Dominique. Just as Thomas was leaving the room to speak with Marie, Dumas entered.

His brother was moving fast and looked agitated. Dumas asked Antoine, "Everything okay with the deal?"

Antoine replied, "It all depends on what kind of trouble Dominique is in again. I am sure it is just Dominique being herself. It should not sidetrack a multimillion-dollar project." Then he added, "But you never know with that girl."

Dumas just stood there in shock; he felt his heart beating fast in his chest. He looked around the room frantically and then settled his gaze on the downtown area outside their room. He stared blindly out at nothing; he had not discussed Dominique's illness with Thomas. Dumas had not seen Marie yet, and Thomas had not asked about things at home.

He got butterflies in his stomach, thinking there may be more to the story than what Dominique shared with him. Then, Dumas tried to draw comfort by telling himself, *As much as I love that girl, she has cried wolf so many times before; maybe that is all it is.*

As Thomas came back into the room, his countenance was intense, and he threw his phone onto the bed and cursed bitterly.

"What is wrong?" Antoine asked sheepishly.

Dumas just looked at his brother, raised his shoulders, and asked, "What?"

* * *

Marie received Thomas's call about half an hour after she left the hotel heading towards home; he was under high stress, complaining about how the deal would fall through and how this was just like Dominique.

After getting off the call, Marie was numb, not panicked; sad, really. She knew she would soon be home and holding Dominique, and that was her priority, but she also knew that when Thomas arrived home, once again, there would be intense family strife as well as Dominique being the catalyst.

Marie went over in her mind the many times Dominique had manipulated them, and yet, her heart was burdened for both Dominique and Thomas; they were so alike and, really, almost dysfunctional together. *How can we continue to do this? We need help. Maybe a boarding school is the answer.* Leaning back in the car seat, she sighed, saying, "Thomas doesn't like problems."

Her thoughts continued. *But this is not business; this is our Dominique, and besides, he knows Colleen. She would not call if it were not a serious situation.* Her thoughts continued cautiously. *But how many times has Dominique raised false alarms? Can I believe what she tells me?* Then Marie remembered Colleen's warning, how she analyzed the situation, and she said to herself, "No, Colleen has a gift at diagnosing dilemmas; if she says Dom is injured and not sick, that is probably the case."

Unsettled by it all, she sat in the dark, afraid. Watching the miles go by brought her no peace, and then she did something; she couldn't remember the last time she had done this by herself: she prayed silently, "Oh, God, help us…"

* * *

Colleen was busy in Dominique's room, cleaning up the bathroom mess. Her thoughts were racing; not knowing what had really happened agitated her. As she walked back to where Dominique was lying, Colleen was burdened and angered by the severity of her niece's condition. Sitting on the bed, Colleen ran her fingers gently down Dominique's ashen cheek.

"Honey," she said, "I know you are hurting; I have run a bath, and we have to get you washed up and into clean night clothes."

Struggling to open her eyes, Dominique winced and said, "Aunt Colleen, I am not sure I can get up."

Fighting back the tears, she sat staring at the suffering of her beautiful Dom. Then she said, "Come on, baby, you can do this." Gently putting her arm around Dominique's shoulder, she pulled her up.

Dominique let out a little cry and grabbed Aunt Colleen's other hand. When she tried to use her stomach muscles, Dominique fell back, wincing in pain. As they worked to get her in a sitting position, Colleen was taken aback by how thin and frail Dominique was.

Slowly, they moved to the bath. Dominique was still hunched over and very weak. Colleen sat her on the edge of the tub and cautiously removed Dominique's soiled T-shirt and underwear. As Dominique's underwear fell to the floor, Colleen noticed a few drops of blood. She quickly looked at Dominique, but Dominique's eyes were still closed, and she was wincing in pain.

Gently moving one leg and then another, Colleen finally got Dominique into the bath water. The bath was hot, and Colleen added some bubbles. The hot bath was therapeutic to Dominique's aching body. After a few minutes, she began to feel her stomach muscles relax, still hurting all over, but the pain began to subside.

Soaking in the tub, Dominique began to run over in her mind all that had happened and the predicament she found herself in. She became angry again and was resolved that she was no longer to blame for anything that took place.

She tried to put the thought of Durand out of her mind but to no avail. *How could he hurt me so?* Then, with emotion taking over, she said out loud, "I hate him." It startled her that she said that out loud. She quickly opened one eye to see if Colleen was in the bathroom. *What if she heard me?* she said to herself. *No, she couldn't hear me*, she surmised. Colleen was in the bedroom changing the bedding.

* * *

Thomas could not find a private plane to get him home; adding frustration to an already impossible situation, he was left stewing in a rental car, racing back to their home. He hoped, almost without hope, that Dumas and Antoine would be up to the task of closing the deal. Then he thought, *I have done all I can to make this deal happen.* Still, he winced at the possibility Dumas and Antoine together could figure out a way to mess it up.

Thomas was a control freak, and he had never felt so out of control. Traveling for some time, he began to realize that he had a death grip on the steering wheel, and his arms and hands were cramping up. Relaxing his arms and hands, he was also able to take a deep breath and let it out. Letting that breath out was like opening a steam valve, and he began to realize the desperation of his situation.

In business, Thomas is most rational and, therefore, most successful. He relishes gathering, analyzing, collating the data, and going for the jugular. He views business as a battle, and his strategy is simple: the winners get the spoils. This battle invigorated him and gave him peace. On the other hand, family dynamic was difficult for Thomas most of the time, and he was lost.

He hated feeling guilty for the family makeup, and whenever those thoughts came in, he would just as quickly push them out. He would tell himself, "My family lacks nothing; I am a good provider. What more could I do?" But today, he began to sense a dull, foreboding ache in his stomach. He had to admit, "I am not the ideal father or husband, nor a success in my family."

With an hour left to get home, he began to reminisce about the days when the children weren't around, and it was just him and Marie. In those days, they had the world by the tail; nothing seemed to slow them down or get in their way. Marie was so happy, and home was almost utopian.

Then he felt guilty again, but this time, he knew there was no pushing it away, no blaming someone else. He said out loud, "You selfish jerk!" Having heard himself say that out loud, he kind of looked around to be sure he was in the car alone. It was a heavy truth for Thomas to swallow, and the implications were daunting to him. He was feeling bad now for how he spoke to Marie on the phone. He knew he had hurt her. He thought, *I was so insensitive; I was blaming Dominique and Marie for having derailed the business opportunity.*

The thought that plagued him most was how he had hurt Marie. He heard her desperation, but he could not empathize with his grieving bride; no, he just yelled at her. She was his lifeline, and his life made sense because of her. Wrestling with his thoughts, he proposed, "What is the point of being, as it were, a land baron and having all this stuff without his baroness?"

She was his real everything, and he said to himself, "One day, the pain I cause her will be greater than the love she has for me." He almost laughed at his sentimentality but then realized, *What would I do without Marie? How do I begin re-prioritizing my home and family?*

Thomas felt odd as if this was not really him talking to himself. Isolated, traveling hurriedly along, separate from everyone, he was lonely, and his heart ached for home. Feeling something that he had not felt since childhood, he wasn't sure how to assess it all, but the best way to describe it was that he was feeling melancholy; he hated melancholy people, but this new clarity of thought betrayed his hypocrisy and forced him to reconsider his life.

He thought to himself, *This is not about me; for once in your life, Thomas, this is not about you.* And he realized it wasn't about guilt this time, which always racked him terribly in these situations; rather, it was about what is important.

Swallowed up in the truth of his thoughts, Thomas drifted back to the early days at home; he was very young, and his mom and dad cared for him; he missed that love which he knew then, love from both

God, family, and the church. Then, as if to push it all away, he said, "Oh, why think about that now?" But deep inside, he could not deny he needed to change, and right now, something was changing.

His home was close now, and he began to reflect: "The love of business has taken my soul and left me wanting. How can business be my 'precious'? Precious is home, especially right now, because of the pain Dominique is suffering. Whatever this may be…" He paused and looked up sheepishly, acknowledging his feebleness, and said, "I am not a good husband or father; help me to rise up for them." Sitting there silent, with his heart in his hand, straining to arrive, he ached for home and being with Marie and Dominique.

It was not long after their disastrous trip to Philadelphia, coupled with the uncertainty of what had happened to Dominique while they were gone. Thomas and Maire agreed that they did not feel good about their daughter in public school, so they enrolled at William James.

CHAPTER 7

The deception with Mrs. Martsen had worked for now. Leaving the dispensary and heading to her dorm room, Dominique was still in deep thought. She knew she had messed up, not staying with her team on the hike, and was feeling too tired for another skirmish with Mrs. Martsen.

Her thoughts somehow meandered back to the pain in her life and how she ended up at William James. She began to wonder if it was worth continuing the fight when she did not even know what she was fighting for. She never allowed herself to remember what happened with Durand, but today, even those thoughts kept creeping in.

Inside her room now, she felt exhausted and depressed, overwrought with emotion. Suddenly, she threw herself down onto the bed and began to cry. Then, without remedy, she began to sob uncontrollably. She couldn't stop; the anguish poured out in tears, wetting her pillow and hair. For nearly thirty minutes, this went on, and then she sat up, took a few deep breaths, wiped the tears from her eyes, and brushed back her long black hair away from her face, which was now wet and clinging to her.

The pain and suffering remained, but she could cry no more, Dominique concluded; she had no answers. She was too emotional to make sense or a defense of anything. Then she remembered what her aunt, Colleen, told her when things became too hard. "Dominique," Colleen told her, "when things don't make sense to me, and I have come to the end of my rope, I pray and write down my thoughts." Dominique decided the first part of Aunt Colleen's advice concerning prayer would not happen, but she was so depressed she thought, *Maybe writing my thoughts out will help me.*

Dominique slowly, painfully slid off the bed to the floor. She had no strength; her head was pounding, and when she stood, she nearly fell back down onto the bed. Bracing herself, she moved methodically over to her desk and sat down. There on top of the desk was a mess: makeup and curlers, creams and lotions, stuff she hadn't used in months.

With her desk a mess, there was no place to even begin to write down her thoughts. Frustrated, she angrily thrust it all off the desk onto the floor and then looked up triumphantly at herself in the mirror attached to her desk. She reached inside the desk drawer and pulled out a notebook and pencil. She paused, looking at the notebook, and then slowly looked up into the large mirror again. She was surprised to see her reflection with such pain etched on her face. She hated the image before her and wondered who it was staring back at her.

Still mesmerized by the image set before her, the reflection in the mirror became ominous. She was staring at a red-faced demon with swollen cheeks, sunken eyes, and an uncontrolled head of locks; fearfully, she said, "Who are you?" That stopped her for a moment, and she just kept staring. Then, slowly looking down, she focused on the empty lines before her, and she wrote these words: "Who are you?" Having written it down, she paused again to look up at herself. Still there, glaring at her, was the same pale aberration mercilessly staring back at her.

Dominique could not think of anything else to write; there were no more thoughts, there was nothing more to add to her story, and this was all there was to her premise. Depression set in and began to numb her mind, and she thought to herself, *What is the point of going on?*

Gingerly, she turned away from the ghostly figure before her and moved slowly back onto her bed. As Dominique was lying there, her face felt like it was swollen, like when all the blood has rushed into your head. Lethargically, she lodged her pillow up under her head and brought her knees up to her chest. While she was beginning to pull the covers up to her chin, her next thought surprised her, and she said to herself, "Maybe it is not worth it." That thought, strangely, gave her peace, and she fell asleep.

Her dreams startled her, and Dominique awoke frantic in the dark. After coming to grips with her surroundings, she calmed, lying there enjoying the privacy and the pitch black. Dominique could see nothing, not even her hand in front of her face. It felt weird, but this opaque sphere was not frightening but rather calming. The peace of it seemed limitless, and the pain of the light of her reality was nonexistent. Dominique did not want to move and destroy the serenity of this moment. "Finally, a place for me," she said to herself.

All of Dominique's life, she forced the world to revolve around her. Her dad made sure she was the center of his universe. She was too selfish to think about enduring any suffering, but this was a new concept: being alone in the dark was refreshing, and it came without any hassles, a built-in bubble, a safety net.

How tranquil, she thought, *to just turn out the lights on life*. Dominique felt small and insignificant, completely alone, but she felt no pangs of suffering in it. It seemed almost uncomplicated for her; rather than think about how to endure, it was time to begin thinking about how not to exist anymore, and she dosed back to sleep.

Awakening in panic, Dominique sat up, frightened by the anxiety of another bad dream. She was instantly despondent as she opened her eyes to find herself still in the insanity of another new day. From her window, the sun blared into her peace and exposed what her eyes longed not to see. The thought of a school day was impossible to imagine.

Dominique had more sick days than any student on campus, and she knew faking sick with Mrs. Martsen would not fly. Dominique was sure that Mrs. Martsen would be chomping at the bit to interrogate her concerning the hiking incident. Dominique had contrived so many excuses with Mrs. Martsen that she said to herself, "There is no way for me to win this battle." Then she stopped her conniving, and a fresh and wonderful thought entered her mind: *I don't care what Mrs. Martsen thinks*. Suddenly, she was not afraid of the consequences; she thought, *What can they do to me? What can they take?*

Refreshed by the peace of not caring, she fell back asleep. Not long after her nap, there came a knock on her door. Dominique was slow to respond to the noise of knocking, and not even opening her eyes, she yelled, "Get lost." On the other side of the door, Mrs. Martsen was instantly hot. She quickly reached for the master key on her hip and opened the door.

With her thoughts instantly scuttled, Mrs. Martsen could only see red. Having once again to deal with the never-ending drama that was Dominique, she had reached the limit. She did not raise her voice, but she was burning inside. "Dominique," she said calmly, "you are late for breakfast. Why are you still in bed?"

With her new confidence, Dominique did not respond. Mrs. Martsen stepped closer and said, "Dominique, answer me." Dominique, still lying with her back to Mrs. Martsen, did not move or respond. Then, Mrs. Martsen moved quickly over to the other side of the bed to see Dominique's face; from there, she stared at Dominique.

Dominique's eyes were wide open, with no expression on her face, staring at nothing. "Young lady, I am talking to you!" Mrs. Martsen exclaimed. Still, Dominique remained silent, unmoved.

At this point, Mrs. Martsen thought, *Why do we continue to allow this child to exploit our good senses?* She moved forward, reacting to the situation, and was just about to pull the covers off Dominique to force her up, but she stopped and thought, *Wait a minute, this is not Dominique's way; she loves confrontation and the opportunity to make a case; she has given no excuses for her insolence.* So, Mrs. Martsen backed up and calmly responded by saying, "Dominique, if you do not dialogue, I will have no choice but to call for the school nurse to come and visit you." Dominique continued to act stoically defiant, so Mrs. Martsen called the nurse.

The nurse was busy handling the needs of another student and told Mrs. Martsen that she would be there soon. Mrs. Martsen grabbed the chair from Dominique's desk and pulled it up in front of Dominique, still lying in her bed, still staring motionless. Mrs. Martsen began a new approach in trying to understand Dominique's needs. She began by saying, "Dominique, I know you hear me because I heard you yell, 'Get lost.' Why are you doing this?" Dominique did not reply.

Mrs. Martsen did not trust Dominique at all but was beginning to think something was different, and she felt Dominique was showing signs of being closed off. Being trained and familiar with "individuation" (a normal closing off of children who are coping with becoming an adult), Mrs. Martsen started to become alarmed. So, she began again and said, "Dominique, has something happened that you cannot talk about?"

Dominique would not look at Mrs. Martsen, but she was thinking, *Mrs. Martsen seems at a loss at what to do here.* She smiled inside and said to herself, *This new outlook of mine has some positive benefits.* She continued in her thoughts: *How about that? I am in control of the situation and not Mrs. Martsen.* But that thought wasn't nearly as pleasing for Dominique as she thought it would be because apathy had won the war, and Mrs. Martsen was no longer an issue.

Dominique began to understand: she wielded the power by not caring any longer. Still talking to herself and becoming more pleased with herself, she said, *This new power alleviates the need for energy spent on manipulation strategy. This is safe and simple.* She thought, *And I am going to stay right here.*

Mrs. Martsen tried again. "Dominique, I know I am not the person you would feel most comfortable confiding in, but if you don't help me know what is happening to you, I will have to call our doctor. Is that what you want me to do?"

Dominique was unafraid and unmoving, and she said to herself, *This new perspective is what is best for me.*

The nurse arrived but had no more success than Mrs. Martsen in getting a response from Dominique. Mrs. Martsen asked the nurse to remain with Dominique while she went to visit with the school doctor. Having discussed the situation with the doctor, she suggested that Mrs. Martsen and the nurse transport Dominique to the dispensary. Mrs. Martsen was beginning to feel something was truly amiss with Dominique, so she took a wheelchair from the dispensary with her back to Dominique's room.

Moving the wheelchair over to the side of the bed that Dominique was facing, Mrs. Martsen said, "Dominique, we are really concerned about what you are experiencing and believe it is best that we take you up to the dispensary for evaluation."

Dominique heard but did not care and did not respond. At that point, the nurse on one side and Mrs. Martsen on the other slowly pulled the covers down toward the end of the bed. Dominique was still wearing the clothes she changed into after the hike, and she did not move.

Dominique was closest to the side of the bed that Mrs. Martsen was on, so the nurse moved over there to help pull her up. As they each grabbed an arm and began to pull Dominique over to the edge of the bed and into the wheelchair, Dominique jumped nearly off the bed and screamed for about ten seconds at the top of her voice.

This behavior startled Mrs. Martsen and the nurse; they were forced to let go of Dominique, and she threw herself back to where she lay. Not sure what had transpired, Mrs. Martsen and the nurse just stood there lost and looked at each other.

Mrs. Martsen tried to reason with Dominique and said, "Honey, we need to help you get to the dispensary; please let us help." Dominique recoiled back against the bed headboard, lying on her back; her facial expression was frantic, her eyes darting wildly and hatefully at Mrs. Martsen. Mrs. Martsen has had to help girls who have been depressed, angry, and even somewhat combative before, but she realized Dominique's reaction was something new. It was like a possession.

Mrs. Martsen asked the nurse to step out into the hallway. They both stood in the doorway in the hall, not taking their eyes off Dominique, and discussed how to move forward. The nurse suggested they make no more efforts at physically removing Dominique from her room. Mrs.Martsen agreed but then asked, "What do we do now?"

The nurse told Mrs. Martsen that Dominique was showing classic signs of paranoia. The nurse continued, "If that is the case, we have two options: One, attempt to talk her into receiving help, and two, sedate her for transfer up to the dispensary." The nurse warned, "If this is paranoia, there is a good chance that Dominique will not receive comforting words and could become even more combative."

The entire time the nurse and Mrs. Martsen were in the hall, Dominique never took her eyes off them, and her facial expression remained eerie. Mrs. Martsen asked the nurse to go and prepare a sedative while she attempted to talk Dominique down off the ledge of whatever this cliff was.

Coming back into the room, Mrs. Martsen slowly moved toward the bed. Dominique was pensive and silent, her eyes never leaving Mrs. Martsen as if a wily and dangerous adversary had slunk back into the chair by her bed. Knowing her history with Dominique, Mrs. Martsen was sure this would be a very difficult de-escalation.

She started to go over in her mind who was close to Dominique on campus. She finally had to conclude that most of the teachers have also had to confront and deal with Dominique's behavioral drama. Then she remembered that during one of the parent-teacher conferences, the Meuniers (Thomas and Marie) shared with her how much they appreciated Mrs. Allard, Dominique's science teacher. She recalled how the Meuniers were thankful for Mrs. Allard's care and encouragement. Dominique told her parents that Mrs. Allard was her favorite because she seemed to know kids and where they were coming from.

As that conference came back into focus, Mrs. Martsen's recollection of the conference gave her a new idea and a new hope. After that meeting, the Meuniers confided to her that Mrs. Allard was the only teacher Dominique really trusted. They were hopeful that Mrs. Allard would have some special time with Dominique to build a relationship. That being the case, Mrs. Martsen said to herself, "We need support, and we need it now."

Just then, the nurse came back in with the sedative. Mrs. Martsen asked the nurse if she would sit with Dominique while she left to get some help. The nurse started to say something but stopped, realizing by her body language and the expression on her face that Mrs. Martsen was on a mission.

On the way back to her office, Mrs. Martsen was torn between calling Dominique's parents or trying to resolve this at school. She was hoping to discern which would garner the better outcome. Then she thought, *Dominique's past is full of phone calls home.* As Mrs. Martsen was taking that into consideration, she remembered it always appeared that phoning home just frustrated the Meuniers.

She thought back to the many meetings with Dominique's parents. They would sit in her office, berate Dominique, and tell the school it should handle things better on this end. She remembered Thomas saying, "We spend an awful lot of money here. Isn't handling this what we are paying you to do?" *Marie was more sympathetic*, Mrs. Martsen remembered, *but Thomas always seemed to react as if his being at school was a huge inconvenience. He had other priorities, and he wanted us to know it.*

At her office now, she sat at her desk, still anguishing over the best option; Mrs. Martsen put her head in her hands and wrestled in futility. She finally came to the conclusion that this was over her head.

Her thoughts turned inward, and she started to feel remorse. Then, the obvious set in, and she realized that over the last year, she had not offered a single soft word or a word of comfort to Dominique. In fact, she had shown so little compassion for Dominique that guilt was starting to set in. As she pictured Dominique suffering in her room, she said to herself, *Even if we have Mrs. Allard on board, that is not enough if I am not on board.*

This heavy revelation touched her deep in her soul, and emotion she had not felt in years made her chest ache. She groaned, and the tears began to well up in her eyes. Feeling very unnerved and not wanting anyone to see this vulnerability, she quickly stood up and shut her office door.

She thought to herself, *Dr. James would be so disappointed with me today.* Staring out the office window, she wiped the tears away and found herself saying, "Oh, God, I have become so cold." She was coming to grips with her own frailties, and her pride was fighting back. She was sadly surprised by the deceit, which she had allowed, and now ruled her ability to oversee school matters. This was painful, but this was real, and she said to herself, *Janet, this is not a ministry for you; it is just an occupation.*

She was coming to grips with the possibility that all these years of supposed bathing children in love was rather just a parched desert of indifference, which had dried her soul to the real needs of children. She could not get over the desperate state that Dominique had come to, and she wondered, *What have we done? What have I done to contribute to this suffering? How have I become so blind as not to see the needs of this precious life?*

After a period of wallowing in this new revelation of herself, Mrs. Martsen realized that now was not a good time for her to be self-absorbed; now was the time to begin a support team for Dominique. She quickly called her secretary to send someone over to Mrs. Allard's classroom to relieve her, and she said, "Tell them to have Mrs. Allard come to my office immediately."

Dominique was surprised to see Mrs. Allard step into her room. Seeing the nurse and Mrs.

Martsen standing there with Mrs. Allard, Dominique felt danger. She thought, *Why has Mrs. Allard joined the enemy? The one person I can count on is now also against me.*

Never taking her eyes off the threesome, Dominique drew back in a defensive posture. She thought, *Bring it on; you will need more than three to take me.* Just as Dominique was getting fully ready to go to war, Mrs. Martsen touched the nurse on the shoulder and said, "Let us leave Dominique and Mrs. Allard to themselves." And they turned into the hallway and closed the door.

Though being briefed by Mrs. Martsen of the situation, Mrs. Allard was very uneasy as to how she could help. As they were leaving Mrs. Martsen's office, heading to Dominique's room, Mrs. Allard began to pray. She prayed because she knew the severity of this situation, and she was not sure how God wanted her to proceed. So, she prayed, "Oh, Lord, You are sovereign over this situation, and for some reason, You have invited me into Your workplace. Please remove my anxious thoughts and move into Dominique's suffering and relieve her pain and fear that we may both know Your power over this situation, which, of course, is allowed by You and orchestrated by the enemy of our souls. I pray this in Jesus's name, amen."

Entering the room, Mrs. Allard was staggered by what she saw. She had never seen Dominique with such a crazed look on her face; in fact, she was sure she had never seen anyone who looked so, but as she focused on Dominique's agony, her heart was instantly moved to great compassion. She couldn't understand it, and she also could not help it, but tears began to flood her eyes, and through those tears, a genuine longing to help Dominique came alive, and she said, "Dominique, it is Mrs. Allard. It looks like you need help, and I am here to help, if you want me to be."

Dominique did not budge from her stance; she just stared, with caution, at Mrs Allard. Mrs. Allard continued, "Mrs. Martsen felt it would be better for me to be here alone so you and I could talk. Mrs. Martsen and the nurse have gone back to her office, so it is just you and me."

Dominique was going over every scenario in her mind as to why Mrs. Allard was in her room and what she really wanted. She thought to herself, *Don't they get it? This is where I want to be, and there is no place else.*

Dominique was surprised that Mrs. Allard was weeping, and her hands were shaking too. She thought, *Maybe I frightened her since they left her all alone with me.* She continued her thoughts, saying to herself, *She should be afraid if she tries to remove me from my new place.* But then, looking closely, Dominique could see that Mrs. Allard was not threatening her, just smiling at her and crying.

Not feeling intense pressure from Mrs. Allard, Dominique realized that, having been stuck in one position for so long, her body was now starting to ache from exertion. Mrs. Allard had not moved or exhibited any intimidation except being there, so Dominique relaxed her grip from the bed sheets and rolled over onto her side facing Mrs. Allard, but her eyes remained fixed and wary. As she stared at Mrs. Allard, it felt so good for Dominique to relax her muscles, but there was no way she would relax her disposition.

Mrs. Allard, still looking warmly at Dominique, asked, "Dominique, can I come closer? I have no intention of trying to remove you from your room, and that is not why I have come." After saying that, she thought, *Lord, why have I come?* Mrs. Allard observed that Dominique was no longer bristled, so she asked again, "Please, Dominique, allow me to come closer and speak with you."

This approach was so different from Mrs. Martsen's, and Dominique was feeling more in control, but she thought to herself, *If she tries anything, I think I can take her.* So, Dominique nodded her head giving permission for Mrs. Allard to move closer. Mrs. Allard's smile broadened; wiping the tears from her eyes, she asked, "How about if I grab the chair on the other side of the bed and bring it to this side of the bed and sit there?" Dominique nodded again, but while Mrs. Allard moved to get the chair, like a trapped animal, Dominique's position moved in sync with Mrs. Allard's every step.

CHAPTER 8

Still, in her office, Mrs. Martsen could not get past her failure in this situation, and she began to recall other examples of failures with other students. She realized she had tricked herself into believing that an effective administrator just needs a firm and strategic disciplinary system. She also had herself fooled into believing she was achieving the results the school desired. Now, in remorse, she admitted, *All these years, all my training, and all my credentials…* She dismissed herself, saying, *I am equipped to see children only as I want them to be, not as they are; I am so deceived.*

She just kept beating herself up until she finally asked herself the question, *Maybe I am not the person for this job, and how do the students really see me?* It didn't take long before she knew the answer concerning how the students felt. It hurt as she said to herself, *I am a person of authority only, not a person you can trust.*

She tried to stay focused on Dominique's suffering, but she kept coming back to her own pain. Then she thought, *What is it that makes Mrs. Allard a student favorite? How does she captivate their attention? They all seem to trust her.* Mrs. Martsen thought back to several classes of Mrs. Allard, which, as her supervisor, required her to sit in on and observe.

Science, typically, is one of the more difficult classes to keep everyone's attention. Few of the girls had their sites set on a career in the sciences. Mrs. Martsen drew back to her memory of one class session, which she remembered sitting in on. It was a most interesting eleventh-grade anatomy lesson.

Mrs. Martsen remembered arriving a little after the lesson had begun; sneaking quietly in, she sat in the back of the classroom unnoticed by the students. What immediately caught her attention was an overhead and, on the screen, a naked woman. The students, though, were focused on Mrs. Allard sitting on the edge of her desk.

Mrs. Allard was sharing with the girls the amazing differences between the sexes. She was very calm when describing the female anatomy. She asked her class, "What makes the female anatomy so attractive to the male sex?" At first, the girls were kind of silly and offered the obvious outward extremities of the female anatomy as the attractant. A few bold ones puffed up their chests. Mrs. Allard laughed with them, and the girls all looked at each other somewhat sheepishly and then back to Mrs. Allard. Expectant of where she thought this might go, Mrs. Allard said, "Yes, those are the obvious allurements, but it goes much deeper than that."

She continued, "You need to know, as the opposite sex, how a male sees you." She paused for a minute to ensure that she had everyone's attention. "You need to know how your physical attributes affect males." Mrs. Allard shared with the girls the scientific term for the physical differences between males and females. She continued, "It is called 'sexual dimorphism.'" This was a major area of study for her degree, and she told them how much time she spent learning about how humans, male and female, are amazingly made for attraction to each other.

She alerted the class to the need to know the scientific terms in this area of study, like gender dichotomy—"The perception of the two genders as mutually exclusive, even diametrically opposed, but today," she said, "we will discuss the emotional and physical impact of why we are attracted."

She began again, "More than just my education, but as a married woman, I also have a practical experience in this area. I know what physically attracts me to my husband, and I am thankful to God for those physical differences, which he ordered into each sex, male and female. So, let's begin." She said boldly, "But let's start with a biblical perspective on those differences, and we will start in the Garden of Eden."

At that juncture, some of the girls wrinkled their noses and looked around the room to see if anyone else was turned off by adding God to their discussion. One girl spoke out, "*Awww*, just as this was getting good." Mrs. Martsen sat up in her chair to see how Mrs. Allard would handle what seemed to be the beginning of a mutiny.

Excited about the opportunity of this diversion, Mrs. Allard said, "How many of you girls are interested in having sex?" Most of the girls were shocked at the question. Mrs. Allard continued, "Come now; show me your hands if you are interested in having sex." For fear of admitting such a thing in a Christian school, not one girl raised their hand. Mrs. Martsen was shocked as well; nearly falling out of her chair, she looked on in awe.

Then, one of the bolder girls spoke up and said, "Yes, but not now."

All her classmates turned toward this brave peer, each one contemplating what they just heard. Observing the classroom commotion with renewed interest, Mrs Allard asked the class, "Is that a good answer? Raise your hand if you feel the same way?" Though somewhat embarrassed, all the girls raised their hands, even the one who complained about adding God to the conversation. Mrs. Allard said, "Way to go, Bella," speaking of the girl with the brave answer. Mrs. Martsen marveled, too, at how mature this brave young lady with the bold answer was, and she remembered her and her parents. *Bella Corbin*, she recalled, *and her parents are in real estate.*

Grasping the moment, Mrs. Allard said, "Getting back to *the garden*, can we begin again? Let's explore intelligently the fact that God designed us for sex, and by the way, He says it is good." With new vigor, the class leaned in and refocused again on Mrs. Allard as she moved from sitting on her desk over to the overhead of the naked woman. She began by pointing out the differing body parts of the caption on the overhead.

"For our discussion," she said, "we will look at just outward appearances, other than the obvious extremities; let us examine what makes a woman a woman. Rather than reproductive organs, we will start with form, but remember none of these differences are subtle."

"So," Mrs. Allard began, "generally, women are smaller and have less muscle mass. Our bone structure is smaller as well." Again, speaking generally, she continued, "Women carry more fat than men. Though men and women all have the same muscles and bone similarities, there is a huge contrast in why they are arranged so." She continued, "Unlike most males, the greater part of a woman's body is not covered with hair." At that point, cries of "*ewww*" spewed from the girls! Mrs. Allard reminded the girls that this is how men are designed. "Keep that in mind as we look at the differences," she said.

"Again, remember we are discerning what attracts the male to you, not you to him. We will discuss what attracts you to a male in another session. Try to remember we are speaking generally; some men will be attracted differently, but we are talking about the average male."

She paused a moment, assuring she had good eye contact, and began again. "Most would think that beginning with facial features would be the best place to start talking about what attracts men to women, but I believe that would be wrong, and here is why: at the end of Genesis chapter 2, God put the man to sleep and took a rib from him. While he slept, God created the woman from the rib. After creating the woman, God brought her to the man, and since humans do not naturally sleep standing up, we can assume that he awoke, lying down, to see her standing before him naked. So, for this discussion, we will start from the ground up, yes, her feet. Adam had to look up to see Eve; therefore, he first saw her feet. And only after capturing the complete perfection of the package, every intricate part of her, did he truly see her."

Mrs. Allard paused and posited a question: "What did Adam see in *the garden* when he first fully saw Eve?"

All the girls began pondering the question. After some time, and this surprised Mrs. Martsen, Dominique spoke up, "Something different, other," she said.

Mrs. Allard stopped, looked around the room to ensure all the students were alert to that answer, turned to Dominique, and said, "Great answer, Dominique." The rest of the girls who really didn't like Dominique turned to look at her. Dominique remained slouched in her chair, showing little deference for the class, but Mrs. Allard was moved and said excitedly to herself and out loud, "Other. What a great descriptor. From now on, when discussing the differences in the sexes, we will use Dominique's term 'other.'" She concluded the discussion by saying, "Males and females are 'other to each other.'"

Knowing that Dominique's phrase had changed the dynamic for the class, Mrs. Allard was thankful, and she looked longingly at Dominique as if to say, "Well done."

She finished the lesson by adding, "When trying to understand the differences between the sexes, we should remember they both qualify for having what it takes to be uniquely human, and yet, they still are 'mutually exclusive, even diametrically opposed.'"

There was no way Mrs. Martsen could know the impact that class had on Mrs. Allard. On the way home that night, Mrs. Allard could not get Dominique's descriptor out of her mind. "Other," she said to herself and continued the thought. *God's creation is truly amazing. He made men and women so uniquely different and yet so wonderfully compatible.*

Still in awe, she thought to herself, *I will never truly understand the differences between me and my husband, and I will never fully understand how the difference in our sexes is what draws us to each other. I cannot fathom the depth of his maleness, and he cannot fathom the depths of my being female. In every way, we are other but made for each other to explore in depth that which is the unfathomable.* And she marveled at God's wisdom.

* * *

Mrs. Martsen, still in her office, going over her personal plight and Dominique's dilemma, was engrossed with the memory of Mrs. Allard's anatomy class. She was startled when, suddenly, there came a knock on her door. Having been so caught up in deep thought about Dominique, she didn't know how much time had elapsed since arriving at her office.

She was surprised to see Mrs. Allard coming back so quickly. Opening the door, she was drawn to Mrs. Allard's eyes, red from crying. Mrs. Martsen felt instantly defeated, and she leaned into the doorjamb of her office for support. Her first thought was, *Dominique has kicked Mrs. Allard out of her room; now what? I am running out of options.*

Mrs. Allard, sensing Mrs. Martsen's consternation, smiled and said, "Dominique is in the dispensary."

* * *

Dominique awoke disoriented; the room was unfamiliar to her, and she became tense. Anxiously looking around for something to associate with, she sat up tentative to her new surroundings. She gazed down and, seeing the hospital bed, gathered she was in the dispensary. Fear began to build in her heart, and she had a foreboding feeling of what came next. Not knowing how long she had been sleeping, Dominique figured it must have been quite some time. Her body ached all over, and she was dying of thirst. She thought to herself, *They must have sedated me.*

Lying back down on her pillow, she began unraveling her thoughts as to why she was there. Slowly, some clarity began to emerge, and the image of Mrs. Allard started to come into focus. Though her head was stationary, her eyes darted back and forth as a new revelation entered her mind. The vision she sought was beginning to materialize, and she pictured herself back in her room, lying on her bed, talking with Mrs. Allard.

Now things started coming back together for Dominique; she recalled Mrs. Martsen and the nurse trying to rip her from her safety and Mrs. Allard caring so much for her pain. She paused on that thought, *The concern of Mrs. Allard.* She remembered thankfully thinking, *Mrs. Allard wanted nothing from me except to be my friend.* Her thoughts were coming in clearer, expanding. Dominique was beginning to see the amazing role Mrs. Allard played in reviving her desire to live on. *It was a lovely bonding together.* As she remembered, tears began to fill her eyes.

As if she was back in her room, Dominique allowed the scene to replay in her head, and she said to herself, *How gentle Mrs. Allard was, as she slowly moved over to my bed. How cautious she was not to hurry me, and when she took my hand, with tears in her eyes, I felt her tears drop on my hands as well; then she surprised me and said, "Dominique, I love you."*

Dominique continued to remember. *We just sat there for the longest time, holding hands, not forced to say anything. I could not take my eyes off her gaze; she never looked away from me, and her smile continued to widen.* Dominique remembered that she was not embarrassed and did not want to hasten into dialogue, and neither did Mrs. Allard. *What a moment,* she said to herself; she finally knew someone at her school cared.

Her thoughts went on. *We both wept softly, never turning away, and we sat there for several minutes until I had to ask Mrs. Allard, "Why do you love me?"*

Dominique hadn't spoken in twenty-four hours. It felt strange to talk, but she had to know, fearing and hoping at the same time, that it could be real.

Before speaking, Mrs. Allard paused, ensuring what she said next would validate Dominique's need but also open the door for dialogue. Then, Mrs. Allard said, "Because you reminded me of someone else who was desperately hurting, and love is what healed them."

It all came back clearly, with a deep feeling of compassion in Mrs. Allard's response. Dominique remembered she was forced to look away to contemplate what she just heard. Mrs. Allard took one of her hands away from holding Dominique's hands; she reached up and tenderly lifted Dominique's chin with her fingertips. Making eye contact again, Mrs. Allard said, "That someone was me."

The entire conversation was becoming translucent. Not expecting that response, Dominique still never broke eye contact. She leaned back a little, and at the same time, she sat up a little taller; while her mind was racing, she thought, *No way… No way was Mrs. Allard ever, at one time, like me.*

This news took Dominique by surprise, and caution began to creep back into her thoughts. She didn't have a response, but something changed; a doubt started to form. She thought, *Maybe this is just a ruse to get me to the dispensary.* She didn't move her hand, but she let the pressure of holding Mrs. Allard's hands go. Sensing the release of the pressure on her hand, Mrs. Allard reached back down from holding her chin, grabbed both hands tightly again, and said, "Let me explain."

Dominique remembered how fixed she was on each word as Mrs. Allard began to explain how love healed her. She began her story by saying, "I did not arrive where I am today through much joy but through much suffering. Dominique, I do not know all of your story, but I do know your pain. As a small child, my life seemed normal to me. Busy parents, busy siblings, we all made the most of each day. Church life, though boring, was our weekly ritual, which kind of kept us all in balance. Both my parents worked, and as we became older, my siblings and I took care of each other a lot of the time.

"I was pretty popular in school and had lots of friends; like I said, I had a pretty normal life, and then one day, my life tragically changed…" Dominique remembered how Mrs. Allard's demeanor altered at this point, how her remembering seemed to place her back into the moment and the pain.

Mrs. Allard continued, "I was left alone at home with someone that my family and I trusted. It was my uncle. He raped me and continued to do so for about a year; I was fourteen years old." Hearing those words, Dominique recoiled and pulled away from Mrs. Allard. She recalled how this intimate revelation took her back to Durand, and she was instantly angry but primarily afraid.

Dominique looked away for a second to quell her anxiety, but when she looked back at Mrs. Allard, Mrs. Allard was now looking down, trying to gather her thoughts; her pain was exposed, and darkness seemed to enter their domain. Dominique felt a foreboding presence.

Just then, Mrs. Allard looked up with a weak smile and even a twinkle in her eye. She continued, "Dominique, I thought I would die; at times, I wanted to die. Nobody knew my suffering, and I was all alone. My uncle told me if I ever told anyone, he would hurt me or one of my younger sisters. I started to act out badly at school and at home. My parents were baffled and did not know what to do."

At this point in the story, Dominique was beginning to discern that Mrs. Allard was legit; her loving countenance betrayed her likelihood for duplicity. Dominique remembered clearly at this juncture. Mrs Allard was so shaken that Dominique had to stop and ask her, "Do you really want to do this?"

Mrs. Allard paused and said, "Sorry, I am okay; this is just hard to relive again." She settled herself by clearing her throat and focusing keenly on Dominique's eyes. She continued, saying, "I don't know what your story is, but it appears it has led you to the same place I once found myself."

Tears began to flow again into Dominique's eyes. Mrs. Allard stayed on course, unveiling more of her personal darkness, but at the same time, she was exposing Dominique's own experience. This was scary to Dominique, and she thought to herself, *No one but her and Durand could know.* Dominique recalled how Mrs. Allard just seemed to know where to go, and for Dominique, this was the first time she encountered someone with a plight like herself but appearing healed and happy.

Dominique went back into her own life, remembering the painful stories of her friends. They were willing to open up and share the extreme abuse that they suffered at the hands of their attackers, but she also remembered that sharing their stories did not change their situation or their pain. Having never revealed her situation to anyone, Dominique began to feel a sense of relief, as if she had just shared her story with someone, someone who could help.

Again, the tears began pouring from her eyes, and a weak but reticent smile cracked her parched lips open, and she said to herself, *How could she know?* Reliving that wonderful scene again, Dominique recalled how tender Mrs. Allard was as she reached for her hands again; grasping them, she pulled Dominique into her arms and held her. Dominique was surprised with herself; she did not resist but melted into the safe affection of Mrs. Allard's warm embrace.

CHAPTER 9

Anxious about what had befallen Dominique, Marie looked up with anticipation and dread; it was dark, but she was finally home. The lights shining from the house made her feel warm and thankful for a safe place to call home. She jumped from the car and ran to the door. As Marie opened it, there was Colleen.

Hopeful, she embraced her sister and said, "How is she?"

Colleen shared with Marie the struggle of getting Dominique bathed and in bed. Colleen was sure to caution Marie about how difficult it might be for her to see Dominique in this condition. Colleen reiterated again to Marie, "I do not believe this is sickness."

Colleen paused, turned to her sister, grabbed her hands, and said, "Well, mom, she is expecting you."

The sisters held hands as they walked up the stairs. Marie looked tentatively into the wall mirror as they walked by. That reflection revealed a frightened and unsure person. Marie tried to brace herself and smile, but the image she just saw bore the truth of the situation; coping with Dominique, whatever the situation, was always scary.

Just as they arrived at Dominique's bedroom door, Colleen said, "I will wait out here; she needs her mom an awful lot right now."

This admonition made Marie even more timid; thinking to herself, she said, *I need to help her. How do I help? Where do I begin?* Just before she opened the door, she looked down to clear her thoughts, and for some reason, her thoughts coalesced around Chloe's phone conversation and the peace of that prayer in her hotel room. These thoughts lifted her spirit, and she said to herself, *I love my daughter; that is all I need right now.*

Marie boldly opened the door and moved quickly over to the bed and Dominique. Dominique looked up and, though excited to see her mom, she was fearful and dreaded what she thought would be an interrogation. Though surprised by how feeble Dominique appeared, Marie looked past that and gently reached down to embrace her daughter.

Dominique responded likewise, and they held on to each other, rocking gently back and forth. After some time, Marie pulled back and looked into Dominique's tear-soaked eyes and said, "How are you, my darling?"

Dominique, fixed on her mom's eyes, full of tears as well, responded by saying, "I am good now." She paused, and they enjoyed just looking at each other. Then Dominique said, "Mom, I am glad you are here, but you didn't have to come home. I am just sick, and Aunt Colleen has been so helpful in getting me better."

Marie looked at Dominique compassionately but firmly and said, "Please, tell me what has happened."

Dominique was always good at telling Mom lies. It came so naturally, but this time, it felt so deceptive she could hardly put her thoughts together. Still, she gave her mom the same story she had told her aunt and finished by saying, "I am feeling so much better now; I am even starting to have an appetite."

Marie weakly smiled and hugged her daughter again. Holding on tightly and staring blindly out into nowhere and over Dominique's shoulder, Marie thought, *Oh my, something is not right. I am not convinced that she is just sick. Why is she sticking to this tale?*

Physically, Dominique really was feeling much better, and having her mom and her aunt with her did give her emotional comfort, but she knew there was no way around the dreadful internal suffering she was experiencing. She told herself, *This is a lie that must remain intact; there is no way the truth will ever make this better.*

Dominique was sticking with the "being sick" story and thinking her mom was buying it too. She asked tentatively, "Where is Dad?" Marie explained he would be home soon; she could tell Dominique was apprehensive about having to share this ordeal with her dad. Marie tried to comfort Dominique, so she grabbed Dominique's hand, made sure they had good eye contact, and said, "Your dad is rushing home because he loves you and wants to be with you when you are hurting."

After making that statement, it was hard for Marie to keep eye contact with Dominique, and she looked down as she finished speaking. She did this because she did not completely know why he was coming home or how he would react. Looking up into Dominique's eyes again, Marie smiled uncomfortably, then turned away. She quickly looked back at Dominique again, but it was awkward for both of them. They were uncomfortable; they both smiled weakly but had to look away from each other again. Dominique read her mom's nimble explanation perfectly, and she knew her dad was hot about having to come home.

***

After arriving home, Thomas rushed in to find Marie. He found her standing in the foyer. Marie was somewhat tentative at having to explain to Thomas that Dominique was just very sick, and that was all. She figured he would fly completely off the handle and go after Dominique cruelly for upending a very important business deal. Instead, Marie was surprised when he reached out and gently hugged her. She was even more pleasantly surprised when he softly whispered in her ear, "I am sorry for how rude I was to you on the phone; please forgive me."

Marie leaned back from the embrace and just stared into Thomas's eyes. His appearance puzzled her because his face was not frantic like it normally is; he appeared emotionally broken, and sadness etched his expression. Marie's heart calmed; she needed Thomas so much right then, and a tear ran down her cheek. She reached up, kissed him gently, and said, "Thank you." Thomas, worried about how Marie would respond, let out a breath, rolled his shoulders forward, leaned down, placed his forehead delicately on Marie's forehead, and said, "I love you."

Colleen, hearing the door open, walked into the foyer to see Marie and Thomas in an embrace. Seeing Colleen enter, they both looked up sheepishly and smiled at her. Colleen's first thought was, *Thomas does not smile in these situations; what is up?* Thomas reached over and gave Colleen a brief hug. This surprised her as well because Thomas does not hug, and then he said, "Thank you for being here for Dominique."

Thomas looked at both sisters, one then the other, and said, "How is she?"

Marie and Colleen looked at each other as if to say, "Who starts this?" Colleen nodded to Marie, and Marie gave Thomas a rundown on all that had transpired. When finished, Marie looked at Colleen and asked her to share her take on the situation with Thomas. As she told Marie initially, Colleen reiterated her conclusions to Thomas as they pertained to her having injuries and not sickness.

Clear with the input but lost on how to proceed, Thomas looked again at both of them and said, "What now?" Marie told Thomas that the best thing he could do right now was to go see his daughter.

Thomas turned from the sisters, who were now holding hands for comfort, hoping for a peaceful connection between father and daughter. As Thomas started up the stairs, Marie was tempted to say to Thomas, "Be gentle, honey," but for some reason, she held her tongue.

Moving toward Dominique's room, Thomas was surprised that he was not mad but quite concerned about how Dominique was. When he reached the hallway leading to Dominique's room, he realized that this empathy he was feeling was new, and it left him nearly clueless on what to say to his daughter.

With his mind swirling, he reached Dominique's door. Having no concept of how to begin comforting her, he paused, holding on to the doorknob. Thomas looked around to see if Marie or Colleen would show up to rescue him, but there was no one there. So, he relented to the fact he was all alone. Then, he stared at the door for a moment. Seeing Dominique in his mind, something broke open in his heart; a picture of her formed in his mind; there she was, his little girl, smiling at him; his emotions overwhelmed him, and he stepped into the room.

Dominique was startled by her dad's unannounced entry, and she sat up, fearful. She had spent some time worrying about how to prepare for this scrimmage with her dad. She knew he would be angry, having to come all the way home only to find her feeling already better.

Their eyes met for a second, and Dominique could not read him; she wanted to blurt out what she had planned to say, which was, "Daddy, I am sorry you had to leave the business meeting and come home for me; please forgive me." Just as she started to say something, she stopped; she couldn't speak, and she was shocked to see tears welled up in her dad's eyes. She had never seen her dad cry; it disarmed her, and she didn't know how to respond. Thomas walked to the bed, sat down, looked adoringly into Dominique's eyes, and said, "Hello, baby. How is my girl?"

All that Dominique feared would happen from Mom and Dad because of this awful situation did not happen. As Thomas pulled Domonique in for a hug, she could not remember the last time her dad had held her. In fact, for a long time, Dad would not hug her at all. This hurt Dominique very much because she always loved Dad's nonstop hugs; then, one day, he just quit hugging her. At the time, Dominique felt she must have done something wrong, and she tried harder to be good, but that did not work; that did not change things.

Dominique remembered asking her mom if Dad was mad at her because he did not hug her anymore. Marie noticed that Dad's hugs stopped just after Dominique reached puberty. Marie tried to talk to Thomas about how important it was for daughters to get physical affection from their dads. Thomas told Marie that he felt very uncomfortable holding Dominique now that she had blossomed into a woman. At first, Marie could not grasp what he was implying and thought him silly; she said, "Dominique needs her dad's affection, especially now that she is a young woman, so she doesn't go looking for it from some other man."

Thomas tried to explain to Marie, saying, "This is very hard; she has all the woman stuff now, and I don't know how to hold her. When she sits on my lap and hugs me, I…" He paused. "I don't know what I am saying."

Marie stopped, looked at Thomas sternly, and said, "Are you saying you are aroused by Dominique?"

Thomas was completely embarrassed by Marie's question. His face began to flush, and he became frightened as well. He didn't want to remember the times when his thoughts were not right. His embarrassment quickly became anger. He glared into Marie's eyes and said emphatically, "No, I am not aroused by Dominique, and I never want to be either. That is what I am trying to explain: why I struggle with hugging her."

Marie decided it was time to give this topic a rest. She realized she was somewhat angry and puzzled with Thomas's remarks. She said to herself, *How can a dad be sexually attracted to his daughter?*

That night, Marie did some research, and she found that almost all psychologists agree it is normal for dads to shy away from maturing daughters. All but a few are in agreement; the experts suggest, "If a dad is not a deviant, then doing what makes you excruciatingly uncomfortable is what you signed on for. This is what is best for your daughters. A dad's job is to show their daughters that no matter how much they change, dad's love is constant and unconditional."

Marie shared her research with Thomas. Thomas seemed to understand, and it appeared that he knew it was normal for dads to be uncomfortable, but try as he may, he never did get comfortable enough to hold Dominique, so he quit completely. At that time, Marie was not sure how to share with Dominique her dad's change without exposing too much intimacy, so she didn't.

***

Still evaluating what this hug from Dad was, Dominique could not get past the fact that she wasn't in trouble. Thomas just held on to her. Dominique could feel his sobs. Until just then, she could not remember a real loving moment with her dad, and she realized how much she missed and loved this about him.

Feeling the wonderful warmth of her dad's love, Dominique let go of her fear, closed her eyes, now filling with tears, and clutched him tightly, which led him to hold her even closer.

In her dad's embrace, Dominique felt love and acceptance, and her circumstances, so dreadful, for this moment anyway, were forgotten. Holding her close, Thomas was in bliss. He finally realized how important this embrace was. Sorry for how he had neglected Dominique, he choked up, thinking about how foolish he had been, not loving her as a father should.

***

The first few days after Mom and Dad returned from Philadelphia were the best days Dominique could ever remember with her parents. Dad could not get enough of being with her, and whenever they were in the same room, Dominique would look up at her dad. There, he would be staring at her, and when their eyes met, he would smile.

Likewise, Mom didn't just nurse her; she held her, talked with her, and even laughed together, which hadn't happened in such a long time. For the first time in her teenage years, Dominique felt no judgment or condemnation from her parents. She even began to be thankful for them instead of wishing to be away from them.

Then, one night, in the midst of this profound family joy, just before dosing off to sleep, an alien scheme was forced upon her heart and mind. Dark memories of Durand, the pain and suffering rolled back upon her soul, and anger, like she had never known, gripped her. Her chest started to hurt, her head began to pound, and she became so warm she had to throw the bed covers off her.

She tried talking to herself, saying, *I cannot be here; I do not need this now.* Then, she stopped in panic and realized she was a phony; everything was not all right. She said to herself, *Mom and Dad know nothing about what has happened to me. I am deceiving them; I am using them.* The alarm in her heart was blaring—telling her, "You have to tell them what happened." Then, the dread set in; she knew if she shared with them, everything would change. She knew what she had longed for and now has with her parents would vaporize. This disclosure would destroy them all.

***

After the breakdown at school, Thomas and Marie got Dominique settled in at home for rehabilitation. Their first priority was to contact their mental health professional for evaluation. Thomas and Marie were frightened for Dominique and unsure if home would be a safe place for her. They had never seen her like this before and wrestled over placing her in an institution for help.

Mostly, though, Thomas and Marie were caught somewhere between brokenhearted and fearful for their daughter. Try as they may, they could not figure out what had happened to Dominique. These emotional collapses began that night when they had to hurry home from Philadelphia. They also knew that Dominique was not truthful about being sick. They both felt guilty for not probing more about what had happened. At the time, they were so overjoyed at seeing her loving and kind that they didn't want to talk about the injuries and ruin it.

They could not forget and longed for the joy of those first days after returning from Philadelphia: how wonderfully different she was and the days of loving Dominique and each other, but that all ended quickly.

They remembered how strangely Dominique changed and how sad it was; she became vicious and uncontrollable. They were unprepared to have Dominique hurting and being so hateful. Feeling unable to help and unable to cope with their own inadequacies, not knowing what to do, Thomas accepted Marie's premise for boarding school, and they enrolled her at William James.

At the time of Dominique's overarching rebellion, William James seemed like the only remedy. Now, with her breakdown at school, they were both feeling unsure of that choice. Something must have happened at school. They were looking for answers but also were wondering if there wasn't someone to blame for Dominique's suffering. Knowing the answers would not come from Dominique, they began to turn their attention to her school.

***

One positive change that took place after arriving home from Philadelphia and while waiting on Dominique to heal at home, Thomas and Marie would often reflect on the changes in their lives since that fateful day when they arrived home to be with Dominique. These changes prompted them to lean into each other for day-to-day support as they anxiously but hopefully waited for the day when Dominique would be well.

Thomas remained a bulwark at the office, but now he knew he must taper that with his number one concern, which was Marie and Dominique. Marie loved this revived husband. He was not the same driven tyrant he used to be. Now, whenever they were together, he was soft like never before. Marie would occasionally catch Thomas reading family help books and even the Bible, which, with his family history, was a real shock to her.

Marie found great solace in Chloe. Chloe was faithful to call Marie several times a week. Marie would call Chloe when she felt inadequate at helping Dominique or when she just felt lonely. When Chloe told Marie she would always be there for her, she was true to her words. Most of the time, Chloe wanted to know how Dominique was doing, but she also wanted to know how Marie and Thomas were doing. Chloe would say to Marie, "I have not stopped praying daily for your family. I love bringing you before the Lord, and He loves hearing from me for you."

At first, Marie was uncomfortable talking about God, but little by little, since that is what Chloe did, Marie began to rely on the things Chloe said and prayed. Marie was no longer embarrassed when Chloe wanted to pray over the phone; she looked forward to it. Marie began to see and trust that God was making a difference in their lives.

Church was different as well. At first, Thomas and Marie were embarrassed about Dominique's troubles and sharing them with others. It never failed; someone from the church would always ask how Dominique was fairing. This made Thomas not want to go to church. He figured, *How could I ever tell anyone all that had transpired with Dominique?*

Then, one day, one of the businessmen from the church asked Thomas to lunch after Sunday service. Thomas was hesitant, but he knew this man well, and they had much in common with the business world. Plus, he saw him weekly at church. So, they met, but Thomas was leery, fearing his spiritually overzealous friend would take advantage of the intimacy of just the two of them meeting.

His name was Hal Sealy. Lunch was going well; they were going over business ideas and small talk, and suddenly, Hal said, "Thomas, I have noticed a change in you lately." Hal paused and didn't say anything else.

Thomas felt trapped in the moment. Looking skeptically at Hal, Thomas said, "What changes have you noticed?" Thomas was not ready for this kind of conversation, and he became instantly wary.

Hal continued, "Well," he said, "I don't know; just, maybe, I see you more at peace. Maybe surer of who you are, I can't put a definite finger on it, but it is evident."

Surprised that this conversation did not sour him, Thomas, instead, saw Hal's input as a perspective he needed. Hal's evaluation helped Thomas to realize that there was some validation for him; he really had begun to make family his priority. That day, Thomas was comfortable for the first time sharing with someone and confiding in someone about the suffering that he, Marie, and Dominique had been through.

CHAPTER 10

Dominique, on the other hand, was at peace with being in her room, planning nothing, and not even talking unless she had to. She went over, again and again, the episode at school and how everything had now changed. What used to be important was not; what used to be fun was not. There was no purpose for Dominique, and that was fine. She tried as she may to do things she knew would please her parents, but she did not sense a conviction, nor did she have the wherefore to do so.

She even began to ponder why it was no longer important to conspire and get what she selfishly wanted for herself. Her favorite game of manipulation had become so trivial. Dominique was finally in a place where it wasn't about what she wanted; it wasn't about her being popular, nor was it about things she thought she needed, and yet, she felt so empty, and she had no idea why that was.

Occasionally, Dominique would go back and relive that dark place, that peaceful place in her dorm room at school, but she could not stay there. Mrs. Allard had opened up something inside her: a light that pierced into her darkness and exposed it for what it was; that world was a death trap. Dominique found herself different but lost. She no longer contemplated the indifference of life but was beginning to yearn for the meaning of it but had no answers.

***

After the school incident, Mrs. Martsen made it clear: if Dominique made a full recovery, William James wanted her back. Therefore, after enduring nearly two weeks of constant poking and prodding to make sure nothing could thwart her resuscitation, Dominique was found fit and ready to return to school life.

Dominique continued to struggle with lethargy, but what she found most difficult was that she had started acting again, trying to please everyone so they would think she was all right. She thought to herself, *If I don't play this game, I will be homebound forever.*

She had to admit things were not as difficult as before, but she felt like the controlling forces around her life were striving again to stick her back into a mold that she could not and would not continue in. She also knew she had to be careful; if she messed up again, Mom and Dad would take drastic measures to protect her, which would mean long-term care.

Last but not least, Dominique really did not want to go back to school to finish the school year. She had no interest in classes and had little desire to be with her classmates, especially now, since they all knew she had wigged out, but that was a better option than home.

She tried to envision how she could ever share with anyone about what had happened to her. How could she ever trust anyone with that information? First, she thought of Rachel and Sarah; they played at being her friend, but they really only cared about her drama; it made for good gossip. The only other student that tried to be friendly was Bella Corbin. Dominique liked Bella but thought there was no way they could be friends.

It was Bella's distinctive temperament that Dominique found appealing; Bella didn't care what others thought about her. She was really smart and didn't appear to need the high school drama; she seemed secure in herself. She would wear shirts with Jesus on them; this drove many of the other girls bananas. They would laugh at her and point. Dominique thought this was so weird; she reasoned, *You attend a Christian school, but you laugh at someone with Jesus on their shirt; what is that?*

Some of the girls would try to bully Bella, but she would laugh at the effort and remain calm and noncombative; she was so sure of herself. Though they would never admit it, most of the students admired her, but what was even better was that Bella didn't care if she was admired or not. The word that Dominique used to describe Bella was "undomesticated." She was free and did not have to play the games to be happy.

Religion was the one place Dominique was sure she could not trust herself to Bella's safe keeping. It is not that she forced religion down students' throats, but she personally applied God to all situations. Dominique felt she forced God into circumstances where He didn't need to be applied. Though Bella was the only one at school who stood up for her, Dominique kept her at a distance just to ensure she would not be forced to encounter Bella's radicalized worldview.

***

Finally, the day came, and it was time to head back to school. Dominique was divided in her thinking: she could not stand it at home, but school was not her thing either. Watching Mom and Dad exit down the campus driveway made Dominique feel relieved and sad at the same time. When she first came home, family life was wonderful. She was accepted and loved; she had meaningful time with her parents as they helped her heal. Things turned quickly, though, as the guilt of lying to them about Durand haunted her every thought.

At first, it was hard being so belligerent because her parents had changed, and she knew they loved her so much; still, because of her pain, she could not help but push them away. Now, as she stood on the sidewalk in front of the school office, melancholy disconnects raced through her thoughts.

Dominique strongly opposed her parents coming into the office; she wanted to do this on her own. To keep this from becoming a feud, Mom and Dad honored her request. She bid them farewell and watched them depart. She thought to herself, *I am so worthless, I cannot even raise my arm to wave goodbye.* So, she stood there and watched. Just before the car disappeared, she caught a glimpse of Mom waving through the backseat window.

***

Mrs. Martsen was expecting Dominique, and so was the rest of the school staff. As she watched out her office window, Mrs. Martsen saw Dominique exit the car. The picture she saw of Dominique as she stood there watching her parents leave was a stark one. She was slouching, and her winter clothes seemed to hang on her like they didn't fit anymore. She had stuffed her long hair up under a baseball cap, which she had on backwards.

Mrs. Martsen had not seen Dominique in two weeks; she was shocked at the sight. She thought, *Is this the same girl? She looks so frail.* The picture Mrs. Martsen was looking at made her sad, and she said to herself, *Has a child ever looked so alone?*

Dominique was not looking forward to engaging Mrs. Martsen again. On the other hand, Mrs. Martsen was anticipating a new beginning with Dominique. Leaving her office quickly to meet Dominique on the sidewalk, Mrs. Martsen said a silent prayer: *Oh, Lord, give me another chance with Dominique.*

Lowering her head, Dominique turned to the office entrance. Unbeknownst to Dominique, Mrs. Martsen had arrived, standing behind her. In taking her first step, Dominique was startled to see feet so close to her. She looked up, and there was Mrs. Martsen, which startled her even more.

When Dominique saw who it was, she muttered, "Oh," and instinctively stepped back. Mrs. Martsen knew right away that surprising Dominique this way was not what she had hoped for. The negative impact was plain to see; Dominique's body language spoke volumes, and she was already in defense mode.

Knowing she needed to make this work, Mrs. Martsen smiled. She was surprised that the smile came so naturally. She not only smiled with her lips, but she smiled with her eyes, and although Dominique was well rehearsed in her plan to evade contact with Mrs. Martsen, rather than looking down, something forced her to remain staring into Mrs. Martsen's eyes. After a few moments, Dominique caught herself and looked down and away, but as she did, Mrs. Martsen grabbed the opportunity to initiate dialogue and warmly said, "Welcome back, Dominique."

***

This first day of school seemed different. Classmates were different and more friendly, but it almost seemed like they had been warned about being otherwise. It wasn't long before Dominique was feeling right back in the rut of school. One thing she did appreciate was her new roommate. For some reason, Bella Corbin now bunked with her. Dominique asked Bella why she had moved in with her. Bella explained, "I don't fully know; all I can come up with is my ex-roommate didn't really like living with me; maybe she complained to Mrs. Martsen?" She added, "I also think the administration thought you needed a friend."

Dominique didn't know exactly how to process Bella's last comment. She thought to herself, *I can only take this one of two ways: either I am a welfare case, which the school has agreed to take on, which forces Bella to help, or they really want to help me?*

Not sure she wanted anyone fixing her, Dominique went into her default mode, not trusting the motives of people who say they want to help. So, she was sure it must be the first scenario. But in her heart, having Bella around gave her at least some hope for the latter; something about Bella was believable.

As much as Dominique refused to accept that this place was where she needed to be, it beat the alternative of being elsewhere, like a forced, mandated, in-house therapy. Having arrived Sunday evening, she tried to prepare herself for Monday's grind. It was only small talk, but visiting with Bella helped relieve the anxiety.

One piece of the requirement for reentry to William James, which pleasantly surprised Dominique, was that she must have daily scheduled time with Mrs. Allard. She glanced at her schedule and found her time slot with Mrs. Allard; it was every school day after breakfast. Dominique thought to herself, *We will see how Mrs. Allard handles a non-morning person as her first student each day.* Exhausted, she finally lay down on her bed, only to rekindle the negative past. Her mind wandered from pain to pain, and she could not sleep. It was just as well; Bella snored all night.

Morning found Dominique more exhausted than when she went to bed. She heard noise in the background, and in an attempt to not have to deal with a new day, she threw her pillow over her head.

Bella was bouncing around their room, fixing her bed, changing into her school uniform, primping in the mirror, and all the time humming something Dominique found irreverent. *Oh, great*, she thought, *a morning person.*

Dominique hadn't moved, the pillow still over her head, so Bella walked over and said, "Hey, lazybones, breakfast in ten."

Dominique didn't move; she made like she didn't hear, which caused Bella to grab the pillow off her head. Still, Dominique didn't move, but she began to simmer, thinking, *Who do you think you are?*

Bella began again to say, "Hey—" but she got no further than the word "hey" when Dominique rapidly spun over onto her side. With her hair flying wildly and the look of a possessed person in her dark eyes, she glared at Bella. Bella just laughed; turning to walk out, she muttered, "Okay, don't eat breakfast."

But she paused, turned to look at Dominique, and leaned back into the room. Bending down and staring directly into Dominique's eyes, she said, "You know what, Dominique? You are your own worst enemy. It is so obvious, even right now, that you are telling yourself that I am your problem. I woke you up for breakfast; how dare I. The reality is, I have watched you for two years now, and the only truth I see is that you need an excuse for life. Yeah, your life has been hard, but guess what? You are not the only one who suffers. Your problem is you, and you can't get out of your way. You have no purpose for living except to blame everyone else for your failures. Tell me, is the image I see before me what you hoped your life would turn out to be?" Not closing the door, Bella turned abruptly and left the room.

After Bella left the room, Dominique became enraged. She was instantly wide awake. She sat up quickly on her bed and stared hatefully at the doorway where Bella just stood. Then she thought, *I wonder if anyone out in the hall heard Bella yelling at me.*

Dominique was impressed by Bella's ability to confront others, but now that it was pointed at her, she hated it and said, "How dare she talk to me like that?" She ran over to the door as if to yell out in the hall at Bella, but as she moved across the room, her eyes caught the clock on the wall, and she stopped and cried out loud, "Breakfast!"

One of the requirements for re-enrollment was that she had to eat all the meals prepared each day. She panicked and said to herself, "I will have to deal with Bella later; right now, I need to get to breakfast." Dominique began racing around the room trying to get her uniform on and her backpack filled for the day's classes. She didn't have time to brush her teeth or hair, and as she passed by the mirror, she looked at herself and said, "Oh, to hell with it," and down the hall, she raced. Running now toward the cafeteria, Dominique looked down and noticed her shoelaces were untied; she thought to herself, *Who cares?*

Just as she burst through the double doors going into the cafeteria, she realized how weak she was, and her head became very light. She kept herself from falling by leaning up against the wall inside the room. Dominique bent her head down, not knowing if she was going to faint or not. Slowly, the lightheadedness began to subside. Though she continued to be very weak, she was better and didn't feel faint any longer. Slowly, she raised from the waist back to upright, leaning against the wall with her eyes closed tight.

Slowly, Dominique opened her eyes; things were blurry at first, so she closed her eyes once more. As she opened them again, things began to take shape, and now the vision became clear; it jolted her. There before her, all eyes, the entire student body and staff, were staring at her in disbelief. It was deadly silent in the room, and not one person was still engaged in eating; every eye was fixed on this disheveled intruder.

Not only was she disruptive, but to her classmates, she looked scary and abnormal. The horror of this moment began to creep into Dominique's soul. She looked right and then left, affirming that all eyes were on her. In her heart, she began to bolt, but her feet would not move. Then, from the corner of the room, she caught a glimpse of a figure striding toward her. She turned again to run but still could not move. When Dominique turned back, nothing had changed except that Mrs. Allard was now standing at her side. Mrs. Allard reached out and touched Dominique's hand and said, "Good morning, Dominique. Is everything all right?"

Still petrified, Dominique looked longingly at Mrs. Allard. Desperate for someone to help her, Dominique became riveted on this friendly face before her. "I know these eyes." Calming herself with those words, she continued, "These are the same eyes, the same touch that rescued me from my room two weeks ago."

Slowly reaching up with her other hand, Dominique tightly gripped onto Mrs. Allard's welcoming touch. Mrs. Allard never stopped smiling and said, "What do you think? Shall we find you a place to sit?"

Dominique was hesitant, but Mrs. Allard reassured her that all was well, and Dominique allowed Mrs. Allard to lead her forward. As they moved toward a table and with the help of staff, the cafeteria debacle fell back into its normal routine.

Never missing an opportunity, like evil does, some of the girls couldn't let it go and began to snicker quietly and even point at Dominique. Angered by their insensitivity, Bella quickly stood up at her table and stared the culprits down, saying, "You brood of hypocrites, do you think you will never need a helping hand?" Bella remained standing, staring defiantly, daring anyone to test her. Dominique looked over her shoulder at the commotion, and there was her angry, redheaded roommate, reaming this unsympathetic mob.

Dominique looked away, continuing to move with Mrs. Allard toward a dining table, but she had to turn back again to see what was happening with Bella; as she did, Bella turned to her, and their eyes met. Dominique was surprised that Bella would defend her after what happened in their room. Self-consciously, she looked away.

Not so upset now, she continued along with Mrs. Allard to her table. At this point, Mrs. Martsen, with other staff, stepped in, moving from table to table, refocusing the girls to return to their meals. Bella slowly returned to her seat but kept her sights on the lingering crowd, ready to move on any remaining dissidents.

Eating helped a lot, but sitting next to Mrs. Allard is what gave her strength. Dominique sat nibbling at her breakfast, staring back and forth between the back of Bella's head and Mrs. Allard's warm smile. Neither of them said anything for the longest time. Finally, after noticing that Dominique was settled calmly into the breakfast setting, Mrs. Allard asked Dominique, "Are you ready for our first meeting this morning?" Dominique took a drink of her water and stared over at Mrs. Allard; she slowly nodded her head to acknowledge that she was ready.

* * *

After breakfast, Dominique and Mrs. Allard walked together toward Mrs. Allard's classroom. Strengthened by the meal and the restful time at breakfast, Dominique did not need to lean on Mrs. Allard for support any longer, but Mrs. Allard put her arm inside of Dominique's arm and placed her hands together, cuddling Dominique's arm in hers; they slowly walked arm in arm to the classroom.

Wondering again what made Mrs. Allard tick, Dominique would briefly look up at her as they continued toward the classroom. Dominique thought to herself, *It is almost as if she purposely doesn't question me like that isn't as important as just being together here.* Thought-provoking as that was, Dominique couldn't help but believe this was just another strategy to bend her will.

Mrs. Allard had a private office in her classroom, and they moved between the desks past the whiteboards to the office door. Mrs. Allard opened the door with her key, turned on the light, and motioned for Dominique to enter. Unsure of what this all meant, Dominique hesitated and motioned for Mrs. Allard to enter first. So, she did and moved over to her desk, looking back at Dominique.

Starting into the office, Dominique was pleasantly surprised with the office décor. It kind of reminded her of her dad's office. She remembered the many days as a young girl playing in Dad's office. He kept toys and snacks in the desk drawers, and she was always welcome. Dad's desk was dark wood and very big, and he kept pictures of family on the desk so he could see them.

Dominique recalled her favorite thing to do in Dad's office; she loved to climb under his desk. There was so much room under there, like a fort. She smiled as she remembered the days when she was under his desk, and people she didn't even know would come in, sit in one of the chairs in front of the desk, and visit. Sometimes, unbeknownst to his guests, right in the middle of a conversation, like feeding a little bird, Dad would cater bits of Lucky Charms into her welcoming mouth. It was their father-daughter secret.

Caught in that moment, still smiling and not knowing how long she had been dwelling in this fond memory, she looked up, somewhat embarrassed to see Mrs. Allard musing in the moment as well. Mrs. Allard asked, "What do you think, will this do?" Dominique nodded, and she came around to sit in one of the chairs. She could not help but notice several family pictures on the walls and on Mrs. Allard's desk.

Still unwilling to let her guard down, Dominique was unsure if she could trust anyone. Nervous, she ventured to ask a question: "Who are all these people in your pictures?"

Mrs. Allard said, "Great idea. Hey, you are pretty good at this; what a wonderful way to begin getting to know each other."

Mrs. Allard went through all the pictures, explaining the significance of each. Dominique was wondering if this was what counseling was going to be like; if so, she liked it so far.

Impressed with how much time Mrs. Allard spent on each of the individuals in the pictures, Dominique watched Mrs. Allard closely. It was enduring watching her facial expressions change as she shared the significant details of each one. Dominique could see the love she had for her family.

When She came to a picture of a little boy, maybe three years old, Mrs. Allard's countenance changed. She held it in front of her and stared long at it, then turned it so Dominique could see it. Mrs. Allard remained smiling, but this was a different smile, a sad smile. She turned the picture back to herself again and placed it down, lingering there a moment, then looked back to Dominique. Dominique could tell this was someone special, so she asked, "Who is this little boy?"

Mrs. Allard paused, took a breath, and said, "This is my son, Oliver, but he is no longer with us."

Dominique wasn't sure what she meant. Mrs. Allard picked up the picture again and said, "He died in a car wreck with his father four years ago." Dominique was shocked to hear this; she instantly felt uncomfortable, not wanting to know. Her eyes opened wide, and she stared at Mrs. Allard, whose expression had not changed. Dominique started fidgeting in her chair.

Sensing her fear, Mrs. Allard reassured Dominique by saying, "It is okay; I am okay."

Knowing nothing about empathy, Dominique froze. Handicapped by the situation, flight was all she could envision. She just stared at Mrs. Allard, and she started to get angry. She couldn't control the anger; she felt herself boiling, and she blurted out, "How is that okay? How are you okay?"

Still smiling, Mrs. Allard reached out, wanting to hold Dominique's hand. Dominique recoiled, leaned back in her chair, and said, "No, no, I do not want to get this close to you. I want this session to be over."

Mrs. Allard, still smiling gently, leaned back into her chair and said, "That would be fine; I will see you tomorrow."

Exiting the room, Dominique was so shaken that she banged into the doorjamb and nearly knocked herself down. She spun sideways, caught herself with the door, looked back again at Mrs. Allard, and ran out.

Mrs. Allard bowed her head and began to pray for Dominique. She prayed, "Oh, Lord, thank You for orchestrating today's session. You know how much Dominique has suffered. Please help her and help me to help her."

CHAPTER 11

Mrs. Martsen was delighted with the connection that Mrs. Allard and Dominique appeared to have made. She lingered a little while in the cafeteria to measure how accepting students were of having Dominique back in school. She stopped several girls to see if the student population was respecting Dominique's special situation, and she asked if they were reaching out to help her. Some of the girls just gave Mrs. Martsen the answer they thought she wanted to hear, but several others said, "We know this is an opportunity to help Dominique." But they also said, "We are not sure how to best do this." Mrs. Martsen encouraged them to be natural and do what was right for her. Then she said, "If you do that, everything will be all right."

She smiled at those girls and wished them a good day. Then, she headed over to where Bella was standing, visiting with a classmate. Bella was comfortable talking with anyone, and Mrs. Martsen was no exception. Mrs. Martsen stepped up in front of the girls and smiled at them. She was beginning to realize that smiling had a wonderful effect on students. The girls turned to her and said, "Good morning, Mrs. Martsen."

Mrs. Martsen returned the greeting. She asked Bella if she could have a word with her. The other girl smiled and left, saying, "Hey, I gotta go." Bella turned to face Mrs. Martsen and waited to hear what she had to say. Bella was thinking, *Mrs. Martsen is not happy with me for my outburst during breakfast.*

She had been warned several times before concerning these abrupt verbal discharges. Just as Bella was ready to defend her actions, Mrs. Martsen leaned toward her and half-whispered, "I am proud of you. You set a positive tone today in beginning the process of Dominique's healing here."

Bella was pleasantly surprised by Mrs. Martsen's encouragement and said, "Thank you. I will do my part."

Mrs. Martsen asked Bella, "How are things going with your new roommate?"

Bella responded, "Hard to tell in just one day, but I think it's good." She continued, "Dominique does not trust people and will not let anyone in untested. It will take some time, but she does not scare me. In fact, I will probably drive her crazy before she gets to me." Mrs. Martsen laughed, but Bella, sensing it was getting late, looked at her watch and said to Mrs. Martsen, "Is there anything else? I need to get to my first-period class." Mrs. Martsen shook her head no. So, Bella headed off to class.

As Mrs. Martsen turned to leave the cafeteria, she paused and reflected a moment, still remembering Bella's courage to confront evil; she smiled as she realized how much fresher and more rewarding her position was becoming, how much more relaxed she was. She thought to herself, *I am enjoying this; it is fulfilling to really care about the needs of others.* She began to leave the cafeteria, but she stopped and caught herself, like when you forget something. She looked up and said, "Thank You, Lord." Still smiling, she calmly moved down the hall to her office.

***

Shaken by her time with Mrs. Allard, Dominique made it to first period. She remained agitated throughout the entire class period. She heard nothing the teacher taught and couldn't wait for the bell to ring. Finally, when it rang, she nervously grabbed her backpack and headed into the hall toward second period. Out in the hall, not even noticing other students, Dominique began to hatch a plan, an excuse, so she would not have to go to classes for the rest of the day. Normally, this was right up her alley; she was a convincing actor, and if she wanted it badly, she could play any role.

Still plodding to the next class, dreaming up this deceptive but worthy scheme, all of a sudden, without notice, somebody snuck up behind her and slapped her on the rear end. Dominique turned in anger only to see Bella's smiling face. Then, Bella, in a jolly voice, said, "Hey, roomy." Just as quickly as Bella came, she turned and ran off to second period.

Dominique was torn between two thoughts. On the one hand, she really disliked the fact that she was stuck with this crazy girl, but on the other hand, she liked Bella's contagious outlook on life, and it seemed like she didn't play favorites. Dominique concluded, *What you see is what you get with Bella.* That little interlude with Bella in the hall threw Dominique off the scheming track, and she could no longer concentrate on fabricating a way to end her school day.

Dominique stood back in the hallway, watching her peers pour into her second-period classroom. In a daydream, she began to relive the moment with Bella in their room. She couldn't believe how cold-hearted Bella was. *What does she mean, "I need an excuse for life, and I have no purpose"?* Dominique started to get angry again, but then, all of a sudden, and out of nowhere, a saying Aunt Colleen had taught her years ago and shared with her often burst into her thoughts.

Feeling uncomfortable, Dominique said to herself, *Aunt Colleen only used this saying when she thought I wasn't being honest with myself. Now Bella is using Aunt Colleen's very words against me too.* With unyielding precision, Aunt Colleen's quote fractured her thoughts. It was like a reader board flashing in her mind. Dominique was perplexed, and she thought, *Why is this going off in my brain now?*

She had no thoughts, but these words, they alone, remained alive and visible. She read them in her mind, recalling Aunt Colleen's calm delivery, and they said, "Excuses are the tools with which persons with no purpose in view build for themselves great monuments of nothing." Then, the quote repeated itself again. As it started to run through her mind the third time, Dominique shook her head, wondering, *What is going on?*

Still standing outside the classroom, trying to come to grips with this subliminal encroachment, she looked up to see that she was the only one not in her seat when the bell rang. Her teacher leaned out into the hall and said, "Dominique, would you like to join us?" Then, for a second time that day, Dominique was standing alone, like a portrait framed in the doorway, exposing herself again to her peers' ridicule.

She lowered her head and sheepishly crept over to her desk. Trying to shake it off, Dominique rallied inside and remembered Bella's breakfast rebuke, which helped. She even thought, *Bella knows my suffering, but it is like food for the others. Why do I give them this power over me?*

And something changed. She couldn't put a finger on it, but she felt different. She went back over the pervading feelings she used to have when someone teased her or just looked at her; she would fake it and say it didn't matter, but it did matter. Today, however, she was not feeling the pain of it, and it really didn't matter.

Now sitting in her seat, with even less learning going on than last period, Dominique was captivated again by Aunt Colleen's quote. She began to tear it apart. At first, she thought it was speaking about the fragility of having to use excuses for life, but then her mind became fastened to one word, "purpose." It was saddening and hard to admit, but she had to admit it: all she had in life was "great monuments to nothing."

Sorrow began to untie her emotions, and she felt so shallow. The echo of emptiness screamed into her hearing, and she said to herself, *I have lived my entire life building great monuments to nothing.* Then she spoke to herself, saying, *What is my purpose?* Finally, she told herself, *I have to quit thinking about this stuff; it is driving me nuts.*

The rest of Dominique's school day was a blur; she didn't even remember lunch, and at the end of the school day, she found herself hurrying to get to her room. It was not like she felt completely safe there, but at the same time, she thought, *After watching Bella defend me today, this is the safest place on campus.* It was also becoming evident that she did like her, but how much of her could she take? Right now, her greatest concern was to get away from the crowds that seemed bent on her destruction.

* * *

Hoping to arrive before Bella, Dominique walked double time to her room. Hating confrontation, she thought it would be easier to control the roommate tension by getting settled in first, but as Dominique cautiously peered in through the slightly open door, there was Bella already out of her uniform and sprawled on her bed.

Dominique's first thought was, *I won't go in.* So, she pulled her head back from the doorway to leave. Then, she thought, *But if I leave, I will end up running into classmates who are surely out to get me.* She turned back to the door, and as she did, Dominique scraped her backpack against the open door. Bella heard it and came over to check on the noise.

Bella peeked out, which frightened Dominique, and she shrank back against the hallway wall. Staring wide-eyed at Bella, Dominique could not remember ever feeling so alone. Bella just smiled and said, "No safe place, huh?" She turned and went back into the room.

Dominique stood leaning against the wall. She looked down the hall both ways, and she could see other students busy talking, goofing around, and moving in and out of their rooms. Suddenly, other girls began to notice Dominique looking lost and afraid, standing alone in the hall.

Two girls started moving toward her. Not knowing their intentions, Dominique stood up tall and quickly entered her room, closing the door behind her. The two girls came down to the door and looked at each other. One said, "Should we knock?"

The other girl said, "No, she is probably all right, and besides, Bella is in there."

The first girl nodded, agreeing, and they headed back to their room.

After entering the room, she saw Bella once again sprawled on her bed. Hoping to stall the inevitable, Dominique snuck into the bathroom to change out of her uniform. In the bathroom, she felt trapped; she had no quick trick, no manipulative plan to put into motion, and no escape from this uneasy moment she found herself.

She realized she could not stay in the bathroom until supper, so after about five minutes, she relented, acknowledging that all was lost and she would have to surrender to the moment. She unlocked the door and peeked out; Bella had not moved. She nimbly moved over to her bed and sat staring at the back of Bella's head, which was turned away from her.

Dominique sat there silent for what she thought was way too long and concluded she would have to speak to Bella. She knew Bella must be upset with her; Dominique was anxious about the tension of that moment. She thought about how to start, and she decided she would have to address how she overreacted this morning before breakfast. Just as the words were forming on Dominique's tongue, Bella began to snore.

Supper wasn't for another hour and a half, so Dominique was left listening to Bella falling into an even deeper sleep. It was funny; Dominique smiled to herself, thinking, *How little, if anything, affected Bella.* She felt a sense of safety in her room.

Settled into her bed, propping her pillow up so she could sit, Dominique began going over the day's events in her mind. Starting with how poorly she treated Bella prior to breakfast, she said to herself, *That was wrong.* She quickly moved on to the cafeteria scene and found she was not upset at the mockers; in fact, she felt kind of sorry for them after hearing Bella put them in their place.

The most important part of the cafeteria segment was that Mrs. Allard rescued her again, and she said to herself, *She is so kind.* Then, she moved on to the counseling time in Mrs. Allard's office. Here she had to stop and ask the question, *Why did I freak out? Mrs. Allard is so good to me, and as she was sharing her deepest pain with me, I blew her off. How do I face her again tomorrow?*

Wrestling with the awkward feeling of caring for others, Dominique was caught between having faith in others and doubting their sincerity. She made up her mind right then: Mrs. Allard was a friend whom she could trust. Bella, on the other hand, was somebody who you better have on your side, so she decided she would make the effort. Having these thoughts was strange for Dominique and, at the same time, comforting. She rested her head back a little and slouched down to get more comfortable, and even though Bella was bellowing, Dominique dosed off.

About an hour later, Dominique woke startled, not knowing where she was or if she was safe; she jumped up. The first thing she heard was Bella still "sawing logs," so she knew she was in her room and safe. Then she looked at the clock, and it was time for supper.

Not knowing what to expect, she walked over to where Bella was lying, hesitated for a second, and took the plunge; she leaned over and touched Bella's shoulder. Much to her surprise, Bella rolled over, looked at Dominique, looked over at the clock, and said with a smile, "Hey, roomy! Looks like it is time for supper. I am starved."

Dominique said, "Yeah, me too." Though rarely hungry, Dominique thought saying "me too" would be a bridge-building statement.

Jumping up like a spring, Bella bounced into the bathroom for a minute and came back out smiling, saying, "Shall we go?" Dominique agreed, and Bella held the door for them as they left. Going down the hall to the cafeteria, Bella said, "How long did I sleep anyway?"

Dominique responded, saying, "Long enough to get a good snore going."

Bella laughed. Her laugh was contagious, and for the first time since enrolling at school, though no one saw it, Dominique chuckled to herself.

As they moved toward the cafeteria, Bella was silent, content with no dialogue, but Dominique was nervous, trying to decide if she owed Bella an apology for being so rude before breakfast. Right on cue, though, Bella looked over to Dominique and said, "You know what? I think I like having you for a roommate."

To Dominique, that statement was like Bella reading her mind. Dominique decided right then there was no one like Bella. She didn't need an apology for offenses posed against her; rather, and almost inhumanly, she willingly overlooks offenses for the sake of relationship.

Puzzled, Dominique glanced at Bella, thinking, *Who is this person? Why is she so?* Just then, Bella turned and looked at Dominique; their eyes met. Bella wasn't smiling but looking warmly and intently into Dominique's eyes. In that moment, with their eyes fixed on each other, Dominique sensed a warm flush come over her, and she realized Bella was willing to offer her unconditional acceptance, an acceptance that she only knew with two other persons: Aunt Colleen and now Mrs. Allard.

* * *

Bella could sit and have supper with anyone. She didn't have an assigned table, and it would be normal for her to just sit at any table she chose, listening and occasionally interjecting input on the topics of the day.

As they entered the cafeteria together, Dominique was very self-conscious and not really excited about another school gathering. Much had taken place in their one day as roommates, and even though Dominique was beginning to take courage being at Bella's side, she still remained emotionally vulnerable.

As soon as they walked through the doors to the cafeteria, they had everyone's attention. Making eye contact with anyone daring to stare, Bella gave the room a quick once-over, and without incident, everyone went back to their meals. Dominique was thinking to herself, *What an ally.* As she went through the chow line, she was thinking to herself, *I have never known anyone with such presence.*

The last meal of the day went without a hitch. Dominique looked around at several of the girls, and they smiled at her. She looked over at where she used to eat, at the self-exile table, and there was Sarah and Rachel; they never looked up to acknowledge her.

As they were sitting there together, thoughts ran through Dominique's mind. Surely, everyone was acting nice to her, but it had something to do with not wanting to cross Bella. At the same time, she knew Rachel and Sarah really did not care for her. They were not people you could trust.

Moving slowly down the hall, back to their room after supper, Dominique made a decision: she had to talk to Bella. She was not sure what to say; Dominique knew she had "Valley Girl" social skills and was afraid that Bella would throw up in a conversation with so little substance.

Dominique was nervous because she knew trying to get an advantage over Bella by manipulating the conversation would be useless. And besides, Dominique had no idea what a normal conversation looked like. She had no frame of reference. What she did know, and this was hard to admit, was that she was a phony with glaring weaknesses in her character. She remembered how Aunt Colleen could, so lovingly, dispatch fatal criticism about her lack of character.

Not knowing how to have this conversation, Dominique waited until she felt they were comfortably settled, and she just blurted out loudly, "Bella, I need to talk with you."

Bella looked up, somewhat surprised at the noise level of the request, and scooted herself around to face Dominique, saying, "Here I am."

Dominique was on her bed, sitting cross-legged, and Bella sat on her bed with her feet on the floor. They were maybe four feet apart. Having Bella's attention was one thing, but knowing what to say was another. Dominique paused a moment and looked up to see Bella staring directly into her eyes.

She knew Bella's eyes were green, but until she was stuck staring deep into them, she had no idea they were so big and beautiful. Dominique never really saw Bella as beautiful; her beauty was the essence of her character, but looking at her up close and straight on, her beauty was mystical.

By looking at Dominique's expression, Bella could sense that something big needed to be said, and so, to prompt her roommate, she said, "Okay, let's have it."

Dominique nearly choked trying to speak, and she just let it out, "Bella, I do not know how to talk to people about real things." Bella didn't flinch; listening carefully, she tilted her head slightly, waiting for Dominique to continue. Dominique looked down, pleased with her beginning. She smiled, thinking that was all she needed to say.

She waited for Bella to say something, and when she didn't, she looked up, but Bella remained staring patiently. Dominique shook her head a little as if to say to Bella, "Did you not get that?"

A whimsical smile started to form on Bella's lips, and she turned her head again. She quickly resisted the smile, sensing Dominique's body language was tightening, and continued to look pleasantly at her. Becoming frustrated, Dominique said, "Are you going to answer my question?"

Bella smiled and said, "You didn't ask me a question."

Beginning to sense that starting a real conversation was much harder than she imagined, Dominique threw her hands down on the bed and said, "See, I don't know how to do this."

Bella smiled again, remained focused directly into Dominique's eyes, and said, "Do you have a question you would like to ask me?" Dominique had about a million questions for Bella, but she didn't know where to start. Sensing Dominique's dilemma, Bella said, "It takes a willingness to be vulnerable to have a real conversation. I don't mind; you can ask me any question you like."

Dominique hated it when people asked her questions because she was unsure of the intent as if they might use the information against her. Bella's invitation was exquisite; she was inviting Dominique into the depths of herself, and Dominique was delighted. Knowing Bella didn't care if she knew her well made Dominique smile, and she said, "You don't mind?"

Bella laughed and pointed at Dominique, saying, "Hey, we are having a real conversation." She smirked at Dominique and said, "Ask me something; this is boring."

Dominique knew what the first question to Bella had to be, but she also knew this question was too intimate to begin with. She paused, gaining strength, and just said, "When I was so rude to you before breakfast today, why did you forgive me? I didn't even ask you to forgive me, and I knew you had forgiven me. I was hurt by what you said to me before you left for breakfast. I figured you and I would be the worst roommates, but all day long, I have been thinking about what you said, even though it hurt me. Now, after spending the day with you, I think you would make the best roommate ever."

Bella smiled, paused a second, and said, "That was a big question. Good job." Then she continued, "I forgave you because there was nothing you owed me. I know you are hurting; I don't know why, but, Dominique, it is evident. I should apologize to you. I say what is on my mind way too often, but having watched you suffer so, I felt it was necessary to challenge you to really take a look at yourself rather than look at others as an excuse to stay buried inside yourself. Trust me, you have nothing to apologize to me for. My goal is to lift you up and nothing more."

Part of Dominique wanted to run; this was way too real, but as she stared into Bella's eyes and listened to her share her thoughts, she knew Bella really cared for her. For the most part, excluding the Durand incident, Dominique wept for effect. It always helped her experience fewer consequences, but being immersed in Bella's raw honesty and love, she looked down and began to cry.

Not like she cried when she was so all alone and wanted to end her life, but tears of joy, like when she first came home, and Mom and Dad loved her so. She began to sob, and with each tear, a liberating transformation began.

Bella came over and put her arms around Dominique. They didn't speak, but Dominique turned and put her arms around Bella, and she cried like a child. Bella knew they had opened a floodgate of pain, and feeling Dominique's pain, Bella wept too. As they held each other, Bella looked up from where her head was buried under Dominique's long black hair and prayed, "Oh, God, help my friend…"

CHAPTER 12

That second night, as Bella's roommate, Dominique slept like a baby. She even had sweet dreams, which never happened to her. She heard Bella moving around, and as she became more awake, she actually welcomed the day. This was something new for Dominique because most days were nothing for her to look forward to. Not wanting a repeat of yesterday's morning, Dominique sat up and, finding Bella at her desk, said, "Good morning, Bella."

Bella smiled and said, "Wow! Who is this? Their day starts with a pleasant conversation?" They both laughed, and Bella turned back to writing something on her desk. Dominique slid out of bed and headed to the bathroom. She was warm in her soul, and she looked at herself in the mirror. It instantly struck her that she hadn't really seen herself in a long time. Staring at herself and really seeing herself, Dominique paused, standing there with her hands on the sink. She thought to herself, *This is the same peace I knew at home right after Mom and Dad came back from Philadelphia.*

It had been so long since she liked what she saw in the mirror, and she smiled at herself. Stopping to admire the one in the mirror, she began to analyze what she was feeling, and suddenly, out of nowhere, a thought burst in and caused her to shiver; fear began to creep into this beautiful scene.

As if like clockwork, the same old hideous thought that always took her peace forced its way in. Durand appeared in the mirror, standing between her and the reflection of her peace. She froze, staring, trying to bring back that beautiful reflection of herself, but Durand continued to fill the picture until she was no longer visible.

Instantly, like flipping a switch, Dominique was transported by agony to exile. She looked down into the sink; she stared there for a long time, and as she did, fear and anger started to pulse in her veins. She froze and couldn't look up again into the mirror. She turned her back to the reflection that was holding her captive.

With clenched fists, she raised her hands slowly over her head and took a deep breath. From that position, she threw her hands down and, at the same time, bent over and screamed until she had exhaled all the air in her lungs; it was a torturous scream. Instantly after the scream, she started throwing anything she could get her hands on directly at the image in the mirror.

Bella was startled when she heard Dominique scream, and then she heard things being broken in the bathroom. She jumped up from her chair and ran over to the bathroom door. She said forcefully, "Dominique, what is going on?" Dominique stopped breaking things and turned to the door, then she backed up and sat down on the toilet. Her heart was racing, and her pulse was pounding, and she started to become light-headed.

Bella asked again, "Dominique, what is happening?" Dominique could not answer Bella and started to sob. Getting ready for action, Bella said, "Dominique, I will not ask you again; I will break down this door if you do not answer me."

Dominique knew Bella was there, but she was lost in her own world of doubt and pain. She looked back and forth, trying to focus, but was unable to. She looked down onto the bathroom floor and then up to the ceiling, trying to find a point of reference. She slowly began to pace her breathing, and she could see more clearly. Focusing better, she realized Bella would do what she said she would do and tear down this door, so Dominique gathered herself and weakly replied, "I am okay, Bella; please give me a minute."

Keenly alert and listening intently, Bella backed away from the door and sat on Dominique's bed. Dominique sat there in the bathroom, trying to compose; knowing she had an ally on the other side of the door helped her focus. She stood up, trying to avoid the glass breakage on the floor, and moved to the door. She was embarrassed and unsure how to begin explaining to Bella what had just taken place. Dominique knew Bella was waiting, and that minute Dominique had asked for was just about up.

Afraid, Dominique unlocked the door, and as she did, Bella sat forward on the bed. Not sure what to expect, she prayed, *Give me strength, Lord.* Then, Dominique turned the doorknob and opened the door. Bella was shocked to see, there before her, that same estranged girl who stood so bitterly in front of her the morning before.

Fearing this entire situation, Dominique knew this incident would lead to a meltdown for her parents and the school, and that would lead to her being placed in private care for recovery.

Defeated and forlorn, Dominique slowly looked up and into Bella's eyes. She wished she could be all alone, but at the same time, she longed for help. To her surprise, Bella's expression was not horror but questioning and comforting. Bella didn't say a word; she just walked over and grabbed Dominique's hands, pulling her out of the bathroom and past the broken mess on the floor. Then she led Dominique over to sit on her bed, still holding hands; Bella settled in next to her.

Dominique didn't want to cry; she wanted to scream again, and she said to herself, *What is going to become of me?* Then she thought, *If Bella tells anyone what happened, I am gone.*

Her desperate situation forced her to settle back into what comes naturally for Dominique: to scheme her way around Bella. With her eyes and face red from crying, Dominique looked up at Bella and pleaded with her, saying, "Please don't tell anyone what happened in the bathroom; they will kick me out of school again."

Leaning back a little to survey Dominique's face, Bella knew what she just experienced with Dominique was for adults to fix, not teenagers. Continuing to stare at Dominique, Bella could see the fear and the tragedy that engulfed her new roommate. Captivated by Bella's stare but wary of the betrayal that could be coming, Dominique began to tremble.

Finally, Bella spoke. As she did, Dominique moved her head up so she was level with Bella's eyes; still holding hands, she squeezed Bella's hands even tighter. Very calmly, Bella said, "What happened in the bathroom?"

The question Bella asked almost put Dominique over the edge; she thought, *How do I answer that?* Then she thought, *Why didn't Bella just say she wouldn't tell anyone?* Her pulse seemed to race again, and Dominique began to question if Bella really was an ally.

Dominique's body language began to alert Bella that she was nearly at the end of her wits. So, Bella seized the opportunity to interject and said, "Dominique, something happened to you, which really concerns me. I cannot be put in a position where what I do now puts you in more danger. So, with your history and your parents and our school doing all they can to help you, unless you help me understand what happened, you are forcing me to get the adults involved."

Wrestling her hands away from Bella's grip, Dominique looked angrily at her. Just before Dominique spoke, Bella jumped in and said, "Hey, you can trust me. Last night, we cried together, holding each other. Do you now not trust me?"

Dominique's first inclination was to smack her for wanting to betray her, but then, she let what Bella just said sink in. She said Bella's words to herself, *Don't you trust me?* Caught between two responses, Dominique was torn. She could employ her old response, which was to strike out, or this new response, which was just coming to fruition, which was to trust because these people cared for her.

The problem for Dominique was that she trusted no one, but a new revelation was playing out right in front of her, and as scary as it was, a more chilling thought took over, and she said to herself, *What is going to become of me if this doesn't work?* She rested her thoughts and tried to imagine that Mrs. Allard and Bella were trustworthy, that they really only wanted her best.

Calming herself, Dominique hoped upon hope, and she carefully chose her words and said to Bella, "Do you mean, if I tell you what happened in the bathroom, you will not let my parents know?"

Bella could see the hope in Dominique's question, but at the same time, she knew she would have to decide on what to do only after she heard Dominique's story.

The school offered semester-long ministry opportunities off campus, and Bella chose to minister to at-risk teens at the nearby community center. She was well-versed in the proper protocol dealing with abuse. So, Bella said to Dominique, "A confidence is only a confidence when physical safety is a surety. I will need to know those details, and if I am not convinced, I have a responsibility for your welfare past confidentiality."

Dominique didn't like hearing all the what-ifs and started again to doubt Bella's sincerity. Then she thought, *I don't have to tell her the facts; I can make it up. Most people think I am a nutcase anyway.*

With the plot in place, she started to tell Bella what she thought Bella wanted to hear, but just before she began, she abruptly stopped and thought, *How is telling a story, a lie about what is hurting me, going to help me?* Then, as if she was holding her own shoulders and straightening herself up, she said to herself, *Now I am lying to myself.* Finishing the thought, she said, *Why can't I trust anyone with my pain, and what will happen if I never do?*

CHAPTER 13

With the Bible lying still open on her bed, Colleen sat for a few moments, just looking at the book. She hadn't closed it because she didn't want to lose the red ink section. She could not remember the last time she had even held a Bible, let alone read it. Now, as she continued to examine just the physical characteristics of the book, she concluded: *It doesn't look that dangerous.* As a child, she had a Bible, and she read it, but she could not remember a single line she had read.

Her thoughts moved back out into the family room with Marie and Thomas sitting together. That picture was so peaceful, and Colleen knew that more of that calm was the key to keeping this family together.

Then she thought, *How do I help facilitate that scene on a daily basis?* Then, she allowed a thought to slip into her brain, and she said it out loud, "By taking me out of the equation." She pondered long on that reveal and wrestled with how to make that happen practically.

All along, Colleen thought she was protecting Marie from Thomas; he was such a loser to Colleen, but after hashing that thought over at length, she finally caved, realizing she was the problem. What she had been doing for so long was separating them, not bringing them together.

That reality was huge; it revealed her pride, and Colleen finally relented and said to herself, *This is not about me.* With a peace she could not fully understand but felt so warmly, she pulled herself under the covers and picked up the Bible.

She reached over to her nightstand, grabbed a fingernail file, placed it where the Bible was open to the red ink section, and closed it. She held it close and then looked at it out at arm's reach. Observing the size of it, she said to herself, *I'll bet there is a lot more good stuff in here.*

She puffed up her pillow so she could sit and read; expectantly, she opened it to the very beginning. It didn't take long, though, before she was hating every second of it. Nothing made any sense. Somebody begets someone, and another begets someone else, and very few of these names meant anything to her.

After all that had transpired earlier, Colleen was so looking forward to more insight, but she was very disappointed at what she read and closed the book. She thought, *Did I just luck out and get the only gem in this entire book?* Disheartened, she leaned over to lay it down on her night table, but because she had to reach quite a way to set it down, and it was heavy, it flipped out of her hand and landed on the floor. She leaned over to pick it up, and to her delight, there glowing before her was another red ink section. She quickly picked it up and sat on the edge of the bed to read what was printed before her.

She first looked at the top of the page, and it read: "The Book of Luke." Next, she read down to the red ink section. It began at verse 11 through verse 13 of chapter 1. It was talking about an angel who heard a guy named Zechariah praying, and the angel said to him, "Do not be afraid, Zechariah; your prayer has been heard…"[2]

Finding that section about prayer inspired Colleen; she wanted her prayers answered for Marie and Thomas. Holding that section open, she climbed back into bed, propped herself up again, and laid the book in her lap. She lifted her knees again so she could cradle the book at the right angle to relax and read.

Holding the place in the Bible with her fingers, she opened it, and with new vigor, she looked again at the red ink section. This verse really caught her attention because she believed she had received an answer to prayer today and wanted to know more about prayer. After reading that section several times, she went back to the beginning of the book of Luke and started reading.

***

After that first night of having the Bible in her room, Colleen found it difficult to go to bed without reading it. Most of the time, it made very little sense, especially in the beginning of the book, but since she had found the red ink underlining in Luke, that is where she spent most of her time reading.

Strangely, little by little, she began to remember from her childhood reading about biblical characters, characters beyond Mary, Joseph, the baby Jesus, and the nativity scenes. It was most exciting to hear what Jesus had to say, and she read His words over and over again. She began to believe that getting along with Thomas was directly related to what she read.

In fact, Thomas was transforming into someone she could not only tolerate but was thankful for; it was a God thing, and Colleen knew it. It was not that Thomas had completely quit treating Marie poorly, but as Colleen worked at getting along with Thomas, she knew that was God's purpose for her. Colleen finally came to the conclusion that it was her changing, not Thomas, who was healing their home.

Though Thomas knew Colleen was acting differently, not so hostile, he still did not trust her completely. One evening after work, Thomas was reading the paper in the kitchen. As Colleen entered the room, they were both startled to find themselves in the same proximity.

It was instantly uncomfortable in the kitchen for both of them; when Thomas saw Colleen enter the room, he scooted his chair a few inches away from her and raised the paper up so as to not see her.

Immediately angered by his obvious disdain, Colleen thought to herself, *I should just walk over there and slap him in the back of the head.* She was so angry. Then, without warning, she heard the words again from the Bible: "Be content with what you have…"

Moving away from where she stood staring at her nemesis, Colleen's demeanor changed, and as she moved past Thomas to the refrigerator, she asked him, "What do you feel like for supper."

Not wanting to respond, Thomas was surprised by the gentle question. He shuffled the paper and turned to look at Colleen, but before he could answer, Colleen said, "How about a big taco salad? I know you really like that."

Feeling very uncomfortable with the tension in the kitchen, Thomas put the paper down; he had to get out of this odd pleasantry, so he said abruptly, "Fine, that would be good."

Hurrying out of the room, Thomas made brief eye contact with Colleen. She turned to face him and smiled, saying, "I will call you for supper."

As he was leaving the kitchen, Thomas felt forced, but he said to Colleen, "Thank you."

Continuing the conversation, Colleen said, "Oh, Marie has been looking forward to your arrival home; I believe she is awake now." Turning to begin dinner, Colleen smiled inwardly and outwardly, thankful for God's intervention.

* * *

After reminiscing about the blessed encounter in the kitchen with Thomas, Colleen came back to where she was struggling to understand what she was reading in Luke. Colleen understood from childhood that the baby Jesus had come to save the world, but she must not have paid much attention when He spoke of dying on the cross. She also came to the conclusion from reading Jesus's words that He was quite demanding.

One section that was almost too hard for her to believe was the conversation He had with the disciples on His way to fulfill His destiny in Jerusalem. It sounded like He was saying, "Unless you are willing to die yourself, you cannot be His follower." Colleen knew about the cross but had no idea of the suffering Jesus endured. She read ahead in Luke to understand how this suffering could happen to Jesus. She also read footnotes at the bottom of the page and was shocked at how cruel the Romans were. She finally understood that if you carried a cross in Rome, you did not come back alive. Now, she was learning that Jesus expected the same of His followers. If you put on the cross, you cannot go back.

Somewhat baffled by Jesus, Colleen continued to read on, and she came to where He had conversations with several men.

> As they were walking along the road, a man said to him, "I will follow you wherever you go."
>
> Jesus replied, "Foxes have dens and birds have nests, but the Son of Man has no place to lay his head."
>
> He said to another man, "Follow me."
>
> But he replied, "Lord, first let me go and bury my father."
>
> Jesus said to him, "Let the dead bury their own dead, but you go and proclaim the kingdom of God."
>
> Still another said, "I will follow you, Lord; but first let me go back and say goodbye to my family."
>
> Jesus replied, "No one who puts a hand to the plow and looks back is fit for service in the kingdom of God.[3]

At first, Colleen thought, *How harsh Jesus is. He seems to be pushing these men away rather than drawing them in.* Undeterred, she pushed on in Luke until she came to other stories of the unbelievable compassion of Jesus, healing people, raising people from the dead, and the feeding of thousands of people with only a boy's lunch.

It was becoming evident to Colleen that Jesus did not request but demanded allegiance, and His miracles of love were the proof of His authority to demand such. Her greatest quandary revolved around Jesus's promise of eternal life and the kingdom of heaven. But she continued to read and take it in.

It became like food to her, and she became famished without it. The more she read, the more her attitude changed with Thomas and Marie. With Marie being sick all the time, she could be quite a pill, and it was hard for Colleen to have her baby sister yelling at her unthankfully. *After all, does she not know what is being done for her?*

About six months into the healing process, which God was working out for her sister's family, Colleen suggested to Marie that Chloe, Marie's best friend, come for an extended visit.

Chloe, Marie, and Colleen had become good friends years ago. They all ran in the same circles, which intertwined around their husbands' business dealings. They all traveled together, partied together, went to church together, and Chloe's and Marie's kids played together. They all were like family.

With Chloe being Marie's best friend, Colleen thought it would be a good thing for Marie to have her dear friend around to lift her spirits; Chloe, and Chloe alone, had that ability. Chloe was like sunshine; she brightened a room by just walking in. Chloe had not seen Dominique yet, so it made the best of sense. Colleen thought to herself, *I could use a hand as well.*

It wasn't long after Chloe arrived that Marie began to heal. Chloe would make Marie laugh, and you could see the light in Marie's eyes starting to shine again. Almost every night, Chloe would sit in a chair next to Marie, holding her hand, brushing her hair, and talking for hours. Colleen had little time to sit and gab with both of them, so she wasn't sure what they talked about, but many times, she heard bits and pieces that were Bible related.

Chloe was also a great help with Dominique, and that freed up Colleen for other family matters. With so much going on, Chase was getting left out, and he was beginning to act out. Chloe's help with the baby afforded Colleen more one-on-one time with him.

Thomas was incapable of understanding Chase's needs and was always on his case about something. Chloe also felt something was missing with Chase, and she mentioned it to Colleen. Colleen shared with Chloe that Chase's dad treated his older boys the same way, and they stayed away because of it. The two of them made a pact to reach out to Chase and enhance his position in the home.

Colleen remained true to her mission, though, as much as Thomas could do wrong, she did not let it discourage her from helping the family heal, and with Chloe alongside, it just became easier to do so.

On a regular basis, Colleen let Chloe know how thankful she was for sacrificing her family to be here with hers. Chloe said to Colleen, "I know you are thankful, but do you know what a joy it is for me to be here? This is not a burden. Chloe had a way of making everyone feel better about themselves, and she knew this was why Marie so loved Chloe.

One night, when Marie was feeling well enough to sit out in the family room, the entire family gathered around her. All could see that Marie was healing, and this made everyone grateful. Chase was even able to get really close to Mom; he missed hugging on her so much; it was a big deal for him. Everyone passed Dominique around; she was growing so fast, and there was a bliss that even Thomas was able to enjoy. They all must have wondered if they would ever see Marie well again, and now that she was healing, they were overjoyed.

Colleen was especially joyful for what played out that night in the family room. She lingered for a while, relishing the family dynamic, and then she realized it had been a long day. She had to get up long before anyone else, even Thomas, so she stood up, walked over to Marie, leaned down, and kissed her forehead, saying, "Good night, Sis. Love you."

Marie said, "Are you leaving so early? We are having such a good time…"

Colleen replied, "No rest for the wicked." Even Thomas had to laugh. Colleen said, "Yes, it is time. Should I put Dominique down?" Chloe could tell Marie wanted the baby to stay, so she offered to put her down later. Colleen nodded her head and left for her room.

Lying in her bed, Colleen was exhausted, but she was so joyful she bowed her head and said, "Thank You, Jesus, for what You are doing in this home." She grabbed the Bible on the nightstand and held it for a moment. For some reason, her thoughts jumped back to when she was married. Maybe because of the bliss she was experiencing here with Thomas and Marie. She could recall some wonderful moments of being married, but quickly, those moments were erased and overshadowed by the terrible moments she endured in that union. She wondered if she would ever know love again and if it was too late for a family.

Just then, she heard a knock on her bedroom door. It was Chloe, and she said, "Can I come in?"

Colleen sat up, still holding the Bible, and said, "Sure, come on in."

Entering with a big smile, Chloe said, "I hope I am not bothering you."

Smiling as well, Colleen said, "Not at all; please come in," and she invited Chloe to sit in the chair by the bed.

Chloe sat down, still smiling, and said, "I just wanted to stop by and thank you for how you have ministered to this family. You are like a healer."

Not expecting the accolades, Colleen was embarrassed. She looked down and felt herself blush. Looking up, hoping to appear humble, Colleen was about to speak, but Chloe stopped her and said, "I know the difficulty that Thomas and Marie have been through, and I know how difficult it is here for everyone, with Thomas being so… well, you know Thomas." Continuing, she said, "Thomas is different; he remains pretty worthless around the house, but I see how he looks at Marie now, and something has changed him."

Still sharing, Chloe said, "I think the change started with you. I also see how, like before, you are not at war with Thomas, and that has put Marie at real peace. So, what is your secret ingredient?"

Not sure of what Chloe was talking about, Colleen looked up at Chloe and said, "I guess I just decided to be thankful for what I had and where I was."

Looking down into Colleen's lap, Chloe said, "Does that book have anything to do with it?"

Colleen looked down at the Bible and then quickly back to Chloe's eyes. She wasn't embarrassed at all, and she said, "Yes, yes, I believe it does."

Chloe said to Colleen, "Can I confide in you?" Not sure what was coming, Colleen nodded uncomfortably. Chloe began by saying, "I know you know that I am in love with Jesus, and from what I see, I think you are beginning to love Him too." Sitting up a little, Colleen smiled. Continuing, Chloe said, "What you are doing for this family is not happening because you are preaching Jesus at them. You are making a huge difference because you are being Jesus to them. You, better than anyone, know Marie is not comfortable with, in her words, 'religious people.' I know your family and Thomas's family have difficulty with church people. So, I want to encourage you to continue as you have, to be led by thankfulness, and let God work the miracles into this family's life. Marie will not accept Bible talks until she sees the Jesus she needs in other people. There is a wall there for both Thomas and Marie, so our job is to pray for them."

Chloe and Colleen talked for a few more minutes, and just before Chloe left, she reached out and grabbed Colleen's hand and said, "Can I pray for your continued success here?" Colleen knew Chloe was very religious, and so did Marie, but Colleen was beginning to see it wasn't religion; it was Jesus living in her.

Colleen wanted more of that for herself, and she was learning that prayer works, so she said, "Yes, thank you. I could use all the help I can get." Chloe bowed her head, so Colleen did too. It was scary and wonderful at the same time. Colleen didn't know what to expect; she had only heard herself pray lately, but she was expectant. Chloe spoke to God like He was in the room, and she poured her heart out for His help with Thomas and Marie. Then, she prayed for Colleen that Jesus would continue to use her and give her wisdom and strength. Colleen had never felt anything so powerful; her heart was overwhelmed. She didn't want to end this prayer, in which Jesus was so present.

CHAPTER 14

Bella continued to stare at Dominique, waiting for her to explain why she went crazy in the bathroom. Bella did not want to rat on Dominique, but she knew it was not up to her; it was really up to Dominique to convince her otherwise.

Having observed Dominique manipulate and embellish so often in the past, Bella was beginning to doubt if, in the heat of the moment, Dominique was capable of telling the truth. So, she prayed to herself, *Oh, God, let this be a beginning for Dominique.*

On the other hand, Dominique sat there trapped. She knew Bella had her future in her hands. She wrestled so hard in thought that she began to perspire, and beads of sweat formed on her forehead. Completely unaware of the concept of the inevitable, Dominique was grappling with having to accept it.

Finally, she looked up again into Bella's eyes. Her shoulders fell forward, and she let out a sigh. Bella could see more than fear in Dominique's face; she saw horror. Hoping to reassure her, Bella said again, "You can trust me."

With the last vestige of hope burning in her heart and mind, she said to herself, *How can I do this? If I tell Bella what Durand did, she is going to have to tell the school, and the school will have to tell my parents. Bella will not believe me if I tell her a lie, and she will have to tell someone. And if I say nothing, Bella is still bound by protocol to report my meltdown in the bathroom.* She completed her thoughts with: *I have no options; I am over.*

Dominique could not take her eyes off of Bella; tears began to well up in her eyes again. Her forehead wrinkled, and her chin began to quiver. Sensing a dam was about to burst, Bella leaned forward, ready to catch whatever came. Then, the dam broke. Like the weight of the whole world being lifted from her shoulders, tears streaming down her face, Dominique said calmly, "My cousin raped me."

With her face placid but wet from crying, Dominique sat there numb, completely exhausted, too tired to move. She continued to stare at Bella. All at once, she felt released from the anxiety of keeping such a terrible secret. She closed her eyes, tilted her head back, and said to herself, *There, somebody besides me knows.*

With her head tilted back, letting it all sink in, she stayed there for a moment. Then, she slowly lowered her head to make eye contact with Bella. At last, she was experiencing an emotion not built on guilt, but she was still uneasy, not sure of the future, and she asked Bella, "What happens now?"

Having been held spellbound, waiting and wondering if Dominique was going to share, Bella let out a sigh of relief; she reached over and threw her arms around her. In agony for comfort, Dominique collapsed into Bella's embrace.

Holding on to Bella, Dominique felt strangely free, and the guilt was gone. Even as they held on to each other, Dominique was able to think and to feel, to feel so instantly different than just seconds ago. She was relieved that this was no longer just her secret.

Feeling such a release of pain, Dominique didn't want to end this peaceful moment, but then, a thought pricd its way into her bliss, and she had to stop. She said to herself, *This exposure will have unintended consequences.* She pulled herself back and held Bella's arms in her hands. She just stared at Bella, and a thin, nervous smile crept onto Dominique's face; she shuddered and said, "Really, what now?"

Overwhelmed by the enormity of this revelation, Bella reached again for Dominique's hands and said, "First, I want to thank you for trusting me to share your story; I am so blessed that you confided in me. You are so brave, and starting today, you proved yourself ready for healing and moving forward. Bella reached up, held Dominique's face in her hands, and said, "You did nothing wrong; you are the victim here."

Wiping the tears away from Dominique's face, then Bella brushed her thick black hair back behind her ears, and while still holding her face in her hands, she said, "Dominique, how do you feel?"

Taking a deep breath, Dominique knew something was different, better. She looked quizzically at Bella's warm and tear-streaked face, then she looked down. She contemplated for a moment, and it was clear to her: she felt free. She looked up again at Bella and said, "I am not afraid. I don't know where we go from here, but with your help, I believe I can handle whatever comes next." She continued, "Knowing that I no longer bear this alone gives me hope. I have for so long carried this awful truth, which I wanted to be a lie. In fact, I thought the only way to continue my life was to continue this lie. This will be so hard on my family, but I want them to know; they need to know what has happened to me." Then she stopped, cringing at the thought, and she asked Bella. "What will happen to my cousin?"

Bella looked at her firmly and said, "Your cousin is not your responsibility. He did evil to you, and he must face the consequences." Dominique couldn't help but think about how much Bella sounded like her aunt, Colleen. She was so wise for her age, and Dominique trusted her.

Noticing that Dominique was calming and that they would soon be late for breakfast, Bella told Dominique, "Now, we have to tell someone." This stark revelation pulled Dominique up short; even though she knew this had to happen, she began to dread her decision. She started to look around the room for answers, but Bella quickly reached out, grabbed her, and pulled her in close, saying, "Do you still trust me?"

Dominique froze and looked straight into Bella's eyes. She thought, *This is all happening too quickly.* But fixed on Bella, right there before her, some of that peace and freedom entered back into her, and she was strengthened. She squeezed Bella's hand and nodded.

Steadying herself, Dominique said, "Fine, who do we tell?"

Knowing how hard this was going to be for Dominique, Bella also knew she was now responsible for following proper protocol, and she said, "We must tell your counselor."

Dominique's first response to the news frightened her, and she recoiled against it. She was embarrassed, remembering how awful she treated Mrs. Allard at their first session. Trying to come up with an alternate choice, Dominique questioned Bella, saying, "Can't it be someone else?"

With a look of disbelief, Bella turned her head sideways and said, "Who do you suggest, Mrs. Martsen?"

Dominique looked down and then at the door. Thinking clearly was difficult, and she gazed quickly back and forth around the room; she was hoping for a way out but found no escape route. She looked up at Bella and nodded. "You are right; there is no one else."

Hoping to boost her confidence, Bella told Dominique that she would be going with her to meet with Mrs. Allard. Dominique smiled and hugged Bella, who said, "Hey, we got to go."

So, they both rushed around the room, prepping for the school day. They met at the door. Bella reached out for Dominique's hand, and with excitement in her voice, she said, "Let's pray before we go."

Dominique stepped back in shock and let go of Bella's hand. She thought to herself, *Right now… right now, she wants to pour her religion on top of this.* Bella could see that Dominique was offended, so she reached back for Dominique's hand and said, "I thought you trusted me. This is how I deal with things that are bigger than me. I take them to God."

Dominique had no reason to not trust Bella, but she was still offended that she wanted to bring God into her world. As far as Dominique was concerned, there was no place for God in her world. While Bella stood there looking at her for a response, Dominique's skin began to crawl, and she nearly yelled out, "Let's call this whole thing off," but just before the rebel in her began to yell, she looked again at Bella, and she saw a friend, someone she could trust, and there was no one else to trust. Even if she didn't trust God, she did trust Bella. She gripped Bella's hand and, sounding disgusted, she said, "Fine."

Frozen in her tracks, Dominique just stood there captive and hostile. When Bella bowed her head to pray, Dominique stared foolishly off in the distance. As Bella began her prayer, Dominique's attention was fixed on the top of Bella's red head.

She couldn't believe this was happening. Bella began her prayer by saying, "Dear God, thank You for knowing this situation and how much Dominique has suffered. Thank You, too, for letting Dominique feel safe enough to share her suffering with me. I don't have the answers, but I know You do; please move in our lives right now so that we might see Your mighty hand in what comes next. In Your name, Jesus, I pray. Amen."

With a huge smile on her face, Bella squeezed Dominique's hand. She grabbed the door, threw it open, and held out her hand as an invitation for them to head to breakfast. Bella was so excited and moving so fast up the hall that she was dragging Dominique along, and she said, "Come on, lazy bones, let's go."

Being pulled along, Dominique remained upset about what had just taken place in their room. Then, she started to go over Bella's prayer in her mind. She thought, *Bella's words were short and sweet, and she didn't get all mystical.* Then, Dominique looked up to see Bella, half dancing and singing as she pulled her along. Dominique tried to fight it, but Bella was just so funny. She realized that she was not as offended as she thought she would be with praying. There was no doubt in her mind that this silly but wonderful new roommate really did care for her. Bella looked back with a stupid look on her face. Their eyes met, and Dominique could contain it no longer; she burst out laughing. This wonderful emotion, so foreign to Dominique, felt so real and so good.

***

Though Bella made the trip to breakfast fun, Dominique was still unnerved about meeting again with Mrs. Allard. She was confused about why she freaked out at her first counseling session.

Breakfast went well; it was comfortable with Bella at her side. She wasn't sure if it was Bella demanding the girls to be accepting or if they really were warming up to her, but either way, the atmosphere was pleasant.

Several times during breakfast, Dominique slid a glance over at Mrs. Allard, and every time she did, Mrs. Allard would be looking right at her, smiling. The comfort of breakfast quickly became uncomfortable. Feeling like she was avoiding Mrs. Allard, Dominique made eye contact again, but this time, instead of looking away, she smiled at Mrs. Allard, and Mrs. Allard smiled back. This bond with Mrs. Allard was wonderful, but even with Bella at her side, Dominique couldn't imagine starting this awful conversation with an adult, even if the adult was Mrs. Allard.

Just as Dominique was taking in her last bite of breakfast, she looked up and was startled to see Mrs. Allard standing next to her. Reacting nervously to Mrs. Allard being in her space, Dominique became tense and wary. Mrs. Allard bent down and whispered to Dominique, saying, "I am excited about our meeting this morning. Shall we walk together?"

Calming from Mrs. Allard's surprise encounter, Dominique smiled weakly but could not keep eye contact. Then she nodded, acknowledging the invitation, and said abruptly, "Can Bella come with me to our meeting?"

Mrs. Allard looked over at Bella, smiled, and said, "Of course."

As the three of them exited the cafeteria, Mrs. Allard grabbed both girls by the arm and led them toward her office. Both girls were somewhat subdued; this was especially odd for Bella, which led Mrs. Allard to wonder what was going on with Dominique's request to have Bella present.

CHAPTER 15

Chloe's stay lasted for two months, and everyone benefited greatly by her presence. Marie became stronger with each day and didn't need to spend as much time in bed. Marie and Thomas's marriage became stronger as well. Chase made great headway in relationships with both his parents, and they both took on a new perspective on knowing and meeting his needs. Now eight months old, Dominique was growing like a weed.

Using words that she only knew, she would carry on lengthy conversations with anyone who would listen. She crawled around the house, but she was also able to stand and hold on to the furniture; everyone was enlisted to keep track of her.

Colleen and Chloe had become great confidants and relished time together. They met mostly in the evening after Marie retired to bed. Colleen had so many questions about the Bible and about life in general, and Chloe loved the fellowship. Chloe marveled at how changed and mature Colleen was becoming.

One night, while visiting in Colleen's room, Chloe told Colleen of her soon departure. Colleen knew she would have to leave sometime, but she did not want it to be soon. Chloe assured Colleen that all would be well and that God would not be leaving with her. Colleen laughed, but inside, she knew things would be so different without Chloe.

Sensing Colleen's trepidation, Chloe reached over to touch her hand, and she said to Colleen, "Remember the revelation, the first thing you read in the Bible, the underlined red ink section? What did it say?"

Colleen paused a minute but knew it by heart; it was the beginning of a new world for her. She looked up confidently and said, "God will never leave me or forsake me."

Chloe asked Colleen, "Do you still believe that?" Colleen nodded her head, and a big smile settled across her face. "There you go then." Chloe continued, "Keep on trusting that you are where you are supposed to be and that God wants to use you in this family. I will never be more than a phone call away, so take courage and be strong."

That message resonated with Colleen, but it also revealed the lack of confidence she had in being courageous and strong. That week, Chloe left for Philadelphia.

Having learned so much from Chloe, Colleen wondered if she could continue to grow without her. After Chloe left, Colleen drew strength from remembering those early days when Chloe first arrived. It was so exciting to expose her life to the teachings of the Bible.

After Chloe left, Colleen succinctly remembered one day above all the others. That day, Chloe explained to Colleen what Jesus meant when He said, "I am the way and the truth and the life. No one comes to the Father except through me."[4] Colleen believed that God had revealed Himself to her that day she picked up the Bible, but she was not sure what that statement implied: "No one comes to the Father except through me."

She believed that God was real and was helping her live with Thomas and Marie, but she also couldn't forget what she had read about how stern Jesus was with those who drew near to Him. Jesus appeared to make it harder to follow Him rather than to make it easier.

Chloe was careful to explain to Colleen the full message of God that from the beginning, God had a plan in place to free us from the penalty of our sin. She continued and told her that this plan was the main theme of the entire Bible. God's plan was that Jesus would willingly go to the cross and die; He took on Himself what we deserved.

Chloe also showed Colleen in the Bible where Jesus said, "For God so loved the world that he gave his one and only Son, that whoever believes in him shall not perish but have eternal life."[5] Colleen remembered asking Chloe, "What does it mean 'to believe in Jesus'? Don't I believe in Jesus?"

Chloe told her what the Bible says: "Anyone who comes to him must believe that he exists and that he rewards those who earnestly seek him."[6]

Becoming confused, Dominique asked, "What more can I do to seek Jesus?"

Again, Chloe was alert to not deviate from God's Word, and she told Colleen, "The Bible says, 'For all have sinned and fall short of the glory of God.'"[7] She continued by saying, "The wages of sin is death, but the gift of God is eternal life in Christ Jesus our Lord."[8]

At that point, Colleen remembered asking Chloe, "So, Jesus thinks I am a sinner?"

Chloe responded, "Not just you, but every human who has ever lived."

Colleen asked, "So, what do I do to make Him happy?"

Chloe smiled and said, "Allow Him to love you as only He can and remember His requirements." She continued, "He knows what is required; we must repent of our sins and agree with Him that we are sinners, that we need forgiveness."

Colleen asked Chloe, "Where in the Bible does it say that?"

Smiling, Chloe grabbed the Bible off of Colleen's nightstand and turned to Matthew 4:17. And she read to her: "From the time Jesus began to preach, saying, 'Repent, for the kingdom of heaven is at hand.'"[9] Then she also read in Luke 13:3: "Unless you repent, you will all likewise perish."[10]

Colleen wanted to please Jesus, but she was not sure she was the sinner He made her out to be. She asked Chloe, "If I don't say I am sorry for my sins, will I perish?" Chloe affirmed that was true. At this juncture, Colleen started to balk; she began to feel like one of those people Jesus told to come and follow Him when they responded, "Lord, first let me go and bury my father."[11]

Chloe could see that Colleen was wrestling with being considered unworthy because she was a sinner in Jesus's eyes. Leaning forward, Chloe looked Colleen straight in the eye and said, "We are all sinners according to Jesus; unless we repent, we will not go to heaven." She went on, "You, like every person on the planet, have to make a decision: is Jesus speaking the truth? Does He have power over life and death and heaven as His reward? Does He choose to forgive that which would send us to eternal death?"

Looking hard at Chloe, Colleen questioned her, saying, "What have you done with this information? Have you repented or asked for forgiveness?"

Chloe smiled and said, "Yes, I have, and ever since that day, I have found peace about my purpose for life."

Colleen had to admit Chloe was the only person she knew who was completely at peace. Colleen said, "It sounds too simple, but it sounds too hard to believe that I am not good enough just the way I am."

Coming to the conclusion that for that night, they had spoken enough on this subject, Chloe looked at Colleen and said, "Let's end our discussion tonight with this. Everyone has a decision to make. If you believe that Jesus is speaking the truth, then you are left with one choice: repent and be welcomed into heaven. If, however, you do not believe Jesus is speaking the truth, you would be a fool to repent, but according to Jesus, you would not get into heaven. I guess what I am saying is that Jesus has made a way to be with Him in heaven, but it depends on us choosing to do so; we can say no to Him."

Colleen opened her mouth to continue the discussion, but Chloe raised her hand and said, "There will be another time to talk; let's end this for now." She smiled at Colleen, said, "I love you," and walked out of the room. Then, she poked her head back in and said, "Continue reading in the book of Luke; find out all that Jesus said to the people and how they responded to Him." She smiled again and said, "Good night."

* * *

After that discussion, Colleen started to get frustrated with the whole "forgiveness thing"; it was eating on her, and with Chloe no longer available to talk to, it started to impact her daily dealings in the house.

The first thing she noticed was that she was not as tolerant of Thomas's failings; she found herself ready to explode on him rather than tolerate him. Then Colleen realized she was also angry with Chloe; she couldn't understand why, but she looked for ways to blame her for her lack of peace. And for the first time since discovering the Bible, she found it hard to pick it up and read.

One night, after all had turned in for the evening, she lay there in her bed, still upset about Jesus being so demanding. The more she thought about it, the more frustrated she became. Colleen stopped in her thoughts and looked over at the Bible on her nightstand. She was saddened by what had become of the joy she had known for so long.

Rather than remaining angry, though, her heart began to ache, and she had to admit she was lonely for Jesus. The Jesus that she first met, the one who spoke so gently to her in His Word. She couldn't control her emotions, and she started to cry.

Devastated by how quickly things had changed with her family and Chloe, she rolled over on her side and wept. She thought to herself, *I can't keep up with the demands here without help, and it seems God and Chloe have abandoned me.* As she tried to focus on something in the room, she could hardly see through the tears. As Colleen wiped the tears aside, her vision cleared, and there before her again, on the nightstand, big and bold, as if it was the only object in the room, was the Bible.

She instantly started to turn the other way when, suddenly, a strange flicker of hope burst into her heart. The hope she thought she had lost and so longed for began to grow as she stared at the Bible. The longer Colleen stared, the more comfort she felt. She began to remember again those magical days when she first opened that book before her.

She began to sob, and an intense guilt started to rule over her. Colleen knew she had not talked to Jesus since her talk with Chloe. She was so happy before that day, and now she missed Him so much, and she thought, *What has happened to us, Jesus?* Then she realized she was not talking to herself but to Jesus. She sat up, staring at the ceiling, closed her eyes, and prayed, "Dear Jesus, I am a sinner; please forgive me for my sins. I am so lonely without You."

Colleen stayed there with her eyes closed for some time, hoping she would hear Jesus say, "I forgive you," but she did not hear His voice. She opened her eyes, longing to see Him, but He was not there either. Frantic, she reached over and took the Bible into her hands, then opened it to where she had used the nail file as a bookmark.

The red ink section jumped out at her, and she ran her fingers gently over the words. The joy of reading the truth filled her heart, and she read His words out loud, "I will never leave you nor forsake you."[12] Relieved and at peace again, Colleen said to Jesus, "Thank You for meeting me here." Her heart was swelling with thankfulness, and she knew God had not left or forsaken her but had been waiting on her to accept eternal life on His terms. Then she said to herself, *I just asked Jesus to forgive my sins; that is exactly what Chloe said Jesus needed me to do.* Feeling brand-new, she quickly turned to the book of Luke and set about seeking Jesus in the pages before her.

CHAPTER 16

The closer they came to Mrs. Allard's office, the more Dominique began to regret sharing her secret with Bella. She started looking around, hoping for a way to escape. She felt her heart beating in her chest, and her face began to flush. She started going over in her mind how her parents and Aunt Colleen would respond to this news and the suffering that would be unleashed because of it.

Beginning to feel the pain of the death grip that Dominique had on her arm, Mrs. Allard put her hand on Dominique's hand and said, "Dominique, are you all right?"

Dominique was taken by surprise; she released Mrs. Allard's arm and looked up, saying, "Yes. I am sorry, I am just a little nervous today."

With that said, Dominique looked at Bella for support. Bella gave Dominique a reassuring smile, and hoping to appease any fears about the counseling session, she turned her head and projected that same smile into Mrs. Allard's eyes. Bella knew how hard this was for Dominique, so she prayed, *God, right now, please help Dominique.* Just as she finished her prayer, she looked, and they were standing at Mrs. Allard's classroom door.

"There, we have arrived," Mrs. Allard said. They walked through the classroom and over to the office door. She unlocked the door and held it open for the girls to enter. As before, Dominique signaled that Bella and Mrs. Allard enter first. Dominique hesitated before entering, and Bella, sensing she was about to bolt, reached out into the classroom, grabbed her by the arm, and pulled her into Mrs. Allard's office.

Being forced into the room, Dominique shot a stern glance at Bella, and Bella, continuing to hold her arm, shot the same stern glance back at Dominique. Then, turning to Mrs. Allard, who was now looking at both girls cautiously, Bella said, "Well, should we all sit?"

Mrs. Allard slowly moved over to the door and closed it. Trying not to overanalyze the tension that seemed to be building in her office, as she moved to her desk, she smiled and kept her eyes on the girls, but then she said to herself, *Why are these girls acting so strangely?*

She remembered how uncomfortable Dominique was at their last meeting. She thought, *Maybe Dominique does not want to meet with me, and that is why Bella is here.* Mrs. Allard put both hands on her desk, leaned forward, made direct eye contact with Dominique, and said, "Dominique, are you afraid of meeting with me? Would you like to meet with someone else?"

Quickly glancing over at Bella, Dominique thought, *Hey, this is my way out.* She turned back to Mrs. Allard to affirm she was not comfortable, but just before she spoke, Bella stopped her by grabbing her hand and said, "Hey, you cannot run from this; remember our deal."

Now, Mrs. Allard was truly at a loss about what was going on. She leaned back into her chair and asked, "Will somebody please tell me what is happening here?"

Still holding on to Dominique's hand, Bella placed her other hand around Dominique's hand and firmly embraced it. Then she turned to Dominique, looking straight into her eyes, and said to Mrs.

Allard, "Dominique has something she would like to share with you."

* * *

After hearing Dominique's secret, Mrs. Allard was not shocked by the news. The day she shared her own rape with Dominique, she knew her pain was somewhat like her own. Dominique's behaviors were so typical of someone enduring this kind of awful in their life.

Graciously embracing her secret, Mrs. Allard stepped from behind her desk and knelt down beside Dominique. Wide-eyed and petrified, Dominique followed Mrs. Allard's movement toward her. Fearful and near panic, she pictured in her mind the fury coming her way. All she could see were the consequences she would endure for being so forthright.

The horror in Dominique's face remained fixed, staring at Mrs. Allard. Mrs. Allard never took her eyes off of Dominique's face, and she softly touched Dominique's knee with her hand; Dominique's knee was shaking frantically.

The three of them, connected physically and emotionally, were frozen in the moment. It seemed to Dominique that time stood still, and then, like a crack in a dam seeping open again, Dominique's face wrinkled, and her lip began to quiver. Mrs. Allard instantly reached up and held Dominique's face in her hands. She said, "Thank you for trusting me to share this most intimate part of your life."

Tears began to well up in Dominique's eyes, but instead of bucket loads like before with Bella, two large tears ran down along her nose, off her cheeks, and onto Mrs. Allard's wrists; Mrs. Allard was still holding Dominique's face.

Finally, Dominique looked down into her lap. She let out all the air in her lungs, sat up, took in a deep breath, and shuddered, and when she did, her whole body shook. Mrs. Allard rubbed her right thumb against Dominique's cheek and then let her hands drop down to hold Dominique and Bella's hands.

Dominique was surprised that she began to feel relief. She looked over to Bella for comfort. Bella's face was a mess of tears, but she smiled, proud of her friend, and hugged Dominique tightly. Mrs. Allard put her hands on both girls' backs and began to rub them affectionately. The hugs ended after a short while, and the trio began exchanging glances back and forth at each other. Then, something amazing happened; they each began to smile as if a victory had been won. They remained smiling, not saying a thing, basking in the joy of this secret exposed. Then, Dominique's face became serious, and she said, "What happens now?

Mrs. Allard told Dominique that because she was now aware of what happened to her, by law, she was forced to begin an immediate disclosure to her family, to law officials, and to the school.

First, though, she wanted to help Dominique and Bella to not worry about what happens next. She praised Bella for her courage and for being such a good friend. She thanked Dominique again for sharing this tragic, secret event with her and Bella. Then, Mrs. Allard dismissed the girls to go back to their dorm room.

She demanded they stay there until she could meet with them later, and she forbade them from attending any classes for the rest of the day. Standing up, Mrs. Allard looked firmly at the girls and said, "Do not leave your dorm room; stay there until I come and get you." She opened her office door and walked the girls to the hallway, which led to their room.

Bella and Dominique grabbed hands and headed to their dorm room, but then, automatically, as if in sync, they both stopped and glanced back up the hall where they had left Mrs. Allard. And there she was, still watching them from her classroom door. She smiled and winked at the girls, then she soberly pointed down the hall, reminding them of their charge, and they turned again and headed briskly toward their destination.

* * *

At first, they were just relieved to have spilled the beans to someone they could trust. Now that they were sitting in their room, with the door locked, they felt secure, but after staring at each other for some time, dreadful thoughts began to creep into Dominique's mind. Watching Dominique carefully, Bella picked up on it immediately. Dominique's body language changed, which sent a clear message that doubt was growing in her soul.

Bella asked Dominique calmly, "Is everything all right?" Startled by the question, Dominique looked quickly at Bella and tried to give a reassuring smile, but to no avail; Bella was reading her like a book. Bella said, "I know you are scared. I know you feel out of control, but I also know that you have opened up your old life to let new life in."

She continued, "Disaster like you cannot imagine was waiting for you if you would have chosen to remain in silence. I have had friends who kept silent, and their lives were destroyed, and some of them even committed suicide."

Dominique was paying close attention to every word Bella shared. Bella went on. "That is one of the reasons why I started volunteering at the teen center, to help young women cope with their pain."

Seeing Dominique start to relax, Bella went on. "You and I coming together has not been an accident. I believe God meant for us to be in the same school and eventually to be roommates. I also know, now that I have brought God into the conversation, you are starting to become uncomfortable because you do not want to factor His sovereign work into your life."

Dominique started to squirm cautiously on her bed. Bella was on a roll, and since she had prayed much for Dominique in the past, she was not detoured. Instead, she felt empowered to move forward and said, "Dominique, how has God let you down?"

Dominique nearly choked on these words. Her tongue felt so dry in her mouth that she couldn't swallow. All that had ever come before her, as it pertains to God, started rolling through her brain, and she was left with only one thought; she bristled and stared at Bella. Then she sat up, laughed hatefully, and said, "How can you trust a god that when you need Him, He never shows up?" She just continued to stare belligerently at Bella, as if she had Bella trapped in her own words.

Bella smiled and said, "Thanks for being so transparent. I now see that in the past, you have spent some time with God."

Bristling, Dominique countered, "Yeah, but it was like talking to the ceiling. You would not believe how many times I cried and pleaded with God to help me, but what a waste of my time."

Bella continued to engage and said, "Tell me then, Dominique, from your experience, what is

God like? How do you know Him to be? Where did you first learn about Him, and what do you know about His life and time on earth?"

Confused and angered by all the questions, Dominique wanted this conversation to end, so she shot back at Bella, saying, "What do you mean?"

Bella responded, "Who first told you about God, and how do you know what He is like?"

Throwing her hands up in the air, Dominique said, "I just told you what He is like, a myth, someone people use like a genie in a bottle. My dad goes to church every Sunday, but he only goes to look good with his friends, and my family only prays for show. Dad forces us all to go to church, and God fits nicely into our family routine, but our home is empty of His presence."

Seeing an opening, Bella jumped back in, saying, "So, your dad is the one who explains God to you?"

Dominique countered, "No, my Sunday school teacher is the one who really told me who God was." At that point, Dominique felt she had just backed herself into a corner. Talking about her Sunday school teacher opened up memories of the days when she thought Jesus was real and was comforted by those thoughts.

Her countenance softened, but she flippantly told Bella, "I don't want to talk about this anymore."

Smiling, Bella looked lovingly into Dominique's eyes and said, "Yeah, maybe you are right, but you know what I think? I think you are running from Jesus, just like you have been running from your experience with Durand, hiding in the pain, hoping it will all go away."

At that point, Dominique began to feel fear and again a little tentative about Bella's loyalties. She stared long at Bella, who continued to smile, which made Dominique even more unsettled. So, with a groan and a flip of her hair, she jumped off the bed and ran into the bathroom.

***

Dominique didn't know how long she had been in the bathroom. She sat on the edge of the bathtub, steaming about Bella. She was thinking of ways to not be roommates anymore and how she could get back at her for being so mean. Dominique was most resourceful when seeking revenge. Unaware of time spent in her "self-exile," Dominique was engrossed in her growing contempt for Bella.

Suddenly, out in the other room, she heard Bella close a door. Dominique was instantly back in touch with what was really happening in her life, and she panicked, thinking, *Mrs. Allard told us not to leave our room.*

She stood up and put her ear to the door to hear if Mrs. Allard had returned, but she heard nothing more. She stood there for a moment, straining to hear anything, and then a familiar voice started singing gently across the room. It was Bella; she had not gone anywhere, but Dominique thought to herself, *How can she sing after having a huge blowout fight just minutes ago?*

As she continued to listen to Bella, Dominique couldn't help but hear the beauty in her voice, and the lyrics seemed to resonate through the bathroom door; Bella was singing to Jesus.

She moved back over to the bathtub, but it was no longer comfortable, and she said to herself,

This bathtub is hard and cold. Then, something strange happened; she could not maintain her contempt for Bella. She tried to muster the same resentment she had when she first went into the bathroom, but her heart was not the same. That scared her, but what scared her even more was the descriptor she used for the bathtub when she sat back down. She said those words again to herself: *This bathtub is hard and cold.* The words came back, crushing her attempt to blow it off. Then she knew that the resentment she tried to muster for Bella came from her own "hard and cold heart." She wrestled with herself, realizing that since Bella and she had become roommates, she was a different person.

She was not angry all the time, and she felt safe; she knew without Bella, she would still be suffering all alone in the awful memories of Durand. It frightened her to contemplate the person she had become in the bathroom disaster; she was Dr. Jekyll, completely devoid of Mr. Hyde. Remembering that fierce anger and lack of control, she didn't like that person anymore. Then, she heard someone knocking on their dorm room door.

***

Dominique opened the bathroom door and peeked out sheepishly to see Mrs. Allard talking to Bella. "There you are," Mrs. Allard said as she noticed Dominique peering around the door. The memory of her fight with Bella was gone. She was seized with fear, but it was more than just fear; there was also anticipation about outcomes. Mrs. Allard, sensing Dominique's trepidation, looked at her and then at Bella and suggested they all sit down.

Looking back and forth at both girls, Mrs. Allard said, "I have done what I am required to do in these situations. All parties have been notified." Then she focused in on Dominique, who, by observing her, was stricken with doubt and apprehension. Mrs. Allard smiled and reached over to grab Dominique's hand. Dominique pulled her hand back and sat back at the same time. Seeing the opportunity, Bella reached over and firmly grabbed Dominique's hand. Dominique started to withdraw her hand, but seeing Bella's smiling and reassuring face, she relented and moved a little closer to Bella.

Acknowledging Bella's commitment to Dominique, Mrs. Allard said to Dominique, "You have a dear friend here, don't you?" Dominique nodded but remained unmoved. Knowing it was time to get into it, Mrs. Allard said, "First, Mrs. Martsen and I called your parents." Dominique's eyes opened wide, and she tried to swallow but could not. Mrs. Allard continued, "They are devastated to hear about Durand's betrayal, but all they really wanted to talk about was how you were doing and when they could see you. Of course, they were weeping and struggling with having you so far away, but I reassured them you were in good hands." At that, she looked proudly over at Bella and then at Dominique.

Not knowing what to think, Dominique began to shudder, but then the shudders stopped, and silent tears began to run down her cheeks. She looked up at the two faces before her, those faces that had helped her finally arrive at a place she didn't believe could exist, and she reached out for both of them. Weeping, they embraced, and for the first time since that horrible day with Durand, Dominique relaxed, relishing a moment she had rarely known; it was called peace.

As Dominique continued to hold the two of them fervently, a smile started to form on her face. This was a foreign smile to her because it was born out of being thankful. Thankful that there were no more painful secrets, thankful that her parents still loved her, and thankful that she had two friends who were faithful to her.

She pulled back from their embrace and, with that same smile, which neither of them had observed before, a genuine Dominique's smile, a manifestation of someone new, said, "Thank you both." There was no need for Bella and Mrs. Allard to respond; they both quickly looked at each other as if to say, "Thank God," and then they just smiled a smile of gratitude.

Dominique's facial expression changed quickly when she started to think again about the outcomes of this disclosure, and she looked concerned to Mrs. Allard, saying, "What will happen to Durand?"

Mrs. Allard, trying to remain positive, took Dominique's hand again and said, "Darling, that is not your concern; Durand has earned the outcomes headed his way. The authorities have already contacted his dad, who is the one Durand needs now." Not wanting to dive into the legal ramifications of Durand possibly denying the allegation and the ensuing court battles that could arise, Mrs. Allard deflected those outcomes by saying, "What is important now is you and how your parents and this school will partner together to help in your much-needed healing."

Dominique had spent extra time worrying about how this situation might impact her relationship with the school, which was becoming more and more a harbinger of good things to come. After hearing the notion that her parents and the school were partnering for her good, she smiled that thankful smile once again, and Mrs. Allard and Bella rejoiced; her smile was good news.

There was so much to be done, so Mrs. Allard started laying out the plan for Dominique's sabbatical, which her parents and school had put into place. The first part of the plan was for Dominique's parents to pick her up that evening. She would be staying with them for an undetermined time until she was ready to return to school. The school would follow the lead of her parents and would be ready to accept her back whenever the family saw fit to have her return.

Reacting to the plan, Dominique said, "I know I have to go home, and I am looking forward to it, but don't I have a say in when I come back to school?"

Picking up on Dominique's concern, Mrs. Allard assured her that Bella and she would be available to talk to every day. She told her, "This plan includes your parents and all who love you here working on the same page for the same goal: to get you back with us as soon as you can."

Dominique took this explanation at face value, but she paused, thinking to herself, *They don't understand how terrible it will be for Uncle Dumas and Aunt Colleen. It will be so hard to look them in the eyes and tell the truth about what happened.*

Dominique was sure a brief time at home would be better than an extended one. She did not want to deal with the family dynamic and the possible drama, which would drive her crazy if she was left home too long.

Mrs. Allard asked Dominique if she had any unanswered questions or concerns about the plan. Though feeling like the guinea pig in a scientific experiment, Dominique knew with what had already been achieved; this could morph into, like Bella said, "A changed life." She turned to Mrs. Allard and Bella and said, "I guess my concern now is, how will I get along without you two? You have proven yourselves trustworthy, and I don't have anyone like you at home."

With smiles beaming from the three of them, they gathered into a group hug. After a brief time and a few more tears, Mrs. Allard said, "I have things still to do in preparation for your departure; your parents will be here around 3:00 p.m. So, Bella, would you help Dominique pack? We don't have much time." At that, she hugged Dominique again and quickly left the room.

CHAPTER 17

Two months after Chloe left the Meuniers' home, everyone still moved around, somewhat lost and disconnected. Even though Marie was much stronger now and needed less bedtime, Chloe's absence left her depressed, and it didn't take much for her to just stay in bed.

Bolstered by her commitment to Jesus, Colleen went about her daily routine, but it was difficult; she couldn't keep her thoughts from coursing back to Chloe.

Thomas, too, sensed the loss. He wasn't sure how things had deteriorated so quickly, but he sensed a difference, like something was out of place.

As he walked around the house, it felt like a morgue. It was eerie; it was so still in his domain that it was uncomfortable. Chase felt it too; a void had taken the realm and its occupants captive. Though it remained their dwelling place, a void had taken over, and what once had been a vibrant home, a darkened hue had taken over, and joy had vanished.

It appeared that they all had lost their way and didn't know how to get back what they once had. Then, one day, suddenly and without warning, a dreadful scream burst out, ringing through the silent caverns of the hallways, and the place came alive. That day, Dominique decided to change things up.

Chase had just arrived home, and that was the first thing he heard when he entered the house. Colleen was in the kitchen getting supper started, and Thomas had not quite made it in to see Marie after getting home from work. After hearing the awful scream, they all pivoted and spun, heading to the baby's room. Marie, frightened, called out from bed, "What is happening to Dominique?"

Panicked, they all arrived simultaneously at Dominique's bedroom door. They bumped into each other, trying to see what in the world had caused her to scream in such a way. And there in her crib, she stood smiling from ear to ear. She clasped her hands together, then threw them over her head and jumped up and down on her mattress, clapping her hands with each jump.

They all looked at Dominique; then, they looked at each other. She was a sight to see, and they all started to laugh. The only one not laughing was Marie, and she yelled out, "What is going on out there?"

Dominique chose this day to have her coming-out party. She had never done anything like that before, but with the success of the endeavor, it became her new calling card. She would scream bloody murder when she did not want to be unattended. The missed excitement that Chloe brought to the family dynamic was instantly replaced with another strange source of energy.

***

Dominique's newfound vocal vibrancy soon was no longer a laughing matter. When not in her crib, Dominique was your typical toddler; she was hard to keep up with and never stopped moving. If Colleen put her in the playpen to slow her down, she would just use her calling card and scream till she was lifted out, and off she would go again.

Everyone was busy trying to control the chaos she created. It wasn't long before Marie decided they needed to have a family meeting to hand out assignments so that by the end of each day, they weren't all worn out. With Marie still not well, keeping Dominique somewhat subdued was important for her health. Marie loved Dominique to death, but with this new Dominique, she almost loved her more when she was sleeping.

No matter what they tried to control Dominique, she had a way around it. Needless to say, it wasn't long before the family was coping with Dominique rather than enjoying her, and that upended the much-needed peace that the beleaguered clan had lost with Chloe's departure.

To say that Dominique was demanding is an understatement. There was no season of terrible twos and then moving on to a calmer stage of child development. It did not matter what stage of development she was growing through; Dominique was terrible.

From that first day in the nursery, where she had the entire family eating out of her demanding hand, the family was trained to be at her beckoned call.

Not that she wasn't beautiful and cuddly, or that she wasn't affectionate at times, but she became so good at manipulation; they didn't know they were had until it was too late. In spite of the ugliness of her personality, the entire family loved Dominique to pieces, but she was so good at playing on each family member's weaknesses that they tripped over themselves, trying to gain her approval and affection, which left a toddler in complete control.

The greater burden fell on Chase to care for her. This was a heavy lift for someone only four years older than his sister, but not being as busy as the adults, he was called upon most to be the sitter, or maybe better said, keeper, of this wildly busy and overindulged mini-monarch.

At first, he just resented the time it took to manage such a demanding menace, but it wasn't long before he felt this was forced, full-time servitude, and it left him hating his elite little sister.

Time at school became a haven for Chase, and his grades dramatically improved, but his parents never guessed his incentive was the joy of being away from home and Dominique.

At home, Chase learned quickly to not have out in the open conflict with "Her Highness." It didn't matter what happened or who was at fault. Dad would always yell at Chase, "What did you do to that baby?" So, Chase was left with no choice but to develop subversive tactics to quell the uneven balance of power she held over him. Only Colleen was aware of the battle raging between the two siblings, and she made it her mission to facilitate a peaceful interaction between them.

With all the dysfunction floating around her, Colleen found time in God's Word and prayer as the antidote necessary to manage the tension building in the Meuniers' home. She would start her morning prayer for Thomas and Marie, who, after Chloe left, seemed just to put up with each other. Then she would move to prayer for the children, who were becoming self-trained antagonists, and then she would pray for herself to have wisdom and grace to help her broken family.

Colleen longed for Chloe's fellowship and insight, which had always manifested itself in the family as comfort and peace. She prayed daily for herself, that same kind of wisdom and strength that Chloe brought to each situation. Then, one day, as she continued to observe the family dynamic deteriorating even further, she realized she was not Chloe, and hoping to be a Chloe clone was not the answer.

So, she prayed, "Oh, God of heaven and Lord of me, make me what You need me to be to serve

You best here." Almost immediately, Colleen felt empowered. It reminded her of the days prior to Chloe's visit, how the power of the Lord moved in her, and how the family was transformed.

After prayer and getting Dominique laid down for a nap, Colleen decided to have a talk with Marie. On the way to Marie's room, she thanked God for creating humans with a built-in sleep regulator; she didn't know what she would do if Dominique never slept.

Just prior to arriving at Marie's room, she heard soft sobbing. Colleen slowed down, crept up to the open door, and peeked in. Marie was lying on her side, turned away from the door, and her body shook as she wept.

Seeing her sister suffering so, Colleen could not help herself, and she began to weep as well. So as to not embarrass her sister, Colleen turned to leave, but one step away, she knew that was not what her sister needed. She turned back and walked slowly up to the side of the bed, where Marie lay and sat down beside her.

Marie was surprised and turned to look up at Colleen. Her face, distorted and oozing with pain, spoke clearly to Colleen about the turmoil she was enduring. Colleen cupped Marie's hand in hers, and staring at each other, they both wept.

It was like they were talking, only not saying words, and both understood the dialogue. After some time, Colleen said, "I love you." Marie nodded as if to say, "Thank you, me too." Colleen was not sure how to even begin a conversation that made sense since she could not make sense of what was happening. She finally said, "How can I help you today, Sis?"

Marie rolled over onto her back and tried to sit up. Colleen pulled her to the sitting position and pushed the pillow under her shoulders. Marie just kept staring at Colleen and didn't seem to know where to start. She looked down and then back up again. She wiped the tears from her eyes and shook her hair as if to freshen her outlook, but then she said, "I am so lost."

Not sure if she meant eternally or physically, Colleen smiled and said, "I am sorry you feel so alone." Marie stiffened when she heard her sister interpret what she said as she felt so alone. Then, she thought back to her statement, "I am so lost." Marie had to admit that "lost" meant she needed to be found.

Feeling misunderstood and hoping to clarify her statement, she opened her mouth to speak, but the excuse she had patently used her whole life to berate God as a no-show didn't seem to cut the mustard. There was no explaining how she felt or what to do about it.

Knowing this was a tense moment, even for sisters, Colleen said, "Maybe you do not know how to explain how you feel; you have been through so much pain."

Pausing briefly, Marie looked up at Colleen and said, "Besides the obvious, I know everyone suffers. It's just that my suffering has taken me to the point of despair, and I don't even know how to come back from that." She trailed off, saying, "And I am not even sure I want to."

Realizing the depth of her sister's despair, Colleen prayed for help and decided to jump into the deep end of the pool. She said, "Can you talk about it?"

Becoming somewhat frustrated, Marie said to her sister, "What is this that we are doing if not talking about it?"

Hoping to be sensitive, but after hearing her sister say, basically, "Life was not worth living," Colleen said, "Maybe a place to start is not in the depths of what you are experiencing but rather what is your heart and brain yearning for and start there."

Contemplating her sister's statement, Marie nearly laughed out loud but held it back, saying to herself, *Are you kidding? How about not being sick and having a family that is normal?*

Staying alert to her sister's body language, Colleen could tell Marie was about to be more than sarcastic. Then, Marie's face became somewhat serene, and she said nothing. For the first time, Marie was truly considering her plight; it was obvious life was not changing, and she had no way of making it happen.

Looking desperately at Colleen, Marie said, "I truly want out of this mess, but I will not leave my family to deal with this alone, so my heart tells me I need help, but my brain tells me, 'Where does my help come from?' I am out of options."

Knowing this was a tremendous opportunity because her sister had just said, "Where does my help come from?" Colleen was drawn back to that first wonderful day when she walked over to the Bible lying on the table in the living room and all that had transpired since then.

Calmly and carefully, Colleen began sharing with her sister the change that had come about since the day she stopped and looked at the Bible. She told Marie that change had taken place, not because she just looked at the words He spoke but because they seemed alive, and she was able to apply them to her circumstances.

She ended with saying to Marie, "When I first came to live here, I had such a contempt for Thomas. I am sorry for that now, but it was that contempt that God used to change my heart. I read your Bible on the table, and God asked me in His Word to be thankful, and if I did, He would never leave me nor forsake me.

"If you remember, after I arrived, during those first days of family struggles, I actually tried to get you to support me rather than your husband. I was hoping you would agree with me and admit that Thomas was wrong.

"Well, the day I applied thankfulness to my life for what Thomas was providing for me, my whole life changed. I saw him differently, and the battle for household supremacy ended. You yourself know the change that took place; peace came to your home. I believe God empowered me to forgive and also be thankful in spite of my circumstances. He did that for me, and He will do that for you if you allow Him to love you."

Sarcastically staring at her sister, Marie said, "Chloe has gotten hold of you, hasn't she?"

That statement put Colleen on the defensive, but she checked herself and said, "Chloe loves you more than the world. Why would her influencing me be a bad thing for you?"

Before Marie could react, Colleen continued, "You and I both know for the last two months, we have all been struggling, and I believe it is because Chloe went home." Colleen gave Marie a nonthreatening glance and said, "Admit it: Chloe brings peace and joy wherever she is, and we are missing that. And what is it that she relies on other than God?"

Fighting the impulse to allow this truth to emerge, looking down and then back up at Colleen,

Marie said, "I do not want to trust God."

Colleen countered, "What will you trust then? How will your life change, continuing on as you are? You just said, 'Where does my help come from?' Where else will you go? To what end will you search? Why is God not the answer?"

Before Marie could comment, Colleen began again. "I have been struggling too. I miss Chloe so much. She inspires me to do the next right thing. And it was just today that I realized since she has been gone, instead of trusting God, I have been trusting Chloe to keep me at peace. She told me she had to leave but that I would not be alone because God had said, 'I will never leave you nor forsake you.' I believe that, and I believe Chloe wants you to be at peace, and you know that too. Chloe only speaks the truth; she doesn't know anything else."

Looking sternly at Colleen, Marie said, "That is enough; I am through talking in circles about how God will fix me if I am thankful. Why do I have to be thankful to someone who, rather than dwelling in people's lives, dwells on a table in the living room?"

As hard as it was to end their conversation, Colleen knew there would be another day. So, she smiled at her sister, squeezed her hand, and said, "Sorry, I did not mean to upset you."

**

Back in the kitchen, Colleen was thanking God for what took place with Marie. Even though it appeared Marie was turned off by the flavor of the conversation, Colleen sensed an inroad had been achieved.

Time moved quickly past that day when Colleen and Marie had discussed God's promises of help for their family. Colleen tried several times to engage Marie again but to no avail. Marie seemed to be in better spirits, and her health began to improve, but she remained, at least outwardly, disinterested in God's desire to help her.

Things around the house did begin to change and change dramatically. Colleen found herself daily in God's Word and prayer, and she was able, again, to be thankful for her circumstances. She found herself, once again, more willing to cope with Thomas in compassion. And in return, Thomas began again to appreciate Colleen's help with his family. As much as she missed Chloe, Colleen finally realized that Chloe was right; God wanted to work through her to reach her loved ones for Christ.

Praying for her family became her greatest joy, and Colleen lived each day with anticipation of what God would do. As she came close to God, He made things clearer about how to move forward with wisdom. One of the things that God made clear was that Dominique needed special care. Colleen was sure of that truth but had no idea how to even get her attention.

So, Colleen decided if she was going to have impact on Dominique's life, she would have to spend more time with her. Loving Dominique was not difficult. Colleen loved her dearly, but loving her rightly was more difficult. She would pray each night, "Oh, God, please help me and prepare Dominique for what You want to do."

At first, it seemed impossible to reach Dominique. She could not respond correctly to normal input. Her first and only concern seemed to be her and what she wanted. After several attempts at appeasement, Colleen realized appeasement only made things worse. So, Colleen began to just observe her daily rituals and routines. After some time, she started putting the pieces together. Dominique was not thoughtful nor showed any compassion. Colleen devised a plan to help her see the need for those character qualities.

First, she knew she would have to have Thomas and Marie in on the plan. Initially, they were opposed to the plan because Colleen was requiring the entire family to not indulge her tantrums. Then, she wanted to have a time-out area that Dominique earned by not complying to family structure and protocol.

It seemed like a good plan, but the hardest part for everyone was even though Dominique was receiving consequences, she let everyone know she was not going down without a fight; she would scream for hours, confined in the time-out area.

Colleen finally won the day when she told Marie and Thomas, saying, "This has to be done; having this child without limitations on her lifestyle is child abuse." After that, they succumbed, and the battle lines were drawn.

It was hard work for everyone because Dominique was a formidable opponent. As she missed opportunities to do the right thing, the consequences fell into place. As Colleen explained to everyone, even Chase, "Dominique desires to rule, and she will throw a fit every time she does not get her way." Colleen had to explain the need to control her in the time-out area. Her suggestion to build a small enclosure was frowned upon at first, but she explained that Dominique would not be neglected and she would have everything she needed for comfort other than freedom.

At first, it was harrowing. Every time she found herself in the time-out area, which was in her bedroom, she would scream until she fell asleep. Completely closing the door was not part of the plan, and so the family was left cringing for hours as Dominique loudly made her displeasure known.

Colleen became the enforcer and the comforter. When Dominique realized that seeking Mom, Dad, or Chase for moral support did not work, she was devastated. She started to actually cry and not just throw a fit. This nearly drove Marie crazy, and she would go to her room and cry.

A big element of the plan required that anyone who was home during one of her moments in solitude must step in and tell Dominique that they loved her and they were sorry to see her in time-out. Engaging her in dialogue was permitted, but no amount of begging could relieve her from the consequences.

Colleen spent the most time with her during time-outs, but at times, Marie would go inside the enclosure to sit and hold her while she cried. These visits were so hard on Marie. Dominique did not want Mom's comfort but wanted out of the enclosure, and she would add fury to her fit. This hurt Marie, but she was not going to cave in, and she would put her down and leave the room.

Colleen spent most of her time in the enclosure explaining to Dominique why she was there and how she could remedy her situation. After about a week, the family called it "hell week." Dominique started to see the futility of her belligerence. One day, she surprised everyone. After only being in her room for about twenty minutes but crying all the time, she stopped crying. Marie and Colleen were the only ones home, and they both rushed for the baby's room. Arriving there together, they peeked in to see Dominique sitting there, holding a teddy bear and turning the pages of one of her books.

The sisters looked at each other, and Marie nearly jumped for joy. She started to run into the room to rescue Dominique, but Colleen pulled her back into the hallway and said, "Give her a moment; she could be testing to see what we will do." They stood outside the room for a few moments and then poked their heads around the corner again. Just as they did, Dominique looked up to see her mom and said very sweetly, "Momma."

Smiling from ear to ear, they both walked in and over to the enclosure. Dominique stood up and held out her hands for her mom. Marie looked to Colleen for approval, which Dominique picked up on, and she looked hopefully up at Colleen as well. Colleen smiled and said, "You are doing the right thing now, and we are very proud of you." At that, Marie bent down, picked her up, and hugged her warmly. Colleen said to Dominique, "Shall we go out to the kitchen and see if we can find some cookies and milk?" With tears still in her eyes, Dominique smiled and nodded.

* * *

Dominique needed the time-out on a regular basis, but she finally figured out that being quiet would get her out of prison. In most of her time-out situations, she was there for something she refused to do, which put her in prison in the first place. Now, Dominique was learning that if she was going to stay out of time-out, she was required to complete what she refused to do or go back to time-out.

The plan and the effort were paying great dividends, and the entire family rejoiced in the progress. Within a month, Dominique had seen the light. Not that she was perfect, but she was learning to consider consequences for bad behavior and the needs of others. Thomas was relieved the torture was over, but he had to admit she was a changed little girl, and he was happy for the outcome.

Colleen spent as much time with Dominique as her day would allow. Marie was not completely healed, but she was much more able to help than before. Chase even came to the place where he would enjoy playing with his sister again.

Though Dominique knew Aunt Colleen was the warden at large and it was she who held her accountable in all things, she still knew that her aunt loved her very much. Colleen made time for her like nobody else. She would read to her, play on the floor, take her for walks, and give her baths, which Dominique loved because Aunt Colleen put bubbles in the bath and all her toys as well.

The thing that was most enduring for Dominique, though, was that her aunt would hold her and talk with her for hours, rubbing her back and stroking her hair, and when she put her to bed, she would stay there telling her stories until Dominique fell asleep.

With Marie improving but not completely well, Aunt Colleen was the first person Dominique saw in the morning and the last person she saw at night. Of all the gifts that Colleen could bestow on her niece, she knew the greatest gift she could share daily with Dominique was the knowledge that Jesus loved her. Every morning when she rose and every evening when she went to bed, Colleen would tell Dominique, "God will never leave you nor forsake you." As Dominique grew and started school, their bond grew greater and greater. Dominique loved her momma and daddy, but she trusted her aunt, Colleen.

CHAPTER 18

Colleen so enjoyed her time with Dominique. She would talk with her after Sunday school to see what Dominique was learning. She shared the Bible with her on a daily basis and never forgot to tell her how much Jesus loved her. Dominique trusted what Aunt Colleen said. She did not doubt her because she never felt judged by her, and she knew her aunt loved her unconditionally.

After her time-out training camp, Dominique was a normal kid with all the baggage that comes with growing up, but whenever she was in trouble, Aunt Colleen, who was unafraid of disciplining Dominique, still remained faithful and loving, never gave up on Dominique. Sometimes, Aunt Colleen's words were hard, but Dominique knew they were words meant to help her, not hurt her.

Time went by quickly, and the entire household flourished in the peace that was maintained under Aunt Colleen's prayer and service. Then, one day, when Dominique was seven years old, she was forced to endure the most painful thing she had ever known.

The bliss of family life began to fade. Dominique picked up on it first, though she didn't know what body language was; she knew things between Aunt Colleen and her mom and dad were becoming strained. She didn't know why, but at times, she heard them sharing angry words.

Dominique felt she needed to help make peace, so one night, she grabbed Aunt Colleen by the hand and pulled her over to sit on the couch with her mom, and she said to her dad, "Don't you think Momma and Aunt Colleen look good sitting together?"

Dad shrugged and said to Dominique, "Don't you think that is up to them?"

Marie just stood up and left the room. This tension scared Dominique, and it wasn't long before all her attempts at peace-making became futile.

Not long after that episode in the living room, Aunt Colleen came into Dominique's bedroom. She seemed sad, and Dominque had never seen this look on her face before. Aunt Colleen asked Dominique if they could sit on her bed; Dominique nodded, affirming her request. Aunt Colleen reached over, took hold of Dominique's hand, and said, what she always says, "How are you, my love?"

Dominique was afraid; Aunt Colleen looked so somber and not herself, so she said, "Aunt Colleen, are you okay?"

Colleen bowed down and rested her forehead on Dominique's forehead; staring deep into her eyes, she said, "I have some sad news."

Dominique's eyes widened, and she winced as if she already knew what the news was. She said to Aunt Colleen, "You are not leaving, are you?"

Colleen pulled her head up a few inches away from Dominque's forehead and cradled her face in her hands. Just before she spoke, tears welled up in her eyes and poured out and over onto her face; unable to say a word, Aunt Colleen nodded yes.

Never taking her eyes off of Aunt Colleen, unable to understand what she just heard and terrified by the thought, Dominique's eyes filled, and her heart raced. She opened her mouth to scream, but nothing came out.

Still holding Dominique's face in her hands, Colleen tried to look reassuring and said, "I am so sorry, darling…"

Dominique was in panic mode. Finally, she closed her mouth, and with tears pouring down her face, trembling, she said, "Did I do something wrong?"

Colleen's heart was breaking, and she was still unable to speak. She just shook her head. Dominique wrestled free from Aunt Colleen and ran out of her room, screaming, "Noooo!" She found Mom and Dad in the living room nervously sitting together on the sofa. Still screaming and weeping uncontrollably, Dominique pleaded with them, saying, "I will be good; I will try harder; please don't make Aunt Colleen leave."

Still sitting on Dominique's bed and listening to her plead with her parents was excruciating for Aunt Colleen. It was more than she could bear, and she rushed out of the room sobbing terribly. As she continued to plead with her parents for mercy, Dominique did not see Aunt Colleen leave.

Instinctively, Thomas and Marie reached out to pull Dominique in close to console her, but she pitched backwards, and with her eyes staring wildly at them, she ran back into her room, only to find Aunt Colleen gone. Instantly, she turned and ran out of the room, screaming Aunt Colleen's name, and just as she came tearing through the door, Thomas arrived, picked her up, and cradled her in his arms. Marie joined him, and together, they tried to comfort her.

Shaking and having trouble trying to unlock her car, Colleen could still hear Dominique screaming her name from inside the house. She screamed it over and over again; it was like torture.

Finally getting the car unlocked, she jumped in and shut the door. The screaming stopped, but the vision of the encounter remained stark in her mind, and she could still see Dominique screaming desperately for help; the silence in her car was acute and agonizing.

With pain destroying her soul, she put her head on the steering wheel. Lost at what to do, hoping that Dominique would hear her reply, she screamed at the top of her lungs Dominique's name, but alas, she knew there was no way to reach her; she could not help her. Powerless to achieve anything on her own, she cried out to the only source she knew that could help. Crying aloud, she yelled, "Oh, God! Oh, God! Oh, God!"

* * *

Barely remembering leaving the house and with no idea where to go, Colleen found herself aimlessly traveling along in an older subdivision close to Thomas and Marie's residence. She stopped the car to contemplate, *What now?*

As she sat frozen in her pain, her thoughts started to collate, and she had to admit she knew this day was coming but hoped against it. Colleen went back, trying to pinpoint what led to today; what had she done? The only thing she could think of was her passion for Jesus and her making sure Dominique knew about Him too.

She recalled a day when Marie found her in the kitchen, just shortly after Dominique tried to make peace by having her and Marie sit together on the sofa, and she said, "We need to talk." Marie's countenance was solemn, and at first, she wouldn't make eye contact, but then, she looked straight at Colleen, and with steel in her stare, she said, "You know that Dominique only has one mom, right?" Colleen remembered being sorrily frightened but unable to speak, and she just blinked her eyes in confusion. Marie stood firmly awaiting a response but tired quickly of waiting and stormed off, saying, "This is not working."

Not wanting to admit it, Colleen's thoughts went back to Chloe's warning about pushing Marie toward God. She scolded herself for being so unwise and hung her head sobbing. Her heart could not fathom the finality of leaving behind all that had happened through the years living in the Meuniers' home.

So, hoping to catch a glimpse of Dominique, she drove out of the subdivision and slowly by the Meuniers' home. As she drove by and the house came into view, the truth came rushing into her heart, and then, clearing up the confusion in her brain, she said to herself, "I cannot go back there."

* * *

Though she had a new dwelling, Colleen felt lost and lonely, and time dragged miserably by. It took several weeks of this suffering before she could sense God's presence again. Many times, she thought about calling Marie, but she could not muster the courage. She kept reliving the scene of Dominique's suffering, and that memory kept her locked up in her own pain.

One morning, she found the strength to seek God, and while reading God's Word and praying, she suddenly lifted her head, and her favorite verse scrolled through her mind. She said it out loud, "I will never leave you or forsake you." Instantly, God's presence became real again; she never was really alone. Weeping, she fell to her knees and thanked Him for His residence in her heart. The peace of the next thought surprised her; she felt good about calling Marie.

As the phone was ringing, Colleen found herself nervous, pacing back and forth around the kitchen. There was only one thing she wanted Marie to hear, but it was scary because she didn't know if Marie would receive it.

* * *

It was days after Colleen left before Dominique could compose herself enough to leave her bedroom. Thomas and Marie would not let her call Aunt Colleen, so she remained angry with Mom and Dad and would not be comforted. To Thomas and Marie, Dominique had morphed back into the little girl who, when she didn't get her way, threw fits and screamed incessantly. The only difference between then and now was that there was no remedy; with her heart being so shattered, time-out was not a humane option.

It had been a ruthless two weeks, and they were about ready to start pulling out their own hair. Thomas and Marie were fixed in their own conflict, and neither of them could bend to the other. Dominique was so angry with her parents that she misbehaved purposely; she used their conflict to inflict more suffering on them.

It was in the midst of this constant turmoil that one Saturday morning, the phone in the kitchen rang. Dominique was closest to the phone, and she rushed to it, hoping it might be Aunt Colleen. Answering it anxiously, she said, "Hello." When Aunt Colleen heard Dominique's voice, she instinctively clasped her hand over her mouth and was frozen, not knowing what to say. With some anticipation, Dominique said again, "Hello?" She followed with, "Is that you, Aunt Colleen?"

Colleen's heart jumped up into her throat, and she almost started to cry but caught herself and said, "Yes, my darling, it is me; how are you?"

Dominique squealed into the phone and said, "Oh, Aunt Colleen, I have missed you so much!" Having heard the phone ring, Marie had just entered the kitchen to answer it. When Dominique saw her mom, she screamed, "It is Aunt Colleen!"

Colleen's plan was to talk to Marie, whom she needed to talk to. She was surprised and not ready to talk to Dominique because she didn't know how Marie would feel about Dominique talking to her aunt without their permission.

Marie looked at Dominique and said, "I will take the phone."

Dominique handed her mom the phone but glared at her the whole time, saying, "Don't you mess this up, Mom."

Colleen had prepared herself to talk with her sister, but Marie was not prepared to talk with Colleen. Marie took the phone and coldly said, "Hello." Dominique kept the glare on her face, still pointing up to Mom, continuing to warn her.

Colleen said, "Hello, Marie; can you talk?"

Wanting to remain angry, Marie said, "About what?"

This gave Colleen the opening she was hoping for. She just jumped right in and asked Marie if she would forgive her for being so insensitive. She told Marie she was sorry for being so pushy concerning her faith and the Bible. Colleen started to cry and said, "If you will forgive me and allow me another chance to prove that I love you, I will never force my faith onto you again."

Marie was taken by surprise; she was angry with Colleen for trying to guilt her into submission to God and for arguing with her about how important it was for Dominique to follow Jesus. Colleen apologizing and crying on the phone shocked Marie, and she realized how sad and lonely she had been without her sister, but because of her anger and still holding a grudge against Colleen, her first thought was, *No, I will not forgive you. Religion is a personal thing, and I will not be lectured by you.* But her second thought and the overriding thought of love for her sister, who was now apologizing, she relented and said, "Yes, I will forgive you."

Hearing that, Dominique squealed again and said, "Now, can Aunt Colleen come back and live with us?"

Marie looked down at her and frowned, then turned her back on Dominique and said to Colleen, "I don't know where this will lead, but I am glad you called."

Colleen said, "Thank you, Sis. I love you. Goodbye."

***

As much as Dominique wanted Aunt Colleen to move back in with them, Colleen and Marie both knew that would be difficult. There was much healing that needed to take place. Now that they were talking, Dominique was sure everything was back to normal, but normal had a way to go for the sisters.

Slowly, though, the relationship began to unthaw, and Colleen asked to come over and visit on a semi-regular basis, to which Marie consented. The first time she came back, after the initial conflict, Dominique was so happy to see her aunt that she wept and clung to her the entire visit. Colleen was so happy to see Dominique as well, but even Dominique knew something had changed between the sisters.

The casual coldness was so blatant that Dominique had to ask Aunt Colleen, "Do you not love my mamma anymore, and does she love you?"

Unsuccessfully, Colleen tried to explain to Dominique the adult side of the healing process and how it would take time, but eventually, things would get back to normal; that just frustrated Dominique.

One day, Dominique and Aunt Colleen walked into the family room. Marie was in the living room, sitting on the sofa staring into the fireplace. Taking the sisters by surprise, Dominique just blurted it out and said, "You know what?" Looking suspiciously at one sister and then the other, she continued, "I don't think you two love each other anymore."

Both sisters felt the manipulation in the statement, but they also could feel the real heartache that their estrangement was causing Dominique. Marie looked to Colleen about the same time Colleen looked at her. They both looked quickly down and then back up to Dominique. Dominique looked so small, but they both knew that for someone so young, she was an imposing figure. There she stood, with her hands on her hips, as if to say, "Well?"

Knowing that she was the one who had disrupted the family and hoping to save her sister some embarrassment, Colleen began to explain that it was not her mom's fault but her aunt's fault.

Just as Colleen began making her case, Marie interrupted and looked directly at Dominique, saying, "Colleen and I are sisters, and that will never change. I love her like no one else, and I know she loves me the same. Initially, your father and I invited her to live with us to help us with you and Chase. I was very sick when you were born and, most days, could not get out of bed. We don't know what we would have done if it were not for your aunt, Colleen. Your aunt's loving sacrifice made our house a home. We were all changed for the better, and your mom has forgotten how good it felt to be loved in such a way."

Looking deeply into Dominique's face, she finished her explanation. Then, she turned to look at Colleen. Colleen's face was frozen; her mouth was half open, and her eyes were welled up with tears. And Marie said, "I am so sorry, Sis. I love you and need you."

Squealing with joy, Dominique bolted over to where Marie sat and dove into her mother's arms. Colleen, running right behind Dominique, landed on the sofa next to them. With Dominique snuggled tightly between them, the sisters embraced, rubbing and patting each other's backs.

＊＊＊

It soon became normal for all of them to be together as family. The relationship was now healed, and except for Dominique, everyone was happy. Dominique was unhappy because Aunt Colleen was no longer living in their house, and no matter how hard she tried, Dominique could not talk Mom or Aunt Colleen into making that happen.

She even went to her dad and tried to manipulate him into forcing Aunt Colleen to return. He basically told her it was out of his hands and he could not make it happen. With that not being what she had hoped to hear, Dominique just puffed up at him and stomped off, mumbling under her breath.

Dominique had no way of knowing that it was Aunt Colleen who would not consent to returning to live with them, and Colleen had no way of explaining that to her niece. She would not understand, so, to not inflict undo pain, the sisters chose not to reveal her decision.

Colleen knew she had made the mistake of not heeding Chloe's warning. By sharing her new life in Jesus in a preachy and pushy way, she alienated Thomas and Marie. In the zeal of her new life, she was not careful and lacked wisdom. She came across to Marie as just judgmental. Marie was not ready; she did not have ears to hear.

Therefore, Colleen decided she first needed to love her sister unconditionally and, second, let God seek Marie Himself. As hard as it was to not move back in, she felt it was best to wait on God. She also knew she was welcome and could go to see them at any time, so she put a plan in place to do just that: to be there as often as she could.

* * *

Colleen moved into a house that was in proximity to her sister, and at first, the plan worked out well. She was there three or four days a week. She would come to visit, and where needed, she would offer herself to help around the house. Marie was excited about the sister's time and the help at home, but it was Dominique who dominated all of her aunt's time.

Dominique used her aunt's presence as a way to manipulate her mom and dad to get her way. At first, Colleen really enjoyed all the time with her niece, but she soon realized that Dominique was playing her sister and her against each other. The more evident this became, the more Colleen was forced to admonish Dominique for manipulating the family dynamic. Dominique would respectfully listen to her aunt's reproof, but her attitude did not change.

Marie was thankful for Colleen's insights, and they discussed how to maintain a united front against Dominique's maneuvering. Still, the tension started to arise again, and Colleen decided it would be best to make her visits less frequent. This gave rise to a new strategy for how to help Dominique overcome her morose attitude.

Colleen asked Thomas and Marie if Dominique could spend more time at her home. At first, they didn't like the idea of her being out of the house. Soon, overnight stays became a relief because they knew Colleen relished having Dominique with her, and their lives became less stressful with her gone.

Chase, being an academic, was busy adjusting to junior high school. He had been promoted two grades and was now in the eighth grade, and it was much easier for him to study with her gone.

Whenever Dominique was at her aunt's, it was all about her, and she loved it. Colleen loved loving on her niece, but her love was not a foolish love. Colleen prayed constantly for Dominique for wisdom to love her the way Jesus would have her love.

Colleen made a decision early on that she would not be Dominique's judge but would let God do that. Her goal was to love her and keep her accountable. Dominique came to know she was loved unconditionally by her aunt, but she also knew that Aunt Colleen was a tough cookie and not someone easily manipulated.

So, they came to an understanding about mutual respect and value judgments. Colleen made it her life's goal to help Dominique see life through the lens of God's Word and, within that framework, to see that God created the world and then us so we could have a relationship with Him.

Taking on the challenge of mentoring Dominique forced Colleen to grow spiritually herself. Knowing on her own she was unable to do this, she sought God continually. She prayed for Thomas and Marie daily as well that God would draw them to Himself, but they seemed more apt to drift away from faith than draw near. Something had changed, and the glue of God, which held them all together before, was no longer adhering. It became nearly impossible for Colleen to exchange peace into the tension rising between Thomas and Marie, and she prayed all the more for God to intervene.

* * *

As Dominique grew older, she became a regular guest at her aunt's home, and their relationship flourished. Even while Aunt Colleen was planting seeds of God's love into her niece, Dominique became more and more alienated from her parents. To her, they seemed to hate each other.

For Dominique, it was like living in two different worlds. She knew Dad loved her, but he seemed so distant and disappointed with her all the time. Knowing that her mom loved her as well, it still seemed that they both just could not let her be herself. They wanted her to be something else.

Like going to church, Dominique used to love church, but now it just seemed like a litany of dos and don'ts. On the other hand, Aunt Colleen made her feel more than loved; she made her feel free. There was nothing that she could not share with her aunt, but it seemed to her there was nothing she felt safe sharing with her parents.

One day, out of nowhere, Marie was awakened to the fact that her estrangement with Thomas was alienating Dominique from both of them. Dominique continued to use their pain and frustration with each other to manipulate them. She would go to Mom when she wanted something, and if Mom did not comply, she would go to Dad and ask for the very same thing, saying, "Mom said no." So, Dad would let her do the thing she wanted just to win a marital battle. And Marie would do the same thing with Thomas.

When Marie tried sharing this revelation of Dominique's ploy with Thomas, he would not listen. Privately, he was actually enjoying the consternation he caused Marie in overriding the discipline she was trying to employ, and he also liked the idea of having Dominique as an ally in the war zone.

It scared Marie that Thomas could not see what was happening. She did not know what to do, and each day, more and more, she felt a foreboding darkness covering their marriage.

On another day, Marie stopped right in the middle of a thought, and she asked herself, *Why am I so mad at Thomas?* Then, she wondered, *At this point, why does that even matter, and why am I asking myself this question?* That thought trailed off in her mind as she focused back on the routine of her busy day.

That night, she went to bed before Thomas and could not sleep. She lay there, and the question came back again: *Why am I so mad at Thomas?* The next thought frightened her, and she said to herself, *Do I still love Thomas?* Not knowing the answer to the why, she was forced to think back to when this new struggle in their marriage began.

She was unable to pin it down to some incident they disagreed on or come up with a certain time or place where Thomas did or didn't do something right, but she was able to frame the beginning of their estrangement around the time Colleen and she were fighting over religion. It finally appeared to Marie that the downhill slide in her marriage started the day of that big blowup with Colleen over religion.

She came to the conclusion: *It was like Thomas and I had to turn on Colleen to keep her from pushing Jesus down our throats. We stood together, not wanting her input in our lives, but what it did was take the glue out of the family dynamic. That decision put Colleen on the outside and left Thomas and me alone to manage or mismanage family affairs.* Marie did not know what to think or do about this conclusion, but it appeared like there was no other explanation. That thought rolled around in her head, not allowing her to fall asleep.

Marie finally decided to just get up; there was no way to put these thoughts to rest. The sun was not up, and she looked at her clock; it was four thirty in the morning. Thomas was not in bed, which did not surprise her; he had begun sleeping in one of the other bedrooms.

Sitting silent and forlorn in the family room, she realized she was right back where she was before Colleen had come to stay with them, completely alone, with no one to help.

She started to cry, and the pain of her loneliness poured out of her soul. Through the tears, she thought to herself, *Here I sit in this big beautiful house, lacking for no earthly thing, and yet, my life makes no sense.* And for the first time in a long while, she wasn't angry, just afraid of the future, and she wept.

Thomas awoke for some reason and saw the light on in the family room. He heard Marie crying and silently moved closer to hear what was happening. Looking into the dimly lit room, he saw Marie in her nightgown, lying on her side, with her legs pulled up to her chest, sobbing softly on the sofa.

He wanted to turn and just walk away, to let her suffer, but he couldn't move; he was frozen, holding his hard heart in check. The picture before him sent shivers through his body. Marie looked so small and fragile lying there in the spacious room. Seeing the agony of his bride, so alone, so vulnerable, he nearly gasped out loud and quickly raised his hand up to cover his mouth. Tears filled his eyes, and he began to move toward her. His frozen demeanor, melting away with each step, softened, and he found himself moving quickly to her side.

Unbeknownst to Marie, Thomas stood over her, weeping. He was unsure what to do, but he got on his knees next to her, put his hand on her knee, and spoke, "Marie, I am so sorry."

Marie didn't move when he placed his hand on her knee, and she didn't look up when he spoke; she just gently let her hand slip from her chest to rest on his hand. Thomas moved his head down until it was resting softly on Marie's temple; his tears mingled with hers, and they wept together silently.

CHAPTER 19

When Marie finally woke, she was startled to find herself so late in bed. She was also surprised to see Thomas shaving in the master bath. She lay there for a minute, coming to grips with what happened between them, and looked again at Thomas. Just as she looked at him, Thomas turned his head, and they made eye contact. Thomas smiled and raised his chin to acknowledge her gaze. Marie felt embarrassed and looked away.

Thomas came out of the bathroom and sat on the edge of the bed next to Marie. They had not spoken a word until now, and Thomas said, "Good morning."

Marie mustered a faint smile and said, "Good morning." Sitting up and pushing herself back against the headboard of the bed, she looked long at Thomas and he at her. Then Marie's face became stoic, and she said, "Thomas, what are you sorry for?"

Thomas was forced to look down as he measured his response to her question. He looked up and gently said, "I am sorry because, for so long now, I have not been a good husband to you." Marie was not sure where this was going to go, but she was surprised to see tears welling up in Thomas's eyes. Thomas continued, "Last night, I saw the end of us, and it broke my heart."

He reached out to grasp her hand, and Marie reciprocated, and as she did, she said, "Where do we go from here?"

Thomas responded, "I don't know, but wherever we go, I want to go with you. In the family room early this morning, my eyes were opened, and I saw my life as it should be. And I remembered who you are and why I love you. I am willing to go as far as we need to because I love you and do not want to lose you."

Trying to accept this proposal at face value, Marie was not sure, wondering what mending would even entail. She said to Thomas, "We cannot just say we will not be hurting each other anymore and know for sure that will happen."

Thomas agreed and said, "What do you suggest?"

Softening, Marie countered, "I don't know. What I do know is I love you, and I am sorry for how I have treated you." Thomas could not contain his emotions, and he pulled Marie to him and embraced her tenderly, but that was not enough; she could not be close enough, and he wrapped his arms around her firmly. Feeling her frailness so tight to him, he felt complete and at peace; what he needed was locked in his embrace. As they held each other for the first time in years, Marie felt peace too, but she also knew something was missing and that this brief moment of blissfulness could fall apart at any time.

That evening, Marie felt comfortable calling Colleen and sharing with her the dynamic of what had transpired between her and Thomas. She went on by confessing her animosity toward her sister and asking for forgiveness. Colleen was giddy on the other end of the phone, praising God, but she only listened to Marie share.

At the end of the conversation, Marie asked Colleen to consider helping them become a family again. Marie closed by telling Colleen, "We need you, Sis."

That day, Thomas and Marie fell in love again, and to Colleen's joy, they became more open to her ministering into their lives. She knew unless God intervened in their marriage, it would not be long before they could be back at each other's throats, so she began praying anew for God to move.

Dominique was mesmerized by the abrupt change in her parents' lives, and though it took away much of her power in the home, she was glad to have them love her and each other.

* * *

Except for Aunt Colleen not moving back in with them, this arrangement for Dominique was a treasure, and those blissful days with Aunt Colleen quickly turned into years.

Just before her fourteenth birthday, Aunt Colleen came up to her room. Dominique's bedroom was now up the stairs; she liked the privacy. Colleen knocked lightly and said, "Can I come in?" She was hoping to get some kind of idea about what to buy her niece for her birthday.

Dominique yelled out, "Come in."

Stepping in, Colleen saw Dominique sitting on her bed, brushing her long black hair. Colleen stopped just inside the door and was taken by how beautiful and grown-up she had become. She said to herself, *She is nearly a woman.* Colleen just stood there mesmerized by her beautiful Dom.

Dominique stopped brushing her hair, confused by the look on her aunt's face, and said, "What?"

Colleen said, "Nothing, it's just that you have become a very beautiful young woman. I do not know if I am ready for you to be all grown up."

Dominique blushed a little and looked at herself in the mirror on her dresser. Then, she laughed and said, "Naw, I looked just like this yesterday." They both laughed, and Colleen walked over and sat down on the bed.

They chatted about nothing and everything; that is just how they were together, and Colleen, being so engrossed, forgot to ask about the birthday gift. She knew she had to be heading home soon, so Colleen asked Dominique, "How are you doing, my darling?"

That was their normal protocol. Aunt Colleen would ask how she was, and Dominique would say, "I am good now that you are here."

Colleen reached over and kissed Dominique on the forehead and said, "See you later." As Dominique watched her aunt leave the room, she realized she was happy. She knew her parents loved her, and she could cope with life because having Aunt Colleen so close meant she wasn't left all alone trying to live completely in her mom and dad's dominance.

* * *

No one could foresee that which was hovering just beyond the horizon of their lives; things were about to change dramatically. One day, Colleen received a call from her and Marie's mom. Their mom and dad had just begun retirement, moving into a fifty and older community in Frankfort, Delaware.

Colleen was excited to hear her mom's voice, and she said, "Hi, Mom! How are things going?"

Her excitement was quickly shattered as her mom shared that her and Marie's dad had just been diagnosed with terminal cancer. Colleen cried out, "Oh, no!" Her thoughts were racing, and she said to herself, *How can this be? Dad has always been so healthy.* She said to her mom, "Did you get a second opinion?" It was too difficult for Colleen to imagine. Her mom confirmed the diagnosis was accurate and final.

The truth of this diagnosis submerged her instantly into a hollow grief. Her mom went on to tell Colleen she could not manage her dad's care alone and asked if she would come to Frankfort to help. She told Colleen it would be unreasonable to ask Marie to come with Dominique and Chase at home.

Colleen agreed to the request, but as she ended the phone call, her knees became weak, and she had to sit down. She looked up to God and raised her hands, then bowed her head and wept.

Marie was emotionally destroyed by the news, and she and Colleen spent the next day on the phone making plans with Mom to coordinate when they would arrive. Marie knew she could not pack up and leave with Colleen and stay with Dad until he passed, but she decided she must travel with Colleen to see her dad now.

Thomas tried to put up a good front for Marie, but he was unable to grasp the pain she was suffering. Even as he was consenting to the weeklong trip, he began to have second thoughts about them leaving him alone with Dominique.

He could not imagine, with both Marie and Colleen gone, how he would manage the turmoil he envisioned just around the corner after they were gone. Chase would be available part-time, but he was busy managing his sophomore year of college.

Thomas nearly panicked as he thought to himself, *The one most unable to handle the news about Grandpa was Dominique. She will have neither her mom nor her aunt home to torture, and I will be stuck alone with her and her endless demands.*

Thomas was right. Dominique had already started to complain to her mom. She could not understand, nor could she empathize with Grandpa's suffering. In her mind, this was a real rip-off. Grandpa and Grandma, who hardly ever visited and now live 200 miles away, were selfishly taking Aunt Colleen from her.

The night before they left, Thomas cautiously confronted the sisters and asked, "How will I survive Dominique while you are gone?"

They looked at each other, then sarcastically at Thomas, and Marie said, "Our dad is dying; I don't have time to babysit you and Dominique. You will have to figure it out."

* * *

Though she was able to speak daily on the phone with her aunt, Dominique was beside herself. She took her frustration out on Colleen as well, blaming her for not being close when she needed her. Colleen tried to reason with Dominique, telling her that their dad was dying and she needed to be patient. Hoping Dominique would understand, she told her how her mom was devastated and cried daily for her dad.

One night, in one of their phone conversations, Colleen, beginning to dread the loss of her dad, confided in Dominique how sad she was. Not able to understand how hurt her aunt was, Dominique became nervously unsettled and persisted in feeling sorry for herself.

At that, Colleen became stern on the phone and said, "Dominique, your mom and I have only one dad, and we will not have him on earth very much longer. What would you be doing if it was your mom or me dying and you only had a few days left to be with us?"

As Dominique had to reflect on that question, her heart softened, and she became saddened instead of angry. Then, she had nothing to say. She just sat there holding the phone. It was so silent and eerie that Colleen was forced to ask, "Honey, are you there?"

Dominique just responded, "Hey, I gotta go."

That night, while thinking about Grandpa dying and Aunt Colleen being gone, Dominique surprised herself; suddenly, she felt compelled to seek God for His help. She started her prayer like this: "God, I don't usually trust that prayer works because I am not sure You are really there, but Aunt Colleen really believes You are. So, today, I need You to help me. I need You to stop all this suffering. And if You will do this, I will try to make church fun again." She finished her prayer by saying, "Don't make me doubt You."

Marie finally returned from Frankfort. She felt she could not stay any longer; it was just too hard watching her dad die and her mom suffering through this illness.

While she was gone, she spoke with Thomas; he was careful not to divulge too much information about how things were really going with him and Dominique. When Marie returned home, she was saddened and angry to hear the horror stories of the battles fought between father and daughter while she was gone.

They both blamed each other, and Marie felt like she was arbitrating between two teenagers. With all that was going on with her mom and dad and Colleen not being there to referee, she finally blew a gasket and decided to let them both have it.

Starting with Dominique, she took away every privilege she had and demanded that unless things changed and she started honoring her dad, life as she knew it would end.

With that kind of heat in the house, Chase just laid low. It was actually kind of scary. He didn't know if he was next, so he spent most of his time in his room studying or out with his friends.

Marie was very disappointed with Thomas, but she knew her approach with him had to be more measured. After sending Dominique to her room, she went searching for Thomas. She found him in his den sulking on the sofa. She poked her head in and said, "Hey." At first, Thomas didn't look up but grumbled inaudibly. Marie knew that Thomas was more upset with himself than at Dominique. She also knew that Dominique was an expert in the use of subversive countertactics, and he had no chance at winning against her.

Letting out a deep sigh, Thomas finally looked up to meet Marie's eyes, and at the same time, as if to admit defeat, his shoulders slumped forward. Marie could read the signs plainly, so she moved slowly over to sit down with him. She reached out and put her hand on top of his.

Thomas was so moved by her gesture that he began to tear up. He looked deep into her eyes and said, "I know I have let you down again; you have been dealing with so much, and by adding to your suffering, I have made things worse."

Marie was still angry and wanted to harangue him soundly, but his confession helped her see how really confounded he was. She grabbed his hand tightly and said, "Thank you for being so honest." Then she sat up straight and said, "Thomas, we have so much going on right now, and we don't have Colleen to help. I am not sure how to fix all that is going on, but we must be together in our attempt. I know Dominique is in trouble, but I think we will have to rely on us to help her get past this stage in her life."

Thomas seemed relieved to hear there was still an "us" in her rebuke. He said, "I am at a loss. I try to force her to comply, and I get angry when she does not comply. I think she knows she is winning."

Marie responded by saying, "With Dad slowly dying, I am an emotional wreck and do not have the stamina to endure this onslaught of family fervor. Before I left Mom and Dad, Colleen shared with me how Dominique was translating all that was going on. She encouraged us to maintain a very strict environment for Dominique, kind of like when she was a toddler and we were forced to keep her in time-out.

"Colleen suggested we enforce the rules of our home, but without the drama, and we do not react to her fits. We will tell her that she is not the focus of our family right now, and she will not be allowed to disrupt or disallow the grieving process of us losing Grandpa."

Thomas looked kind of strangely at Marie and said, "How do we do that?"

Marie jumped in and said, "According to Colleen, the conversations she has had on the phone with Dominique have been hard but productive. She believes Dominique is starting to soften her heart. She has asked Dominique several times how she would feel if her mom and dad or her aunt, Colleen, were dying; how would she respond? Colleen said that Dominique had never contemplated that idea before and finally said, 'I wouldn't want to be left alone.'"

Thomas nodded his head and said, "I'm in, but this will be very hard."

Marie said to Thomas, "Life is very hard; we are living it." Marie ended the talk by saying, "One thing we cannot do in our discipline of Dominique is not to deprive her of time on the phone with Colleen. Colleen is our ally, and she has Dominique's ear." Marie added one more thing: "Let's keep Mom and Dad as our family's priority right now, and we need to help Dominique buy into that scenario."

**

At first, Dominique became hostile and maligned her parents and their new discipline. When that strategy did not work and ended up costing her more than she bargained for, she then began beguiling them in an attempt to lessen the consequences pouring in on her freedom. After much suffering, it finally became evident to her that her parents were serious, and they were not going to budge from this regiment.

What became really frustrating for Dominique was how even Aunt Colleen would not enable her during her woeful tantrums. She had no idea how much time her mom and Aunt Colleen spent collaborating on the phone to maintain a united coalition, combatting Dominique's schemes.

Colleen prayed continually for God's wisdom to achieve the family's goals and, at the same time, not alienate her precious niece, and that strategy was successful. During Colleen's absence, Dominique actually became more trusting of her aunt. Though she longed for her physically, she still had her voice in her ears and her words growing in her heart. Due to the suffering she was experiencing in missing Aunt Colleen, she began to understand the pain that Mom and Dad were suffering in Grandpa's decline.

***

It seemed like forever since the last time Dominique had physically held and talked to her aunt, Colleen, and her heart ached. Then, just seven weeks into her aunt's departure, the family received the hard news: Grandpa had died. At first, Dominique was excited, and it became urgent that she call her aunt to see when she would be coming back. Hearing Aunt Colleen's voice crack and then listening to her cry on the other end of the phone was not what Dominique had expected. She thought that Aunt Colleen would be as excited as she was to end their lonely separation.

Left listening to Aunt Colleen trying so hard to talk through the tears and heartbreak, Dominique started to feel remorse for her aunt, a feeling she had never known. This was not about her, and then, for the first time since hearing about Grandpa, she had a forlorn moment, and she said to herself, *My grandpa is dead.* For some reason, this revelation crushed in on her emotions, coupled with hearing Aunt Colleen trying to cope with the loss, made her realize how death made her feel so vulnerable, and tears filled her eyes.

This was the first time in her life that Dominique was forced to face the finality of death. She was not unaware of the idea of death, but she had never come to grips personally with the devastation of knowing that a life had ended and was no longer viable. It scared her terribly, and the fear made her doubt everything. She quickly apologized to Aunt Colleen for her abruptness and said, "I have to go."

Dominique listened to her mom crying most of the night; then, just before bedtime, Marie came to her room. She peered in and asked, "Can I come in?" Dominique had feared and dreaded the idea that sooner or later, Mom was going to come up and want to talk.

Not knowing what to do, Dominique went into panic mode. She just stared wildly at her mom as she came across the room to her bed. When her mom sat down, her first thought was, *Do I hug her? Do I let her hug me?* So, without thinking, she said, "What are you doing here?" Marie leaned in, stroked Dominique's long black hair, and said, "How are you doing, my darling?" Dominique was taken aback by her mom's plagiarizing use of Aunt Colleen's signature greeting, but it was very evident to Dominique that her mom was hurting terribly.

It felt so odd; she had no idea how to emote correctly in this surreal moment. Marie felt odd as well. Most of their interaction lately had been just confrontational. She knew, in these moments, it was a mom's responsibility to comfort her children, but she felt so inadequate; there was no rehearsing the dialogue for such a terrible moment.

They both sat there thinking about how to proceed when Dominique thought to herself, *Mom just lost her dad; even if I do not completely understand this, I must say something.* She started to say something, and then she stumbled at the beginning, so she sat back a little and started again. Marie was looking intently and lovingly at her daughter, not sure what she was trying to say. Then, Dominique just blurted out, "Mom, I am so sorry."

Hearing that, Marie looked lovingly into Dominique's eyes. As she did so, Dominique was caught trying to re-evaluate what she had just said. She was quickly going over in her head: *Does mom think I am sorry for how I have acted lately, or does she think I am sorry for her dad dying?*

To Marie, those words covered over a multitude of sins, so with tears of mourning and joy, she grabbed Dominique and hugged her tightly. Dominique thought she would hate this moment, but she found herself needing her mom and this hug so much, so she embraced her mom firmly and said, "You really miss Grandpa, don't you?"

* * *

After spending another week with Mom and helping her and Marie get through the memorial, Colleen finally arrived back in New York. She was at peace and grieving in a positive way. She missed her dad, but she was thankful for the quality time they spent together.

She was actually overjoyed, not because her dad was gone but because she believed he was now in heaven. She knew God had orchestrated their time together, and in the last week, she was led to share with her dad Jesus's call for him to receive eternal life. He did that unashamedly, and trusting God, he received forgiveness for his sins.

This was Colleen's first experience with leading another person to Jesus, and she thought back to her time with Chloe and how Chloe led her in the same way; now, she had led her dad to Jesus. She paused and said, "Thank You, God of heaven and Lord of me." In the midst of her prayer, the phone rang. She had just arrived, but she knew a certain young lady would soon be calling.

* * *

As time passed, Colleen rested comfortably in the peace God had arranged between her and Marie. The healing was complete, and their relationship continued to grow, even beyond what Colleen had hoped. Thankful, she continued to pray for Thomas and Marie that God would open their ears to hear His loving call.

Now, with unhindered family support and God's help, Colleen poured herself into the task of molding character into her niece, the love and the joy of her life. Dominique was unaware of the spiritual battle being waged for her soul, but Colleen was aware. To Colleen, each day, it became more evident a celestial enemy was entrenched and taking captive all who dwelt in and around Dominique's life.

It also became clear, now more than ever, that Colleen needed Chloe's feedback. Time on the phone with her was both precious and refreshing. Colleen often needed encouragement to continue to live humbly and faithfully before her sister and family.

Together, they committed to doing spiritual warfare for their loved ones, and together, they came up with a life verse to battle the enemy who overtly paraded himself as light in the Meuniers' home. The verse they chose was 2 Corinthians 10:4–5: "(For the weapons of our warfare are not carnal, but mighty unto God to the pulling down of strongholds;) casting down imaginations, and every high thing that exalteth itself against the knowledge of God, and bringing into captivity every thought to the obedience of Christ."[13]

Colleen kept pleading with Chloe to see if there was any way she could leave Philadelphia for a short time to visit Marie. Colleen believed things would change more readily if Chloe was there. Chloe, on the other hand, felt differently. She believed God was moving and using Colleen as His catalyst to open their eyes to Him. Colleen disagreed but trusted Chloe to have the pulse of the situation.

***

Thomas and Marie had little time to flesh out all that they had just become aware of. Dominique's disclosure to the school and of Durand's evil caught them off guard, and it left them feeling guilty and angry. All that made any sense was they had to get to Dominique as quickly as possible. As soon as they got off the phone call from school, they were in the car and on the road.

At first, they didn't speak; they were overwhelmed with grief, and as they hurried over the road to Dominique, the only words spoken were Marie telling Thomas to slow down before he would get a speeding ticket. About thirty minutes into their excursion, a sullen gloom overtook Marie, a mother's worst nightmare, and she began to cry.

Thomas had issues of his own. His vision was a red blur; he could only imagine, over and over again, the evil and the suffering that Dominique endured at the hands of Durand, her cousin. He wanted to hurt Durand and curse his brother, but most of all, he was suffering the pain of knowing it was he who set up the Durand summer visit; it was he who put her in harm's way.

What tore him up most was how weak he was as a father. When Dominique's injuries were first exposed, he hoped he wanted her injuries to be just as she said. Though he had doubts, he didn't want to think that someone had inflicted this pain on her.

The anguish of this last consideration took him over the edge and spilled out from his brain and into his heart. He cried in his soul, admonishing himself, saying, *For so long now, my precious Dominique has been coping with this horrific nightmare alone.* As the tears began to run down his face, the road became blurry; he could not see to drive, so he pulled off onto the side of the road.

When the car finally stopped, Thomas looked out in front of him through the windshield. In the distance and slowly overwhelming the landscape, a storm was brewing; ominous clouds filled the sky, forcing a darkness. The coming storm made him feel small and insignificant. He sat there holding the steering wheel, numb and lost.

The darkness of this storm was reminiscent of the darkness of their lives right now. He looked over to see Marie clutching a damp handkerchief and staring out at the same darkening sky. She slowly looked in his direction, and simultaneously, they reached out and held each other. The storm opened up its fury, and the rain plummeted the car and everything around it. Other than the rain, the only sounds that could be heard were the tire noise coming from the cars passing by on the rain-soaked thoroughfare.

As the cars passed noisily by, Thomas pondered the question: *I wonder how many of these travelers, on this same road, are as lost as we are?* As the storm continued to ravage the daylight, they sat there weeping together, devastated and alone.

CHAPTER 20

At first, Dumas was furious with his brother's incendiary claim. He thought to himself, *How dare he blame my son? Dominique has her side of the story, and Durand will have one as well.* It wasn't long, though, before he was transported back to his brother's house, going over all the details of the night before they left for Philadelphia.

He also recalled the next night when Chloe called to alert Thomas of the need to get hold of Marie. The rest was a blur because, after hearing of Dominique's injuries, Thomas left the hotel so quickly that they never really did get to speak about Dominique's strange behavior at their home.

Then, a sickening feeling gripped his soul. Dumas's legs became weak, and he had to sit down. An awful thought shot into his mind, and he said to himself, *Am I just being naïve? What if Durand did do this? Is it possible?* The next thought crippled him, and as he pondered the possibility of his son committing this evil on his precious niece, he retched, nearly vomiting on the floor, and he ran to the bathroom.

As he stood at the sink washing his face, Dumas slowly raised his head and looked into the mirror. The depiction before him terrified him. He yelled out loud, "Who are you, and what have you done?" Then, he became sorrowful and ached for Adelle, and at the same time, he blamed her for leaving him and Durand all alone.

The more he thought about it, the more Dumas contemplated the possible outcomes and the more he was left with a worst-case scenario for his son. He had to confront Durand about the allegations, but he thought, *Surely, he would deny it. Why wouldn't he?*

Dumas waited anxiously for Durand to arrive home from school. Then, the school called to let him know they had received a call from the authorities and they would be remanding Durand to the county jail.

Entering the jail, Dumas was lost in his thoughts and hollow of answers: he had no idea how this would work out. To his amazement and horror, when confronted about the allegations, Durand admitted that he had finally gotten even with Dominique. He felt his actions were righteous, and he was justified due to all the harm she had inflicted on him over the years. He confessed to the rape.

Though still in high school, Durand was eighteen years old and considered an adult. After Durand was taken into custody, Dumas was despondent. He felt the dread of having this all fall directly on his shoulders; he wasn't sure he could go on, but he was yet to know the totality of his agony. Just two weeks into Durand's incarceration, Dumas received a dreadful phone call; he was informed that Durand had taken his own life.

***

Dominique stood up when her parents stepped into Mrs. Martsen's office. It was instantly awkward, and neither Dominique nor Marie and Thomas were comfortable. They just stared at each other.

Prior to their arrival, Mrs. Martsen gave Dominique a heads-up about how her parents would be feeling. She told her they would be angry because of the attack, but more than that, they would be feeling guilty because they were unable to protect Dominique from that attack. Mostly, though, they would be hoping to make her feel safe and secure in their embrace. Then, they entered the room.

Not knowing what to do, they just stared at each other, each set of eyes focused on their own emotional presuppositions. Marie saw fear in Dominique's eyes, and she began to weep. Thomas saw a little girl who needed her daddy, and Dominique saw love pouring out from her parents' faces. She could not control her holding back any longer, and she burst from where she stood into her parents' arms.

On the way back home, Dominique felt safe just to ride and enjoy being together. From the back seat and holding hands, Marie and Dominique made intermittent eye contact. It was dark, but when the light of a passing car poured into their darkness, they would turn and look at each other, each catching a glimpse of the light reflecting from the glistening moisture in their eyes.

Dominique felt safe, and she stretched out. Not long on the journey home, exhausted, she fell asleep. Marie reached up and grabbed Thomas's shoulder and softly said, "Turn on the interior light." Thomas did, and as he did, he looked into the rearview mirror to see Dominique's face.

He was overwhelmed by his love for her, and looking into the mirror at Marie's face, he smiled. Marie smiled back at Thomas, then in the dim light coming from the car ceiling, she looked down, and while gently caressing Dominique's face, she said tentatively to herself, *Thank You for this moment, and, God, please protect us and this precious gift you gave us.*

***

As she waited at Thomas and Marie's home, Colleen felt strange about her soon-to-be in conversation with Dominique. As she waited for them to return, her thoughts exploded into fragments. She was saddened that Dominique had not confided in her, and she felt guilty for not being the one her niece could trust to share her pain.

Time moved slowly as she nervously paced back and forth in front of the big window, which peered down their long driveway. She used the ample time of waiting to blame herself for not following her suspicions concerning Dominique's injuries. She chewed on herself, saying, *Why didn't you press more? How could you see but not see?*

The blame and the waiting were taking their toll, and Colleen became frustrated; then, she remembered the conversation she had with Chloe right after the news broke. Colleen recalled the discussion with Chloe; she couldn't believe that Dominique would not confide in her and would not trust her with her suffering. Chloe told her not to blame herself. Chloe said to Colleen, "God orchestrates trials for His good purposes." Chloe finished the conversation by saying, "Have you thought, though, that maybe Dominique felt there was no way she could tell you for fear of losing something in her relationship with you?"

Chloe always saw things from God's perspective. Colleen didn't know how she could remain so trusting, but then she caught herself saying, *Chloe has a faith that I have never seen.* Just as she finished that thought, she anxiously looked again down the driveway, and coming her way was a set of headlights.

***

That night, aunt and niece rejoiced at seeing each other, and they wept holding each other. Dominique felt as safe as she had ever been. Aunt Colleen decided to stay the night, and later, at bedtime, after precious goodnights, they exchanged warm smiles, but as her aunt turned to leave the room, Dominique thought she caught a glimpse of sadness on her face.

The next morning, Dominique and Aunt Colleen were in the kitchen; Dominique wanted all of Aunt Colleen's time. Trying to catch up, she talked up a storm, and Colleen tried to stay warm and engaged, but Dominique began to sense something was wrong; her aunt's smile seemed forced.

Suddenly, Dominique became fearful; she quickly reached over and grabbed Aunt Colleen's hand. They looked at each other, and a trepidation they had never known crept in between them. Aunt Colleen knew instantly that she had exposed Dominique to the void she was feeling in their relationship.

Dominique could not speak; she began to think the worst: *Is my aunt, Colleen, upset with me? What did I do wrong?* Colleen sensed Dominique's fear and tried to change the impression on her face by putting on a genuine smile, but it did not work. Frantic, Dominique gripped her aunt's hand tightly and screamed, "What is wrong?"

Marie heard Dominique scream and rushed into the kitchen. Staring at the two of them, she saw something she had never seen before: they looked estranged. Marie spoke up and said, "So, what is happening here?"

Colleen reached out with both hands to hold Dominique's hand, but Dominique's eyes rushed full of tears; her mouth opened slightly, and she let out a painful "oh." She stared heartbroken into Aunt Colleen's eyes and abruptly let go of her hands. Terrorized, she turned and ran up to her room.

Colleen yelled after her, "Dominique, please…" She rose to follow her, but Marie grabbed her by the arm and said, "What?"

After listening to Colleen explain the dilemma between her and Dominique, Marie stared in unbelief at her sister. She opened her mouth to speak but could not and walked out of the kitchen. Colleen started to panic; she knew she had just turned the entire family upside down. As she hurried to catch up with Marie, she prayed, *Oh, God, what have I done?*

Marie heard Colleen following her, and as they entered the living room, Marie came to an abrupt stop and turned to face her sister. Colleen stopped wide-eyed in her tracks and started to explain, but Marie held out her hand and said, "Do you know what you have done? After all that she has endured, she finds out today that her favorite person in the world does not support her. Do you feel like Dominique has let you down? I cannot believe you; you had better make this right." And Marie turned and walked away.

With her heart feeling overweight in her chest, Colleen physically ached; she had hurt Dominique so badly. She turned to go upstairs, but she thought to herself, *How will I make this right? What have I done?*

She reached the bottom of the stairs and looked up. She could not move, so she sat down on the first stair, hoping to have an epiphany as to how to proceed. Then, she bowed her head and prayed, *Oh, God, I have no words; I am so sorry for being so selfish with Dominique. Please help me.*

Not sure what had just happened, Dominique was in shock, crying on her bed. She realized that by not telling Aunt Colleen about Durand, she had let her down. She agonized and said to herself, *Aunt*

Colleen is the person I tell everything to; she must be so ashamed of me. This is what I get for sharing; I knew this couldn't work out. She was instantly angry with herself and with Bella and Mrs. Allard for talking her into disclosing what happened.

There was nothing she could do, so she decided to quit school and began devising a plan to leave her home and get out on her own. Her thoughts were coming faster than she could manage them, and everything started to swirl around her. She put her head in her hands and tried to slow things down, but nothing worked.

She jumped up to get a suitcase out of the closet to begin packing. Just as she swung it off the top of the closet, she heard Colleen knock and say, "Can I come in?" Still holding the suitcase in her hand, Dominique froze but turned her head to look at the door. She didn't know if she could bear hearing from Aunt Colleen that she was disappointed with her.

Completely at a loss at what to do, she threw the suitcase onto the bed. Somehow, she mustered the courage to say, "Yes, come in." As she envisioned Aunt Colleen entering her room, Dominique imagined a different aunt would appear, one that would think less of her and want less to do with her. As the door swung open and Colleen entered, a peace also entered the room, and when Dominique saw her aunt's face, she squealed with joy. There before her was the same old wonderful Aunt Colleen, her face beaming with pride and joy.

Running quickly toward each other, they met at the foot of the bed and held each other at arms-length, their eyes locked, and they blurted out simultaneously, "I am so sorry."

Dominique started to speak, but not wanting her to have to explain why she didn't tell her about Durand, Colleen said, "I know why you didn't tell me, and you have nothing to explain. I have been so selfish, darling, and I have no right to be upset with you. Instead of where I have been, I should have been aching only about how to help you get through this terrible injury. Please forgive me."

Dominique nodded her head and said, "I do." She just stared at the amazing person before her, and she thought, *I must be growing up because this is the first time in my entire life that Aunt Colleen was wrong and apologized to me instead of the other way around.*

Colleen said, "Let's go find your mom; I think she needs to see us happy together." Holding hands, they ran out of the room and down the stairs, looking for Marie. As they rushed out, Colleen happened to glance at the suitcase on the bed, and a solemn thought entered her heart. Even as they ran, holding hands, Colleen prayed, *Dear God, she is so fragile. May I never do what I did to her again.*

***

As the whole family sought to support Dominique's healing, conversations, which could have been so hard, seemed to happen quite naturally. One difficult conversation that needed to be resolved was securing a family therapist. Since she and Mrs. Allard were already meeting, Dominique was opposed to securing a family therapist.

Wanting to build trust with her, Thomas and Marie relented and agreed that Mrs. Allard would be fine. This allowance went a long way with helping Dominique trust her parents. And for the first time in her dad's and Dominique's lives together, Thomas didn't feel the need to control each and every difficult situation. The last few days were exhausting for Thomas. He felt so out of control, but with each new day, he became less anxious.

At first, with all the family and school support, Dominique relished the outpouring of love. Her life was becoming peaceful, a new dynamic. The peace made it easier to not have to manipulate situations to get her way. She believed those close to her wanted what was best for her, so she didn't doubt as much as she did before.

Even her sleep was peaceful, but then, after two weeks of home care and the night before she was scheduled to head back to school, she had a terrible nightmare about Durand. She awoke screaming and in a deep sweat. Calming, she laid back down, wondering, *How long will this go on?*

The entire family was confused and angry about Durand. For the two years that Dominique suffered alone, they had no idea of the cruelty he was capable of. When they learned of his evil, naturally, they were angry and dismissed him, but after receiving the news of him taking his own life, they could not maintain the anger and animosity needed to hold him in contempt. All but Dominique began to soften, and their fierce anger directed at Durand was turned to empathy for Dumas, a grieving father.

The nightmare about Durand ended Dominique's rest, and she could not sleep. Neither could she sit in the dark, alone in bed; she was physically shaking. She turned on the light, but that did not dissuade the growing fear. The anxiety that sought to destroy her was eating away at her solace. She turned to look at the clock; it read two thirty in the morning.

With Dominique leaving for school the next day, Colleen prepared herself for bed and had just begun to pray. She was thankful for being able to stay at Marie's for the last two weeks. She was also very thankful for the headway Dominique was making, but her heart was not at full peace because she knew Dominique's greatest need was not met; was she going to heaven?

Colleen was experiencing a warning in her soul; how would Dominique cope with school and the trauma of having been raped at the same time? She concluded her prayer by saying, *Dear God, You know Dominique's greatest need; please meet her there.*

She felt like she had just dosed off to sleep when Colleen heard a knock on her door. She looked over at her clock and found it was two thirty in the morning. Then she heard Dominique say, "Aunt Colleen, can I come in?"

Colleen turned on the light and said, "Yes, dear, please come in."

As Dominique came into the room, Colleen cautiously surveyed her face; she saw fear and quickly said, "Are you all right, darling?" She hadn't quite finished her question before Dominique rushed over and sat close to her aunt. Colleen could see how frightened she was, so she reached out and caressed Dominique's head and laid it on her shoulder.

Since she had just prayed before going to bed, Colleen was sure God was orchestrating a divine appointment. As she held her, Colleen's thoughts were the same as they always were when it concerned Dominique, and those thoughts repeated themselves again in her mind: *My Dom is nearly eighteen years old; how will she ever get healed and functioning correctly for life?*

She paused the caressing and put her hand under Dominique's chin. She slowly lifted her head up so they could make eye contact. Then she said, "Tell me what happened?"

Dominique's fear and anxiety poured out as she shared the dream and how real it was. She felt like she experienced the whole ordeal all over again. Then she said, "Durand seemed so real in my dream…"

Remembering what Dominique shared concerning her counseling time with Mrs. Allard, Colleen said, "Sweetheart, this awful thing that has happened to you must not defeat you."

"How do I defeat my dreams?" Dominique responded. "I have no control over my dreams."

Colleen came back and said, "Prior to tonight, when was the last time you had this dream?"

Dominique was surprised by the question because she had not had this recurring dream since she came home. Dominique's last bad episode with Durand was in her room at school in the bathroom before the disclosure with Bella. She realized that she had never gone this long before without having one of these nightmares; normally, they were daily reminders.

Staring lovingly at Aunt Colleen, Dominique's countenance became brighter. She realized something was different and better, and she almost smiled.

"You see," Colleen interjected, "healing has begun because you are not bearing this pain alone." Dominique had to agree; something was different at home, at school, and even in her dreams.

Trusting that God was leading her to speak, Colleen just jumped in. She looked deep into Dominique's eyes and said, "You know my favorite verse, right?" Being surprised by the direction of the question, Dominique feigned a wry smile and nodded while turning her head down a notch. Colleen intervened and said, "No freaking out, you have heard me say this verse hundreds of times, but today, I want you to hear it for yourself."

It scared Dominique to have her aunt pushing religion on her. Yes, she had heard this verse a hundred times but always attributed the verse to her aunt's life, not hers. Colleen forged ahead, saying, "I pray for you every day, that you would know the peace of that verse. No human can ever keep the promise of this verse; only God can promise this, 'Never will I leave you; never will I forsake you.'"

Dominique puffed up and sat back, saying, "Where was Jesus when Durand raped me?"

Colleen foresaw that response and came right back at Dominique, saying, "Darling, unless you are willing to be honest in your battle with God, you will never have peace. I know you think God is just a fantom, a fairy tale, and that's because you want God on your terms. You want Him to be how you think He should be."

Dominique said, "How do you see Him to be?"

Thoughtfully, Colleen replied, "First of all, He is not frustrated by humans who say they hate Him or don't believe in Him. Second, He is familiar with suffering; He knows all you went through and the evil done to you. He suffered the torture of the cross so we could be redeemed back to God. His death was the price, the only sacrifice great enough to appease God's wrath for sin."

Trapped, Dominique remembered how many times these same conversations came up between the two of them, but this one seemed more intense. Desperately looking for a way to change the subject, Dominique said, "I know Jesus is important to you, but what if I cannot see Him changing my life for the better?"

Ready for that response, Colleen wryly smiled and said, "He already has. Look at the peace you have experienced these two weeks. What is it that Bella, Mrs. Allard, and I all have in common?"

Not wanting to admit it, but it was true, she said to herself, *The ones who love me most are the ones who love Jesus too.*

Colleen continued, "I believe without Jesus's intervention, you would still be trapped inside yourself and dealing with Durand by yourself. Honey, Jesus is calling you to Him."

***

Though getting little sleep due to the night spent with Aunt Colleen, Dominique awoke early, excited about seeing Bella and Mrs. Allard again. She quickly packed her luggage to get ready to head back to school. In the middle of all the hubbub whirling around her soon departure, Dominique stopped, and her thoughts unexpectedly took her back to the conversation last night with Aunt Colleen.

She stared out into the backyard from her bedroom window and reflected on all that had taken place since that day with Durand. Durand taking his life haunted Dominique, not because she felt sorry for him but because she felt others were now using his mental issues as an excuse for his behavior. She could not excuse the evil he had inflicted on her, not even with him dead. She thought, *Am I at peace?*

Though over the top and way too long, Aunt Colleen's talk last night had an impact on Dominique, and she thought to herself, *If, for no other reason, I finally know the evil that happened to me is better revealed than kept secret.* As exposed as she was, she felt the exposure was safe in the hands of the right people.

It was invigorating, having the support she now had, but still, her heart told her something was missing, and according to Bella, Mrs. Allard, and her aunt, the missing ingredient was Jesus. As simple as their remedy was to them, Dominique could not see the reality of Jesus in her world; instead, she felt a code of cold demands that she could not decipher.

Continuing to look out the window, she pictured herself in the backyard again, standing before Durand; the thought gave her chills, and she asked herself, *How will I ever be free from the fear and the despair of that day?*

Hating where she just let her mind travel, she banished those thoughts and turned quickly away from the window and back to get ready for the journey. Taking one more look to ensure she had everything, she slowly closed the door and thought, *I hope I don't have to leave school again. As much as I am loved and cared for here, I need to be at school; home reminds me too much of the horror still alive here.*

She turned and headed briskly down the hallway, but just before she got to Durand's room, she moved slowly to the other side of the hall, avoiding the proximity to that dreaded place. Once past the room, she glanced back toward the door and was relieved to be leaving not only the place but the codified memory of her suffering.

CHAPTER 21

As excited as Thomas and Marie were, with the evidence of Dominique's healing, they feared and even anticipated that this would not be the end of her suffering. They sensed her excitement about getting back to school and were excited for her, but they knew her calm was only a moment away from another whirlwind. They could not grasp, nor had she revealed it to them, how anxious Dominique felt living in the place where her nightmare began.

As she reached the bottom of the stairs, Aunt Colleen stood there, smiling and welcoming as usual. Dominique smiled back, and as she did, Colleen sensed a real excitement in her countenance, and she prayed, *Oh, God, make her fearless by Your constant presence.* Colleen, Thomas, and Marie had spent little time talking together about Dominique's departure, but in the waning moments till that departure, each one felt uneasy about the future.

***

Arriving and getting Dominique settled back on campus went smoothly. After saying their good-byes, the car slipped slowly down the darkened driveway, and the three of them sat silently, dreading the dreary drive home. Speaking up first, Colleen said, "What a precious cargo we just delivered."

Still very emotional, Marie just nodded, and Thomas said, "Home feels too distant; what happens the next time she struggles and needs our help? Can we really say we are available for her?"

The entire time Dominique was home rehabilitating, Mrs. Martsen was rehabilitating as well. She had not been the same since that day when she cried hard and long in her office. Confessing who she really was and coming to grips with the disdain she had for the girls in her care, her soul was revitalized, and her heart changed.

Days before Dominique's return to school, she started to pray. Not that she didn't pray often, but now her prayers were pointed and sincere. Dominique was the first girl she prayed for each day. She also began to individualize her prayers for each student. Another change she made was staff prayer for the school, and the girls were on the daily agenda. Led by Mrs. Martsen's new zeal, even the staff began to see things anew for their students.

One day, after a staff meeting, Mrs. Allard pulled Mrs. Martsen aside and said, "These changes in staff meetings are having a huge impact on the staff and carrying over to the girls; thank you so much for your insight."

It felt good to have her changed life confirmed, and she thanked Mrs. Allard for the kind words. Then, off-handedly, she said, "Why we haven't done this earlier is beyond me, but now that this is who we are, would you help remind me, should I ever forget, this is how we do it?" Mrs. Allard nodded and thanked Mrs. Martsen again for the new commitment to their students.

That night, lying in her bed, Dominique's thoughts were everywhere. Still resonating fresh in her mind was the scene as she entered their room. There was Bella screaming at the top of her voice, "*Roooomy,* it's you! Welcome home." Dominique thought Bella was going to break her neck as she jumped on her; she hung on and threw her legs around Dominique's waist, then spun in circles, ending the greeting with a big kiss planted on Dominique's forehead.

Normally, Dominique tried to play down these kinds of emotional outbursts, but with Bella, there was no way to keep her zeal for life from overtaking your inhibitions. Dominique could not contain her joy at seeing Bella again; she fell headlong into the festivities, hugging her and laughing out loud.

Dominique mused again in her thoughts, and she said to herself, *I don't laugh out loud, but I hope I can learn to do this more often.* She paused, thinking hard; she queried her mind and said to herself, *It is really strange; I have never really had a reason to laugh like this.*

The thoughts were still warm in her heart as she recalled that right after their joyous reunion, they both paused and held each other at a distance and just stared at each other. Once again, Dominique was mesmerized by those big green eyes and the tiny freckles sprinkled around Bella's nose. Dominique responded first, saying, "I missed you."

Bella quickly came back and said, "I missed you more."

They laughed again and settled onto their beds. They talked all night long.

Rather than rushing back to the classroom, the plan was to arrive back to campus on a Saturday, allowing Dominique time to settle into school life slowly. Tired now, after all the reminiscing, but due to the thin howl of Bella's snoring, she was unable to sleep. She smiled and whispered out loud, "What a girl." That thought warmed her all over, and then she continued silently with her thought: *And she is my friend; no doubt, she loves me.*

This reality was so overwhelming and, at the same time, so transforming Dominique wept tears of joy. She could not understand all the peaceful changes erupting inside her, and it was scary and wonderful all at once.

Prior to dozing off, her last thought centered on Mrs. Martsen. Dominique was pleasantly surprised by the change she saw in her and wondered if this might be the end of the feud that had plagued their relationship since entering school. So many things had changed so quickly; she was caught up in so much, but she realized she was happy. *Imagine me happy*, she said to herself. But in the back of her mind, she wondered whimsically, *When and how will this, once again, all come crumbling down around my head?*

***

Dominique was not sure if it was Bella's insistence or if her classmates were different, but they seemed more cordial. Then, she had a weird moment; she stopped and evaluated the dynamic of that thought and said to herself, *Maybe the catalyst, which is rearranging my relationships, is a change in me.*

While she and Bella headed for lunch, she continued to wrestle with the thought she just had. Looking down, she imagined so many things changing in her life, and as she passed through the double doors of the cafeteria, she wasn't paying attention to people leaving the cafeteria and ran straight into someone exiting; they nearly bumped heads. So surprised by the collision, Dominique uttered a brief "oh," and then she looked quickly up. Hoping to make amends for not paying attention, Mrs. Allard stood there before her.

They instantly hugged each other and spun around into the cafeteria. Dominique could not believe her eyes, which were now filled with tears of joy, holding her at a distance. Dominique just stared at her. Finally, she settled and began to analyze their chance meeting. She thought, *This is Sunday and not Monday.* Then she said out loud to Mrs. Allard, "What are you doing here today?"

Gleefully responding, Mrs. Allard said, "I came to see you."

Wonderfully surprised, Dominique reflected on the days leading up to coming back to school. Now it was clear: what had been drawing her away from home and back to school was Bella and Mrs. Allard, and now she stood holding on to both of them.

As they sat together having lunch in the cafeteria, they laughed and cried, and all three were consoled. Sharing the amazing outcomes that had taken place at home and in her heart, Dominique said to them, "I had no idea what freedom felt like until I had the courage to share my pain with someone else. Now, even while it is still very hard, I don't have to deal with it alone." She bent her head down slightly and smiled, looking at one and then the other, and she said, "Thank you."

Leaning into the center of the table, Mrs. Allard said, "I thank God for you, and I think I can speak for Bella." She looked at Bella, and Bella nodded. Then, she continued, "We want to thank you for trusting that you would be safe in our care; thank you."

When Mrs. Allard said she thanked God for her, like always, when someone mentioned God, Dominique felt instantly uneasy, and it put a damper on her reunion with Mrs. Allard, but looking deep into her eyes and remembering how much this woman loved her, she let the God thing go and reaffirmed Mrs. Allard with a loving stare.

Unable to help herself, Bella threw her hands into the mix and rubbed Mrs. Allard and Dominique's arms; healing and bonding happened all at once, and their joy together was complete.

The other students in the cafeteria did not seem to be bothered at all by all the bonding that was happening right there before them. From time to time, some of them even smiled and nodded approvingly in the direction of the threesome.

Though the time together had been wonderful, it was also getting late, and Mrs. Allard needed to be heading home, so she stood and said, "This has been a blast, but if I am going to show up for my classes' tomorrow, I need to go home." Just before she turned to leave, she leaned down and whispered in Dominique's ear, "Don't forget our meeting in the morning." Dominique jumped up and gave Mrs. Allard one more hug, and then, she let her go.

* * *

Just like the night before, Dominique could not slow her brain down enough to sleep. She knew she needed to be rested for classes tomorrow, but there was nothing she could do; she was reliving every moment of her life since moving in with Bella.

The only sound in the room was Bella's soft snoring. Dominique smiled and considered the idea: *Maybe Bella's sleeping habit, like her fan at home, will have to be the sleep aid, which helps her to find rest.* Now, with her mind on Bella, she was frightened to be drawn back to the day and the conversation when Bella told her she was running from God, just like she was running from having to come to grips with Durand's evil.

She remembered how offensive that comment was, and just thinking about it again, she started to bristle. Shortly after, though, she realized that Bella was right about running and not confronting herself with Durand. This peace she knew now, and the support she has now, would never have happened had she remained bound in her fears.

She didn't like the idea of someone thinking she was running from anything, but she had to admit it: talking about God in any way upset her. Then she remembered the day when she told Bella about Durand raping her and the peace that came from sharing. She also remembered that just before they left the room, Bella said, "Let's pray."

Dominique became angry again, just thinking about the timing of Bella's comment, but she quickly refrained, alluding back to what Bella said. It echoed in her heart and mind as if she was standing next to Bella again, and she heard her say, "This is how I deal with things that are bigger than me. I take them to God."

Exhausted in her thoughts and actually becoming sleepy, Dominique said whimsically to herself, *Yeah, that might work for Bella, but who would go to God if you didn't trust Him?* And with that last thought, her eyelids became extremely heavy, too heavy to hold them open any longer. Not hearing Bella snore, not afraid of the night, she dozed off to sleep.

***

Maybe it was the bad memory of her first visit with Mrs. Allard, or maybe it was that final thought she had before falling asleep last night. *Am I running from God?* she asked herself. For some reason, Dominique felt uneasy about her counseling appointment this morning.

She had to admit she felt good about being back at school, and she loved rooming with Bella. She looked up from her bed to see if she could locate Bella, and there she was with her headphones on, dancing, almost spastically, oblivious to the world. Dominique could not hold back, and she burst out laughing, falling back onto her bed. As she fell back on her bed, Bella noticed the movement and stopped to look over at Dominique. Bella could see that her roommate was having a great time at her expense, so she gave Dominique a thumbs-up, bobbed her head, spun a couple of times, and, just exaggerating her gyrations, headed off to the bathroom.

Still laughing and thankful for her crazy roommate, Dominique sobered quickly as that same thought crept right back in: *Am I running from God?* Still trying to understand why going to see Mrs. Allard this morning was scary, she began to evaluate the trust factor with Mrs. Allard. She came to the conclusion that though she was not as close to Mrs. Allard as she was with Bella, she had to admit there was no reason to distrust her.

As she arrived at Mrs. Allard's office, she could hear her singing inside. She listened for a moment and was amazed at how beautiful her voice was. Captivated by the concert streaming from the other side of the door, Dominique pressed her ear a little closer to hear better. Just as she moved close, Mrs. Allard opened the door. Startled, Dominique leaned back; she couldn't help but look flustered. Mrs. Allard was surprised as well but just smiled and said, "Welcome! How is your morning going?"

Gathering herself together, Dominique smiled and said, "It is good."

Mrs. Allard waved her into her office, and she stepped in behind her desk. When she turned to sit down, she noticed Dominique was still standing outside the door. They just stared at each other for a moment, and Mrs. Allard said, "Is everything okay? Please come in."

Dominique slowly slid into the office and awkwardly settled into the chair in front of Mrs. Allard's desk. Reading "body language" is a key asset when digging deep into a hurting person's psyche. Mrs. Allard assessed quickly that Dominique was not her normal self and that something major was wrong. She continued to smile as if everything was normal and reached over for Dominique's hand, saying, "I sure loved visiting with you in the cafeteria yesterday. Since you left school for home, you have been on my heart and mind continually."

Having not broken eye contact, Dominique flinched slightly but allowed her hand to reach out for Mrs. Allard's. When their hands touched, Dominique's heart leaped, and tears filled her eyes. Not falling, the tears gathering made her eyes glimmer, and Mrs. Allard's heart nearly burst, wondering what other evils were tormenting this precious child.

Finally, the tears rolled out of her eyes, and Dominique wiped them away with her other hand and said, "I am sorry; I don't know why I am crying."

Reaching over with her other hand, Mrs. Allard covered Dominique's hand and, smiling, said, "Maybe that is what we will discover as we meet regularly." Maybe she didn't know why she was crying; there was so much she didn't know or understand, but again today, Dominique knew that Mrs. Allard had proved herself a trustworthy ally.

Relieved and beginning to relax, Dominique said, "I heard you singing before I came in; you have a beautiful voice."

As a methodology, Mrs. Allard's preferred style of counsel is conversational. With Dominique opening their time with a compliment, she measured her approach accordingly. She knew that, eventually, just by talking about life, Dominique would reach the place where they needed to go. So, she said, "Thank you. I am always singing. As a little girl, I nearly drove my parents crazy, screaming songs around the house. Do you sing, Dominique?"

Embarrassed, Dominique bowed her head slightly and shook her head. Mrs. Allard pushed a little and said, "Not at all?"

Dominique smirked a little and said, "Well, I do sing solo." Then she got a big smile on her face and said, "So low that no one can hear me." An old joke her dad told her.

Although Mrs. Allard had heard this quip many times before, hearing Dominique use it in such a corny way, she burst out laughing. Dominique never considered herself a jokester and rarely tried, but seeing Mrs. Allard losing it right before her, she became excited, and her smile turned into a big belly laugh too.

They sat laughing and enjoying each other, so Mrs. Allard grabbed the opportunity and said, "How do you feel now?"

Catching her breath and without thinking, Dominique casually said, "I feel good." Having said that, she had to stop and admit she had felt better at times, but she had not felt good in a very long time.

Seizing the good vibe, Mrs. Allard asked, "I know you have been through and are still going through so much. I am so proud of how you have responded to help. It will take time to process everything, but I feel you are making such great headway. I was glad to hear yesterday how well things are going at home." Still smiling, she paused and said, "Is there anything you need to share with me that is not going well?"

The question felt like an instant betrayal. Dominique's smile slowly ebbed away, and she became tight-lipped. She started to become fidgety sitting in her chair, and she broke eye contact with Mrs. Allard. More than fear gripped her, anger started to replace the joy she had just experienced. She knew she could tell Mrs. Allard anything she wanted, but she also knew the thing that was most unsettling now was Bella's comment: "You are running from God."

Mrs. Allard did not have to know the topic of what was causing her to suffer, but she did know that Dominique was ready to explode due to it. She didn't say anything; she just continued to stare lovingly at Dominique. With so many thoughts blazing haphazardly through her mind, Dominique could not hold it in any longer, and she just blurted it out, "I do not like to talk about God."

Wisely and still smiling, Mrs. Allard said, "We do not have to talk about God." That comment should have given Dominique the closure her countenance demanded, but instead, she knew she was exposed and in danger and that she would remain in danger if she chose to not talk it out.

Dominique was starting to see that trying to figure out how not to talk about God had made Him the center of her attention. She looked quizzingly over at Mrs. Allard, and it was becoming evident to her that her counselor was very wise.

She smiled a wry smile and said, "You know, that for me to not want to talk about God, it becomes the only thing I should be talking about? You know that, don't you?" Mrs. Allard just smiled and said, "Is that what you believe?" In any other case, Dominique would have felt victimized by such a blatant setup, but with Mrs. Allard, she just smiled and said, "I guess I do believe it is time I start talking about God."

∗ ∗ ∗

Without waiting for ground rules and as if she was angry at the world, Dominique began sharing the litany of disappointments she had experienced with God. She shared how, in the beginning, her early exposure to Him was exciting, and she believed God loved her. Then, she paused; her face took on a strange look. She said, "Then one day, it all went away, and I knew He didn't exist." As she said that, her features seemed to take on an air of confidence. She sat up tall, nearly reeling in the joy of a victory won; she had dispatched the God myth.

This wasn't necessarily where Mrs. Allard felt they should start the initial query, but Dominique had finally found an attentive ear, a sounding board, and she was making the most of this opportunity. Mrs. Allard knew just getting this weight off her heart was the beginning of real therapy.

Catching Dominique's eyes again, Mrs. Allard said, "So, if you think God does not exist, what is your dilemma? Is this why you don't like to talk about God?"

Dominique looked hard into Mrs. Allard's face, but it was evident to Mrs. Allard that she had lost some of her bravado. The harshness in her voice peeled off, and she quietly said, "My problem is…" And having said that, her voice trailed off as she completed the thought. She said, "The people who love me most, who I trust most, trust that He exists."

After hearing Dominique's problem, Mrs. Allard nearly jumped off her seat and had to quell her excitement. Dominique had just made a gigantic leap toward belief, and Mrs. Allard wanted to track with her, so she said, "Let me see if I hear you correctly. You are saying that in the past, God has been unreliable to you, and therefore, He is untrustworthy, but you cannot deny the evidence of the belief of those closest to you? Is that correct?"

Silently, in her mind, Dominique surveyed the question inside and out. One word that Mrs. Allard used kept flashing like a neon sign inside her head: the word "evidence." She was forced to consider the definition of evidence. Her thought processes went like this: *Since Mrs. Allard teaches science, she would have to admit true science needs evidence/facts to support a premise.* She continued in her thoughts, *Therefore, where is the evidence that God really exists?*

Restless in her chair, Dominique continued to contemplate the possibilities, and she continued inside her head, *How can you have faith without evidence? Isn't that intellectual suicide?* Then she stopped as if turning in another direction and said to herself, *How can I deny Aunt Colleen's love for me? How can I deny Bella and Mrs. Allard's unconditional love for me? And that's not all; it is impossible to deny the peace where they all live.*

Dominique didn't realize it, but as she wrestled with her thoughts, she had been staring right through Mrs. Allard. Suddenly, she realized where her gaze had landed, and she opened her mouth to speak. Stopping quickly, seeking clarity, she reexamined her conclusions, then said, "Faith is a funny thing. It's almost like, if you see the evidence, faith cannot exist."

As Dominique downloaded her thoughts into words, it became apparent to Mrs. Allard that Dominique had spent a good portion of time contending in the arena of faith but without coming to a solid understanding of the topic.

Believing that Dominique was on new ground, as far as her faith goes, and believing she had just now passed through some previously unopened spiritual door, Mrs. Allard decided to turn things up a notch.

She asked Dominique, "What do you think my role in our time together should be?" Dominique thought to herself, *Now, that seems like we just switched gears. We were talking about evidence versus faith, and now she alludes to her role in all this.*

It seemed to Dominique a weird question, so she had to reboot her brain to move where she felt Mrs. Allard wanted her to go. Then she thought, *Where does she want me to go?* Continuing her thoughts on the quiz, Dominique mused, *This is definitely a loaded question; she just fed me an allurement to fit her purposes.* So, Dominique threw out what she thought Mrs. Allard wanted, and she said, "To help me become like you, Bella, and my aunt, Colleen, right?"

Mrs. Allard read the sarcasm in Dominique's voice, and she heard the voice of a skeptic. Then she spoke to Dominique, saying, "In the long run, yes, I want you to be like me, Bella, and your aunt, but I do not want you to accept a Jesus that you do not fully understand. If you cannot really trust Him, I don't want you to be handicapped by an easy 'believism.'"

Confused, Dominique came right back and said, "So, you do not want my believing in Jesus to be too easy?" Beginning to feel somewhat frustrated, she followed up by saying, "Trust me, it is not easy to trust someone who promised, 'I will never leave you nor forsake you,' (recalling Aunt Colleen's favorite saying) when that promise has never been a reality for me."

Moving her head up and down so as to affirm Dominique's question, Mrs. Allard said, "Correct, we are in agreement; I do not want you saying yes to Jesus just because you feel pressured to do so from anyone, not me, Bella, or your aunt." Mrs. Allard could see that Dominique was tired of the mental gymnastics and said, "Well, that was a good session. Shall we meet again tomorrow?"

* * *

Leaving Mrs. Allard's office, Dominique felt somewhat let down by her counselor's therapeutic skills. She tried to rethink what they discussed, and it was a jumbled mess. The only thing that stood out to her was when Mrs. Allard said, "I don't want you handicapped by an easy 'believism.'"

Heading down the hall and still thrashing through her thoughts, she looked up to see Bella run into their room. Refocused on Bella, she smiled and quickly navigated the hallway, ready to join Bella in their room. Just as she was about to yell through the door a welcome to her roommate, she heard Bella weeping.

Dominique stopped dead in her tracks, and she said to herself, *This is not right; the only time I have heard Bella cry was when she was comforting me.* Dominique didn't know what to do, but she did know that Bella was too tough to let things get her down, and she said to herself, *What could have happened?*

Right in front of her, one of Dominique's greatest fears just took place. The dread of not knowing what to do to help someone who is suffering. She thought about turning and high-tailing it out of there, but the sad sounds pouring out from her beautiful Bella gripped her heart, and her fear turned to concern.

Dominique walked into the room, and there was Bella, sitting at her desk with her head in her hands, weeping softly. Emotions that Dominique had never known began welling up inside her, and she felt real pain in her chest. It physically hurt Dominique to see Bella this way.

Unable to do anything else, she ran over to Bella, fell to her knees, put her hand on Bella's head, and said, "Bella, what has happened?" Fearful of what she might say, she waited, but Bella said nothing. Dominique touched Bella's hand, leaned in softly, and said, "Please tell me what is wrong?"

Bella reached over, took Dominique's hand, and slowly turned her direction. As Dominique looked onto the terrible pain in Bella's face, she felt like she was frozen in time, and it was unbearable. Barely able to speak through her sobs, Bella made eye contact and said, "My grandpa died today." Instinctively, Dominique took Bella by both shoulders and pulled her close. At that, Bella started to tremble. Unable to cope alone, she fell into the comfort of Dominique's embrace.

As she held Bella, Dominique was sad, but she also felt strangely alone. There were so many things she wanted to share with Bella concerning her counseling session, and there were so many questions to ask. Alas, she knew Bella needed her now, not the other way around, and she felt strangely guilty for having such a selfish thought.

She stopped right in the middle of her selfishness to reconsider what she had just said. She repeated it in her mind, and the thought burst ripe with significance. She said it again: *Bella needs me.* There had never been a time in Dominique's life where this was the case. She marveled at the thought: *Someone needs me!*

CHAPTER 22

Bella left for home the next day, and Dominique was beside herself. It wasn't that Dominique did not feel good about helping Bella through this terrible time; in fact, she felt empowered and stronger than she ever remembered. She knew she had made a difference in someone else's life and that Bella was thankful for her. Even after all the caring and bonding, not to mention the healthy change that was taking place in Dominique's heart. It wasn't long after Bella left that the fear of being left alone set in.

Mrs. Allard stopped in after school to see how Dominique was doing. She told Dominique how proud she was of her to care for Bella the way she did. Dominique needed the encouragement and told Mrs. Allard how good it felt to be needed rather than to be the needy one all the time. Then, with a troubled look on her face, she confided in Mrs. Allard, sharing how much she relied on Bella and how she wasn't sure how she could make it without her.

Mrs. Allard seemed poised over Dominique's statement, holding for just a moment, then she said, "What did Bella say to you before she left?"

Dominique could never tell where Mrs. Allard was going with her questions, and this one was no exception, but she remembered perfectly what Bella said. "Well," Dominique began, "the first thing she did was to thank me for being a good friend and for comforting her in this bad time. After that, she told me she knew she could count on me and that because she needed her friend, she would call soon. The last thing she said was she would be praying for me and that I could call her any time I needed to, but the main thing she wanted me to remember was how much positive change was happening in my life and that I was capable of great things, even without her here."

"Is that all?" Mrs. Allard queried.

Then, Dominique remembered: "As Bella was heading out to her parents' car, she turned back and smiled at me, saying, 'Please do not forget me.' And I said, 'I won't.'"

After finishing what she remembered of Bella's farewell, Dominique looked up to see Mrs. Allard with a big smile on her face. Dominique could tell from Mrs. Allard's look and demeanor that she felt there was some hidden message in Bella's farewell. Dominique was becoming frustrated, and her face flushed because she was not good at interpreting subliminal messages. So, she just looked back at Mrs. Allard with a blank stare on her face, waiting for the punch line.

Mrs. Allard allowed the silence to sink in a little and then calmly said, "Dominique, who needs someone the most right now, you or Bella?" As Dominique was letting that question sink in, Mrs. Allard continued, "You are making a difference in Bella's life, and she in yours. What she is saying, what she wants to remind you of, is that even though she is gone for a while, you are stronger than you think you are. When she turned and said, 'Don't forget me,' what was the point of her last words to you?"

Dominique knew, by the finality of Mrs. Allard's question, that she was left to come up with the answer on her own. While her mind went blank again, it was apparent that Mrs. Allard was in no hurry for an answer. Then it hit her, and as it did, something wonderful happened: a transforming change filled her soul; the thought of Bella gave her peace and warmed her being.

Dominique made sure she had Mrs. Allard's full attention, and with a new confidence, she said, "Bella is telling me, 'Don't stop thinking about me.' And as long as I keep Bella on my mind, I will be at peace."

Nodding her head, Mrs. Allard said, "You may not completely see it, but since sharing your incredibly painful story, your life has changed dramatically, and the evidence is in the peace you bring to Bella and the peace she brings to you."

Dominique paused to take it all in, and as she did, she heard a knock on her door; it was Mrs. Martsen. Dominique said, "Come in."

As she entered, Dominique could tell by her smile that this was a new, softer, more caring Mrs. Martsen. Looking truly concerned, she said, "I just stopped by to see if you needed anything." Looking over at Mrs. Allard, she continued and said, "But I can see you are in good hands."

Dominique smiled, and as she did, she realized for the first time this smile wasn't faked. She warmly responded, saying, "Thank you, Mrs. Martsen, but I am doing good; I just wish Bella wasn't in such anguish."

Mrs. Martsen glanced over at Mrs. Allard as if to confirm Dominique's pleasant state of mind and said, "We all are saddened by her loss."

Watching Mrs. Martsen and Dominique build bridges back to each other was a joy for Mrs. Allard to observe. Then, she interjected, saying, "It is getting late, and I need to be going home."

Mrs. Martsen said, "Yes, I need to be leaving as well." Then she looked at Dominique and asked, "Is there anything you need before I go?"

Dominique responded, "I know it is not possible, but it would be great to have Bella here tonight." Then she smiled, knowing both of them understood her longing.

Mrs. Martsen looked straight into Dominique's eyes and said, "Yes, honey, that would be great for us all. We will miss her so much, but she will be back soon." Then she added, "I know what we can do for her; how about we say a prayer for her and her family before we leave?"

Mrs. Allard knew what Mrs. Martsen didn't know: Dominique's hesitancy with trusting God for real answers. As Mrs. Martsen waited for a response, Mrs. Allard looked over to Dominique for a reaction, and Dominique was staring right back at her. In the middle of that silent exchange, Mrs. Martsen said, "They must be hurting so badly; shall we ask God to help them?"

Dominique was feeling coerced, just like she did when Bella prayed in their room, but she remembered how loving Bella's prayer was, and she nodded a cautious approval. With that, Mrs. Martsen reached out for both their hands, bowed her head, and began to pray.

At first, Dominique was just hoping to get this quickly over with, but as she listened to Mrs. Martsen talk to God, it was like hearing this part of her for the first time: love and compassion flowing through words. Dominique found herself accepting the petition and desiring it to be answered. Mrs. Martsen ended the prayer by saying, "We know You—You who have promised, so we trust You will help Bella's family. In Jesus's name, we pray. Amen."

Dominique had heard amens her entire life. She had even said amen herself many times at church, but the word never meant anything to her. It was like adding an unnecessary tag on the end of a thought, but when she heard herself say amen at the end of this prayer (which surprised her), she wanted more than anything for the prayer to come true. She opened her eyes, but since she had never closed her eyes before while praying, she was embarrassed to see both ladies staring at her. She lowered her eyes and smiled self-consciously. They smiled back, hugged her, said good night, and left.

As Mrs. Martsen headed to her car, her heart was full of joy. Getting into the car, she paused, stared out the front window, and prayed, "Dear God, thank You for allowing me, by Your grace, to love, to really love." She started the car and headed home, but she could not stop thinking about the prayer they just had together and the magic of holding Dominique's hand. The touching of her hand wasn't just warm; it was electric. This touch was a bond, a connection, which she had lost but needed so badly.

Then, she thought about the hug she gave Dominique prior to leaving: how real it was. It was a cleansing hug because it felt like a wave of guilt lifted from her shoulders. Not necessarily that Dominique had forgiven her, but that God had changed her, and this was who she wanted to be.

After her two guests were gone, Dominique was instantly pummeled by frightful thoughts. She feared the walls of the room would start closing in on her and the memories of Durand would suffocate her, but to her surprise, they didn't. Although the ramifications of everything that was pouring through her head were colossal, she chose to hold her thoughts to the memory of Mrs. Martsen's prayer for her and Bella. Slowly, the fear subsided, and she began to tire. She went to bed confident and focused her mind on Bella, as she promised she would.

***

Though the morning found her alone, Dominique awoke unshaken and refreshed. Her first thought was, *I wonder how Bella is doing right now.* Those thoughts permeated her morning as she prepared to meet with Mrs. Allard. Just before Dominique headed out the door, she paused and looked around the room. She did not like being abandoned to herself and needed affirmation that she was not alone. Then, she remembered her two visitors from last night and how odd it was to be holding and hugging Mrs. Martsen, but at the same time, she felt that Mrs. Martsen's concern was real. Bolstered by some confidence she didn't fully understand, she turned out the light and left her room.

As with every school morning, the foot traffic in the hall was intense, so she looked carefully in both directions and entered her lane, but to her surprise and chagrin, there, waiting for her in the hall, was Sarah and Rachel. They both smiled and said, "Good morning." Then, Rachel said, "Can we walk you to breakfast?"

Shocked by their cordial greeting, Dominique did not know how to respond. She backed up slightly, surveyed both their faces, and, with a forced smile, said, "Why?"

Without missing a beat, Sarah jumped right in and said, "With Bella being gone, we thought you could use some company."

Sarah and Rachel were never up front with Dominique, and she instantly felt this was a setup. Knowing they were both highly unreliable, she couldn't believe her ears when she heard herself say, "Okay." They both grabbed her arms and shuttled Dominique down the hall, talking as if this was something that happened every day.

* * *

She could not remember much of what was spoken at breakfast; in fact, she was not sure she said anything during the entire meal, but she did sense that Sarah and Rachel were different. They both remarked several times how hard it must be for Bella to have lost her grandpa, and they both asked, "Without Bella being around, will you be okay?"

Part of her wanted to doubt anything they said, but on the other hand, they didn't have to do this, and here they were, attempting to make her feel better. Not sure where her next thought came from, she said to herself, *Maybe it is not them changing so much as it is me changing.*

As she headed to Mrs. Allard's office, that last thought took over her entire thought process, and she was forced to admit her entire life was littered with people with whom she could barely tolerate at all.

As those thoughts continued making inroads, fresh ideas came to her, and she said to herself, *The reason I hold people at a distance is so I don't have to deal with them.* This revelation was an unsolicited and disturbing enlightenment. Frustrated by where this was heading, she asked herself, *Does this need for estrangement just come naturally for me? Has my subconscious developed a mode of operation whereby I turn people away from me so as to make myself unapproachable?*

With that calamity racing through her mind, she looked up to see a smiling Mrs. Allard standing in the hallway. Not startled but still balancing the crazy thoughts blowing through her conscious, she brandished a weak smile and nodded to her waiting confidant.

Mrs. Allard kept smiling, but the coldness of Dominique's demeanor caused Mrs. Allard's antenna to signal concern. "You are right on time," Mrs. Allard said encouragingly. She continued, "How did you sleep?"

Dominique did not answer but moved into the room. Coupled with these new thoughts, she had not stopped wrestling over the direction of her last session with Mrs. Allard. She continued to be baffled by the comment Mrs. Allard made about not wanting her to trust in an "easy believism." Now, with these latest disclosures flowing in her mind, Dominique was starting to feel anxiety about where this counseling would eventually lead.

Seated in their customary chairs, Mrs. Allard stared at Dominique, but Dominique was somewhere else, and Mrs. Allard did not feel her gaze; she stared ahead, not engaged. Sensing the disconnect, Mrs. Allard reached across her desk and, taking Dominique's hand, asked, "Are you all right this morning?"

As if being called back from a long mental journey, Dominique looked up and forced herself to focus on Mrs. Allard. As she did, she quickly looked down to see her hand in Mrs. Allard's hand. Like awakening from a dream, she smiled and said, "Oh, I am sorry. What did you say?"

Mrs. Allard squeezed her hand and repeated the question, "Are you all right this morning?"

Awake now and in the conversation, Dominique paused for a moment to consider the question. She started to speak but didn't know what to say. Mrs. Allard gave Dominique a puzzled look and said, "Just tell me what is going on in your mind right now."

She paused again to clarify her thoughts and said, "It is like I am seeing myself for the first time. It is hard to acknowledge my insecurities and admit that, for so long now, I have shunned people with cruel deference. I have kept people at a distance to ensure my own safety, to keep them from seeing who I really am and from becoming vulnerable." She closed her thoughts by saying, "Then, to make things even harder, you tell me you do not want it to be too easy for me to believe in Jesus, the one who, you say, is the only one who can help me. I am confused. I am frustrated, and Bella is not here to help."

Completing her thought, Dominique just stared at Mrs. Allard as if to say, "This is partly your fault." Mrs. Allard was no longer smiling but remained pleasant in her demeanor and asked Dominique, "Has something happened recently that has led you to this self-disclosure?"

Hesitating, Dominique slowly said, "Well…" Then, she continued, "There have been several things that have happened; the freshest situation was at breakfast today with Sarah and Rachel. They escorted me to the cafeteria, and they were really nice. I have never trusted them to really care about me, but today, I saw them differently. They were concerned for Bella, they were concerned for me, and because I have never been good to them, they did not have to do that. She paused again to gain the courage to make the next statement and said, "What if I am the problem that leads to poor relationships?"

Now Mrs. Allard was smiling, and she responded, "Dominique, you are changing. You are softening, and that never really happens without self-examination." Dominique looked haphazardly at Mrs. Allard as if to say, "I need more input." Mrs. Allard continued, "Bella not being here has put you in a place where you have to evaluate yourself on your own, but without Bella's prior, faithful commitment to your life, you would not be ready to do so. You have found someone you can trust, and because of that, Bella has become someone other than an acquaintance, not someone you just use and dispose of. She is your friend, and I know you love her, and you are ready to sacrifice yourself for her."

Trying to read how Dominique just interpreted her response, she stopped to look closely at her, then said, "Maybe that is why Rachel and Sarah appeared so different because you are different; you see things differently now."

"Why am I different?" Dominique asked.

Mrs. Allard steadied herself and prayed, *Dear God, order my words.* And she said, "I believe it is because you have an aunt who loves you dearly. You have Bella, who loves you dearly, and you have me, who loves you dearly, and the thread that holds all of us together is Jesus. You are different because you have seen the love of God; you have experienced God's love. He is loving on you."

Initially, Dominique said nothing; she sat there analyzing and enduring the unsettling exposure just revealed concerning her life. Trying to put it all together, she made eye contact with Mrs. Allard and said, "If Jesus loves me, why do you say it is hard to believe in Him?"

With that question, Mrs. Allard thanked God for answering prayer and said to Dominique, "That is a great question, but you have to go to class now, and we will pick up tomorrow where we just left off."

Dominique couldn't believe her ears. Then, she thought to herself, *This is second time Mrs. Allard has done this, ending right in the middle of something big.* And she said to Mrs. Allard, "Why can't we just go on? I need that answer…"

Mrs. Allard smiled and said, "Yes, this has been a wonderful time; your presence makes me happy, but how about we pray together and ask God to help you and me find the answer, starting tomorrow? Besides, I have a class full of students waiting for me, and you have a teacher waiting for you. Can we pray together?"

Dominique stood up and said, "Will our prayer together really help me understand?"

Mrs. Allard reached for Dominique's hand and said, "I believe it will; God loves to answer prayer."

Not even thinking about it, Dominique allowed Mrs. Allard to grasp her hand, and as Mrs. Allard bowed to pray, so did Dominique. The request to pray made her feel a little uncomfortable; she was still not sure about this praying thing, but she listened intently to Mrs. Allard's prayer, and her words were soothing.

She found herself, once again, comforted and at peace in God's presence, but even in the midst of that comfort, her thoughts drifted to the real question, and she said to herself, *Is this prayer thing really getting through? Is Jesus hearing us? Is Jesus changing outcomes?* She tried to focus on Mrs. Allard's voice, but other voices were interrupting that goal.

***

As Dominique started to her first-period class, the thought of schoolwork appeared more like an abstract function of her day, a disconnect from that which had her attention. Deep in her own mind, still coping with the Jesus question, she looked up, and there before her were Sarah and Rachel again. Rachel said, "Everything still good?" Dominique nodded, and once again, almost incoherently like before, the two girls grabbed her by the arms and escorted her into the first-period classroom.

The rest of the day was hard. Due to the consuming question on her mind, classroom interaction was a blurred jumble of nonsense; she could not remember a single thing taught. Then, just before Dominique left her last-period class, one of her classmates approached her to ask her a question, saying, "Hey! If you hear from Bella, would you tell her my family and actually many school families are praying for her? She has been so good for our school; would you let her know we all miss her and wish her the best?"

Dominique didn't know how to respond; it took her by surprise. She didn't even know who this girl was, yet she was asking her for a favor. This was getting too weird. She nodded yes to the request, but she was so baffled by the interaction that she just stood there staring at the girl. The girl smiled, thanked Dominique, and said, "See you at supper."

After changing from her uniform, Dominique felt exhausted. Thinking she needed just to get a little rest, she laid her head down but fell into a deep sleep. She dreamt as she slept, but there was no rhythm nor reason to her thinking, just many disconnected ends. Then, her recurring worst nightmare captured her again; it took her by surprise, and there she was, trapped in the evil of Durand's desire. She could not get away; she wrestled frantically but to no avail. All she could do was scream for help.

The dream was so real; she could smell Durand. The reality of his abuse was once again upon her, and all she could do was scream, but no one heard her. Then, faintly in the far distance, she could hear a ringing. The ringing continued, and she clung to that sound, hoping it would overwhelm the cruelty of the moment. As she held onto the sound, she slowly felt herself lifting away from the clutches of Durand's hold on her.

Finally, screaming and disoriented, she burst awake, free from Durand's grasp but still hearing the ringing, the ringing that she had just realized had brought her safely to her room. She reached for her heart and tried to calm her breathing, and she realized that her blouse was soaking wet from sweat. She turned her head toward the ringing; then she realized it was her phone. She rolled off the side of the bed and rushed to the phone on the table. At the last ring, she picked it up, still disoriented and breathing erratically, and said, "Hello."

The wonder of the most angelic voice gently echoed into her ear, and Bella said, "Hey! I almost hung up; what took you so long?" Not sure of what just took place, but knowing she had been rescued, Dominique could not control herself, and she burst into tears, crying out loud into the phone.

Confused by the reception of her call, Bella just listened for a short moment. Then, she firmly spoke into the phone and said, "Dominique, whatever is wrong?" Dominique heard Bella's question but still continued to cry, clutching the phone and rejoicing in being awake and safe. Not knowing what to do, Bella spoke again, "Dominique, talk to me."

After another short pause, Dominique's voice shuddered, but she was able to say, "Bella, you just saved me from the most horrible situation."

Not knowing where this was going or coming from, Bella spoke softly and said to Dominique, "Please explain what is happening." Dominique explained the entire dream scenario to Bella and how her call brought her to safety.

Bella was thankful to hear the danger was in a dream, but at the same time, she felt guilty leaving Dominique to deal with her fears all alone, and she apologized, saying, "I am so sorry I have not been there for you…"

Dominique started to feel warm inside, and she smiled. It was hard for her to put anything into words. She knew this peace was real; she was no longer dreaming, and the only emotion she could identify was thankfulness for Bella. So, she let out an elongated sigh and said to Bella, "You are my hope when I feel hopeless." She continued, "I know you are dealing with a great loss and cannot be here; hearing your voice is all I need right now."

Dominique quickly brought Bella up to speed on how her classmates were treating her and how they were nice and helpful. She shared that her meetings with Mrs. Allard were sometimes very frustrating, but as they continued to open the dark doors of her soul, they were also encouraging.

She told Bella that Mrs. Martsen appeared to really care about how she was doing because every day, she would ask, "How are you doing?" Dominique attempted her best impersonation of Mrs. Martsen and, mimicking her, said, "Dominique, how are you doing today?"

Bella laughed at that and said, "It looks like you are in good hands."

Hearing Bella laugh forced Dominique to quit talking about herself and begin to consider her dear friend's loss. Her heart ached for Bella, and, like Mrs. Martsen did with her, Dominique knew it was her turn to love on Bella, and she surprised herself when she said, "Bella, how are you doing today?"

Hearing that question, Bella exhaled a deep breath of relief and said, "Aw, you care about me, don't you?" For some reason, tears began to well up in Dominique's eyes. Bella's comment crashed through some invisible, self-preserving barrier that Dominique had erected for protection, and she felt relieved and unburdened.

Since Dominique didn't respond to Bella's question, Bella hesitated briefly and said, "Did you hear me?" Dominique paused and sniffled a little, which Bella caught on to, but just before Bella could ask her if she was okay, Dominique said, "Yes, my dear friend. I love you."

CHAPTER 23

Knowing that Bella would be back soon was all Dominique needed to maintain her daily routine and to wait patiently for her return. The night after talking with Bella, Dominique decided to call her aunt, Colleen. She missed her so much and wished she could come and visit her at school. She was feeling very lonely.

When Aunt Colleen answered the phone, Dominique lit up and talked a mile a minute, sharing hurriedly all that was taking place at school. Colleen listened carefully and, at times, caught herself smiling in thankfulness for how it appeared God was changing her precious niece.

Finally, Dominique paused, and Aunt Colleen quickly jumped into the conversation. She said, "How wonderful it is to hear you excited again; it sounds like you have found peace. Is that so?"

Though not putting a damper on Dominique's fervor, that comment forced her to contemplate the question. She said to herself, *Yes, I am more at peace, but how does Aunt Colleen want me to reply? I know what she is fishing for. If I say yes, she will counter with, "I told you God would never leave you or forsake you."*

The pause on Dominique's end of the conversation left Aunt Colleen wondering if she hadn't pushed too much. She knew Dominique had a way of sidestepping "God stuff." It was like they both knew where this was going, but neither wanted to jump too far and spoil the time together.

After what seemed like forever for Aunt Colleen, Dominique took a deep breath and said, "Yes, my dear aunt, God has not forsaken me." After saying it, Dominique was bewildered by the profoundness of such a statement coming from her mouth. Aunt Colleen had to stop and check herself to make sure what she had just heard. Now, the silence was going in both directions.

Aunt Colleen could hardly contain herself, and she was thinking, *Do I ask a clarifying question to verify what I just heard, or do I wait for Dominique to clarify?* Then she thought, *No, this is in Dominique's court; I will leave it to her.*

On the other end of the line, Dominique knew, after hearing her say what she said, that her aunt, Colleen, would be dancing with excitement in her living room. She even pictured it. Then something strange happened; it was like going back in time. She began to relive all the wonderful time spent with Aunt Colleen and how the evidence of her love poured out in action on a daily basis. She said to herself, *There has never been anyone who cared for me like my aunt, Colleen.*

Dominique was surprised by her next thought, but that did not stop her from sharing it. It just rolled off her tongue like it was meant to be, and she said, "Aunt Colleen, thank you for loving me my entire life. I know you have been praying for me all this time as well, and I believe now, finally, that your prayers have been answered. I know God loves me because I see Him in you."

As excited as she was to hear Dominique say, "I know God loves me," Colleen did not hear excitement in Dominique's voice. It was more like surrender, with some regret, but Colleen remained optimistic because she also knew that was the starting point, which led to joy.

After a short exchange of love for one another, Colleen said, "You have been the greatest blessing in my life, and I thank God for you daily. I cannot wait to see you again." And with that, they ended their call.

Sitting at her desk, where the conversation just took place, Dominique fumbled with her thoughts. She leaned forward and rested her head on her hands, slowly moving her head back and forth, but her eyes remained stationary, fixed on the desktop. She stopped moving her head and began to rub her temples with her thumbs, hoping to soothe her thought processes, and as she did, the desktop started to get blurry until it was not visible.

Aware that her eyes were closed but not completely aware of what she was doing, she surprised herself when she heard her voice saying, "Okay, God, this is it. Here I am." Not hearing God respond, she waited, but the only sound she could hear was the sound of her heart pounding loudly in her ears.

Then, she thought, *If He's not talking, what does God want to hear from me?* Then, she realized she was talking to herself and not to God. She shook her head and refocused on the one she had invited into her belief system, and she began again: *It appears that I am indebted to You. It is evident that You have chosen to move into my life. It is undeniable that You have placed love all around me. I am not completely sure how or why, but I feel Your presence.*

She paused again to consider His presence and that He was truly listening, and she continued, *Aunt Colleen has told me about You my entire life, but I never could believe her. Until recently, You have only been cold and unavailable, and I have been angry with You.* She paused again, and as she did, she could feel tears running down her nose and onto her lips. Then she cried out in her soul and said, *I do not want to be angry with You anymore. I believe You will never leave me or forsake me; please forgive me for who I have become and heal my pain. I cannot do this alone any longer; I need You.*

She didn't look up or open her eyes, but instantly, she knew that something mighty had just happened to her. It wasn't like she could hear His voice, but then again, did she? It wasn't subliminal. Whether audible or not, it was clear; the message was: "I will never leave you nor forsake you."

Just as if someone had spoken to her, Dominique opened her eyes and quickly looked around her room. God was not physically in the room, but His words resonated in her soul, and she knew she was not alone. It was like the slipping of Satan's grip on her heart. Knowing God's presence was real, Dominique started to cry, and her tears were tears of joy. In a peace she had never known, she laughed wholeheartedly and said, "Thank You, Jesus. I believe You."

***

As soon as she hung up the phone with Dominique, Colleen was beside herself; she could hardly contain the joy welling up in her heart. She thought to herself, *I have to tell somebody; I need to call Marie and tell her what has happened to her girl.* Then she stopped, saddened by the fact that Marie may not be excited about that good news; she refocused and knew there was only one person to call. Reaching quickly for her phone, she nearly dropped it. Her fingers were shaking with excitement, and she said, "Chloe will be overjoyed." And she dialed her number.

Colleen was right; Chloe was overjoyed and thankful for having received such good news. They laughed and cried together. After some time, the exuberance of the moment began to wane, and Colleen said, "What do I do now?"

Chloe suggested that she take her time and not push Dominique but rather watch and see how God leads her. Chloe continued by saying, "Dominique needs fellowship, being with like-minded people. She has that at school with Bella and Mrs. Allard, but now, she also needs time alone with God. If He has called her and she has answered that call, He will not stop calling until she is securely, willingly abiding in His embrace."

Sensing Colleen was having a puzzled moment understanding her comment, Chloe remarked: "Don't you remember the days after you first believed? You were confused and even angry. You were angry with me, Thomas, and Marie because you had not yet known the loneliness that takes place when we turn to Jesus to be our all but then try to live on our own."

Chloe became silent, waiting for Colleen to reflect. Colleen's thoughts went back to the days after trusting that Jesus would never leave her or forsake her, and she remembered how sad and lonely she was while being angry with God for not accepting her as she was. It came back clearly; she had no peace until she accepted the fact that she needed to repent of her sin before God could forgive her.

Colleen finally spoke up and said, "Yes, I do remember. You are right: Dominique has so many questions right now, and I need to wait for her to ask.

Chloe affirmed Colleen's summation and said, "Our job has not changed because of this revelation; we are still locked in a battle for Dominique, and prayer is our weapon."

Colleen agreed, and Chloe suggested they pray together for Dominique. Chloe asked Colleen to lead their prayer. This time, Colleen was not afraid to pray; she prayed with courage and determination, and she was surprised by how confident her words were as she petitioned God. She trusted God was listening, and knowing that Chloe agreed with her requests, she went on in power, praying for Thomas and Marie as well. Deep in prayer, Chloe smiled. She was blessed to hear her friend speak with such wonderful confidence before the throne of God.

After the prayer, Chloe spoke up and said to Colleen, "How are Thomas and Marie doing?" Chloe was broaching the thought that they may not fully understand all that has happened.

Finally getting to the point, Colleen said, "They are not doing well. I believe they are both still guilt-ridden for what Durand did to her. They are blaming themselves, especially Thomas, but Thomas is going to church, and Chase is meeting him there, whereas Marie will not go."

Chloe simply said, "God is using this awful thing to draw them to Himself. That will have to be on His time. You and I will pray. Remember what I said about pushing Marie? It must be God now, shining through Dominique, that her mom sees the truth."

Colleen agreed, and after one more rejoicing in God's goodness, they said goodbye.

CHAPTER 24

Hal Sealy hurried up the church driveway as he saw Thomas walking into the church foyer. "Hey, Thomas," he shouted. Thomas turned abruptly and paused; he was pleased to see Hal running to catch up with him. Thomas held out his hand as Hal came close, but Hal had no handshake in mind. He reached out and gave Thomas a firm hug and said, "Good to see you; how have you been?"

Thomas wasn't sure about guys hugging, and he felt sort of uncomfortable, but he also felt, which surprised him, a warmth in his soul. He stared at Hal, and Hal's face lit up. It appeared to Thomas that he was so because he was really glad to see him. Hal asked, "Where is Chase?"

Thomas responded, "He is out of town this week; something to do with his love life."

Hal laughed and said, "I really like Chase; what a great young man he is."

Chatting lightly, they turned and headed down to their Sunday school classroom. After the lesson, before the church service, they headed to the coffee bar for refreshment. The coffee shop was overflowing, so after getting their drinks, they went outside and found a table with an umbrella and sat down.

Thomas was really beginning to trust Hal; they talked about everything, and it was peaceful getting to know him. Thomas was not surprised that Hal sincerely cared about how Dominique was healing. He always asked about her and Marie, and true to form, his first words were, "How is Dominique?"

As he filled Hal in on the latest Dominique news, Thomas caught himself considering the fact that he did not have any real close friends at all, none; the business was his best friend, and for the most part, he hated the small talk it took to maintain a friend.

Hal was different; in fact, Hal was special. Like so many of Thomas's associates, Hal was not glib nor indifferent; everything seemed to matter to Hal deeply. Thomas was sure Hal had God as his source for exuberance, but Hal never wanted to push the issue.

Then, a thought jumped into Thomas's mind to ponder, and he said to himself, *Maybe I like church, not so much because God is here but that Hal is here.* Ending that thought, Thomas realized he had been off on his own mental excursion and that Hal must have asked him a question because he was staring at him, waiting for an answer. Thomas blushed and said, "I am sorry; what did you say?"

Hal repeated the question, "How is Marie handling the new family dynamic?" It seemed to Thomas that every time Hal asked a question, it forced him to think deeply, as if there was no simple answer to his questions. Thomas knew Hal was a confidant and that the question was heartfelt, but with each new opening up of his life with Hal, there seemed to be strings attached, strings that Thomas wasn't sure he wanted to be tied up.

Then, in his heart, something happened, and Thomas just took it for granted. Hal cared about him and his family; there were no ulterior motives. So, Thomas went further than he thought he could and told Hal of Dominique's attack and who did it.

Hal stopped for a moment to make sure he heard Thomas right. Then, he surprised Thomas by reaching across the table and grabbing Thomas's hand. Thomas nearly pulled his hand back, but in the middle of that thought, he realized that Hal was not only reaching out to him, but he also saw tears welling up in his eyes. Somewhat embarrassed, Thomas allowed Hal to grasp his hand, and as that connection happened, with tears running down his face, Hal said, "I am so sorry…"

* * *

Driving home from church alone, Thomas went over his conversation with Hal and wished Chase was with him. Chase was as close to his dad as anyone could be. Chase wasn't afraid of his dad like the rest of the crew, and he could hold his own in any debate. That's what Thomas liked about Chase: he didn't suck up to him, and money was not his top priority; he could take it or leave it.

Chase was occasionally tough on his dad; he often warned him about how his mom suffered at coming in second to the business. With all the issues his mom and dad had with Dominique, Chase also learned it was his place to be second to his little sister.

Chase found his strength in the home from his aunt, Colleen. In so many ways, he could have been damaged beyond repair, but with the love and commitment from Aunt Colleen, he found solace in the midst of this dreadful time in his life.

When Aunt Colleen first moved into their home, Chase was confused and angry with everything, especially his little sister. He felt like a prisoner to her whims, and it was all because Mom and Dad would force him to cater to those whims. Angry with the whole world, but mainly Dominique, he would run to his room and throw anything he could get his hands on; that is what six-year-olds do when they have no outlet for fairness or revenge.

As busy as she was, helping Marie with housework and Dominique, Colleen still found time to comfort and guide Chase.

The summer after Chase had graduated from high school and was enrolled in college, he and Thomas were driving, coming home from church. As Chase was at the wheel, Thomas couldn't help but notice how grown up his youngest son was. All the boys were smart; he knew they got that from their mom, but Chase excelled in everything, not just chasing money but in all aspects. He was highly respected among his peers and could handle any challenge. As he stared at his son, he marveled at this young man who never seemed to need his dad's help. He was square-jawed, tall and handsome, more rugged than the other boys. Thomas was very proud of Chase; he always wondered how he turned out so different from the other children.

Thomas had to admit the rest of his clan were pretty self-centered and needy, but Chase looked out for others. He was a self-starter and seemed at peace with the world. So, as they moved along home, Thomas asked Chase, "What makes you tick, Son?" Realizing his youngest son was special but not sure why, Thomas just had to ask.

Chase glanced quickly at his dad with a look of, "Boy, was that left field?" Then, he said, "What do you mean, Dad?"

Not being a great conversationalist but trying to learn to be with his son, Thomas realized he had asked an obscure question, and he followed up by saying, "You know, you are so different from your siblings."

Staring straight ahead at the road, Chase contemplated the question, thinking, *What is Dad fishing for? Is he really asking me why I am so different from my brothers and sister?* Knowing how much his mom and dad have suffered since the Dominique and Durand saga, Chase measured his words and boldly said, "Dad, I was kind of on my own a lot; I had to learn to survive. I don't blame you and Mom. You had Dominique, and I understand that, but I had Aunt Colleen, and without her, I don't think I would have made it."

Knowing he had not been a good father, Thomas tried not to flinch, but the sting in the comment just clarified what he knew to be true. Thomas bowed his head and agreed with his son, saying, "Yes, you did have Aunt Colleen, and I am thankful for her and for you."

Chase reached over and put his hand on his dad's arm and said, "I love you, Dad."

Feeling melancholy, Thomas bowed his head again and, nearly whispering, said, "I love you too, Son." Enjoying the peace of their father-son time, they remained silent the rest of the way home. Thomas couldn't help but feel blessed to have such a wonderful son. He thought to himself, and he was saddened to think it. He said to himself, *Except for Dominique and just recently for her, none of the other children have told me they love me.*

That thought stayed with him the rest of the night. At bedtime, he went into his room, and there sat Marie, putting lotion on her hands and arms. She looked up when he entered and smiled, which always made his day. He reached over and began rubbing her shoulders, then said, "Chase told me that he loved me today."

* * *

At first, going to church with his dad was compulsory, but spending time around Aunt Colleen helped Chase learn to trust Jesus, and then he wanted to go. He learned more each week in Sunday school, coupled with service sermons. He grew to the place where he could "give an answer to anyone who asked him about the hope he had."[14]

High school was the place where he honed his courage to be faithful to God. Because he went to church and didn't party, most of the students thought he was a wimp, but his antagonists learned quickly that Chase was not someone to overlook when it came to applying critical thinking to life's questions. I guess you could say he believed what he believed and could back it up. They knew he was dangerous but under control.

He prayed every morning before heading to school and asked God to use him around his peers, and God did just that. He was bold, and the more he was able to share the argument for a historical Jesus, the more people were willing to hear about the biblical Jesus. Due to his persistence, and for the first time ever, the school administration allowed a before-school Bible study on campus, and Chase led it.

Most of his peers believed he was a cult leader, and his disciples were all brainwashed. Little by little, however, students who came in contact with someone in the group were eventually won over by how caring they were and that they had answers to the big questions.

* * *

As the weeks went by, Thomas could not stop reliving the moments with Chase and what he had said on that day driving home from church. Though it was difficult to admit his failings as a dad, it was almost refreshing to his soul after all the frustrating days dealing with Dominique's issues.

Thomas could not help but see that Chase was a man of God and at peace. He longed for whatever it was his son had but was dubious about the source of Chase's enlightenment, but more and more, he found himself yearning for further time with his youngest son.

It was in that backdrop of those thoughts that one day, he was surprised to receive a phone call from Dumas. Thomas had purposely allowed Dumas to fade from his day-to-day life. It was too hard to think about Dumas because when he did, he was forced to remember what Durand had inflicted on Dominique. He still loved his brother, and he knew that Dumas was destroyed by what happened, but he could not see a way for them to be close again.

After saying "hello," Thomas was shocked to hear Dumas say, "Hey, Brother." With his mind reeling, he froze and could not respond. After waiting some time for a response, Dumas said, "I know you probably do not want to speak with me, but I had to reach out to you." Stumbling at what to say, Dumas paused and then continued, "Thomas, I don't know what to do."

Going back over in his mind their last conversation, Thomas remembered how hard it was to hear Dumas apologize over and over again and still have it land without meaning, so cold in his heart. Thomas still could not speak; he didn't know what to say. Just then, Chase walked into the kitchen to see his dad standing lost and in shock. His dad's hands were shaking, and he had a look of terror on his face. Chase said to his dad, "What is it? Who is it on the phone?" Thomas just handed the phone to his son and walked out of the room.

Hearing Chase's voice in the background, Dumas quickly moved to end the call, but just before he did, he paused and slowly brought the phone back to his ear to hear Chase say, "Hello. Is anybody there?"

Dumas could not have felt more at a loss, but he knew he had to respond. He didn't know how, and he said, "Hello, Chase. This is your uncle, Dumas." Chase had been praying for Uncle Dumas; he was brokenhearted, knowing how much his uncle was suffering, not just the great loss of his son but the loss of what he thought was Dominique's affection and her brother's bond.

This thought brought tears to Chase's eyes, and he excitedly said, "Hello, Uncle Dumas. It is so good to hear from you."

Dumas was surprised beyond belief by Chase's warm greeting. He thought to himself, *How mature he sounds on the phone.* Then he said, "I called to talk with your dad; I guess you can see how that went."

Chase responded, "Yeah, Dad is lost right now, but I believe he will come around." He continued, "It has been too long; it is so good that we can talk."

Dumas nearly burst out crying, and he fought it off, but Chase did hear a brief shudder in his uncle's voice. Dumas, crying silently now, could not continue, and Chase was keen to the awful suffering that was happening on the other end of the line. Trying to lighten up the moment, Chase said, "Where are you? Are you at home?"

Attempting to gain control of his emotions, Dumas didn't answer right away, but then, with his voice shaking, he said, "No, I am in New York."

Animated now, Chase said, "Wow! That is great. Is there a chance we can get together?"

Hardly able to believe it, Dumas said, "Yes, when and where?"

They decided to meet in the suburbs for lunch. Just as he was heading out the door, his dad walked up and said, "Chase, where are you going?"

Running out the door, he screamed back with excitement, "I am going to have lunch with Uncle Dumas." And off he went.

As he watched his son bounding for his car, Thomas was left with a keen thought: *Who is this son who treads so boldly and gently through the harshness of this world's merciless terror?*

* * *

Overjoyed with the time spent with Chase, Dumas drove back to his hotel smiling. Their time together was therapeutic; the presence of his nephew was healing to his soul. Still unable to take it all in, he started to tear up.

Remembering his conversation with Chase, Dumas found it difficult to believe that Dominique still loved him dearly and wasn't holding what Durand did to her against him. Strengthened by this good news, news he was not sure would ever come, he smiled, thinking to himself, *My family is not lost to me.* Still, he could not help but fear the state of his relationship with Thomas and Marie, and he thought about visiting them, but he did not know how to begin.

On the other hand, Thomas was nervously wondering what was going on in Dumas's and Chase's lunch meeting. Thomas became angry, not at Chase or Dumas but at himself and his inability to start moving forward in the healing process. It was becoming evident to Thomas that Chase had a better grip on the needs of their family than he did.

Thomas paced anxiously back and forth, looking out the front window, hoping to catch Chase coming back. Just as darkness was setting in, Marie arrived home from visiting with Colleen. Light poured boldly from the foyer area of the house, and as she pulled near to the garage area, Marie could see Thomas pacing methodically in one direction and then the other, and she thought, *Something is not good.*

Even though he knew Marie had arrived home, Thomas was caught off guard when she entered the foyer. Thomas jumped when she said his name. He grabbed his chest and said, "Please don't do that."

Marie looked strangely at him and said, "Don't do what?"

"Sneak up on me," he said.

Marie moved past Thomas to the coat closet to deposit her wrap, and as she did, she stared at him, probing his face. After a brief moment, she said to him. "What is wrong with you?"

He countered, "You scared me, that's all; I wasn't expecting you to sneak up on me." Marie knew that when Thomas was like this, it was better to let it go than to try to figure this out. She shook her head and left the foyer for the kitchen.

After about ten more minutes of waiting on Chase, Thomas moved into the kitchen, where Marie sat drinking a glass of water. At first, she didn't look up, and Thomas knew he had blown it with her in the foyer. He cleared his throat, moved close, and sheepishly said, "I am sorry for being weird."

Marie had already calmed herself, realizing she was more concerned for Thomas than she was angry with him, and besides, she knew he would soon be coming in to tell her what was bothering him. Having no idea what to expect, she looked up at him and said, "What has happened?"

As always, Thomas started fidgeting, trying to quiet his nerves, and then he just blurted it out, "Dumas called today."

That was news Marie was unprepared to hear. She quickly looked out the window and stood up, then she walked over to Thomas and said, "Why?"

Thomas knew his bride would need more input after a bombshell like that. He was instantly embarrassed; he could not tell her why Dumas called because he never spoke to him. Thomas was caught off guard and could not muster the courage to talk with his brother.

When Marie heard Thomas's explanation of not knowing what to say to Dumas and that he just handed the phone over to Chase, she nearly lost it. She wondered, "How do I remain sane with a man like this?" She looked at Thomas, and that look scared him; he could see she was about ready to boil over, but she didn't boil over. She took a deep breath and reached for Thomas's hand. Relieved that she was not going to kill him, he tried to lighten the moment and smiled cautiously.

Just then, Chase sauntered into the kitchen; he could see the tension on both his parents' faces, and he was sure he knew why they were so. Both of his parents, aware now that he had talked with Dumas, turned simultaneously toward him. Their look of expectation told Chase he needed to spill the beans about Dumas. Not missing a beat, Chase put a great big smile on his face and said, "Wow! What a day I had with Uncle Dumas."

Chase continued on to divulge the content of the time spent with his uncle. He told them how sad Dumas was and how he couldn't seem to move forward since Durand's death. Chase attempted to draw his parents into the loneliness that was his uncle's life. He shared the daily desperation that Dumas lived, knowing what Dominique suffered at Durand's hands. He continued to force them to see the untenable position that Dumas found himself in and the anguish of his suffering, which never ends.

Chase finished the details of his meeting with Uncle Dumas by sharing his uncle's last thoughts. With tears welling up in his eyes, Chase looked softly at his mom and dad and said, "Uncle Dumas's greatest fear is he will never have fellowship with you two again. He knows he cannot say how sorry he is enough, but he also knows how futile it is to not move beyond being sorry."

As Chase delved into the details of his time spent with Dumas, resentment began to foment in Marie. For the first time since Chase began sharing, she looked down, and she could feel her face begin to flush. Then she looked up rapidly and said heatedly, "What does Dumas expect from us?"

Chase was not surprised by his mom's retort, but Thomas was surprised. He looked first at Marie and then, affirming her thoughts, looked back at Chase as if to say, "Yeah, what does he expect?"

Not in a condescending way but in a benevolent plea for his uncle, Chase stared confidently at his parents and said, "He wants you to forgive him. He needs you to forgive him, and I agree with him."

As if Chase had just sworn at them, they both leaned back simultaneously and peered curiously at their son. They looked at each other and then back at Chase, but before either could speak, Chase continued, "Unless you do forgive Uncle Dumas, you will never be whole yourselves."

Not happy with what she just heard, Marie refocused and began to consider harsh words to continue her onslaught on Dumas, but when she opened her mouth to speak, she was left with no words. Looking intently at his mom, standing there with her mouth wide open, Chase turned his head down slightly, then looked up slowly, and smiling gently, he said, "Mom?"

Thomas, sensing he was caught in a crossfire, took a small step away from Marie, then realizing he had just revealed his allegiance, stepped back toward her even closer. Marie's focus remained riveted on her son's face, but unable to maintain the ire, she turned slowly away and silently left the room.

Thomas stared intently at Marie as she left the room, and then he turned toward Chase. Chase remained where he was, still smiling inquiringly. Unsure of what just happened and hoping, by the look on his face, to send some subliminal message to his son, Thomas stared strangely frozen at Chase. Still focused on the need in the family, Chase stared back at his dad and said, "Dad?" Thomas blinked a couple of times as if he was just waking up, then shook his head and turned to follow Marie.

CHAPTER 25

As she headed to Mrs. Allard's room for counseling, Dominique felt uneasy. Since her prayer with Jesus over the weekend and the change that seemed to be real concerning God, she remained puzzled by Mrs. Allard's statement from their last session concerning "easy believism."

Dominique was never puzzled, though, by the warm reception she could count on at seeing Mrs. Allard. As always, Mrs. Allard was standing in the hallway when Dominique looked up from her troubled thoughts, and there she was, smiling from ear to ear. "Good morning, Dominique," she said joyfully. "How are you this day?" she then continued. Trying not to seem unreceptive but still struggling with the "easy believism" dilemma, Dominique forced a cheap smile but did not speak.

Mrs. Allard, reading quickly the temperature of Dominique's response, said, "I sense you have spent the weekend contemplating our last conversation."

As Dominique entered Mrs. Allard's office, she stared cautiously at her mentor, wondering, *How could she know my thoughts?*

As they sat there together, Mrs. Allard jumped right in and said, "Well, what has happened with you since our last meeting? What new thing have you discovered over the weekend?"

Dominique was never comfortable when people in her life seemed to have her figured out, so she balked. She looked up from Mrs. Allard's desk and rather coldly said, "What makes you think I have discovered anything new?"

This was a dead giveaway for Mrs. Allard and confirmed her suspicion that something was discovered, but she wisely played along, saying, "Oh, I just thought, with you wanting to continue, when our last session ended, you would delve more deeply into it by yourself. Maybe I am wrong. What, then, shall we discuss today?"

Beginning to feel guilty being deliberately contentious with Mrs. Allard, Dominique changed her countenance, peered sincerely into Mrs. Allard's eyes, and humbly said, "You already know me so well. I did discover something over the weekend."

Mrs. Allard remained still and focused on Dominique's eyes but said nothing. Dominique began to sense and admit that she was somewhat embarrassed about her amazing time in prayer with Jesus, as if she was not completely sure about her total surrender.

Then, a peace that was so strange but so exciting overtook her fears, and she felt compelled to tell Mrs. Allard her good news. Not sure how to start, but knowing it had to be shared, she just blurted it out, "I confessed my sins to Jesus and accepted His forgiveness for my sins."

Nearly jumping out of her skin and wanting to jump over her desk and quickly embrace her young friend, Mrs. Allard had to contain herself. She sat forward in her chair, leaning toward Dominique, smiling warmly, and said, "What does that mean, Dominique?"

Dominique loved Mrs. Allard so much but could hate her at the same time, and she thought to herself, *You, of all people, should know what that means; you are the one who told me about Jesus dying for my sins.* Then she stopped and had to admit that what had happened to her had not yet been completely fleshed out. So, she reevaluated Mrs. Allard's question thoughtfully.

She was surprised by the boldness and the clarity that formed in her mind. Then, she looked down briefly and quickly back up again and said confidently, "It means I know I am no longer alone. I know God is alive inside me. I know He has been chasing after me for so long, and I have been pushing Him away, but now I have chosen to let Him into my heart. I have comfort I have never known; I know He will never leave me. I guess that is called peace."

She paused, staring out at nothing, and joyfully reimagined that precious time alone in prayer with Jesus, and then she let her shoulders go limp. She put her hands on Mrs. Allard's desk and reached over for Mrs. Allard's hands. As their hands embraced and their eyes locked again on each other, Dominique said, "What I have discovered is, with Jesus, I am not afraid to live any longer."

At first, Mrs. Allard did nothing; she just smiled softly at Dominique. Dominique stared back, anticipating some confirmation, some acknowledgment to the immensity of what she just shared with Mrs. Allard.

Tired of no response, Dominique said, "Well?" She could not wait for another second and was becoming agitated at Mrs. Allard's silence when suddenly both of Mrs. Allard's eyes began to blink rapidly as if attempting to hold back the undaunted emotion, but to no avail, the tears streamed down her face, and she jumped quickly over to Dominique, and as Dominique stood, they embraced tightly.

Now, both weeping and clutching at each other, they moved side to side as if dancing in bliss. It did not matter how long they had been embracing; they were caught up in the joy of freedom. This freedom brought courage, and that courage brought hope; she delighted in her new life.

Finally, Mrs. Allard pulled back to investigate Dominique's eyes and said, "Oh, my love, you are my answer to prayer." As if she knew exactly what Mrs. Allard meant, Dominique smiled broadly back, but as she peered into Mrs. Allard's face, an unanswered question brazenly assaulted her newfound joy, and she asked herself, *Easy believism? This is anything but easy.*

Sensing some change in Dominique's presence, coupled with the strange look on her face, Mrs. Allard said, "What is it?"

Due to the glorious moment they just spent together, Dominique felt trapped by the question and was unsure what she was feeling. She moved back a step, braced herself, and said, "Is all I have experienced only easy believism?"

Anticipating this change of gears, Mrs. Allard quickly responded, "What a great question." She motioned for Dominique to sit again. Moving back behind her desk, Mrs. Allard sat down as well and picked up the Bible she had lying on her desk. Dominique became suddenly aware of the great significance of the book in Mrs. Allard's hands.

Looking at the Bible open in Mrs. Allard's hands, Dominique watched as she quickly turned the pages, then stopped and looked up at her. Though hardly versed in it, Dominique had grown up with a Bible always near, and though she found it easy to pick and choose the parts of scripture she liked and disliked, she always knew that this book was the one that revealed who God was. She sat nervously, anticipating what was next.

Pausing to reflect on what she was reading, Mrs. Allard suddenly stopped and glanced up at Dominique and said, "This is the very Word of God; do you understand that?" Though she nodded gracefully, Dominique was not sure what she meant. Mrs. Allard continued, "That being the case, we must know what the scriptures say about God and why He has made Himself known to us." She paused again and said to Dominique, "I want you to listen very carefully to what I am going to read precisely from the book of Luke, chapter 9, verses 22 through 24."

Dominique thought to herself, *She must know that Bible well; she knew exactly where to turn to.*

Before Mrs. Allard began reading, she said to Dominique, "God's Word is so powerful and life-changing that we need to pray before we read it to ask God to bless us with hearing correctly what He says." She grabbed Dominique's hand and said, "Let's pray." As she did, she closed her eyes.

Though still a little uncomfortable about prayer, Dominique closed her eyes as well and waited expectantly. Bowed together, Mrs. Allard began to pray, saying, "Dear God, help us to understand what we are about to read; in Jesus's name, I pray. Amen."

She began reading:

> And he said [meaning Jesus], "The Son of Man must suffer many things and be rejected by the elders, the chief priests and the teachers of the law, and he must be killed and on the third day be raised to life."
>
> Then he said to them all: "Whoever wants to be my disciple must deny themselves and take up their cross daily and follow me. For whoever wants to save their life will lose it, but whoever loses their life for me will save it."[15]

Dominique found the coincidence odd because this was the exact verse that Aunt Colleen shared with her prior to going back to school.

Mrs. Allard finished reading, turned to Dominique, and said, "Do you understand what Jesus is saying here?"

Keeping eye contact with Mrs. Allard and trying to draw back on the many things Aunt Colleen taught her about Jesus, Dominique realized she had heard this very hard teaching from her aunt, but until now, she had no way of applying it. She continued staring at Mrs. Allard. The only thought that came to mind was: *This is so hard.* And then she heard herself say the same thing out loud to Mrs. Allard: "This is so hard."

Unchanged in her demeanor, Mrs. Allard calmly said, "Thus, 'easy believism.'"

Fighting the urge to feel ripped off, Dominique struggled for words. She quickly went back over the prayer time she had with Jesus and the words she spoke to Him. The words were clear in her mind, and she said them again to herself, *Thank You, Jesus; I believe You.* Then, she said to herself, *I said the words, 'I believe You.' Did I mean it?* Finally giving up, she shrugged and stopped the wrangling in her head and just looked helplessly toward Mrs. Allard.

As if she knew exactly the precipice that Dominique straddled, Mrs. Allard said, "Do not panic;

let's take this slowly and work through why you feel the way you do right now. It is normal to be uncertain when life and death are in the balance."

The finality of Mrs. Allard's last words struck Dominique fully. Jesus was asking her to give up her life, to sacrifice her life completely for Him, and she said to herself, *How could He ask that of me? Better yet, how could I ever possibly submit to such a charge or have the strength to endure it?*

By Dominique's body language and the look on her face, Mrs. Allard knew she needed to intervene quickly, so she said, "In the midst of this turmoil you are feeling right now, you have forgotten the one thing that makes His request possible." She paused to ensure she had Dominique's full attention. That pause brought Dominique quickly alert as if saying, "What have I forgotten?" Mrs. Allard said, "You have forgotten His promise, His part of the bargain. He has told you, 'I will never leave you nor forsake you.' Remember?"

Dominique remained burdened by the absurd totality of the cost of following Jesus, and she started to balk. Not practiced at taking Jesus at His word, Dominique felt a cold shiver and a strange premonition; something, someone, was trying to jump into her thought life.

On cue, Mrs. Allard boldly jumped over that enemy and said, "How about we do this: let me tell you about how I was forced to trust Jesus in my darkest hours, trust that He would never leave me or forsake me." On the verge of succumbing to her fear and the dark force maligning her new faith, Dominique seized the offer of hope, shook her head so as not to be unsettled, and then focused expectantly on Mrs. Allard.

Nearly entranced, it was as if Dominique was transported physically into the living reality of Mrs. Allard's every excruciating moment, every heartache, and all the suffering endured, which she now claimed had developed her into the person she had become.

Dominique knew about Mrs. Allard being raped and about losing Oliver, but there was so much more. She thought to herself, *How could one person endure so much? Like the pain of your mom not believing her uncle raped her, the suicidal thoughts that plagued her after Oliver's death, and the ridicule that comes from friends and family when they do not care to understand your emotional state and are ashamed of your dependence on psychiatric care.*

It was as if Dominique was viewing the unmasking of a broken soul, a soul that was beaten mercilessly, but the scars were left not by the beatings alone but by being left to suffer entirely alone.

To Dominique, Mrs. Allard seemed somewhat exhausted after plumbing the depths of her many losses, but she revitalized quickly as she averted from the presumed destruction of her being to the treasure of the transformation, which her suffering brought about, of which she now boasted.

Dominique was thinking to herself, *And you still love God? How could you, Mrs. Allard?*

Staying on cue, as the Holy Spirit led, Mrs. Allard once again seized the moment and said, "Dominique, there is a verse that has become such an energizer of my soul; can I share it with you?"

Not sure how anyone could remain faithful after all she had endured, Dominique said nothing but nodded her approval. It was as if Mrs. Allard was on another plane of truth, and Dominique was left bereaved, unable to grasp that truth, but she waited for the verse, hoping for clarity.

Mrs. Allard quoted from memory James 1:2–4, saying, "Consider it pure joy, my brothers and sisters, whenever you face trials of many kinds, because you know that the testing of your faith produces perseverance. Let perseverance finish its work so that you may be mature and complete, not lacking anything."[16]

As Dominique wrestled haplessly to grasp the meaning of the verse, Mrs. Allard interjected, "Do you remember when we first met? I told you I did not find peace in the good times but in the suffering." Dominique just stared, still not grasping the point. Mrs. Allard continued, "You see, you do not need strength to get through the good times; there is no test in the good times. Rather, the test is proved in how you handle difficulty. I am mature and lack nothing, not because nothing has gone wrong in my life but, rather, according to what I have suffered and now count that suffering as 'pure joy.'"

* * *

After leaving Mrs. Allard's office, Dominique meandered slowly, in deep thought, down the hall toward her first-period class. *The peace that Mrs. Allard has is real*, she said to herself. She also had to admit the peace she was now experiencing herself was real as well. Reason told her there had never been peace at home or anywhere else in her life prior to the evil of Durand's deed.

So, what Mrs. Allard said is true: real peace does not come in the good times; there is no need for it. Then, she had a thought: *Jesus said He would never leave or forsake me. So, for that to be true, He must be the power behind the inner workings that lead to real peace.*

As peaceful as this line of reasoning was, Dominique remained detached from the dreadful idea that this same Jesus could inspire peace enough for her to be willing to die for Him.

Still lost in her thoughts and not even sure where she was, reality was catching up with Dominique, and she said to herself, *This is deep, difficult, and exhausting thinking.* Just then, Sarah ran briskly past where Dominique had stopped in the hall. She tried to stop and turn, but her momentum forced her to pass Dominique, and with the halls filled with students coming and going to classes, she just yelled back at Dominique, "Hey, Bella is here." And Sarah continued down the hall.

That short four-word sentence shook Dominique awake, wide awake and far away from her beguiling thoughts. She quickly surmised that something was amiss because Bella was not supposed to be back at school until Wednesday. She said to herself, *Sarah wouldn't say that if it were not true.* And even while that last thought had not yet sunk completely in, Dominique was already running through the hall, dodging students, headed to her room.

As she got closer to her room, her joy overflowed at the thought of Bella being back, and a wide smile beamed from her face. Just as she reached the doorway to her room, Dominique slowed, but her excitement was undiminished because the door was open. She grabbed the doorjamb for support and swung excitedly into the room, but there was no Bella.

Her luggage was not there, and there was no sign that anyone had been in their room. Dominique's first thought was, *I am going to kill Sarah.* Then she reconsidered and thought, *She must be in Mrs. Martsen's office or in her first-period class, but why wouldn't she have sought me out by now?*

Frustration had now dampened her excitement, and she plopped down sadly onto her bed. She instantly began to devise a plan that would put her on the trail of Bella but also keep her from going to her class, which she was now late for.

She rose from her bed and took one step toward the open door, and as she did, something caught her attention; she heard the sweet sound of a song. Someone was moving down the hall toward her singing. The hallways were now empty of any noise; all the classes were in session. As the voice came nearer, the sound of her beloved Bella became clearer, and Dominique's joy returned full force, and she jumped out into the hall.

***

Having wrestled like two toddlers out in the hall, hugging and jumping up and down, they finally crashed through the open-door way into their room and stumbled, falling onto Bella's bed.

Dominique wanted to tell Bella so many things, but she waited until Bella explained her early arrival and whether a healthy grieving process was taking place at home. Bella explained things at home were good. Knowing her grandpa was in heaven with Jesus allowed Bella and her family great peace. In fact, Bella's family was adjusting so well that they suggested she head back to school early.

Dominique could not help but admire again the courage of this beautiful friend, and she said, "You are such a rock."

Bella thanked Dominique, then sat up straight, looked deep into her eyes, and said, "So, tell me, what has my roomy been up to while I have been gone?"

Remembering the phone conversation when Dominique had awakened from a dream, panicked, and was in Durand's clutches, Bella said, "How are your dreams?"

Dominique smiled, puffed out her chest, and said, "Well, since talking with you on the phone that day, I have not had a 'Durand dream.'"

Bella held up her hand, and they high-fived. Then, almost anticipating the answer, Bella asked, "Has Jesus been here for you while I have been gone?"

It was the very place where Dominique was dying to go, and she stared in wonder at this friend who could nearly read her mind. With an inspired confidence, she looked boldly into Bella's eyes and said, "I prayed this weekend to Jesus by myself." Bella's face went instantly into joy ballistic. She had to chide herself to keep from interrupting whatever was next to proceed from her dear friend's mouth.

Dominique went on to explain the entire prayer and the subsequent submission to Jesus and her confession of sin. She concluded by explaining the affair: "I believe I heard Him say, 'I will never leave you nor forsake you,' and I told Him I could not do this on my own, and I needed Him. Then I said, 'Thank You, Jesus. I believe You.'"

Being finally caught up, Dominique said to Bella, "One thing, though…" She paused to clarify her thinking and went on, "Mrs. Allard and I have been discussing 'easy believism' and how Jesus's followers must prepare to even die for Him if need be."

Without hesitation, Bella said, "That is true." She bent her head back a little and then refocused on Dominique, saying, "Jesus is not an addition to our lives; there is no drawer He will fit into. It is radical transformation and is accomplished not by our mustering the fortitude but by saying yes to His offer, which is eternal life. Then His promise is possible, and He can back it up when He says, 'I will never leave you nor forsake you' because He has said He will not leave us as orphans but will send us a comforter until He returns. He, living in us now, is our strength, strength even to die for Him. If this is all true, how could Jesus abandon us at our most dire time of need? Does it make sense that He would leave when most needed?" She concluded by saying, "This is a hard thought, but listen carefully."

Dominique nodded her head and focused in.

Bella went on, "The human condition is, we all die. By offering eternal life, Jesus is throwing the world a life preserver, but only if we submit to what He demands. You and I, in fact, all of humanity, have a decision to make. It is self-preservation; we either accept things as God has said or not. One decision leads to eternal life with Him in heaven, and the other leads to eternal separation and hell; both last forever. What you and I are experiencing right now is His validating presence on earth, which builds out our faith."

What Bella said made sense, but Dominique felt like it was all too overwhelming, and she said, "It appears, though, that Jesus wants us to see what isn't there."

Bella nodded approvingly and said, "Now faith is the substance of things hoped for, the evidence of things not seen."[17]

Dominique was drawn back to her prayer with Jesus and Aunt Colleen's explanation about peace not being needed when everything was going well. Trying to believe all she was learning about God was a big lift, but she relented, and peace once again took over. She looked at Bella and said, "I guess I have no place else to go."

Bella smiled, grabbed Dominique's hands, and said, "Me too."

CHAPTER 26

From that day forward, Dominique began to experience the moment-by-moment joy of God in her life. She struggled all the time with life and people, but daily, she also started to trust God for her circumstances. With Mrs. Allard and Bella as her confidants and Christ as her savior, she could face the world with boldness.

Dominique even came to the place where she saw her classmates as people with needs and found herself having compassion for them instead of disdain. Her classmates could see the transformation as well and began to warm up to her as a person who cared for them.

She was even able to accept Mrs. Martsen's attempts at building peace between them as genuine. One day, she approached Mrs. Martsen in the cafeteria and said, "I know you care for me, and I am thankful for that." Mrs. Martsen could hardly control herself, and in the joy of healing, she quickly reached out, grabbed Dominique, and hugged her.

Dominique hugged her back, and they stood there, embracing for a moment. There was complete silence in the cafeteria, and all eyes, not just the students but even the cooks, servers, and teachers, were fixed on the enduring moment before them. Unembarrassed, they ended their hold on each other and pushed slowly back, and as they did, both were surprised to see tears running down their faces. They sniffled, attempting to compose themselves, and Mrs. Martsen said, "Thank you, Dominique; this means so much to me."

All those in the cafeteria could not believe their eyes. All were fully aware of the many battles fought by these two combatants, and as it turned out now, they had ended the hostility and become friends.

They both raised their heads high and bowed slightly to each other and, rejoicing, went their separate ways. As she left the room, Mrs. Martsen smiled genuinely at each of the girls who made eye contact with her. Life on campus changed that day.

This newness of life spilled out in every direction, and she even called her parents just because she wanted to talk with them. She even suggested they come to school for a visit. Thomas and Marie were ecstatic and giddy as they both listened on the phone. They could hardly believe the transformation in her tone and enduring words.

One day, Dominique called, and Marie answered. After a short debrief of life, Marie said, "Honey, you sound so healed and confident."

Pausing to make sure of her response, Dominique said, "What do you mean, Mom?"

Now Marie had to pause to be sure how to move on from her initial statement. She started speaking, saying, "Well, you seem trouble-free, and that makes me so happy for you."

Dominique paused again, trying to be careful of her response. Knowing that bringing God into the foray, this discussion with her mom could quickly turn ugly, but she boldly said, "Oh, I have plenty of troubles, but I also have one who takes my burdens away."

The subtleness of that statement forced Marie out of the bliss of what they had just shared and into a cold place, alive with instant barriers to dialogue. She thought to herself, *Colleen has finally won her over.*

Just before Marie began to counter this brazen assault, a realization confronted her, and she thought, *Wait a minute, this is not the same Dominique who penalized anyone and everyone who dared to bring order to her life. This does not sound like the same girl who had been brutally raped and left alone to live with the terror of her cousin's evil deed; something is different.*

With the delay in the communication, Dominique was beginning to sense a battle brewing, and she prayed, *Dear God, help my mom.* Fighting back the tears and the guilt of being so inept at helping Dominique herself, Marie calmly responded, "I am so glad that you have someone to take your burdens away."

Dominique let out a small sigh of relief and, with gratefulness, said, "Aww, thank you, Mom. My life is so different now, and I am in such a good place; I need your support so badly."

Marie was so choked up that all she could say was, "You have it, darling."

Dominique knew Mom was crying and dealing with so much, so she said, "Hey, I need to be going. I will call again soon, and she closed the call by saying, "I love you so much, Mom. Bye."

Marie said, "Goodbye, my love."

As the call ended, Marie sat at the table sobbing and clutching the phone; she did not know what to do. She looked quickly around the room and considered throwing the phone against the wall. She turned her chair away from the table, bent her head down between her legs, and wanted to scream. Unable to control her thoughts, she did scream; an awkward, frightening scream, a painful scream of defeat, and her body convulsed in overt sobs; nothing could prevent the outpouring of her suffering.

Having heard the awful scream, Thomas flew to the kitchen, bereft by what he saw. There was his bride, bent over and sobbing uncontrollably. Dealing with hardships was never Thomas's forte, but with all that his family had endured these last years, his first response now was to jump in and evaluate the situation, so he did.

He quickly reached down, grabbed Marie's hand, and began to stroke her hair. Then, he did something that he had not done seriously in years: he prayed. *Dear God, please help my Marie and help me know what to do.*

He did not say anything; he just kept praying. Marie's sobs began to subside, and she leaned up and threw her arms around her kneeling husband's neck. He likewise grabbed her and held on tightly. She felt so frail, and Thomas was amazed at how her small frame fit so perfectly into his embrace.

Unaware of source of Marie's pain, Thomas gripped her even tighter; it felt so good to be so needed. He thanked God and waited for Marie to finish whatever this was.

Marie shuddered one more time and turned her head to face Thomas. Her face was racked with pain and wet from sobbing. Thomas had no idea what to expect, so he braced himself and prayed again, saying, "God help us." Marie was pitiful, and Thomas, aching in what she was suffering, waited for her response.

Finally, succumbing to God's call on her daughter's life, Marie was ready to speak; she gulped, wiped the tears from her face, and said, "Dominique is in God's hands now, and He is taking care of her."

***

It was no longer necessary for Bella to accompany Dominique for her morning counseling sessions. Dominique was as comfortable with Mrs. Allard as anyone, and she knew she could share with her any thought, question, or complaint.

One dilemma that haunted the reasoning for her newfound faith revolved around what she had learned in public school. All her teachers pretty much made fun of Christians who believed Jesus was historical and supernatural.

As she and Mrs. Allard settled into the morning session, Dominique felt somewhat embarrassed by her doubts about evolution versus creation. Mrs. Allard was so good at reading Dominique; just by watching her body language, she knew today that there was an adventure in critical thinking headed her way.

Setting up the debate, she started the session with praising Dominique for the spiritual growth that was becoming so evident in her life. Dominique was also becoming quite good at reading Mrs. Allard's setup comments.

Peering stealthily, fully at each other, they paused to ponder their next move. Dominique not only loved how Mrs. Allard cared for her but also for how she thought. She was the best thinker Dominique knew, and she was always blown away by her abilities in "mental gymnastics." That was Mrs. Allard's phrase for people who are comfortable struggling to find truth.

Both equipped and ready, knowing their time together was always an excursion, Dominique said to herself, *Here goes.* Her question eked slowly out and with inflection on the end, and she said, "What does a Christian do when they have doubts?" It was not that Dominique doubted God as much as she needed to have a solid reason for the hope she had in case someone asked her.

Questioning back, Mrs. Allard said, "Why do you ask?"

Dominique knew that Mrs. Allard would not just jump in and give "easy answers"; rather, she always set the table for conflict resolution, leaving it up to Dominique to spill the beans or get to the point.

Dominique jumped right in and said, "In public school, I was taught that only weak-minded individuals hold to the premise that origins are attributed to a supernatural creator."

Mrs. Allard smiled and said, "Is there a question there?"

Dominique smiled back and said, "Okay, how do we know scientifically that God created everything?"

Smiling, Mrs. Allard said, "What a great question." Then, she said, "Albeit a great question, I think we can answer this question quite simply. Not that this is a simple premise but that we have covered this information previously in your science class."

Dominique pressed her lips together and pulled her head back a little, trying to recall the lesson, but to no avail. She spoke up and said, "I do not remember this lesson."

Mrs. Allard said in reply, "Oh, how sad, what an awful teacher I must be." Dominique caught the implication and realized that Mrs. Allard was being critical of her as a student and that maybe she was not paying attention.

Mrs. Allard started again, "Don't you remember we had several sessions covering the *cosmological argument*?"

Dominique was at a loss, and she said, "Sorry, I do not remember." Somewhat embarrassed, she said, "Maybe I will if you go into some detail."

Mrs. Allard reminded her of a handout that each student was given explaining cause and effect, the "first cause" behind the universe. She continued, "Christians need to be ready to give a reason for the hope they have and real empirical evidence, not just deductive reasoning. We need to know and be able to explain that science and faith are compatible."

She continued, saying, "We discussed the three major objections to the natural or material explanation for the cause of the universe. Along with the universe having a beginning, we also discussed how the fine-tuning of the universe reveals astronomical odds that life began by chance, and finally, we also discussed the rapid burst of the appearance in the fossil record during the 'Cambrian explosion.'"

Seeing that Dominique was fading under the daunting deluge of scientific fact, Mrs. Allard deferred and said, "Find that handout and refresh yourself because this topic is too vast for an hour discussion, but for today we can touch on the basics and see if your question is answered."

Dominique nodded and said, "I will find the handout."

"And do what with it?" Mrs. Allard questioned.

Dominique smiled and said, "Read it."

"Good," said Mrs. Allard. She began again: "How do we know about God?" she asked.

Dominique replied, "From the Bible."

"Then, we must start with what the Bible says." She continued by giving several biblical verses. She read Genesis 1:1: "In the beginning God created the heavens and earth."[18] Then, she moved to Psalm 19:

> "The heavens declare the glory of God;
> the skies proclaim the work of his hands.
>
> Day after day they pour forth speech;
> night after night they reveal knowledge."[19]

She followed with Romans chapter 1 that God's "invisible attributes, namely, his eternal power and divine nature, have been clearly perceived, ever since the creation of the world, in the things that have been made. So they are without excuse."[20]

Mrs. Allard finished with Psalm 14:1, "The fool says in his heart, 'There is no God.'"[21] After quoting those verses, she stopped to let Dominique take them in.

Dominique was thinking, *Wow… She knows her Bible well; I think I would like to be able to pull up scriptures like that myself.* With Mrs. Allard peering expectantly at her, Dominique assumed Mrs. Allard wanted her to comment.

She thought to herself, *She never makes things easy; she always makes me work, makes me think…* Knowing that was the case now, Dominique started, "So, according to the Bible, God said He made everything, and He backed that up with the evidence that as we observe the universe, it becomes clear that He made it. Is that right?"

Smiling, Mrs. Allard quipped, "You are thinking well." Then, she said, "As you research that handout and apply what the Bible says, then add to your thinking a few scientific facts, you will have a good reason for the hope you have."

Dominique said, "Like what facts?"

Mrs. Allard answered, "I will give you a few." She started by saying, "Only a fool would deny there is a God." Then, she gave her the facts: "First, 30 percent of the earth's surface is covered by land, while 70 percent by water. If the percentages were reversed, we would burn up and die. The 70 percent water mass helps control temperatures so we are not annihilated. Second, the earth is 93 million miles from the sun. The earth's revolution around the sun is considered in the sweet slot. If we were any closer or further away, we would either freeze or burn up. Third, the earth rotates at approximately 1,000 miles per hour and revolves around the sun at approximately 67 thousand miles per hour. Our solar system revolves around in the Milky Way at 400,000 miles per hour, and finally, our galaxy moves around in the universe at nearly 2 million miles per hour. Do you understand everything has to be perfect for life? Our planet was designed for life. If the earth did not rotate and revolve, there would be no life on earth.

"Fourth, the earth is tilted at twenty-three and one-half degrees. Without this, most of the world would be barren. Fifth, the ozone layer is only one-eighth of an inch thick. Without this very thin layer, the ultraviolet rays of the sun would scorch us.

"Sixth, our air is made up of 21 percent oxygen and 78 percent nitrogen. If these percentages were reversed, a lighted match would blow us up. Seventh, water freezes at thirty-two degrees above zero. Why don't the oceans freeze over? They have salt. Were it not so, the amount of thawing in polar regions would not balance out, causing catastrophic flooding."

She added, "There are many other scientific proofs that support a creator, like irreducible complexity and the anthropic principle, and you should investigate those, but it appears by the evidence we have discussed the earth was created to sustain human life. Also, you need to know that excessive faith and the lack of humility in the evolutionary scientific community are damaging to true science. These scientists are seeking omniscience. They should be more humble."

Beginning to have a greater confidence in her faith, Dominique smiled and said, "There are good reasons for the hope I have."

Mrs. Allard smiled and said, "Yes, but you know God because He has reached out to you and called you to Himself. That is the greatest faith builder of all. Let's conclude today's session by reiterating several thoughts, okay?"

Dominique nodded her approval.

Mrs. Allard began by saying, "I believe the greatest danger the world faces today is Satan's deceptive lie. Jesus does not really require what he says. Satan offers, free to anyone who will bite, 'easy believism.' Let me explain that: A person drowning in the water needs a life vest. A person falling from the sky needs a parachute. In other words, Jesus is not just a nice thought. All the blessings He bestows and continues to bestow are only available if we understand that hell waits for those who reject His offer.

"Again, this is self-preservation. Jesus is saying, 'Only I can save you.' He is throwing us a lifeline, and every soul since creation has been left with the same decision; we have a choice: heaven or hell." She concluded by saying, "Do you believe this?"

After hearing such a strong message, it was undeniable to Dominique that God would not accept an "easy believism" for entrance into His presence.

CHAPTER 27

Only back for one day, Bella was already settled neatly into her campus routine. She found herself excited about the end of the school year and what was next after graduation. After completing the academic day and deep in those thoughts, she headed to her room. She was suddenly surprised when Dominique came running up from behind and pushed her gently. Then, screaming, she said, "Hey, roomy!"

Bella was never one to be shocked by anything, so she stopped, turned quickly, and yelled into Dominique's face, "Hey," which startled Dominique, and she nearly jumped out of her skin. They both laughed and bounded into their room.

It was always a relief for the day to be done, but once in their room, it became a mad scramble to get out of their uniforms and into something comfortable. Bella was more methodical, and Dominique always found her bed before Bella landed on hers.

As Bella moved around the room, Dominique sat there expectantly, never taking her eyes off her. She marveled that God was so good to give her this amazing friend. Still getting comfortable, Bella looked up to notice Dominique frozen in an adoring stare, and she said, "You missed me."

Finally ending up on her bed, Bella stared across at Dominique. Sensing Dominique's eagerness to share what had happened since she was gone, Bella took this opportunity to play with Dominique's anxiety. She quickly started right in, talking about her time at home. She said, "Well, I'll bet you can hardly wait to hear what happened while I was home?"

Nearly devastated, Dominique weakly smiled and weakly said, "Of course I am."

At that, Bella burst out laughing, and her red hair bounced as she laughed. Her green eyes sparkled, and she said, "Just kidding." Still laughing, she said, "Forget that; tell me about your time here without your roommate. What has been going on?"

Blushing at the good trick Bella played on her, Dominique laughed as well. Then she quickly jumped right in, sharing nearly every detail of the days she spent alone. Bella sat there, astonished by what God can do in so little time. As she listened, she could hear God's strength pouring out of her dear friend. She thanked God as she saw the courage evident in Dominique's countenance.

After rejoicing together about what God had done in Dominique's life, suddenly, there were no more words. They sat there silent, at peace, just looking at each other. It was not an uncomfortable moment; instead, it was reassuring and lovely. They did not need to say anything; in fact, it would have ruined the moment to force something. The comfort of the moment was like victory after an intense battle, and they both savored the significance of the quiet.

Finally, Bella said, "That was refreshing, hey?" Dominique, still unable to speak, just nodded approvingly. Then, a thought burst into her mind, and she felt a twinge of insecurity. She could not believe how quickly she could go from bliss to worry. Bella noticed something amiss and asked, "What is it?"

Dominique tried to appear unshaken, and Bella tried to keep things light but had no idea what was bothering her friend, and she said again, "What?"

This was the first time that Dominique had contemplated the end of the school year and what would happen after that. She sheepishly let it out: "What is going to happen to us after graduation?"

At first, Bella was relieved it was not something catastrophic, and she smiled and nearly spoke too quickly when she realized this was catastrophic for Dominique. She realized that this was big because most of Dominique's experience with the hope of God in her life happened here at school. Then she said to herself, *She must be fearful of being alone after graduation.*

Bella prayed quickly for her dear friend, and in wisdom, she said, "God has begun a good work in you, and He will bring it to completion. He will never leave you or forsake you." Then she added, "And you and I will always be the best of friends." Dominique's fear started to subside, and she looked confidently at Bella.

Trying to lighten the moment because Dominique did not appear totally sold on her premise, Bella said, "Besides, maybe someday after college, or even sooner, you and I will both find some hunk of a godly man to be our helpmeet, as is God's plan. God has said He will never leave us, and God's plan is that He will find us the right partner for life." She looked confidently at Dominique and continued, "In Adam's case, God saw that it was not good for him to be alone, so He created Eve to be his helper."

The unintended consequence of Bella's reasoning sent Dominique into panic. She nearly convulsed thinking about a man in her life, and she thought, *How could I ever again be with another man?*

Bella was still smiling but beginning to sense something was not right, and she said, "Dominique, what are you thinking?" Then it hit Bella, and she thought, *I forgot to factor in Durand. God help me.* She prayed again, looked at Dominique, and said, "I know you are not ready to talk about boyfriends and eventually marriage, but that is God's natural plan for you."

Dominique slumped down and sadly said, "How could that ever be?"

Confidently, Bella said, "Just like He has already done so much in our lives, why would He not continue to never leave us or forsake us?"

Almost afraid to even continue talking about this subject, Dominique glanced quickly at Bella and said, "Tell me of your experience with boyfriends." As Bella put her thoughts together, Dominique was thinking, *Bella and I have never talked about her and boyfriends; how odd.*

Having the confidence that God gave her, Bella began to share those experiences. "Well," Bella began, "I will start by telling you of the difficulty of dating and finding a life partner. I decided years ago that I wanted my marriage to be honoring to God. That meant to me that I would only marry a godly man, and I would be a virgin when I married."

Dominique nearly flinched at Bella's words. She felt instantly guilty; she thought to herself, *I will never be a virgin bride, and how could any man be interested in someone who had been raped?*

Bella could see Dominique's countenance begin to fall, and she prayed, *Oh, God, this is Your work; please don't leave this totally up to me.* So, she set her aim on telling the truth and letting God have His way, then she continued. "When I first began to date, I set some rules in place, simple but unchanging rules. If the guy was not a Christian, there was no connection. If there was a connection, there would be no sexual conduct at all." Bella made sure Dominique was still with her, and she added, "That means no petting at all and no tongue kissing."

Dominique looked strangely at Bella as if to say, "Who could abide by those rules?" Most of the girls Dominique knew were already having sex with their boyfriends, even many of the girls at school. She thought, *Sex is all they want to talk about.*

As Bella continued to share, Dominique was struck again by the willpower of her wonderful friend. Then, Dominique interrupted Bella and said, "So, how many boys have you dated, and what were the results?"

Bella smiled and said, "Not too many because they don't like the rules."

"Tell me about those you did date," Dominique responded.

Bella was encouraged by Dominique's query, and she thought, *Good, she wants to know.* So, she said, "I have only dated two boys." She paused to catch Dominique's reaction, and Dominique remained unphased by the count.

Bella said, "Okay, let me tell you about both young men. The first guy told me he was a Christian; we went to church together several times, and he was a perfect gentleman. He made sure to ask about my thoughts and ambitions; in other words, he put me first."

Surprised, Dominique began to find herself enjoying the conversation, and she leaned in to hear more. Then, as if to hurry Bella along, she jumped in and said, "So, why did you end up dating someone else if things were going so well?"

Now, Bella smiled and thanked God for how it was going. She moved on, saying, "One night, even after reading the Bible together, we settled in on the couch, and he put his arm around my shoulder. At first, I was a little nervous, but he smiled at me and made no further advances. It felt amazing. In fact, the first time he held my hand was the week before." She paused to reflect on the emotion of that day, looked warmly into Dominique's eyes, and said, "I had never held hands with any boy prior to that day. It was the most intimate feeling I had ever felt; it was magic, and something in my soul made me want to be receptive."

Now, Dominique was seeing a part of Bella she had not known, and just being in the conversation made her feel warm inside. Bella continued, "So when he put his arm around my shoulder, I felt tingling in my body, and I wanted to lean into him for more. Then, his hand slid off my shoulder and down to my breast."

She paused, as if reliving the hurt of that moment, and she looked abruptly at Dominique and said, "After he did that, my heart was shaken, and I felt my blood begin to boil at being so betrayed. I grabbed his hand and jumped, standing up and out from under his embrace. I yelled at him, saying, 'You know the rules; how could you do that to me?'"

At hearing this revelation, Dominique's eyes became as big as saucers. She felt her heart racing in her chest, and she nearly stood up but stopped halfway up. Then, she sat back down, staring at Bella, and said, "What did you do?"

Bella calmed herself and stared defiantly at Dominique. She told her, "I told him to leave my house, and I never wanted to see him again."

Dominique was baffled; she could hardly believe the strength of conviction this young woman of valor possessed. So, she said to Bella, "What did he do?"

Bella told her, "He tried to apologize, and he agreed he had broken the rules and promised he would never do that again, but when I did not budge, he looked at me pathetically and said, 'Fine, what a prude you are. With those rules you live by, good luck with finding any guy.' I pointed at the door and said, 'Leave.' He stormed out of the house, slamming the door as he left. He even left his Bible behind and never returned for it."

Dominique looked at Bella and said, "That must have been so hard."

Bella just smiled and said, "No, it was very easy; the rules made my decision easy. My mom came into the room after he left. We sat together on that same couch, and she praised me for being so brave and dedicated to God, but still I cried."

Dominique knew that Bella was not dating anyone now, so she began to imagine the results of her other dating experience. She asked Bella, "So, what happened to guy number two?"

She explained to Dominique how fresh this experience still was, and Dominique could see the pain rising in her face. Bella took a deep breath and said, "No one but my parents and closest friends know how painful this experience has been for me."

Dominique bowed her head, feeling guilty. Due to her own selfish concerns, she was clueless about the pain of her best friend, but she still had to know Bella's story, and she asked, "Please tell me what happened."

"It started much like the first time," Bella began. "He was a very godly young man; he treated me with the utmost respect, and we loved being in God's Word and praying together. He was adamant about church attendance and youth activities. My parents thought he was truly a God-send for their daughter. Just months ago, we began to speak about marriage. He told me he was not dating just to date; he was seeking God for a bride for life. I told him those were my sentiments exactly."

Dominique started to feel pain in her chest for Bella. She could see how much Bella really cared about this young man, but still, it ended. She looked lovingly over at her friend. Bella was looking down as if searching for how to continue but reliving the difficulty of having to do it.

Bella looked up again and could see that Dominique was patiently and painfully waiting for the outcome. Bella said, "One night, after six months of both of us seeking God and loving on each other, we were at my house.

"Months before, we had begun to kiss warmly, nothing passionate or too intimate, just brief kissing. We were kissing on the couch, which never lasted long. We knew better, and he surprised me when he put his tongue into my mouth, and I could feel his passion rise. Just then, his hand slid down my back onto my behind, and he caressed me there."

Dominique could see Bella's ache at having to tell this story, and Dominique felt sick herself hearing of this awful betrayal. Almost not wanting her to go on, but knowing she had to, Dominique said, "And?"

Bella looked up and, with wet eyes, said, "I pulled away from him and stared horrified at his disloyalty. Instantly, he knew he had broken our covenant, and he said, 'Oh, Bella, I am so sorry…' I began to sob uncontrollably, and he tried to reach out and comfort me. As he did, I pushed him away and stood, brokenhearted, staring down at him. I did not know what to say; I felt my heart breaking, and I wanted to not have the rules in my life anymore.

"He stood and tried again to apologize, coming closer. I stepped away and turned my back on him, but everything inside me wanted to forgive him and turn into his arms. But my conviction for the covenant and the God of our covenant held me at a distance, and that distance grew with each passing second."

Dominique was weeping now and wanted to reach over and comfort her friend, but she knew there was more to come, so she sat there overwhelmed and started to feel angry with how God would orchestrate such an ordeal.

Bella ran her hands down over her face and dried her tears. She looked at Dominique and said, "As hard as this is, I do not mind sharing this with you. You have suffered so much more than I, but if my story can help you move forward, then to God be the glory."

Dominique had to admit it looked like God did have His hand in this entire thing, and she repented and said, *Sorry, Lord*. Dominique sheepishly said, "So, you kicked him out?"

Bella nodded and said, "Yes, I did. He began to cry and beg me for another chance, promising it would not happen again. Then he said, 'Do you not believe that in spite of this setback, God still wants us to be together?' I looked at him and felt sorry for him. I said, 'You chose to end this relationship; this is not a setback; this is a betrayal, and now I want you to leave my house.'

"His face seemed to become placid, like he could not believe his ears, and he started to take a step toward me, but seeing my face told him it was over. It looked like he was forming a word in his mouth, but he said nothing and could no longer keep eye contact with me. I turned and walked out of the room, and as I did, I heard him softly say, 'I am sorry, Bella…' Then I heard the door faintly close. And with that, there was another closure added to Bella's dating adventures."

Finding the entire story too hard to believe, but knowing if Bella said it, it was true, Dominique reached out, gently patted Bella's hand, and said, "Did he ever try again?"

Wanting to get back to the moment and put this piece of her life in proper perspective, Bella nodded cheerfully. Smiling, like the same old Bella, she said, "For months, he called me, sent me flowers, talked to my parents, he tried everything; I finally had to tell him, 'How could I ever trust you in our married life, you revealing who you really are? It was God's answer to prayer. I forgive you, but we are finished.' After that, he gave up."

Bella looked at Dominique softly and said, "This is my conviction and how I have sought God for a life partner. Not everyone will be able to do this, but I am confident in my heavenly Father that His choice for me is within the boundaries of my convictions."

Trying to make things a little lighter, Dominique smiled cautiously and said, "I hope I never break a promise with you." Bella laughed, and that encouraged Dominique to join in as well, which seemed to help them move past this sordid timeline and back to the present.

Dominique kept smiling at Bella as she continued talking about being thankful for her decision, but Dominique was deep in thought. Her mind went back to Mrs. Allard, sharing she had been raped by her uncle but still was happily married, even after losing a child. Now, with Bella sharing the devastation of her dating life, she is still trusting God instead of how she feels.

She thought to herself, *How will I ever find the man for me, the one who God has prepared for me?* Then, a peace came over her, and she said to herself, *Thank You, Lord, for putting people in my life who know*

You so well. She sighed and took another deep breath. Then, with more resolve and courage than she had ever known, she thanked Bella for proving once again that God would never leave them or forsake them.

***

The rest of the school year went by so quickly. There were many challenges to face in her last days at school, but Dominique found her faith strong enough to endure through all of them.

Bella spent the last of the school year trying to talk Dominique into going with her on a summer missionary trip. She was quite convincing and argued that this was the way they could continue to be together after school, but she also knew this would grow her spiritually in a way no other situation could. Dominique loved the idea of being with her best friend but knew nothing about being a missionary.

She had extensive phone conversations with her aunt, Colleen, on this topic. With Dominique daily falling deeper in love with the only man in her life, Jesus, Colleen had found the mountaintop of her existence. She rejoiced daily in God's goodness for the work He was doing in Dominique's life, but personally, she could see, without much prayer and training, it was a mistake for Dominique to head off to the mission, and she told her so.

They discussed at length the ins and outs of the decision, but finally, Colleen said, "Honey, you must know that God is calling you to this; it can't be only that you get to be with Bella." She concluded their talk by saying, "Unless you pray earnestly, daily for God's confirmation of a mission trip, you should not go."

At first, Dominique was sensing that Aunt Colleen was conflicted, and she contributed her indecision to wanting her home with her instead of going on mission. Then, she changed her mind, knowing Aunt Colleen was not that selfish. She had to consider her aunt knew what a call looked like next to a whim.

Mrs. Allard told her nearly the exact same thing when she asked her about the mission trip. Mrs. Allard's input added an additional perspective, though. She said, "God could be using Bella to direct your next path as you are led to walk with Him."

One day, Mrs. Martsen passed Dominique in the hall between classes. She stopped and called Dominique over to her. Dominique was beginning to see Mrs. Martsen through a new set of lenses. She knew there was no doubt that Mrs. Martsen loved her and prayed for her. It was so good having her on her team rather than on her case all the time; she even thanked God for Mrs. Martsen.

When Dominique came close, Mrs. Martsen smiled broadly and said, "Hey, I hear you might be going on a mission trip this summer with Bella."

Dominique thought to herself, *How does everyone, so quickly, know my business?* Dominique smiled and said, "Yes, there is a possibility, but please pray for me; I do not know how to hear from God on this yet."

Mrs. Martsen never stopped smiling and said, "I have been praying for you since I heard about the trip last week. It is so exciting to think about you and Bella taking the message of Jesus to the lost."

Dominique smiled but had not yet considered this was what they would be doing, and she thought, *Taking the message of Jesus to the lost…*

Before turning and heading back down the hall, Mrs. Martsen said, "I will continue to pray that you hear from God His plan for you." She said, "Have a good day," and disappeared into the mass of students flooding the hall, all on a fixed destination.

As she stood there like a fixture, Dominique could feel the movement of the throng of people. It was strange; the movement of people was blowing softly on her face. They created a slight breeze as they passed by, and she thought, *Dear God, like the breeze I sense on my face right now, I feel my life is just floating along on a breeze, without a destination, blown whichever way the wind blows. Please make it clear to me: what is my calling?*

Dominique did not realize she had been standing there for some time, for when she looked up, the hallway was completely silent and empty. She felt no urgency to move and end this sacred moment, so she stood still, silent, listening in the calm of His presence.

CHAPTER 28

With graduation just around the corner, Dominique reflected on how much her life had changed in such a short period of time. What struck her most was she was no longer the same person. She could remember the old her, but she seemed such a stranger to herself now.

It was like there was an inner beacon in her soul that prompted her about right and wrong. Mrs. Allard made it plain to her that that beacon was the Holy Spirit, which Jesus promised would come so as to not leave us alone when He went back to heaven. Dominique remembered Mrs. Allard saying, "He takes up residence in every believer who trusts Christ to save them from hell."

She quickly came to understand that the more time she spent with Jesus in prayer and in His Word, the more this inner beacon came alive in her. That being the case, she committed to reading and prayer every day. Not ritualistically, to check a box, but for the joy of being with God and knowing the power that emanated from such a connection.

The greatest calm, or comfort, came to Dominique through confession of sin. This at first baffled her because, prior to Christ living in her, she was always haunted and defeated by the thought of repercussions for her actions, the feeling of being guilty, and the expectation and dread of the consequences of her sin.

She remembered how she lived in fear of her actions, knowing that most of her actions were intrinsically wrong and done intentionally. What used to bring her satisfaction now brought her pain, and what used to be all right had become wrong, but now, she was a new person. The difference was that she knew if she sinned, all she had to do was confess it and trust Jesus's promise that she would be forgiven, and she finally knew what the peace of God felt like.

***

Still mystified that she had accepted Bella's offer of going on mission with her, Dominique knew she had no choice. What could she do? That day in the hallway, standing alone, with the light breeze blowing on her face, but not at all alone, rather in His presence, she heard God say, "Yes."

She remembered that day like there were no other days in her life. After audibly hearing God speak, she frantically looked around to ensure that someone had not come up on her. Then, she stayed herself and stood perfectly still, cocking her head slightly left and then right, hoping to hear more, still trying to believe what just happened.

Unable to move and solemnly shaken, she did not know what to do. Her head was racing, and her heart was pounding, but she felt amazing joy mixed with a healthy fear. This was the same voice she had heard before in her first prayer, and it took her completely captive as if heaven had moved in around her. She could not comprehend it all.

Just then, Bella came running up the hall and said to Dominique, "You are late for class; what are you doing here?" Dominique looked slowly up, not sure who was before her. She tried to focus on the sound of this new voice. Bella spoke again, "Hey, are you listening?"

Dominique began to focus on Bella, and she understood the question, but she thought to herself, *How do I tell Bella that I just heard God speak to me?*

Bella grabbed Dominique by the arm and started pulling her down the hall as she said, "Are you all right?"

Dominique began to smile in such a way that Bella was surprised; she had never seen Dominique appear so alive, and Dominique said, "Yes, I am all right."

Bella said, "Good," but she was still struck by Dominique's countenance; she knew something was going on but had no idea what, so to make small talk, she asked, "Hey, roomy, have you made up your mind about going on the mission trip with me?"

Dominique stopped in the middle of the hall, pulled Bella up close to her, and said, "Say that again."

Bella said, "You are acting so strange right now; what is going on?"

Dominique repeated the question, "Say what you have just said to me again."

Puzzled, Bella shook her head, got right in Dominique's face, and said, "Are you going on the mission trip with me?"

Smiling from ear to ear, Dominique grabbed Bella's face, started to laugh, and then, longingly, said, "Yes!"

* * *

The next couple of days after her encounter with God, Dominique started to feel melancholy and unsure about what had happened. Without a doubt, she was sure God had spoken to her, but now she could not verify if she heard Him audibly or in her head; it was all very confusing. So, she decided to bring it up when she next met with Mrs. Allard.

Mrs. Allard was aware that Dominique had chosen to go on mission with Bella, and as their meeting began, she quickly brought that topic up. The first thing she said to Dominique was, "I was pleased to hear you had made the decision to go on the mission trip with Bella."

It never failed to amaze Dominique; Mrs. Allard was a mind reader. Since her profound encounter, Dominique has not yet been comfortable sharing with anyone about hearing from God. She looked up sharply and said to Mrs. Allard, "Why is that the first thing you want to discuss today?"

Not flinching, Mrs. Allard casually said, "Because when I heard about it, I found that to be good news and wanted to hear about it from you. Why do you ask?"

It was uncanny for Dominique to sit before this almost prophet-like seer and have her mentor read her mind. Dominique just shook her head and said, "Because that was what I wanted to talk to you about, but I did not know how to go about it. Then, you, just like a mind reader, bring it up."

Mrs. Allard assured Dominique that she could not read minds, but she added, "I do believe, though, God has gifted me with reading hearts. I just thought that would be something you would like to discuss." So, she looked solemnly into Dominique's eyes and said, "Okay, what is on your mind then?"

Straining at how to phrase her question, Dominique looked away, and while away, it came to her, and she looked back at Mrs. Allard and said, "Have you ever heard God speak audibly to you? Do you regularly experience His presence like that?"

Mrs. Allard started to smile, and her smile continued to grow, and her eyes started to sparkle. She excitedly asked Dominique, "Has that happened to you?"

Dominique started thinking to herself, *Again, this was just like Mrs. Allard. She did not answer my question but came back to me with a question.* Thoughtfully mulling the question over in her mind, Dominique felt unsure about what really happened, and she stuttered as she began to open up about it. She said, "I-I am not sure… I don't really know… I think maybe I did…."

Mrs. Allard, true to her calling, leaned forward onto her desk and said, "How would you know if you did hear Him?"

Having a conversation with Mrs. Allard was like trying to solve a puzzle. Becoming frustrated, Dominique leaned in herself and said boldly, "I don't know; you tell me."

Mrs. Allard started to laugh but caught herself when she saw the look on Dominique's face; she became stoic and replied, "Why don't you tell me about your experience, and let's see where it goes from there."

Dominique nodded but thought to herself, *Finally!* With some trepidation, Dominique detailed the entire event to Mrs. Allard.

* * *

Repeatedly, that entire school day, Dominique relived the morning session spent with Mrs. Allard. Though things seemed to be somewhat clearer, she still did not know how to apply what she was learning about God. Remembering what Mrs. Allard said, Dominique tried to wrap the implications and the intricacies of communion with God around her heart.

Mrs. Allard told her, "Yes, I have on occasion heard God speak to me," which she thought was audible. But she added, "Those interactions could have been in my heart and in my head; it is hard to know." She followed up with this thought, "But either way, beyond a shadow of a doubt, God was communicating to me, and action was required on my part."

Dominique called Aunt Colleen and shared her experience. Aunt Colleen, as always, was so overjoyed. She told Dominique, "Is there any doubt that you heard from God?"

Dominique pondered the wisdom of that statement and concluded, "Absolutely not. God spoke to me, and it doesn't matter if it was audible to the human ear; it was audible to my soul."

That night, as she and Bella perused her experience together, they came to the same conclusion: God was uniquely reaching out to Dominique. Now she had confirmation from those she trusted most, and it appeared God was orchestrating that she was to prepare for a mission trip.

Late into the night, Bella and Dominique discussed the ramifications of God's calling them to mission. They ultimately decided they needed to get through graduation first and then begin the process of how to be an ambassador for Christ in another part of the world, but they concluded with surety that now was the time to begin fervent prayer, so they made a pact that, until they left, they would pray individually and corporately for their excursion.

As the days dwindled down toward graduation, Bella became aware of a supernatural aura that blanketed Dominique. It was not like she wasn't a sinner like everybody else; she just needed God so much for everything, and He met her expectations right when she was vulnerable and trusting.

Many times, her classmates found themselves wishing they could be more like her. In fact, Sarah and Rachel talked about it among themselves and concluded that this new Dominique was not the one they used to know. They asked themselves, "How could someone who cared so little about others care so much now?"

Each year, the staff designates one student who best exemplifies Christ in their life, and they are given a designation plaque engraved with the words: "The Christ-like Life." They also receive a substantial scholarship endowment. It was no surprise that Bella was chosen as this year's recipient, but it was surprising that the staff chose to add a new designation this year. This new designation, which would be ongoing, honors the student who, though suffering greatly, rose above their pain and became an example of faith under fire. This first recipient of the "Faith under Fire" award was Dominique.

***

With her bags packed, Dominique meandered out into one of the screened areas between the classrooms. She was thinking about the closure of her time at William James. With her head down, she walked slowly, eyeing the ornate tile on the floor and solemnly reminiscing in the two years gone by. During the weekend, most of the other students were in their rooms or out enjoying the warmer days of the outdoors.

She thought about the anger she brought with her here. She thought about the suffering, which nearly destroyed her, but she smiled and thanked God, knowing the Durand ordeal was truly behind her.

The lights were turned off, and the room seemed so expansive, but it felt good to be all alone. Dominique was not quite sure why she was so emotional, and tears began to form in her eyes. Then something caught her attention, and she looked up, trying to focus through the tears; she was surprised, for in the shadows in the back of the room, a blurry figure started to materialize.

Startled, she stopped abruptly and uttered a short "oh!" Her heart was racing, and her feet froze, so she wiped the tears from her eyes, and as she did, the figure before her moved closer and out of the shadows, becoming more visible with each step; there was Mrs. Martsen.

Seeming so fragile, so forlorn, and so vulnerable, with her handkerchief wiping her eyes, Mrs. Martsen moved slowly toward Dominique.

Neither spoke; they just stared at each other, and then Mrs. Martsen said, "I was hoping that I would see you before you left." Relieved that Mrs. Martsen was not a bogeyman or a reincarnated Durand, she was still not sure how to grasp the irony of them being alone there together in that moment, but Dominique smiled warmly.

Dominique was thinking, *What is the principal of the school doing on the weekend, hiding out all alone in the breezeway?* Dominique ventured a small step forward and asked Mrs. Martsen, "Are you okay?"

Mrs. Martsen finished wiping her eyes and nodded, saying, "Yes, thank you, dear."

Not sure what to do, Dominique said, "I am sorry to disturb you. I can leave."

Sitting now in one of the breezeway chairs, Mrs. Martsen motioned for Dominique to join her. Smiling warmly, Dominique moved slowly next to her and took a seat. Mrs. Martsen looked gently but straight into Dominique's eyes and said, "Congratulations on your award; it is most deserved."

This was such a precise moment that Dominique allowed herself to go back to the many days when she caused Mrs. Martsen so much grief, and she felt instant remorse. She looked away and instantly knew she must make amends for her actions. She looked up into the eyes of Mrs. Martsen and said, "I am so sorry for how I behaved; I have treated you so badly; please forgive me."

The tears again began to mount in Mrs. Martsen's eyes, and she said, "Oh, darling, it is I who needs to ask forgiveness. There is no way you could know the evil that I perpetrated on you, and if it was not for you, I would have continued to subjugate other students in the same manner."

She continued, "I know this is beyond what you can understand, but please hear me out." Though baffled, Dominique moved her head slowly up and down, waiting for Mrs. Martsen to explain.

Starting with the first days after Dominique enrolled, Mrs. Martsen shared her disdain for a person like Dominique. She told her how she knew Dominique could never adjust or benefit from a school like William James. She continued telling Dominique that she told Dr. James himself of the futility of having someone like her at school and the detriment she would have on other students. She went on to say, "I even hoped for the day when you would be expelled."

With her eyes widening, Dominique started to lean back away from Mrs. Martsen; she had no idea that she had such disdain for her. Dominique was starting to feel uncomfortable, and she slid sideways on her chair. Just as she did, Mrs. Martsen reached out and placed her hand on top of Dominique's hand and said, "I know this is too much and not a pretty picture for you to cradle as you leave William James, but I must tell you, if it were not for you, there would have been no hope for me."

She went on to tell her of that day when she thought Dominique was faking illness and how she tried to force Dominique out of her room and on out to class, the day when Mrs. Allard took her to go to the dispensary.

She told her, "That was the day when God reached down and revealed to me my treachery toward you. He broke my heart and exposed my lack of compassion, and because of that, the frailty of my ability to lead young women for Him was in question."

She attempted to pull Dominique back around to face her, and Dominique allowed her to do so. Now tears flowed again, not tears of remorse but tears of joy, and she said to Dominique, "God has used you to bring me back to Him; I am now ready to serve young women and their families for God only, and not for my own selfish means. Please forgive me for hurting you the way I did, but I must also say thank you for being here these last two years. Your life, as hard as it has been, is the catalyst that God has used to transform the entire school. With you here, God showed me and many others the real point of this school: to educate, yes, but also to meet the needs of our students, no matter what their situation."

That was more than a morsel of input and a lot for Dominique to absorb. She knew that Mrs. Martsen had changed and was so different from when they first met, but how could she know it would be her life that God used to transform another person? Knowing this anomaly was orchestrated by God, Dominique was forced to acknowledge: *It seems that a very big God chooses to reach into this world and en-*

tertain in the intricate details of everyday human experience.

Dominique set about evaluating the story she had just heard and found herself glad, no, more than glad—joyful; having no idea what God was doing at the time, Dominique now knew God was moving in her, to move into the life of another.

She turned to Mrs. Martsen and said, "There is nothing to forgive; I have seen the great change in you and have known for some time that you love me. Now, aware of how God worked in you, I am grateful and humbled to be His instrument. It seems He has played me well, and you have heard His song." Then, she took hold of both of Mrs. Martsen's hands and said, "We are both blessed then, are we not?"

In wholesome joy, they hugged, and after a brief look at each other, Dominique said, "Thank you," and turned to leave. She moved about ten feet away when Mrs. Martsen said, "I will never forget you."

* * *

To ensure that she could spend a few quality moments alone to assess what not being here any longer meant, Dominique made ready to leave ahead of time. So, when she left the classroom and Mrs. Martsen while waiting for Mom and Dad to pick her up, she just meandered around campus, going nowhere, in deep thought.

Things were becoming so clear. A verse Aunt Colleen always shared with her came to mind. It was Philippians 2:13; she quoted it in her mind: *"For it is God who works in you to will and to act in order to fulfill his good purpose."*[22] *In other words*, she thought, *God works in us for His pleasure, not for our pleasure.*

Then, another verse jumped right in line, along with the first one, and it was Acts 17:26. She quoted it as well, *"From one man he made all the nations, that they should inhabit the whole earth; and he marked out their appointed times in history and the boundaries of their lands."*[23]

Then she thought, *It appears undeniable now that God has placed me right down in time, even into the very family I call my own, and this school as well, to work out His good pleasure in me.* That thought was so immense and yet so believable that Dominique was forced to look for a place to sit and fathom the depths of His desire for her.

Nothing was the same, but with God as her hope and her help, everything was possible, and her spirit rejoiced at the thought. She bowed her head and spoke to God, saying, "I am Yours, now and forever. Thank You, dear God."

As the time drew near for Mom and Dad to retrieve her from school, she began again to move in that direction. Looking back occasionally at the campus layout, she thought to herself, *God used this place to take hold of my heart and my life*, but she knew this was only the beginning, a starting point. But alas, her heart and soul were confident and secure. With that peace, she lifted her head, picked up her pace, and marched confidently out toward her parents' car and her new future.

CHAPTER 29

As she settled back in, Dominique could sense the transitory status of being home. Somehow, she knew this was just a place to layover, not reside. On the other hand, since her ordeal with Durand, her mom and dad had poured all their energy into making home a sanctuary, a fortress, whereby they could protect their precious daughter, whom they had failed before.

Since that night on the phone call with Dominique and her confession to Thomas, saying, "Dominique was in God's hands now, and He is taking care of her," Marie wrestled with what her role was now that Dominique had turned to God. She was dwarfed by the burden of knowing Dominique was in love with God, but the change in her seemed to be marked by that relationship.

It was evident that her dad was rejoicing in her newfound faith, and they talked about it openly. It was not because Thomas fully understood the entirety of what had happened in Dominique's life, but rather, who she had become.

Thomas could not believe his eyes and ears, and his heart was overflowing with joy. She never failed to hug and kiss him. She helped Marie around the house with chores. She was always asking if she could do something for him or get him something. She was the same way with Marie. She was not manipulative or argumentative. She did not play her parents against each other; for the first time in their relationship, it was heaven at home.

For Thomas, the most enduring aspect of his father-daughter reunion was that on some occasions, like just before bed, while he was in his easy chair, she would run over and jump into her dad's lap and hold on to him, putting her head on his shoulder and say, "I love you, Dad."

Without guilt, he was finally able to hold her as a father should. Not always, but every now and again, with her eyes closed, sitting on Dad's lap, Dominique would feel her dad's teardrop fall onto her hand or arm, and she delighted in the safety of his embrace.

***

In the backdrop of that scenic home certainty, there was growing in Dominique a greater certainty, one that was forged in her soul and that permeated everything. She was normal, fallen like all humans, but also empowered, like the freshness of a spring welling up inside her, overflowing with love.

Scripture held her spellbound, and to her heart's content, she found herself buried in the Bible and living in love with Jesus, but being a sinner, at the same time, was excruciating.

One day, while contemplating the willingness of her sinful life, she remembered a verse that Bella shared with her. The main point seemed to be that Christians can "take every thought captive to the obedience of Christ." Thinking to herself that it couldn't be possible, she began to research Scripture for that remedy.

She searched for what the entire verse said. Finding it, she put it to memory. It was 2 Corinthians 10:4–5. When she first read it out loud, it changed everything. It says, "The weapons we fight with are not the weapons of the world. On the contrary, they have divine power to demolish strongholds. We demolish arguments and every pretension that sets itself up against the knowledge of God, and we take captive every thought to make it obedient to Christ."[24] Understanding that it was necessary to know how to fight against her enemy, it was better to know that she had weapons for her warfare.

Next, Aunt Colleen pointed her to a verse from Galatians 5:17. She parsed that verse until it was memorized, and she pulled it up often. Nearly every day, she would quote it to herself, saying, "For the flesh desires what is contrary to the Spirit, and the Spirit what is contrary to the flesh. They are in conflict with each other, so that you are not to do whatever you want."[25]

Still, the calamity of wanting what God wants and wanting to sin at the same time left her cognitively alert but emotionally careless. It was Mrs. Allard who put the final piece in place, and it soothed her soul. She called her one day just to bounce her sin dilemma off Mrs. Allard's insight.

Knowing that Dominique's questions were paramount if her faith was to grow, Mrs. Allard cherished the moment and said to her, "So, have you found, like the rest of us, that sin can be both entertaining and malicious all at once?" Dominique concluded that Mrs. Allard was incapable of answering a question without asking a question.

Still trying to comprehend what Mrs. Allard just asked, Dominique was quickly brought back to the future, just in time, because Mrs. Allard was moving on. Not really wanting Dominique's response, she jumped right in and said, "You need to read chapter 7 in the book of Romans. Call me when you have thoroughly perused that chapter, and we will talk."

Dominique thanked Mrs. Allard, telling her she would call her back, but as she hung up, she marveled at this amazing mentor who never quit teaching because now, she had a new word to look up. And she thought to herself, *I have not used that word before; what does it mean "to peruse"?*

Romans chapter 7 was a lifesaver. She read it repeatedly, and then, one day, the pieces fell in place. She kept repeating the verses, then finally, she was able to summarize her thoughts, and she said verse 20 out loud, "Now if I do what I do not want to do, it is no longer I who do it, but it is sin living in me that does it."[26]

That did it; the problem was solved. She paraphrased verse 23 to herself, "Sin is waging war against my mind, trying to make me a prisoner of the law of sin at work in me."[27] She continued her examination by saying verses 24 and 25, "Who will rescue me from this body that is subject to death? Thanks be to God, who delivers me through Jesus Christ our Lord! So then, I myself in my mind am a slave to God's law, but in my sinful nature a slave to the law of sin."[28]

From that day on, in two verses, Dominique rested with the sin issue. First John 1:9–10 says, "If we confess our sins, he is faithful and just and will forgive us our sins and purify us from all unrighteousness. If we claim we have not sinned, we make him out to be a liar and his word is not in us."[29] She finally concluded, "God loves me, a sinner, and confession of sin is fellowship, communion with God. Not a wallowing in despair, a hoping for redemption, a guilt-ridden existence, but an agreement with God and peace in His presence."

With this revelation from Romans and a new understanding of sin, Dominique called Mrs. Allard. Mrs. Allard listened carefully as Dominique shared her enlightened perspective on sin in the Christian life. After zealously making a case, she waited nervously for Mrs. Allard to dissect her premise.

In her usual form, Mrs. Allard asked Dominique, "Have you done all the research you need to do? Are you satisfied with your conclusions?"

She paused briefly, and as she did, Dominique was left to wonder if her questions were rhetorical. Then, she knew they were not, which caused Dominique's doubts to rush in, but right in the middle of that fear, she turned rather to courage and boldly said to Mrs. Allard, "I am perfectly satisfied with what the scriptures have revealed to me."

Unbeknownst to Dominique, Mrs. Allard was smiling from ear to ear, and she nearly chuckled at hearing Dominique so wonderfully confident. Then, she made one more attempt to dissuade her and said, "Are you sure?"

With this new confidence, Dominique could not resist a pushback and said, "Do you have that same kind of peace about sin that I do?"

"Ahhh!" Mrs. Allard exclaimed. She answered Dominique, saying, "I believe my student is becoming the teacher."

Smiling in triumph, Dominique thought to herself, *What a turn of events!* Then, she said to Mrs. Allard, "If I am ready to begin teaching, I owe it to the one person who never allowed me to think poorly. Thank you, Mrs. Allard."

At hearing Dominique thank her, Mrs. Allard thought back to that day when she walked so delicately into Dominique's room, only to see a devastated and helpless soul torn by life's harshness. She also thought of how God was moving that day, which is apparent; He is still moving today, and she thanked Him.

She came back into the conversation and said to Dominique, "Do you remember what I told you in your room that first day when Mrs. Martsen called me to help?"

Thinking back, Dominique said, "You said a lot of things, and thank God you did."

Mrs. Allard pushed a little harder, saying, "It had to do with what suffering in my life ultimately led to."

Dominique was surprised, but she did remember, and she said to Mrs. Allard, "You told me you did not arrive where you are today through much joy but through much suffering."

Thinking about how to phrase it, Mrs. Allard broke off but came right back in, saying, "Dominique, you are now that same person. You have arrived at the place where God wants to use what you have endured to help others, and you are powerful to do that in Him. Still, you must know that enduring in suffering will still be out in front of you, but God's sovereign plan for your life is His doing."

Those words seemed nearly too good to be true, and Dominique felt the flattery was overblown, but just as she doubted, again she was taken to courage, and she said to Mrs. Allard, "Mrs. Allard, I believe what you say is true. I do know His power."

Mrs. Allard nearly jumped down the phone line and said emphatically, "Truer words were never spoken." And when she finished that statement, she said almost sarcastically, "And when are you going to quit calling me Mrs. Allard? My name is Anne."

***

With the mission training just weeks away, Dominique began to feel somewhat leveraged, like this was not really her idea. She knew the commitment she made must be kept but wondered how in the world she said yes to this plan. She understood little of what this excursion entailed and had to rely on the hype of Bella's enthusiasm for both of them.

To relieve Dominique of doubt about who was orchestrating this calling from God, Bella phoned almost every day. Not just to encourage Dominique but to clarify the details and make sure all was going to plan.

Dominique had to admit this whole thing was a bit too much to fathom, and she was scared. Her fear did not come from not trusting that God was capable of all that He had planned for them; it was more like fear of the unknown, like when she was first enrolled at William James, she didn't know what to expect.

What was really eating at Dominique had to do with her mom freaking out about the mission trip, which poured over into her dad as well. She first told them her plans after arriving home from graduation. Marie just stared for the longest time and said, "Doesn't your mother have anything to say about your decisions now?" Thomas looked at Marie and then Dominique and then back to Marie. By the look on his face, it was evident he did not feel safe getting in between his bride and daughter, so he tried to look stern at Dominique but said nothing.

Later that same night, wanting to talk, Thomas came to Dominique's room, but before he knocked and was surprised by the thought, he felt led to pray and said, "God help me." Then, he looked up and knocked on her door.

Dominique said, "Come in," and he entered smiling. He started to make small talk, but Dominique, knowing that he was nervous, let him off the hook and said, "Hey, Dad, I know why you have come. It is okay for us to discuss it."

Since arriving home, Dominique's love for her dad had re-blossomed, and she looked adoringly at him because she knew he had come to discuss hard stuff, which was not his forte. Dominique was almost sure that her dad was sent by Mom to dissuade her from the mission trip. Thomas, on the other hand, was head over heels at having Dominique home and her being so loving and kind.

His throat was instantly dry; he ran his tongue over his teeth, and to no avail. He tried to swallow; undeterred, he jumped right in, saying, "You know, you have just arrived back home, and your mom and I are so very happy about that." After that, he felt at a loss as to how to proceed and started thinking to himself, *If this were a meeting with the board executives of the company, I would be in full command, but this is not the board; this is Dominique who thrives on confrontational calisthenics.*

As her dad contemplated the next bullet in his presentation, Dominique smiled because, in her mind, it was like she could see the script of her dad's speech in front of her eyes, and she knew what the next line would be before he spoke it.

Knowing things were bogging down, he began again, "Honey, you know you are not quite eighteen yet, and your mom and I are not comfortable with you leaving the country. By law, you are not considered an adult yet, and though you are a very mature young woman, we do not feel like you would be safe.

Dominique was surprised, not by the content of the comment, which was right out of her parents' playbook, but by how sincere her dad sounded. She could read his heart and his body language; his comment was sincere and only an expression of their love.

Not expecting her dad to be so convincing, she smiled again at him and said, "Dad, I hear you. I believe you are truly concerned about me, and I know your reservations about this trip are because you love me." Thomas could hardly believe his ears. He was even thinking to himself, *Oh, Marie will be so proud of me.*

Before Dad could say anything, Dominique continued, and she said, "Tell you what, I will take your concern to prayer. If God is calling me to another part of the world, I am sure He would want me to consult you and Mom and get your feedback. How does that sound?"

Thomas was ecstatic, and he said, "I will tell your mother of your decision." Then, he bent down and kissed Dominique on the forehead, and as he left the room, he said, "Thank you, darling."

As soon as her dad left, Dominique began to pray; it was beginning to look like something was amiss. She thought, *If God is calling me away from home, why are my parents not on board with this idea?* So, she prayed and asked Him to intercede with her parents, and she also petitioned Him for a vision of how this was all supposed to work out.

She called Bella to get her input on what she was experiencing. Bella was very calm and said, "Rather than just strategize over the phone, let us not discuss it any further until after we have prayed extensively about this." So, they prayed earnestly for about a week. She even had Chase, Aunt Colleen, and Mrs. Allard praying for them as well.

During the allotted prayer period, Dominique never spoke a word of the trip to her parents, and they never brought it up either. Dominique was so enjoying the peace at home with her parents, but she sensed trouble brewing over this issue.

Chase was a rock; he was so pumped about her going on the mission trip. Initially, they discussed it at length, and it became the main topic of their discourse in nearly every conversation they had. Since they both believed that Dominique should go on the mission, Chase was praying for God to reveal His will to his parents.

***

After Thomas shared Dominique's concession of wanting her parents' input, Marie was cautiously optimistic that maybe they could help her make a better decision, but at the same time, she was honestly forced to ask herself, *Who is this girl who has come back to us so wise and confident?*

She was torn by the dilemma that confronted her. On one hand, she was blissful. It was evident that their decision to place Dominique at William James made the difference, which is now undeniable. On the other hand, their daughter had come back healed, able, it seemed, even to move beyond the Durand incident and noticeably prepared to go and make a difference in the world.

Marie knew that Thomas would want whatever she wanted, so she felt they had a united front, but she was afraid to ask Thomas what he really believed concerning the mission trip.

As she allowed herself to even consider Dominique's suggestion of leaving on a mission trip,

Marie remained pensive and fearful. Unable to discover a peaceful perspective, she spent sleepless nights wrestling with herself. Finally, after several evenings of little sleep and no solace, she sat up in bed; determined to end her restlessness, she said to herself, "It appears, God, that You are seeking me out."

She paused, remembering the reverence with which Chloe had prayed so often for Dominique, and she checked her attitude, hoping to reflect that same reverence. Then she said, "You know, You have been meandering around in our family for quite some time now, and I am not sure I like it." Pausing, she reflected again on the tone of her petition; feeling His presence, she began to feel very small, but then she rebounded, speaking boldly to the Creator: "If I do not confront our estrangement now, just like the rest of my life has been, I will be forever shrinking in Your presence, afraid and doubting Your goodness."

Starting to feel empowered, she went on saying, "Why do You let us suffer, like my poor Dominique? How has her suffering benefited Your purposes? My sister is always telling me that You will never leave us or forsake us. Dominique could have benefited by Your intervention with Durand. How could You just watch?"

Not even knowing she was weeping, she began wiping the tears away from her swollen eyes and realized if she continued this dialogue with God, she might wake Thomas.

Brushing her long hair back, she leaned over to ensure Thomas was still sleeping. Sure he was still asleep, Marie pulled her legs out from under the covers, threw them over the side of the bed, and put her feet on the floor. She stood quietly and silently left the bedroom.

The dim night-light revealed the many shadows of the family room. Still weeping and feeling forlorn, she moved quickly to the lamp next to the sofa and turned it on, then sat down, pulling her legs up under her.

The sofa light did little to illuminate all that inhabited their large family room, and the shadows appeared like ominous fiends. She looked around as if being watched and was unnerved by how all alone she felt. Then, she sensed an unnatural presence, and her heart started to race. In fear, she bowed her head and said, "Oh, God, what is it You want of me?"

***

The next day, Marie awoke late and cranky from a lack of sleep. Along with that emotion, she was also unsure what, if anything, had been accomplished in last evening's time with God. If nothing else, for some reason, she was certain she needed to know Thomas's genuine feelings about the mission trip.

She made her way to the kitchen and found Thomas and Dominique with their backs to her, preparing breakfast together. As they were talking lightly, engrossed in their chore at the kitchen counter, they did not hear Marie walk in. Enjoying the father-daughter clip reeling before her, Marie just sat down in one of the table chairs and observed their interaction.

She could not help but marvel at the peace and the joy reflected before her as they bonded together. When Dominique spoke to her dad, she looked at him, and her eyes lit up; when Thomas saw the look in her eyes, you could tell he was lost in her presence.

Suddenly, without warning, Dominique put her finger into the pancake batter and rubbed it across her dad's hairy arm. She stepped back a little to take in his response, but Thomas did not react; he did not move or look up. This was disappointing to Dominique; she wrinkled her nose and opened her mouth slightly but said nothing.

Marie, now wondering where this was going, looked intently on. Dominique laughed a little, hoping to get a response from Dad. With him not playing along, she moved back in close where she stood before and wondered if Dad was not happy with her jesting.

As she moved close, without warning, Thomas grabbed both her wrists and pulled her in closer. Surprised, Dominique let out a little scream. She froze, and the memory of Durand's attack came crashing into her mind. She stared terrified at her dad, not knowing what to expect. She trembled slightly, and as she did, she focused keenly on the eyes holding her gaze; these were not the oppressive, dark, and evil eyes of Durand but the calm, soothing eyes of a loving father, and she found her way back to comfort in his grasp. Just then, Thomas took the ladle covered with the pancake batter and ran it down her nose, covering it with white sticky goo.

Seeing the gleeful expression on her dad's face, his joy in the playful banter with his daughter, Dominique prayed, *Thank You, dear Lord, for my dad*. Then, coming back to the moment, with the batter running down her nose, her expression changed; she let out a sigh of disgust, and she considered retaliation.

Quickly, she pulled one hand loose and reached for the bowl of pancake batter; just as she did, Thomas spun her around, grabbed her by the waist, and held her off the ground. She struggled to no avail, and they were both laughing hysterically. Wrestling together, they spun full around, and at the same time, they both stopped, riveted on the presence of Marie, a wide grin on her face, sitting there watching them.

As if not knowing they were in trouble or not, they looked at each other tentatively, and Thomas put Dominique down on the kitchen floor. Just staring at them, Marie was no longer smiling, which made them both wonder about their fate. As they closely watched her face for a reaction, suddenly joy overtook the moment as tears formed in both eyes, and Marie said, "I love how you two make breakfast together."

Thomas and Dominique turned and smiled at each other, then they raced over to where Marie stood, and the three of them embraced. With pancake batter still rolling off her nose, Dominique pulled back, looked at them, and said, "I love you guys."

Blissful, Thomas and Marie turned to look at each other, and as they did, Marie spoke silently to her new and ever-present confidant, saying, *Thank You, Lord*.

* * *

With time running out for Dominique to decide on the mission trip, Marie, tormented by uncertainty, found herself longing for closure. She knew the false freedom in which she had lived her entire life was now in jeopardy. It was like she was in a tug of war: one moment, she would be belittling herself for her gullible meanderings about faith in God, and the next moment, she was thankful for His blessings that were so evident in Dominique's life.

With that frame of mind, Marie set out to confirm with Thomas his true sentiments about the mission trip. She found him busy in his den, pouring over several new business prospects. As she entered, he looked up and smiled, but his smile quickly faded because it was evident that before him stood a troubled bride.

Unsure of her motivation for the visit, Thomas motioned for her to take a chair. She moved over in front of his desk and sat down. As Thomas stared at her expectantly, Marie tried to soften her demeanor, thinking, *If I want Thomas's honest feelings, I must not force him to just go where I want him to go.*

Having faced Marie in these situations many, many times, Thomas was apprehensive. He hated this, and knowing these events usually ended up revealing some flaw he portrayed as a husband, he started to squirm in his chair.

Sensing Thomas's uneasiness, Marie smiled and said softly, "So much has happened to our Dominique and so quickly, wouldn't you agree?" Feeling less intimidated by the direction of the conversation, Thomas smiled and nodded his head.

Marie continued, "She is a different girl, and I am so thankful." She paused and became more animated, saying, "She is happy, Thomas; she is pleasant; she tells us she loves us and wants to please us."

Becoming giddy with the tone of praises lavished on their daughter, Thomas sat forward and said emphatically, "Yes."

Now knowing Thomas was at ease, Marie unloaded the premise of her visit, saying, "She is so changed and so wonderfully different, but is she equipped for being out of the country on a mission trip?"

Not stopping to let Thomas answer, she continued, "I fear she is not, but I am torn." She hesitated briefly to gather her thoughts and the courage to say what needed to be said and started again: "The last few days, it seems that God has been seeking me out." Now that Thomas knew her thoughts, she paused just to read the expression on his face. She looked at him, wondering if she should wait for him to respond. He said nothing, but the look on Thomas's face told Marie he seemed excited about it.

For their entire marriage, Marie knew that she and Thomas had only used God as a social construct, a ritual, a compartmentalized addition to daily life, but in this moment, she was admitting to her husband the reality of His presence in her life.

She looked at Thomas and said, "Yes, God has been prompting me, has been pulling at my heart, and I have been talking to Him." Knowing how Thomas felt about his dad and his dad's God, Marie balked, hoping that Thomas would respond. She paused, as if to invite his feedback.

Thomas reached across the desk and took Marie's hands in his, saying, "How wonderful; God has been doing the same thing with me. I just did not know how to tell you for fear it would scare you or make you upset."

This stopped Marie in her tracks because she thought she was hearing Thomas say it was she who was holding them back from God, but looking at the joy in his face, she quickly dismissed that idea and gripped his hands tightly.

Looking intently and lovingly at each other, Thomas interjected, "Now what?"

CHAPTER 30

Praying every day, and as the week came to an end, Dominique had God's peace that she would only go on mission if her parents agreed to it. She had to admit she was not fully sure how all this mission stuff factored into her life. Maybe she was only excited because Bella was, and maybe it was her parents that God would use to make sure of the call; maybe she was not supposed to be going.

With less than a week to begin mission training and completely a surprise to Dominique, Thomas and Marie sought her out to share their decision. They sat together in the family room, and Thomas opened the discussion, saying, "Well, sweetheart, your mom and I have come to a conclusion concerning the mission trip." He paused to look at Marie, and Marie nodded to him. He continued, "We do not like the idea of you leaving home and the country to go on this mission trip."

He paused as if to gather his thoughts, and while he was doing that, Dominique was thinking to herself, *Well, that is it; I guess this is God's answer.*

Then, Thomas went on, saying, "We have also seen a change in you, a wonderful love flowing from your heart, a desire to do the right things, and a peace we wondered if you would ever know."

Dominique was thankful for the accolades and the acknowledgment that they could see the change in her life, but she just wanted her dad to say, "Maybe not now," was the best answer.

Thomas needed to look over at Marie again for moral support; after having done so, he continued saying, "What is evident to your parents is God has entered your life, and His power is flowing out of you. At first, our thoughts about the mission trip were, 'Absolutely not,' but then, we reasoned together, and God allowed us to see that if He brought you safe thus far, He is capable of the same anywhere in the world."

Dominique's eyes started to widen as she listened to her dad; he was speaking what she thought was nearly unfathomable. Thomas continued, "So, our greatest concern is not that God can keep you safe, but that this is really what you want and not just your infatuation with Bella's vision."

As Thomas paused, Dominique looked first at her mom and then back to her dad. Like never before, they were both staring intently at her. Dominique could not speak; she was caught in a wonderful place. Her dad was taking the lead, and with her mom's blessing, they were saying, "We trust God, and we trust you."

Her first thought after hearing this revelation was to ask her parents, "What has happened to you two?" But her next thought confirmed the answer, and she said out loud, "Well, praise the Lord." And she continued, "Am I hearing you say it is up to me, and if I decide to go, God will be the help I need?" Thomas and Marie smiled and nodded. Dominique smiled back and said, "Okay then, I will let you know."

Thomas and Marie affirmed her comment but sensed some reluctance in her accepting their positive take on the trip. Later, Marie asked Thomas if he felt, as she did, that Dominique was not expecting them to support her decision, and he agreed.

Unsure as to how to proceed, they just looked at each other. Thomas was thinking to himself that they should pray, but he did not know how to initiate a prayer time together with Marie. Looking at Thomas but lost as well on how to proceed, Marie was ready to ask Thomas what they should do when Chase walked into the room.

It was pleasing to see his parents together, but looking at them, he sensed they were nearly at an argument, or they were trying to figure out what to do with Dominique. He had seen his parents many times contemplating the second option and concluded it was Dominique on their minds.

Always upbeat, Chase jumped right in and said, "Hey, you look like you could use a fixer right now. How much will you pay for my services?" They both laughed and looked at him adoringly. They attempted to change the solemness of their countenance into light conversation, but Chase was alert to the hypocrisy and said, "What has she done now?"

Marie and Thomas looked at each other, then back at Chase; he amazed them both with his maturity and his insight. They did not know that Chase and Dominique were praying together about the mission trip, so he continued saying, "Does this have anything to do with you not wanting her to go on the mission trip?"

It was difficult for Thomas and Marie to hear their youngest son assume the obvious about his parents, but Chase could not have known all that God was doing recently in their lives. Not bristling, not hurt, but saddened by Chase's assumption, Thomas said, "No, we have given her our blessing for the mission trip."

That was too much of a twist for Chase; he opened his eyes wide and said, "What?"

Marie entered the conversation and said, "Yes, Son, we have. We are sure God has His hand in her life, and we want what His will is for her, but when we gave her the answer that we assumed she was hoping for, she seemed shocked and unsure about her decision. When you came in, we were discussing what this could all mean."

Chase could hardly believe he was hearing these goings on from his parents. He rejoiced in his thoughts and said to himself, *Oh, thank You, God, for answering my prayers.* He wanted to grab each of them and squeeze them, but he refrained and said, "So, what have you come up with?"

Not sure how to tell his son that he was stumped and that prayer seemed to be the only option, Thomas stuttered but got it out and said, "I was thinking, unless we talk to God about this, we will never know what we seek."

At hearing Thomas's remedy, Marie looked up and made eye contact with him. She stumbled as well and said, "That appears the only way to know." Finding himself in a foreign but wonderful world, Chase got the biggest smile on his face and asked his parents, "Have you ever prayed together other than for asking God to bless our meals?"

They both looked sheepishly at each other and then at Chase. Having to admit that the answer was no, they both looked down and shook their heads. Sensing their guilt at his question, Chase moved quickly to put a positive on the negative surrounding their admission and said, "Hey, then, why don't we start a new family tradition and pray together to find God's desire for Dominique?"

Thomas was aware of Chase's passion for God, which he saw at church and in their private talks, but he was unsure of Marie's insight into her son's commitment to Jesus. So, he nodded his head to affirm the suggestion, and they both turned to look at Marie. They were both surprised when she smiled and said, "That would be wonderful."

* * *

After her discussion with her parents, Dominique jumped on the phone with Bella. As the phone was ringing, she began to realize she was not as excited about this news as she thought she would be. Her parents' support threw her into a tailspin. With those thoughts pouring through Dominique's mind, Bella answered the phone, saying, "Hello." Dominique froze for a moment, and Bella said again, "Hello."

Hoping to sound excited, Dominique said, "Guess what? My parents want me to go."

Sensing a lack of excitement in Dominique's voice, Bella was unsure how to proceed. She paused and thought to herself, *Something is up.* Then, she said to Dominique, "Well, what are your thoughts?"

Now, it was Dominique who did not know how to proceed. She had not considered the possibility of this response from her parents. Weakly and without conviction, she nearly whispered, saying, "I don't know…"

Picking up on Dominique's faltering, Bella said gently, "Hey, before deciding your fate in this matter, it looks like we have a few more days to cover in prayer."

Dominique became sad and said to Bella, "I am sorry, Bella. I was so sure my parents would say no; I was expecting to be obedient to them and not go. This is all too overwhelming for me."

As always, Bella brightened the mood and said, "Hey, we have trusted God all this way; why should we not trust Him now? If He wants you to go, I believe, one way or the other, He will make it plain to you. Do not fret, my friend; we are in God's hands. How are you feeling about that?"

Dominique loved Bella's way of seeing things, and in her heart, she concurred. Even with the trepidation she was feeling at that moment, she knew God would be sure in His decision for her. She said to Bella, "I will pray to know His will." Then, she said again, "I am so sorry, Bella, my lack of commitment must be such sad news for you."

Ever forgiving and understanding, Bella said, "I would not want you going if it was just for me. Unless God has you by the fine hairs on the back of your neck, you should not go. He will make it plain and peaceful; you will know."

She finished by saying, "Your parents are on board; think about that, but you must know the truth for yourself. Until we talk again, I love you." And Bella said goodbye.

With tears filling her eyes and being thankful for such a friend, Dominique said, "There is no one like you… I love you too. Goodbye."

* * *

For the next couple of days, after her conversation with Bella, Dominique found herself forlorn and doubtful. The world seemed a weird place to her. She came up empty-handed, trying to remember times in her life when a decision meant so much. In fact, as she looked back at her life, it was laughable, the things she used to consider a big deal.

The only thing that mattered to her back then was manipulating her way around authority figures, especially her parents. Now, she found herself without boundaries, left to her own wisdom, and she wished it was not just up to her.

She knew how Chase felt about it; he was pumped about how God would use her on mission. He was sure the lives that would be changed due to her presence would have eternal value. Aunt Colleen was so supportive, but she would not push her either way; she just wanted what was best for her niece.

Not wanting to call the one person who would force her to make a decision, Dominique shied away from Mrs. Allard, but it seemed she was the only person qualified to force her into critical thinking and real problem-solving. Grumbling to herself, she said, "If I call Mrs. Allard, she will not come right out and make any suggestions; she will just ask me questions to force me to come to my own conclusions." Then she thought, *That is where I am right now, trying to come to my own conclusions; I hate this.*

As she went to bed that night, she assumed all those who loved her would be praying for her about her decision. Comforted by that thought, she tried sleeping but could not fall asleep. She tossed and turned for hours until she had to sit up. So tired and needing rest, she nearly screamed; then, something happened, a prompting, and she realized she had not spoken to God since her parents shared their support about her going on mission.

She thought to herself, *Is it true that I don't really want to hear from God about this trip?* Knowing that she feared hearing His input forced her to lay calmly back down and contemplate her situation. Her thoughts forced her to reason with herself, and she said to herself, "I am afraid of where this is all going. I am afraid of trusting Him in this place, but to ignore Him is even more frightening."

It was surreal for Dominique. She lay there thinking and knowing that the one who spoke all into being, the one who died to take away her sin and take her to heaven, the one who placed all the loving people in her life, explicitly where they are, was, at the same time, excitedly waiting now before her to hear her voice.

Then, a song that she heard Bella singing one day in their dorm room came into her head, and she sang it to herself: *"To have a love like that, it knocks me off my feet, / to have a love like that, my life is so complete. / Reconciled, and I am free; / why should there be fear in me."*

Not sure what was going on or what she was doing, but still unable to speak to the Lord, she began quoting her favorite verses from Psalm 23. So, she said it to herself:

> The Lord is my shepherd, I lack nothing.
>
> He makes me lie down in green pastures,
>
> he leads me beside quiet waters,
>
> he refreshes my soul.
>
> He guides me along the right paths
>
>   for his name's sake.
>
> Even though I walk
>
>   through the darkest valley,

> I will fear no evil,
>
> for you are with me;
>
> your rod and your staff,
>
> they comfort me.[30]

Halfway through the memory verse, Dominique became aware of God's presence; as she poured out His Word, He poured back His presence into her soul. When she finished the verses, a new calm had quieted her; a warmth was holding her, and she closed her eyes, saying cautiously, "Lord, I am afraid of trusting You. I am afraid that You want me to leave the security of those You have surrounded me with."

Then, as she had heard it a hundred times and as if Aunt Colleen was standing in the room, she heard her voice saying, "Remember, darling, He has said, 'I will never leave you or forsake you.'"

Not knowing how long this discourse had been happening, Dominique found herself exhausted; her eyelids became so heavy she could not stay awake, and she said to the Lord, "Can we talk about this another time? I love You; good night." In peace, it was just seconds, and she was fast asleep but never leaving. According to His word, in her dreams, she pictured the Lord keeping watch over her.

* * *

Morning found Dominique still at peace and rested, but she could not get Mrs. Allard out of her mind. She struggled with the dichotomy of just leaving Mrs. Allard out of the equation, which would be easier, but seeking her input would probably reveal deeper insight.

As she buzzed down for breakfast, she found her mom busy making it ready. She said, "Morning, Mom! I love you."

Instantly after hearing that greeting, tears began to fill Marie's eyes, and because of that, she could not turn and face Dominique, but a joyful and thankful smile filled her face, and she said, "I love you too, honey."

Every day now, with Dominique, was a joy, and Marie knew there was only one who could be credited for her transformation. This transformation was so stark that Marie found herself in daily prayer, thanking God for His goodness, and with each day, her trust in Him blossomed.

With Thomas already at the office and breakfast behind them, Marie sat there saying nothing. She just stared longingly at Dominique sitting across the table. The silence became awkward, and Dominique looked quickly down but then right back into her mom's eyes and said, "What?"

Marie was startled by Dominique's question. Somewhat embarrassed that Dominique had awakened her from a mother's blissful silence with her daughter, she sat up a little and said, "Excuse me, what did you say?"

Dominique smiled fondly and said, "Mom, you looked like you were lost in a dream; you were just staring at me."

Eyes bright and a big smile on her face, Marie said, "Yes, I was staring; I love being with you; you make me happy."

It was like seeing her mom through different eyes; now, Dominique was the one staring and thinking back to just a short time ago when they seemed at such odds. Marie broke into the middle of Dominique's daydream and said, "Why don't you and I get out of the house and go do something together; what do you want to do?"

* * *

Arriving home after spending several hours picnicking, gabbing, and reading the Bible together in Central Park, Marie tossed her light jacket on the back of the kitchen chair, took Dominique by the hand, and pulled her into the family room. She spun Dominique around, and they both landed on the sofa. Marie took both of Dominique's hands and said, "I am going to miss you so much."

More than a little surprised by her mom's comment, not knowing what to say, Dominique just stared at her mom. Thoughts racing through her head, Dominique said to herself, *Mom must think my mind's made up.* Not sure how to proceed, Dominique cocked her head sideways, looking at her mom with no intent. She shook her head as if to say, "How did you come to the conclusion that I was leaving?"

Trying to relieve the tension, Marie said, "Hey, come on, I know this is something you feel led to do. I have concluded that if God wants you there, I would be fighting Him for your loyalties, and that is not right, nor what is best for you."

Dominique's jaw dropped open, like when you cannot control the emotion, and she was instantly ready to tell her mom that she wasn't feeling led to go any longer, but just as those thoughts started to roll off her tongue, taking her up short, another thought jumped ahead in line. Then, she thought, *It looks like God is even using my mom to extract all the hurdles and distractions from His inevitable goal for me: the mission trip.*

Dominique began thinking to herself, and the thoughts frightened her; she opined, saying, *If dad is the only holdout now, I am running out of detractors.* Unwilling to acquiesce, she looked straight at her mom, but before she could speak, her mom jumped in and said, "Hey, do not worry. Dad is on the same page as I am. We want what God wants for you."

* * *

Up in her room early that night, Dominique still could not believe the events of the day. As it stood at that moment, she had not one objector to the trip. As exciting as that could have been for someone seeking God's will, it terrified Dominique to see no obstacle in her way. She tried to think back to when this whole adventure with God began.

Then she realized it had only been half a school year and less than a month into summer since she could even consider it plausible that God might be taken seriously. Questioning everything now, she said to herself, "Doesn't this disciple role take some time to develop? Shouldn't there be more exposure to the workings and evidence of God's realm prior to blasting off into the unknown of the spiritual stratosphere?"

The big rub for Dominique was not that God had not worked miraculously in her life; that was evident. Durand was behind her; her relationship with her parents was amazing; God was thoroughly doing it. And add to that her love for Mrs. Martsen, which was just icing on the cake; who would have believed it? But with all the evidence of God's presence in her life, she knew she was exposed; she did not trust God's provision for this next step on her journey with Him.

It was plain to Dominique that the door was wide open to join Bella on the trip, but she questioned herself, saying, "What is it? What am I balking on? Where is the peace that comes from being obedient and following where God leads you to go?"

At this point, Dominique began to realize she might have to accept the inevitable. The inevitable was really the obstacle. For her entire life, Dominique ran from the inevitable. For her, the inevitable always equaled suffering, not getting what you want, and succumbing to the power structure, which meant servitude.

Contemplating that last thought, Dominique was unable to equate her resistance as disobedience to God, but rather, she wondered if God was not too demanding. Right after that thought, she relented of her brashness and asked God's forgiveness, but it was now out in the open, no doubt; she did not like this decision He had made for her life.

Fearful of the consequences for outright disobedience to God, Dominique's mind searched everywhere for a solution, but to no avail; she was left completely alone before all mighty God with no evidence of his contempt for the mission.

Then, as if a lightning bolt went off in her heart and mind, she thought, *I have not talked with Mrs. Allard about this; maybe her input is the piece in this puzzle that is missing.*

* * *

Once again, Dominique could not sleep. Suffering the angst of not knowing for sure God's plan for her life, she awoke unrested and cranky. Before bed, she had resolved that calling Mrs. Allard was the first thing on her schedule for the next day.

Still, very early in the morning, Dominique was forced, anxiously, to wait for a reasonable time to call Mrs. Allard. Finally, the call was made, but the call went to Mrs. Allard's messages, which really tested Dominique's patience. After several attempts at reaching Mrs. Allard, Dominique forced herself to stop and ask the question of herself, and she said, "Why am I so weary over this mission trip? Why do I feel so alone and far away from God right now?"

That question forced her to rethink the entire scenario. It was like a freshening of thought, and she prayed, repenting of her fear and frustration. There in prayer, the tightness in her chest and the wrinkle on her forehead dissipated, and peace took control.

She let out a deep breath and said, "Thank You, dear God. Help me to trust You with my life in Your hands…" Just then, the phone rang, and it was Mrs. Allard. Dominique did not allow Mrs. Allard to finish her greeting before she jumped in and said, "Oh, Mrs. Allard, I have been waiting to hear from you; I need your help."

Though very excited about the opportunity to talk with Dominique, Mrs. Allard became instantly concerned, hearing Dominique's voice so shaken, and she said, "Slow down, take a deep breath, and slowly tell me what the matter is."

Thankful to finally have Mrs. Allard available, Dominique took a few breaths and started again. "Well," she said, "I need you to give me a few good reasons why I should not go on the mission trip."

Knowing Dominique as she did, Mrs. Allard was instantly alert to what was going on, and it was evident to her that Dominique had been given the green light on the mission trip, but with that free pass, she was left alone to decide for herself the right or wrong of it.

Mrs. Allard said nothing at first. Dying for instant feedback, Dominique rather hastily said, "Mrs. Allard, did you hear me?" Still in no hurry to fix Dominique's dilemma, Mrs. Allard remained silent.

As always, it was becoming clear to Dominique that Mrs. Allard was the same mentor she had always been. Dominique knew Mrs. Allard had no intentions of fixing her wagon. It was hard to stick to the rules for their discussions, but Dominique knew Mrs. Allard would not succumb to subversive tactics.

Remembering who she was talking to, Dominique started again and said, "Please forgive me; let me start over."

"There you are," Mrs. Allard quickly interjected. She followed up by saying, "How good to hear from you, my dear friend. How can I help you?"

Knowing that she had already let the cat out of the bag, Dominique was unsure how to proceed. She thought to herself, *Because of what I said, Mrs. Allard already assumes that I do not want to go on the mission trip. She knows that something has changed from when I last saw her and was so excited about the trip, but can she already know that everyone is backing this trip?*

Dominique felt stymied because, once again, she was doing mental choreography with Mrs. Allard, and she was not prepared to dialogue intelligently. She started again by saying, "I am embarrassed by my outburst; that must have sounded very desperate."

Mrs. Allard said, "Oh, it is just us; let's start over. How are you, Dominique? I have missed you so much."

Dominique remembered again how at ease Mrs. Allard was in conflict, how reassured she was in God's goodness, and how loving she was to her. Dominique opened again and said, "I have missed you too. So good to have you close, even if only on the phone." Then she went on saying, "Well, you already know my premise; I should give you some background, right?"

Mrs. Allard said, "That would be nice." And she added, "It sounds like you are having anxious thoughts; let's find out why."

Even though she always told herself she hated how Mrs. Allard forced stuff out of her, feeling the calming of her presence now, Dominique began to relax.

CHAPTER 31

The next day, Dominique still felt overwhelmed about her decision but was so comforted by Mrs. Allard's input. She awoke, going back over everything that they had talked about in her mind.

It took them a while to get to the bottom line, but with Mrs. Allard's help, it was plainly revealed. It was painful for Dominique to realize that her faith was being tested and that without the testing, it could not be real faith.

Mrs. Allard made it clear to Dominique that with all the obstacles removed, the only obstacle left was herself. The roadblock in her heart had to be removed, or she had to live with the roadblock and accept the delusion that God was saying no to the mission trip.

Rather than struggle in the house, living in the panic of this decision, Dominique went outside for a walk. She took some deep breaths as she moved along, and the summer air helped to clear her thoughts. She needed a quiet place to process, stop, and ask herself what she was thinking. She decided to hold up in the park close to her house.

It might have been just that day, but the park was anything but quiet; everybody seemed drawn to the park. She sat on a bench for a few minutes but soon realized the proximity of people hindered her need for solace. Just as she was about to seek a new, quiet place, she saw a young couple sitting on a blanket about ten yards away. Unaware of Dominique's presence, they seemed very happy and enjoying each other's company.

Because she had too many concerns now, Dominique tried not to envision the possibility that someday, it could be her on the blanket with a young man. She tried to brush that feeling off by equating all young men to Durand, and at first, it seemed to work.

Try as she may, she could not help but glance over at the young couple. She even tried turning her back on them, but that did not work because every few moments, she was helpless to not look.

She thought to herself, *I have got to get out of here; this is not doing what I thought it would.* She gave the couple a quick glance as if to say goodbye, but as she did, her vision was preserved over the scene before her; she could not look away. Now, they were lying on the blanket and the young man was cradling the young woman's head in his arm and kissing her gently all over her face: on her cheeks, her chin, her forehead, and finally, he slowly moved until he was sweetly kissing her lips—not lustfully but gently, barely touching her lips, moving from one lip to the other.

Dominique could not look away. Not knowing it, she even leaned toward the couple to see more clearly. In her experience, there was no way for her to relate to the tenderness she was viewing. She looked away, and as she did, she noticed her heart was beating rapidly, and she felt her face flush.

So caught up in what she was seeing, she had no other thoughts, and the allurement was so strong that she was drawn to look back again, but to her horror, as she glanced back at the couple, the young man had turned his head and was staring straight back at Dominique.

Startled, she quickly leaned back against the back of the bench but could not look away from the young man; wide-eyed and terrified, she sat frozen on the bench. The young man's stare was piercing, and her soul was vexed by it. She was so embarrassed that her leg began to shake.

Then, the young man lifted his chin as if to acknowledge Dominique's presence, and a peaceful smile broadened across his face. With that, the young woman rolled over on her stomach to see what had caught her young man's attention. Now, both were staring at her: one with a smile and one with a questioning frown.

Quickly, Dominique swirled to leave, but halfway around, she stopped and looked back at the couple and mouthed the words, "I am so sorry." About two strides away, she heard the young man say, "Hey, don't run away! Come and join us."

*　*　*

Returning from the park, Dominique entered the house through the kitchen door, and there, sitting at the table reading the newspaper, was her dad. Thomas looked up and said, "Hey, honey! Where have you been?" Shaken by her encounter at the park, Dominique was slow to respond, so Thomas put the paper down on the table and said, "Is everything all right?"

Before she could answer, Thomas said, "I hope you know your mom and I are in agreement about the mission trip being your decision."

She moved up close and kissed her dad on the cheek, saying, "Thanks, Dad, that means a lot to me." And she continued saying, "Hey, I need to get up to my room and clean up a bit before supper."

Thomas nodded and picked his paper back up, but just before she left the room, he let down the paper and said, "Dominique." She stopped and turned to see what he wanted, and as she did, he said, "Do you know how much I love you?"

Dominique smiled sweetly and said, "Yes, Dad, I do."

Not knowing why, but when Dominique entered her room, she found herself somewhat frustrated. She thought, *There is no moment in the day when the mission trip doesn't take center stage in my life.* That frustration, irksome as it was, though, had begun to help clarify her motivation for wanting to stay home.

She threw herself onto the bed and propped her head up with her pillow. The instant she settled into the comfort of her own room, the park incident came fresh back into her thoughts.

She could not believe that she actually turned and went back to the young couple, who were now sitting on the blanket, looking intently at her as she walked toward them. It was surreal to her; the young man, whose name was Jean, spoke up and invited her to sit with them on their blanket. The young woman, whose name was Anelise, who was no longer frowning, greeted her with a friendly smile.

Dominique stood sheepishly over them and said, "Please forgive me for staring at you; that was so foolish of me."

Jean said, "Hey, it's no big deal; please sit down." Jean and Anelise moved to accommodate room for Dominique, and she sat down uncomfortably.

As if the moment was not uncomfortable at all for Anelise, she politely said, "We are glad you could join us; who are you?" Lost at how to proceed, Dominique lowered her head, focusing on the lovely patterns in the blanket, but before she could answer, Jean said, "Please be at ease; we are not mad. In fact, we are thankful for your presence."

Looking up slowly, Dominique said, "My name is Dominique."

It seemed to Dominique that Jean was overreacting to her name when he said, "Wow! What a wonderful name."

Dominique just smiled but thought, *Who are these people? This is getting weird.*

Jean continued and said, "You are aware of the meaning of the name Dominique, right?" Dominique nodded, and Jean went on, "Just think, to have a name that means 'of the Lord.'"

Dominique was thinking, *How can he know what my name means?*

Looking as excited as Jean, Anelise said, "Wow! To have your name, what an honor." Then, she followed up by saying, "And we are honored to meet you."

After receiving their names, Dominique said to them, "Then, you are French as well?"

"Yes," Jean said, "and Anelise means 'devoted to God,' and Jean means 'God is gracious.'"

Still confused by how the conversation was moving, Dominique said, "So, do your names reflect how you live your lives?"

Jean became excited and said, "Yes, we do. Our parents named us, and they have spent the rest of our lives explaining the significance of our names. We were taught that we were born to love God with all our heart, soul, mind, and strength; to this day, we still desire to serve Him with our lives."

Wondering how she ended up on a blanket with this rather odd couple, Dominique decided to go along with the dialogue and asked, "So, have you never said no to God and done what you wanted instead?"

Anelise smiled at Dominique and said, "We are just newly engaged, and we want to spend the rest of our lives together. It has been so difficult knowing for sure that Jean is the man I am supposed to marry. Because this decision is the biggest decision I have had to make in my life, I have had many doubts."

Dominique interrupted and said, "Why? Has Jean done something to make you doubt?"

Looking lovingly at Jean, Anelise said, "He is a sinner just like me; I don't expect perfection. What I expect from him and he from me is an unswerving dedication to our Lord Jesus. We have been spending time together to observe and ensure that his commitment to God is real, and the same is true with me. If we went by just our feelings and our urges, we would probably have been married a year ago, but it would not have had God's seal of approval."

At that moment, Jean jumped in and said, "As you observed, we were having an intimate moment prior to me seeing you." Hearing Jean say that, Dominique instantly looked down in embarrassment, but Jean continued, "We have installed boundaries in our intimate moments to ensure our feelings do not override our commitment to God for our marriage."

Hearing this commitment from Anelise and Jean reminded Dominique of Bella's commitment to God for her future marriage, and she said to them, "This is very interesting; my best friend has these same boundaries built into her search for a husband, and she has ended several relationships with guys who could not keep their promises."

Excitedly, Jean said, "She sounds like the kind of friend one would cherish." Anelise nodded her head in agreement.

"Yes, I cherish her." Dominique paused and then said, "Her name is Bella, and her name means 'beautiful'; she is the most beautiful person, inside and out, that I have ever known. She has invited me to join her on a mission trip to Central African Republic."

Anelise jumped in and said, "Wow! That must be so exciting for you?" Dominique paused, and the look on her face gave away her fear and indecision about the mission. Jean waited a moment to observe Dominique's countenance and softly said, "I sense you still have some reservations about the mission trip?"

Slowly nodding but not looking up, once again, Dominique felt trapped in the muddle of the mission trip. She was thinking to herself, *I should be leaving now*. But before she could say anything, Anelise said, "What do you think is causing the indecision?"

Beginning to feel anger, Dominique slowed her thoughts and her breathing, like she knew Mrs. Allard would want her to be in tough situations. She took a breath, let it out, and said, "Just recently, God has revealed Himself to me in ways that can not be ignored. I know He has intervened in my life. I talk with Him now and am lonely when I do not. He has given me a new life, which I thought I would never know again. He has taken away the fear and suffering of an awful ordeal, and I no longer dread the days ahead. Best of all, due to my decision to follow Him, I know that someday, I will be with Him in heaven. Despite all this, the mission trip scares me because I have just newly experienced all this love and peace. I fear I will have to leave that which has become the comfort in my life, which is all the godly people He has surrounded me with."

***

Back to reality, and on her bed, the park interlude ran in rewind through her head over and over. Dominique found herself unable to get out of her mind the scene of Jean so gently kissing Anelise. Until today, her experience with Durand had forever ended any thought of romance in her life.

It was like beginning anew. She realized she had never even held hands with a guy, and she thought, *What would it be like to hold hands with a young man, to be touched so gently and so intimately?* With that exquisite picture rerunning over in her mind, Dominique began feeling warm inside and even longing, hoping someday… Then, she prayed aloud, saying, "Oh, Lord, is it possible that I, too, could have a Jean in my life?"

This new revelation was at once good and bad. It was good because Dominique was seeing God's hand in her healing from Durand's attack, and it was bad because if she was to be fully healed, she was sure she would not find her significant other out on the mission field; another reason to discount the mission trip.

Then, Dominique recalled something Anelise said, and it came back to haunt her. It was wonderful and awful all at once. Anelise said, "I know this is a big decision, but have you considered what God's Word says about His calling us to serve?"

Dominique almost cringed at the question but nodded unconvincingly and said, "Kind of…"

Anelise picked up the Bible on the blanket and said, "Hear is what God's Word says." And she shared two scripture verses with her. One was Luke 18:29–30:

> "Truly I tell you," Jesus said to them, "no one who has left home or wife or brothers or sisters or parents or children for the sake of the kingdom of God will fail to receive many times as much in this age, and in the age to come eternal life."[31]

The next verse Anelise shared, Dominique remembered hearing from Aunt Colleen, and it touched her deeply. It was Luke 9:57–62, and it says,

> As they were walking along the road, a man said to him, "I will follow you wherever you go."
>
> Jesus replied, "Foxes have dens and birds have nests, but the Son of Man has no place to lay his head."
>
> He said to another man, "Follow me."
>
> But he replied, "Lord, first let me go and bury my father."
>
> Jesus said to him, "Let the dead bury their own dead, but you go and proclaim the kingdom of God."
>
> Still another said, "I will follow you, Lord; but first let me go back and say goodbye to my family."
>
> Jesus replied, "No one who puts a hand to the plow and looks back is fit for service in the kingdom of God."[32]

The light in Dominique's room seemed to dim; she paused in her thoughts and started to reason with herself, saying, "What am I afraid of? If God has brought me this far, will He leave me now?" Then, Aunt Colleen's favorite verse came pouring back again into her mind, and she heard God clearly say, "I will never leave you nor forsake you."

Exhausted and relieved at the same time, Dominique reached over onto her nightstand and picked up her Bible. She turned to the two verses that Anelise had shared and began to read them. Repeatedly, she read them, and it wasn't long before she sensed God's presence and peace she needed so badly.

She closed the Bible, looked up, and said, "It is evident, Lord, the park idea was Yours; my meeting with Jean and Anelise was no coincidence. It is becoming clear that if I continue to run from the mission trip, I will run into You at every turn. It appears You have made up Your mind. So, today, I quit running. Have Your way with me; how could it be any better for me than that?"

She rolled over onto her side, took a deep breath, let it out, and said, "Well, I guess that is that."

But just before she dosed off into a peaceful bliss, she said, "I love You, Lord; thank You for loving me." Her thoughts were peaceful, her soul was at rest, and she slept the sleep that only the faithful know; that God will never leave them or forsake them is a sure thing.

* * *

Waking early the next morning, Dominique lay there in bed, feeling strangely that she was not the same person from the night before. During her dialogue with Jesus, something had transpired. She was living in peace, but a peace she could not describe. She remembered Aunt Colleen telling her that "peace that passes understanding" only comes from complete and total reliance on Jesus.

She even tried testing herself to see if this peace was real; she intentionally forced her thoughts over to dwell on the Durand debacle; it was almost like an imaginary dream. There was no consternation, just a myth from her past. She tried to focus on the worst of outcomes, which might happen on the mission trip, and yes, even possibly dying, but she was no longer afraid to go. What a wonderful surprise for Dominique; her faith stood up to the test.

Unless it had to do with manipulation and deceit, Dominique had never been a confident person, but this new life was breeding assurance, which gave her hope, and she was not disappointed because God had her future in hand.

As she left her room for downstairs, the first thing that caught her attention was the aroma of bacon frying; then, she caught a glimpse of her parents. Dominique thought to herself, *Is it possible that I am actually seeing reality now?* She said that to herself because as they came into view, she saw them differently, clearer than before.

Then, she remembered some scripture verses that Bella shared with her. She recalled the day they were discussing Bella's faith, and Dominique asked her, "Have you always had this strong faith?"

Bella responded by saying, "No, it was not until I made Jesus my everything that I jumped down off the throne of my life and said to Him, 'You and You alone can save my life; Your will be done.'"

Dominique quickly asked, "After that step, when did you know you had a stronger faith?"

Bella smiled confidently and said, "It was like the scriptures were coming alive in my soul, like the verse in 2 Corinthians 5:17: 'Therefore, if anyone is in Christ, the new creation has come: The old has gone, the new is here!'"[33] Bella continued, "I was new, it is hard to explain, except to say that my ever-aching burdens were gone, and instead of doubt, the scriptures began to rule my thinking, like the verse in Mathew 11:28, which says, 'Come to me, all you who are weary and burdened, and I will give you rest.'"[34] She finished by saying, "Now I walk according to His Word, not my thinking or feeling, but His Word."

Trying to clear her thoughts and moving deeper into the kitchen, she came up close to her parents. Dominique marveled at the two amazing people teaming up on breakfast. They were like salve to her eyes, but at the same time, she instantly regretted all the awful things she had said and done to them.

They were startled when Dominique came up close; they all just stood there for an instant and looked at each other. Dominique could not fully understand the emotion of what was taking place; unable to stop it, she reached out and quickly hugged them both. After a brief hug, which was an unexpected joy to Marie and Thomas, she pulled back, and with tears running down her face, Dominique looked at Mom and then at Dad and said, "Please forgive me for causing you both so much sorrow… I am very sorry."

* * *

Later that morning, in the family room, Thomas and Marie cuddled together on the sofa. Neither said anything, but they were both in deep thought, considering what took place at breakfast. Marie pulled her head up from Thomas's shoulder and looked at him. Thomas turned his head toward Marie, anticipating her thoughts.

Not sure how to start and nearly whispering, Marie said, "Well, now we know."

Thomas just nodded but was alert to the alarm written across his bride's face. Not sure if Marie needed consoling or confirmation or both, Thomas spoke, saying, "Yes, she seems so at peace with her decision."

Looking away and down into her lap, Marie muttered a quiet yes. Not wanting to lead where he should not go, Thomas just put his hand over Marie's hand and squeezed it. Thankful that her husband was close, Marie remained silent for a moment; then, not looking up, she said, "You know, when I was telling her the decision was hers, I sensed she really didn't want to go."

At that, Thomas reached down, gently placing his fingertips under Marie's chin. He turned her head up and toward him and said softly, "Me too." He smiled and continued saying, "Our Dominique is nearly eighteen years old, and she has become more than what we had hoped for, wouldn't you agree?" Sensing Marie' agreement, Thomas went on. "For the first time in her life, she is thoughtful, sensitive, in love with her parents, enamored with God, and now, if this is His call, trying to be obedient to Him. What more could parents want for their child?"

Marie just nodded her head, but her heart would not let her be at peace. Not wanting Thomas to sense her anxiety, a thin smile etched onto her face, but just barely hiding the fear etched into her heart.

CHAPTER 32

From that day in the kitchen with her parents, Dominique's world became a whirlwind. Bella was ecstatic that they would be going together to Central African Republic. When Dominique told her the news, Bella danced around her house screaming and thanking God that Dominique was going with her. She had spent much time researching the country and had become aware of the great needs of the people there, especially the need of the Gospel of Jesus Christ.

When Dominique and Bella first started discussing the needs of the people of this region, the real mission of meeting needs was not a top priority to Dominique but rather an excitement for the excursion to a new place in the world with Bella.

About a week before they left for mission boot camp, they sat down together to discuss their goals and how to follow God's lead to meet those goals. Bella began by saying, "Our number one goal is to bring the gospel message to these desperate people, but how we do that is most important."

Looking somewhat confused by the comment, Dominique started to say something. Sensing the confusion, Bella jumped in and said, "Let me explain. We will be working with a group of medical experts. The team is comprised of doctors and nurses with expertise in several fields. They will be supported by medical staff and five or six students like you and me. The main goal of 'boot camp' is to get a feel for what we will be facing in the field."

Becoming more alert, Dominique began to really focus on what Bella was saying, and she started to understand the idea of helping the needy. Her eyes were opened to the fact that God was sending them and empowering them to change lives.

Not stopping, Bella continued to share what to expect. She told Dominique of the dire conditions of these impoverished people and the bleak future for the sick without medical intervention. Then, she paused and looked deep into Dominique's eyes and said, "You must know this." Making sure she had Dominique's full attention, she pulled up a packet of literature on Central African Republic.

Listening intently to Bella read, Dominique tried to envision the people they would serve. Other than knowing it was in Africa, she had no idea where Central African Republic was in such a large continent.

She learned about the large Christian community, nearly four million people, and the threats they faced daily, like organized corruption and crime, but also the threat of Islamic oppression.

Continuing on, Bella described the occupation of various armed militia groups, who are responsible for a range of human rights abuses. These groups and the Islamic extremists specifically target Christians; life for the Christians is constantly uncertain.

Converts to Christianity are persecuted by the Islamic factions. Many, having lost everything, are forced into displacement camps. Bella stopped reading and moved her eyes up to catch Dominique's face. She said, "So, what do you think?"

To Bella's surprise, Dominique said, "We cannot do this on our own." That was all Dominique needed; she was instantly clear about what they would be facing for Christ. Grabbing Bella's hand, Dominique said, "Let's pray; we are going to need a lot of God's help." As they bowed their heads, Bella was just about to pray when, to her surprise, Dominique started passionately asking God for help.

Smiling, Bella knew Dominique was truly seeking the only one she knew who could help, and she prayed, saying, "Oh, God, You have made it clear; You want us with these dear people. How could we ever make a difference in their lives without Your help? Please make us what we should be; please make Yourself known to us and those we will be visiting and prepare the way before us. In Your name, I pray, Jesus. Amen." Then, as if forgetting something, she added, saying, "And oh, yeah, this is kind of scary stuff."

Believing that Dominique had touched all the bases in her prayer, Bella said "amen" as well. Waiting to hear Bella begin praying, Dominique continued in prayer posture, but when Bella said "amen," Dominique peeked up to see her best friend smiling with approval. Dominique smiled too, thinking to herself, *Wow! Bella just trusted me with the prayer for our trip!*

Unsure of what they would face in the months ahead, they looked at each other, and they could not look away from each other. It was as if their souls were locked together in a purpose greater than themselves; there was nothing more to say; they were in God's hands, confident of that and that alone.

***

Excited as Dominique was to be departing tomorrow for the mission field, she found her last day at home troubling. Surrounded by so many moody well-wishers and not enjoying the plethora of farewells, Dominique had to excuse herself from the clinging group of patrons. Pretending to use the restroom, she raced up the stairs to her room, locked the door, and sat down with her back leaning on the door.

She tried to stay positive and accept the love being lavished on her, but something was eating at her, and she could not identify what. She pulled her legs up until her knees were just under her chin, then she placed her head on her knees and stared out toward her bed.

Everything was so familiar in her room, and she found a solitude to think. Childhood memories started to rush in. The good and the bad memories permeated her thoughts. After some time, she closed her eyes and laid her head back against the door, and she said to herself, "What? What are you doing?"

Comfortable now and resting for a moment, with her head laid back on the door, suddenly a thought burst into her thinking. It made her sit up and put her legs down straight on the floor. Then, she said to herself, "I am leaving the only home I have ever known; I am leaving the comfort of a family, who now I dearly love, and the truth is, I don't want to leave them."

It was not a fear but more of a longing, a longing to experience the act of needing her loved ones daily. She could not help but sense an aching in her heart; in fact, her chest felt tight, and the pressure seemed to force the blood into her head.

This was a reckoning like none she had ever known. She looked back into the familiarity of her room, and her body flinched, and she nearly came off the floor as someone knocked on her door. Startled, Dominique jumped up and ended up several feet away from the door, staring wide-eyed ahead. Breathlessly, she uttered, "Yes."

A welcome voice drifted through the door, saying, "Dominique, is everything all right?"

She thought to herself, *Who else but the one who always comes to my rescue?*

Then, Aunt Colleen said again, "Dominique."

Trying to put on a smile, Dominique unlocked the door and slowly opened it. Aunt Colleen stood there smiling, but Dominique could also see concern on her face. She reached out, took Aunt Colleen's hands, and pulled her into her room.

They stood there staring, holding each other's hands, when suddenly, like a freight train passing through her room, Dominique started to feel an intense emotional rush pour over her, and she started to weep. Aunt Colleen pulled her in close, held her, and said, "I know."

It was not a long embrace but a needed one. Dominique pulled back and said, "You know what? You said you know."

Colleen fixed her eyes on Dominique's tear-filled eyes. Dominique could sense the intensity of what was going to happen next. Aunt Colleen closed her eyes until there were slits open just enough to see. She dropped her head down slightly, then opened her eyes wide and said, "Darling, you have been called by God, and the best thing you can do is accept that as His best for you; to do anything else would be foolish."

Knowing that her aunt was right, Dominique could not figure out why she still felt uneasy, but she didn't want to interrupt her wise sage. Colleen paused for just a moment to ensure Dominique heard her, and she said, "Do you understand what this means?"

Dominique started to nod an affirmative but could not do it, and she said, "Why me?"

Colleen smiled, which, to Dominique, looked like the smile of wisdom, and said, "You will have to ask that question of God, but it is a good question."

Not sure where this was going, Dominique tried to appease her aunt and said, "I guess you are right."

Coming forcefully right back, Colleen said, "No, Dominique, it cannot be about me giving you the go or the peace to go. It must be the peace that only comes from God. This cannot be a mystical adventure that becomes a fable someday, placed nicely in your scrapbook. This is about you reasoning with all the particulars and making a sound decision on the facts."

Dominique knew she was in over her head and started to complain about not knowing for sure, and she said, "But—"

Just as she did, Colleen interrupted and said, "What are the facts? Are you the same person you used to be? Do you fear living like you used to? Do you know God's presence and power in your life? Have you heard Him say to go on this mission trip?"

Dominique was forced back to the day when she tested herself to see if she was living by faith and that the mission trip was God's plan for her. That reminder took her back to her favorite scripture companion, who promised that God had called her and that He would never leave her or forsake her, no matter where on the planet she lived.

Stuck in indecision was not comfortable, and Dominique knew God was not pleased with her there, so Dominique relented. Not based on fabricated unknowns, but based on the very word of God, she looked boldly into her aunt's eyes and said, "Yes, God has called me to the mission field, and by His grace, His will be done."

Again, at a peace that was beyond her understanding, she grabbed her aunt's hand and said, "I guess I had better get downstairs to the many well-wishers. They must be wondering where I am." She pulled Aunt Colleen out of the room, and down the stairs they went.

On the way, Colleen prayed and thanked God for the transformation in Dominique. She thanked Him for the peace that now reigned in her heart, and she closed her prayer by saying, *Oh, God of wonders, no matter what she faces going forward, may she never know a day away from Your presence. I claim that promise; please seal it in her heart that You will never leave her nor forsake her.*

***

With her rich French background, not a day passed by when Dominique did not hear French spoken in her home. Her parents were gifted with the uncanny ability to bounce back and forth intermittently between French and English while having a normal conversation without missing a beat. And when Uncle Dumas was around, French was all they spoke.

Dominique was ahead of the rest of the team; she was already proficient in the official language of Central African Republic. Bella was surprised by how fluent Dominique was and mesmerized at hearing French roll so beautifully off her tongue, though she had never spoken in French the entire two years they spent together.

Most of the team had already arrived to boot camp. Dominique was amazed and somewhat overwhelmed by the quality people assembled for their trip. The medical staff was headed up by Dr. Bashirah Haji. She was born in Africa and was well-connected with the government. She was raised a Muslim but converted to Christ as a teenager. She received her PhD in the States and spoke fluent Arabic, French, and English.

The only person who had not yet arrived to camp was Bella's friend, William James the second. He was the son of the founder of their school, Dr. William James. Dominique had never met William but was well acquainted with him since her dad and Dr. James were friends. Bella met William in her first year at school. William was born in Quebec but moved to New York as an infant. It was William who asked Bella to consider a mission trip to Africa.

It appeared to Dominique that William and Bella could be more than just friends. Bella talked a lot about him, and when she did, her face lit up. He was twenty-two years old and studying African culture at Liberty University. Bella shared his passion for learning more about how Christianity and Islam have influenced modern African social, cultural, and political developments.

William had other commitments, which kept him from arriving with the rest of the team, but he was set to arrive in Boston the following day. As head of the support staff, his presence was a priority. On the morning of his arrival, and since Bella knew William well, Dr. Haji asked Bella if she would take the mission van and pick him up at the airport. She felt it would be safer to take Dominique along with her, so they set out together to retrieve William.

After they arrived at the airport, Dominique could sense Bella's excitement about seeing William. Bella told Dominique, saying, "You will not believe how amazing William is. He loves the Lord with all his heart, he cares so much for the lost and hurting, and he is a leader you can follow; he is humble, he sets the example for others."

Just as she finished her praise of William, she looked up, screamed, and ran past Dominique down the terminal to jump into William's arms. They spun around several times, then stopped to look at each other and hugged again.

Dominique moved slowly toward them, smiling about Bella's enthusiasm for her friend. When Dominique came up close, Bella looked over and saw her and said, "Oh, William, this is Dominique; this is the girl I have been telling you about. I am sure you are familiar with her since her dad and yours are friends. She is a brand-new believer in Christ, and I love her to death."

William was tall and muscular, with short black hair and a smile that seemed to expose his thirty-two teeth, all in front. Dominique realized she was blushing as she gazed upon his face but could not look away. Staring directly into her eyes, William put his hand out to greet her, but Dominique did not respond; she remained staring at him. At that point, Bella jumped in, saying, "Dominique, this is William."

Heading back to camp in the van, Bella drove, and William sat in the passenger seat. They talked the entire trip back. Occasionally, Bella would say something to Dominique, trying to engage her, but for the most part, they were engrossed with reminiscing.

With William on board, the team was solidified, and preparations were to begin the next day. That night, Bella was all business, asking Dominique for help in getting the language down and sharing her excitement about meeting the people they would be serving.

It was hard for Dominique to get the airport scene out of her mind. She had never seen Bella so animated with a guy; she seemed almost fragile next to him, and Dominique had never seen Bella fragile. Then she thought, *I have really never seen Bella with a guy, so maybe this is just her being herself; she has an amazing love for people.*

She put the airport scene behind her and tried to figure out why she was so flustered at William's presence. She was still embarrassed, thinking about her encounter with him. Then, a thought hit her, and she questioned herself, saying, "Maybe it was just seeing a handsome young man, like when I first saw Durand after he had grown up. He was so handsome, pleasing to look at."

Then she said to herself sarcastically, "And look at what that got me?" She did not think; it was fearing the Durand thing would happen again, as much as it was, after Durand, how does she ever factor men into her life again?

William was certainly pleasing to look at, and she did not know how to filter that input in, so she bowed her head and said, "Dear Lord, You have called me to serve the people we are preparing to go visit. I was not prepared to be encountering handsome young men. Though I know by Your design, it is normal for men and women to be attracted to each other, this scares me. Maybe because of Durand, but whatever it is, please take my fear away and help me focus on what lies ahead in Africa. I know you hear my plea. Bless my heart with Your grace. I pray in Your name, Jesus. Amen."

* * *

The next morning, Dr. Haji pulled the team together to have each team member share their reason for going to Africa. Introductions were made at an ice-breaker the night before, so everyone knew who was going but not why.

Dr. Haji started by giving her background and then sharing why she had called upon this medical team. She explained the physical needs of the residents, saying, "I am sure by now you know some things about where we are going. Here are the details that concern us:

"As one of the poorest countries in Africa, tens of thousands of vulnerable children are without access to basic services. The average adult has no more than three and a half years of schooling. Nearly half of the country's population is less than fourteen years old. Due to armed conflict, 370,000 of these children are orphaned."

She paused to let the statistics sink in. Then she continued. "Our goal is to start with medical aid to families and the orphaned, which would build trust and eventually lead to spiritual healing in Christ." She stopped again to look out at the team. She made eye contact, pausing for a moment on everyone, then said, "What are your thoughts, and why have you chosen this adventure?"

The experienced team members seemed so eloquent to Dominique. They spoke passionately about prior mission trips and the blessing of seeing lives changed for Christ. They were confident that this mission would abound with God's blessing and lives would be renewed for eternity.

As Dominique waited for her turn to share, she began to fear that she had no marvelous message to bring concerning why she was there. Then, it was her turn, and as she looked around the room, she was surprised that her fear had completely vanished; she was filled with the Spirit of God to speak.

Empowered, she stood up, which no one else had done; she smiled and began to share, saying, "I have no experience in serving the needs of these wonderful people. Even right now, I am unsure of how effective I can be. You might be surprised to hear that initially, I came here because Bella asked me to and no other reason; I wanted to be with her."

Dominique paused and looked at each person, ending at Dr. Haji. Then, she spoke again, saying, "But what I can tell you about me is that just recently, God has brought me from the depths of despair; I wanted to die. He has brought me from suffering that I thought could never be undone, from loneliness that scorched my soul and left me despondent. From distrust and hatefulness, from weariness of soul, and finally, wonderfully, to surrender and peace. Even now, I weep over the joy that is mine."

Tears filled Dominique's eyes and quickly ran down her face, but her smile only widened. "I am no longer the same; I am new." She went on, "I have only one to thank for where I am, and that is Christ, my Savior. If I can share this new life to see the change in someone suffering as I was, then this is my life." Not even knowing the reference, she quoted a verse. Dominique said, "For to me, to live is Christ and to die is gain."[35] She ended with, "So be it."

She stood there for a minute and looked again around the room; every eye was glued to her stare, and then she sat down. Spellbound by her friend's testimony, Bella sat enraptured, wiping her own tears away; she stared at Dominique, who now was looking down. The rest, Dr. Haji included, sat there motionless.

* * *

From that day forward, Bella found herself desiring the same passion for the mission as Dominique had. Every day, Dominique grew in power and boldness. One day, as they were preparing to solicit support for the mission in the downtown area, the van was unavailable, so they chose an Uber instead.

Neither of them had Ubered before, so when the car pulled up, Dominique jumped into the front seat, which she did not know was not where passengers normally ride, and Bella jumped into the back seat.

As the car started to move, the first thing Dominique did was introduce her and Bella. She asked the driver his name. With a thick Arabic accent, he said, "My name is Haider."

Dominique asked Haider, "What does your name mean?"

Haider looked strangely at Dominique and then at Bella in the back seat and cautiously said, "It means 'lion.'"

Then she asked him, "Are you Muslim?"

Haider hesitated but answered, "Yes, I am."

Bella was astonished at how casually this conversation was happening. Then, Dominique said, "Haider, are you practicing your faith?" At this, Bella could not help but see where this was going, and she began to pray for Haider.

Haider shook his head slightly and said, "No, not right now." Bella could see he was embarrassed.

Dominique was undeterred and went on. "Do your parents know you are not practicing your faith?" Bella just kept on praying but wondered when Haider would say, "Hey, I am not comfortable discussing this any longer."

But he did not say that; he just humbly, nearly whispering, said, "No."

Dominique changed gears; you could see her love for him as she smiled warmly and asked him, "What does your faith believe about Jesus?"

Haider started to feel more comfortable, saying, "We believe Jesus is a mighty prophet and that He will return in the Second Coming and establish peace and justice on earth."

Dominique paused and then asked Haider, "Why are you not practicing your faith?"

Haider looked like he wanted to crawl under the driver's seat and said, "It is like my parents and my family's faith, not mine. I do not see Allah making a difference in my daily life. That is why I have moved to America. They still think I am practicing my faith, and I lead them to believe that, but I am hiding out here."

Dominique actually reached over and touched Haider's arm and said, "I believe Jesus is more than a prophet, and I believe He wants you to be like your name, a lion in your faith, strong and confident. He has ordained this day that we would be together, and He is calling out to you, Haider. The Scriptures proclaim that Jesus created all that exists, and those who trust Him alone as their only hope of salvation will spend eternity in heaven, and there is an eternal hell for those who reject Him.

"Salvation is by faith in Christ based on His death on the cross and raising to life. Jesus has said, 'If you confess your sins, I will forgive your sins and cleanse you from all unrighteousness.'[36] You have said, 'Allah does not make a difference,' and you are here hiding out here hopeless in Boston."

Just then, they arrived at the destination, and as Haider pulled up to the curb, Dominique asked him, "Can we pray together that Jesus would reveal Himself in a mighty way to you and give you hope?" From the back seat, Bella had not stopped praying, and she was reveling in God's grace and Dominique's courage to speak His name so boldly. To her surprise, Haider said, "Yes, we can."

As she held out her hands, he looked cautiously at her; devout Muslim men do not touch women, but he placed his hands in hers, and she began to pray. "Dear God of heaven, please reveal Yourself to Haider. Let him know he is not alone and that You love him so much. Bless him to know You and have hope in this world and the one to come. I pray against the spiritual forces in dark places; bind them so that Haider knows the freedom of Your love today and forever. In Your name, Jesus, I pray. Amen."

She looked up from prayer to see Haider slowly raise his head, then he turned and looked at Dominique. His face was different, and he said, "Thank you."

As she left the car, Dominique smiled again at Haider and said, "I will be praying for you daily that someday, I will see you again in heaven." Haider smiled a weak smile and turned to drive away, but just before he pulled out, he looked back again at Dominique, still looking at him, standing on the sidewalk; he nodded his head as if to acknowledge her care, and he drove off.

CHAPTER 33

Bella's perspective:

From that day when Dominique shared her testimony with the mission team, she was never the same. As her closest friend, I realized the amazing change that God had wrought in such a short time in her Christian life. She was the most dedicated person on the team. She spent endless hours helping other team members learn French. She was always full of energy and lovingly pushed the team for readiness. She never turned down an assignment given by Dr. Haji.

One day, I took her by the shoulders, which surprised her, and spun her around to face me. As our eyes met, I could see the startled look on her face, then that angst turned into a thin smile, and she said to me, "Bella, what are you doing? As she stared at me with those dark black eyes, a whimsical but questioning look grew onto her face, but soon, those dark eyes began to twinkle, and I was lost in the stare of her inward and outward beauty.

It became evident that this special moment, which seemed to go on and on, needed to come to a resolution, so I shook my head, cleared my throat, and said, "Dominique, daily I am amazed at God's grace in your life. You inspire me, and this team and I are so excited that we will be serving together in God's work. I just wanted you to know what God has worked in you. He is also working out of you, and I am blessed to be not only your friend but also your sister in Christ's service."

Smiling weakly, Dominique just squeezed my hands and said, "Praise God."

As the team became more ready and the days grew near, Dominique started to envision the grand victories that lay ahead. It was like she took every thought captive to the obedience of Christ and found life to be ecstatic. She was well-focused on the battle her flesh opposed and her spirit desired.

**

The week prior to our departure, I was the only one who knew, so I orchestrated a surprise birthday party for Dominique. She was completely shocked and embarrassed. Everyone sang "Happy Birthday," and the entire team chipped in to get her a gift.

After blowing out her candles, I asked her what she wished for; she said, "I asked God for wisdom and courage for our team." Everyone cheered, and then I handed her the present, which said, "Happy eighteenth!" She blushed and looked at everyone sheepishly. Slowly unwrapping it, not wanting to tear the wrapping, made the team anxious, and they exhorted her to quickly get it open.

Finally, it was open, and as she turned the picture frame toward her, she paused to stare at the caption, then humbly, she lowered her head, and her eyes became glassy. She attempted to say thank you, but she could not utter a sound; she just lipped the words.

The team cheered again, and Dominique turned the picture frame around. In a big, bold French script, it read: "'Dominique' OF THE LORD AND BELONGING TO THE LORD." Then, below that was Psalm 96:1–3. Written in French, it said:

"Sing to the LORD a new song;

sing to the LORD, all the earth.

Sing to the LORD, praise his name;

proclaim his salvation day after day.

Declare his glory among the nations,

his marvelous deeds among all people."[37]

Teammates started yelling, "Speech, speech!"

Embarrassed still but gaining some composure, Dominique, in gratitude, held the gift up again. Then, she paused a moment and said, "I am blessed by your gift and love. Thank you!" Pausing again, she looked around at the group, took a deep breath, let it out, and said, "What legacy lies before one so young? I have been loved my entire life. My family at home have all called and wished me a blessed birthday; each one, in their own way, loving on me passionately. It has not been a year yet since Jesus commanded my attention, and I obeyed.

"His love has exposed and disposed of my fears. Just months before this day, I knew nothing of God's love or the worth of the love expressed through my family and now you, but today, I know love, and I know, the many years prior to that revelation, God has freed me from a worthless collection of self.

"So, today, on my birthday, I want to begin a brand-new legacy that the rest of my days are days of declaring His name to a lost and hurting world. Thank you again."

The birthday celebration did more than just encourage Dominique; everyone seemed to recommit to focus on prayer and God's call.

* * *

The preparation was intense, and we were exhausted wrapping up loose ends; we were only days away from leaving for the small city of Ouadda in Central African Republic. Tiring of the constant push, I told Dominique, "I am tired; we have been busting for weeks now, and I need a break."

She looked at me and said, "Bella, we are so close to being ready; why stop now?" It was plain she did not understand, but she said, "Okay, what do you want to do?"

I suggested we grab William and head into Boston for some food and pedestrian intimacy. She agreed, so I asked William, and he was ready for a break as well. It was a much-needed break, and we all relaxed in good fellowship.

Having experienced the break in Boston with Bella and William, Dominique was even more convinced that there was something other than friendship between them. Bella's feelings for William were more than she led on.

One night after our time in Boston, Dominique straight up asked me, "How deep are you enamored with William?"

At first, I was taken aback by the blunt accusation, but knowing Dominique as I did, I looked straight at her and said, "Why are you mentioning this?"

Dominique lowered her head; I could tell she was struggling with how to proceed. She looked up at me but was unable to say anything. I grabbed her hand and said, "Hey, it's me; what is going on?"

Dominique started by saying, "I don't want to hurt you, and that is why I am hesitant to speak."

I just shrugged my shoulders and said, "Trust me, I trust you; tell me."

Dominique squeezed my hand as if expecting me to pull away, and she said, "William has been flirting with me." Starting to pull my hand away, I stopped, and my mouth popped open, but I could say nothing. Dominique could sense the dread I was feeling, and she said, "I am so sorry."

Having to catch my breath and let the statement sink in, *I asked myself, Did my best friend just tell me that William is smitten by my best friend?* Dominique started to place her other hand on top of my hand, but I pulled it away. Tears began to build up in Dominique's eyes, but I could not look at her. Turning, I left the room.

As roommates, there was no way to avoid seeing and being with Dominique, so I went for a long walk. I did not arrive back until late in the evening. Returning, I walked up to our room; there was Dominique sitting on the porch, watching me come up the walkway. I came close and said, "How long have you been sitting there?"

She replied, "Oh, since you left."

Dominique started to say something, but I cut her off and told her the walk gave me time to think. I said to her, "What would be the worst thing that could happen just prior to the two of us leaving on the call that God has orchestrated?" It was a rhetorical statement, and I continued. "Yes, division; Satan's best weapon."

At first, I thought, *Why is Dominique sharing this info with me at this time?* And I came to the wrong conclusion; it was not to win my boyfriend but to protect me from my supposed boyfriend.

Dominique motioned for me to sit with her, and I did. She touched my knee and said, "William is pretty, but I have no interest in him that way."

I turned her way to look at her, and the dim light of the evening did not diminish the brightness that showed on her face, her love for me. Then, I asked, "What kind of flirting?" Dominique was so shy concerning these topics, and I better than anyone know why, but still, I needed to know.

Like she always does when dealing with hard stuff, she wrinkled her nose and frowned at the same time and said, "He keeps touching my hand when we are in proximity. He tries to get close to my face when we are working on things together." She grimaced at having to tell the last detail, and again, tears welled up in her eyes, and she said, "The other night, while working on a plan to better equip the team to become more proficient in French, we had just finished the plan when I moved to leave the table, and as I did, he reached up and pulled my chin toward him, and he said, 'You have the most beautiful eyes I have ever seen.'" She continued, "I think he wanted to kiss me because he started to move in close to my mouth."

As Dominique was finishing her story, I was left dying. My hands were shaking, and I said, "What happened next?"

Dominique looked almost quizzingly at me and said, "I pushed him back and said, "What are you doing?"

Relieved by that, I then said, "What did he do?"

Dominique answered, "He said, 'I am so sorry… I thought this was something you wanted too.' And I answered, 'No, what gave you that idea?'"

Dominique continued, "He was stumped for a minute and looked like his face glazed over as if he just realized I was not interested in him. It was just him hoping that I was interested in him." Dominique went on to tell me how she thought he was a nice guy and that maybe under different circumstances, she would be interested, but she concluded by telling him, "You know where we are going, and the battle will be fierce; this is no time for romance, wouldn't you agree?"

She went on, "His face looked weird as he came to grips with his gross misunderstanding, and he became very sensitive and said, 'I have overstepped my bounds. Would you please forgive me?' I nodded that I would and excused myself."

It was a good thing for me to have spent the time on my walk with God. With Dominique being the one person I could trust with my heart, I had already concluded that my aspirations for William were misplaced and mistimed.

Later that day, I ran into William in the cafeteria. He was loading up his plate, and as I walked up next to him, he turned, smiled, and said hello. He continued loading his tray; I followed him to where he was sitting and pulled up alongside him.

Engaged in some small talk, William changed the subject and asked, "Have you seen Dominique today?"

Still weary from hearing about him hitting on Dominique, I said, "Why do you need her?"

Turning to look at me, he said, "No, I just thought you might be together."

Staring at him as I was, he realized my demeanor was aloof; his face became placid, and he stared back at me as if to say, "What?"

Not changing my countenance, I sternly said to William, "In case you don't know, Dominique is betrothed. There is only one man in her life, a romance with her Savior."

Shocked but realizing where this reproof was coming from, William thought he would have words to say, but he just sat there, pitiful, too embarrassed to comment. He opened his mouth, but before he could speak, Bella was gone.

Though painful, William, Dominique, and I reconciled the delusions of romance and were quickly back as a team, preparing to go into battle with a fierce adversary. Each day, I became more aware of the hold God had on Dominique's soul. She was maturing in leaps and bounds. Dr. Hagi saw this too and placed Dominique under William as his assistant to staff operations.

CHAPTER 34

Going over the team expectations again, Dr. Haji clarified the medical team's response to the residents and the support staff's outreach into the community. She gave us a rousing speech about our destiny and to remember that the work God has called us to do is done in His strength. We all knew the time had come for war.

Just before closing the meeting, she asked the group if there were any thoughts they would like to share. Most shared their thankfulness for the members of the team and how they had grown being here together for one cause. Just before she dismissed the group, Dominique spoke up and said, "I have been trying to apply two scriptures to my/our journey, and I would like to share them, if that is okay."

All approved, and she shared Philippians 2:17 first, which says, "But even if I am being poured out like a drink offering on the sacrifice and service coming from your faith, I am glad and rejoice with all of you."[38] Then, she shared 1 Corinthians 9:24–25, which read: "Do you not know that in a race all the runners run, but only one gets the prize? Run in such a way as to get the prize. Everyone who competes in the games goes into strict training. They do it to get a crown that will not last, but we do it to get a crown that will last forever."[39]

She looked up after reading the verses. At first, she looked almost sheepish and smiled warmly as she said, "I am truly blessed and rejoice with all of you to share this mission." Then, as if a light switch went off in her soul, her countenance became emboldened, and she said, "We have gone into strict training, but have we prepared to suffer for Christ? Remember, we have a crown that will last forever. Let us run this race to win the prize." Everyone just stared at Dominique. Bella wondered, *Who is this girl that is my best friend?*

Dr. Hagi knew the danger Dominique spoke of; she had witnessed it, but most of the team was just coming to grips with Dominique's scenario.

* * *

We arrived in Quaada running. Try as we may, it was difficult to sleep on the plane, and we were all weary when we got there at 6:00 a.m. their time. After securing our personal items in the dorm, attached to the hospital, we were asked to gather at the administrative office. The facility was just a bare warehouse that the mission had secured. They did their best to convert it into a makeshift hospital/infirmary. Except for Dominique and Dr. Haji, the team seemed somewhat lost at how to begin; even William, who just sat on his bunk staring, seemed overwhelmed.

Dominique was focused, and she pushed the team to make a quick exit from the dorm to the hospital. Dr. Haji pulled everyone together and went back over the strategy again to ensure we were all in sync.

The medical staff who occupied the hospital prior to our arrival had already headed back to the States, but the administrative staff and youth help remained. Appointments and surgical procedures were already scheduled, and there was no time to acclimate. We were thrown from the plane instantly to the needs of these dear people of Quaada.

The old staff was to remain for a week and after that return home. They were an excellent team and quickly brought us up to speed on day-to-day administrative plan of action.

Dr. Haji and the medical team went right to work on the needs of the sick and injured while the existing student staff leader pulled our student team aside for a briefing. Her name was Celise; she was from the UK. She looked haggard and like she could use some sleep, but she was sharp as a tack and very matter-of-fact.

Trying to sense their take on how things were going, I looked at Dominique and then over to William. Dominique looked back at me, and with a smile that said, "Bring it on," she lifted her head as if to say, "Here we go, Bella."

Celise made her first reference to the priority, which was that our team needed to get out into the community as quickly as possible. She said, "Your job is to be the eyes and ears of the medical team; you must know the people and their needs." She continued by saying, "The area is broken up into fragmented groups, Christian leaders and Muslim leaders, as well as the criminal element and terrorists' groups. We will be introducing these groups to you today."

From that moment on, things became real. Celise took us on a tour around Quadda and introduced us to the varying leaders who were familiar with what the hospital offered their constituents. For the most part, they were very kind and appreciative of the partnership they enjoyed with the mission.

Watching Dominique as we traveled through the city, I could sense her excitement growing. When on the ground, she stayed very close to Celise, and because her French came so naturally, I knew she was taking in much more than anyone else on the new team.

After making all the necessary civilian contacts, Celise took us on a detour into the more impoverished areas, some miles outside of the city. We thought we had made ourselves ready for what to expect, but little could we know the extent of the suffering and poverty that existed daily in this corner of the world.

Our first glimpse of the horror plaguing the outer regions of this impoverished nation brought our team up short. Just on the outskirts of one village, the team could see what looked like dark bumps dotting the landscape. As we drew closer, it became evident that these dark bumps were toddlers sitting or lying alone on the parched, dry ground.

We could see the village proper just before us, about a quarter of a mile ahead. Celise and the other members of her staff seemed indifferent to the sight before them and did not slow the van down or look at the children before them.

***

Realizing now the distorted representation of what they were seeing, Dominique threw her hand over her mouth, not believing what she was seeing; her heart sank, and she screamed, "Stop the van!"

Surprised by Dominique's abrupt command, Celise hit the brakes, and the van came to a jarring halt. Quickly looking back at Dominique, Celise called out, "What is wrong?" But before she could get a response, Dominique flung the van door open, and she began to run toward the evil picture before her.

However, she came up short and stopped as her eyes explained to her heart what she was viewing.

She began again to walk slowly toward one child, and as she did, Celise caught up with her and said, "Dominique, there is nothing we can do here." Looking over her shoulder at Celise, Dominique's face was soaked with tears, and she said, "What do you mean?"

Lowering her head and then slowly looking up again, Celise said, "This is a Muslim village; they are unreceptive to Jesus's teaching."

Still unable to accept what she was seeing, Dominique said to Celise, "Isn't this why we came here?" Not sure what to say to Dominique, Celise just turned and started back to the van. At this point, Bella had joined Dominique, and they held on to each other but could not look away from the suffering before them.

Together, they came close to the first child; tortuous suffering edged into her face; it was evident that she was dead. As Dominique gazed across the many children strewn across the terrain, she turned back to Bella and said, "They are all alone." Then, she repeated it, "They are all alone…"

Just then, she saw one of the shadowy figures move. Her heart leaped, and not even knowing she was running, she came close to the little boy before her. Bending down, she put her hand on his back. Naked and afraid, he tried to move his head to see who had touched him, but he could only muster a slight turning of his head, and then it fell forward again, and he breathed his last.

The last breath of this precious life vibrated through her hand, and she quickly pulled her hand away. Then, realizing the utter senselessness of this loss, she grabbed his shoulders and turned him to lie in her lap.

Her body shook, and she wept. The tears landing on the dust-filled face of this little boy began to cleanse the dust away, and with those tears, his facial features started to become clear. She took the handkerchief out of her pocket and wiped the tears and the dust away. She stared down on the little boy; she placed her hand on his cheek and gently caressed the still-warm features of his face.

Coming up behind her, Bella also leaned down to examine the little soul lying in Dominique's lap. Dominique looked up into Bella's tear-soaked face, and without saying anything, she shook her head as if to say, "Why?" Bella shook her head as well.

Walking slowly back to the van, Dominique glanced once more at the field of death before her, and she prayed, "Oh my God, to experience this and have no answers… Please help me." Finishing her prayer, something in the sky caught her attention, and she looked up. Surprised by the aerial presence, she found it unbelievable that these wee little ones were to be a delicacy for the vultures gathering for the feast.

* * *

There was so much that Dominique was not prepared to endure. The visit to the Muslim village was branded in her memory, and she was taken back, and it was hard to see forward.

The next day, the team gathered again to do outreach in the city. Her discussion with Dr. Haji concerning the children dying in the desert was unfruitful, and Dominique could not imagine having meaningful ministry happen today.

Having prayed with Bella, they decided to trust God for that which they could not understand and loaded into the van for a day with these needy people; God did bring their way.

The living conditions were dismal. Most of the housing was run down, and due to the lack of sanitation in this quarter of the city, the stench was nearly unbearable. Bolstered now by God's grace, that very offensive fact did little to dissuade Dominique from jumping wholeheartedly into the aroma of this community. She went from person to person, reaching out to them, holding their hands, and asking questions about their needs.

Surprised by Dominique's candor and concern, it was not long before Celise and her staff saw the sense of Dominique's compassion and joined in mimicking her example. Soon, the entire group was engaged likewise with the residents, which ended up having an unintended consequence; residents started flocking to the clamoring sound of caring.

Celise became aware of the sound of movement. She looked up to see a mass of beleaguered people descending on their party. Realizing they had brought nothing with them to give that would sustain their needy friends, she quickly began getting the attention of the team.

She grabbed Dominique by the arm and said, "We have begun something here; we are not prepared to finish." Looking up, Dominique quickly assessed the situation. She looked sternly at Celise, then at William, and said, "Our team will stay here and explain to the onlookers that you and your team are leaving to return shortly with supplies to help them."

Celise just stared at Dominique for a moment, and she said, "What supplies? All we have at the compound is designated for certain groups; there is no reserve." Dominique, looking undeterred, stood up and grabbed Celise by both hands and said, "We cannot leave here without helping these people. You must go and bring what you can for now; we will figure out how to make up for the shortage later."

Thinking about protocol and the lack of sufficient supplies, Celise started to balk, and just as she began to say something, Dominique moved her hand in a gesture to point out to Celise the throng of people now attending this site, and she said, "You must go."

Seeing the crowd growing on her left and to her right, Celise seemed confused, frozen in the intensity of their situation. Then, as if struck awake by the truth, she yelled at her team and said, "Everyone back to the van."

* * *

Later that night, after the excursion team had returned from their journey, everyone was still talking about what had taken place. There was a joy that had settled in and over the mission team. Finding it hard to believe what she just experienced, Bella kept staring at Dominique, amazed at her fearless friend.

Just then, Dominique looked up to see Bella staring, and she said, "Hey, Bella! What a day, huh?" Moving over to Bella, she gave her a big hug and whispered, "Thank you for asking me to join you on this mission."

Everyone was praising God for the work that had been done to meet the needs of so many people. They received food, water, blankets, and some clothing, but most of all, they received love, which they could not deny. Dominique's decision reminded everyone of the book of 1 Samuel when King David took the consecrated bread from Ahimelech, the priest, and fed it to himself and his companions.

Though tired from the ordeal, most were reveling in the goodness of God and thankful to have been a part of such a divine moment. The medical staff were excited as well, with many needy souls ending up at the dispensary.

The joyous group lounging in the cafeteria looked up to see Dr. Haji coming out of the medical wing, appearing ready to join the festivities in the cafeteria. Something was amiss; she was not smiling. Her presence became more and more obvious to the group until everyone had turned and was looking her way.

Since she had her back to where Dr. Haji came in, Dominique was the last one to acknowledge her presence. Sensing the quiet in the room, she turned to see Dr. Haji standing emphatically in the middle of the group. A hush came over those gathered.

Dr. Haji commanded that kind of respect; she was, after all, the captain of the crew. As everyone stared her way, she just looked around the room, taking in everyone there. Awkward would be an understatement of what was happening in that moment; then, she asked everyone to take a seat.

Everyone turned to find a chair; Bella ran over close to Dominique and pulled up next to her. As everyone was fixed on Dr. Higi, the gayety, so pronounced just moments ago, had become more like a dirge. As everyone was left unnerved, her countenance did not change as she continued to glance from face to face.

Finally, she spoke, saying, "What a first day, huh?" Not knowing the proper response, none of us moved a muscle; still fixed on our leader, we waited for her next thought. She took a deep breath, letting it out as she moved slowly among the group, then she stopped, looked down to the floor, and then quickly back up, saying, "God did an amazing thing today; He took our inexperience, our lack of preparation, our misunderstanding of what manna from heaven is, and despite all that, poured out His abundance on a needy people."

It was eerie hearing her response. Contained in one statement, she had couched a reprimand and a praise. No one was left unaware of her meaning, and the team started to look around the room at each other. It was uncomfortable, and we did not know what to say.

Soon, though, many of the group turned their attention toward Dominique. She began to feel their gaze, and she sat up in her chair. Now, all eyes were on Dominique, and Bella began to pray for her dear friend.

Making eye contact with everyone and finally ending up staring into Dr. Haji's face, Dominique stood up. She looked angelic, and then she spoke, saying, "I have not been here long enough to know the organizational ins and outs of our mission, but I am a quick learner. On the other hand, it would be unthinkable to describe what God did today as a blunder; seeds of the gospel message were planted into the lives of hundreds of lost and hurting people. Still, I see that moments like this one can also be realized with a well-planned strategy." She paused at that point to look around the room again and then finished her comments by saying, "But who but God could orchestrate a day like today?"

At that point, Dr. Haji called the youth leadership team to meet with her in her office. Not fully knowing what to pray, Bella prayed until Dominique returned to their room. When she walked in, Bella peered longingly into her eyes, hoping to sense her demeanor. She just smiled warmly and sat down on her bed, looking intently at Bella, saying nothing.

* * *

Unbeknownst to the team, that same evening in Quadda, a new awareness was filtering into the lives of differing leadership groups within the city. Those who had received the bountiful blessing from God were thankful. Longing to know more about this group of young people who had blessed them so, especially that fiery, dark-haired girl, which they believed had opened heaven's blessing on them.

Another group, or maybe a better descriptor would be "another faction," was just learning that people from the mission had moved into the territory that they controlled. They were not happy about the intrusion, and they also wanted to know, but for other reasons, who this dark-haired girl who appeared to be their provider was.

The entire population knew that lurking in the shadows of the streets of Quadda, there was a dangerous and well-organized criminal element. They demanded of the citizenry undying allegiance to their thievery, or they would suffer the painful consequences.

The leader of this menacing band of outlaws was an apostate Muslim named Sylvain. Hundreds of people were under his control, and their destiny was in his hands. It was completely understood by all that breaking favor with Sylvain was a death sentence.

Controlling his empire was a full-time job, and Sylvain was astute in using evil to meet his desired ends. His father was a devoted Muslim and a minister of the government. His duties included receiving recommendations from the prime minister and passing them down to the assembly for approval.

Sylvain grew up in a very privileged environment, but having two older brothers, whom his dad adored, left him feeling neglected by his father. Tiring of his youngest son's lack of family pride and religious discipline, his dad sent him off to Paris to receive his education.

It was not long, though, before his father was made aware of his son's lack of propriety and immoral wantonness, and he called Sylvain home. Sylvain defied his father's wishes and stayed in Paris, to which his dad cut off his funds. This estrangement led Sylvain to seek other venues for income to wit a lucrative life of crime.

This continued for several years, and his career choice led him to a very lucrative lifestyle, making him a key figure in the dark underworld of the streets of Paris. He had no plans of ever returning to Africa, but then, one day, he got the news that his dad had been assassinated in the streets of Bangui, the capital of Central African Republic.

Due to his mother's pleading, Sylvain arrived back to his homeland, only to find his older brothers, who were unreceptive of his return, fighting over his dad's assets. He stayed just long enough in Bangui to soothe his mother's grief and began plans to return to Paris.

A week before his departure, he ran into an old friend from school who had become quite successful marketing for the criminal underground. This appeared to be something worth checking out, so he canceled his flight to Paris and started running with his friend.

With money flowing generously his way, Sylvain reconsidered his departure to Paris, and to his mother's joy, he told her he would be staying.

To hide his duplicity, he lied to her and his brothers and claimed a legitimate work arrangement had been made; he told them he would be employed by the government, meeting the needs of the poor.

A year later, he had the underground boss of Quadda murdered and assumed his role. He led his army of bandits by one rule: "Cross me, and you die." The focus of interest was the poor urban communities who received subsidies from the government. All he had to do to secure the money flow was to corrupt the local officials, which he did through extortion and the occasional, untimely deaths of a few reluctant leaders.

In complete control of the poor population and without interference from any rivals, Sylvain was keenly aware of the disruption that could arise should this "dark-haired savior get a humanitarian foothold in Quadda."

***

Just sitting on her bed, silent, appearing unconcerned about the meeting with Dr. Haji, Bella lifted her hands as if to say, "Dominique, what happened?"

That caught her attention, and she asked, "What? Do you want to know what happened in the leadership meeting?"

Bella thought to herself, *This girl is going to drive me crazy.*

For some reason, that thought took Bella back to the day she first met Dominique. She remembered how pitiful and self-absorbed she was and how defensive she was. Most of all, she remembered Dominique was a hurting soul God had placed in her life who needed a friend. Bella remembered the times she fought for Dominique, and the memory was good.

What did not seem good was that since leaving for Boston, Bella's confidence in the Lord seemed to be waning. Recently, she was forced to ask herself some tough questions about trust and faithfulness. She felt she was in the deep and over her head, as if the comfort piece of the puzzle was missing. She paused in her thoughts and asked herself harshly, *What has happened to your confidence?*

As if in a daydream and still reeling from that question, suddenly, subconsciously, she started to hear Dominique's voice. Unclear at first, but then more and more clearly, she heard Dominique explaining the events of what took place with Dr. Haji.

Bella stopped her from continuing and said, "Wait a minute; please start over."

Confused and looking at Bella, somewhat puzzled, she said, "Why?"

Bella sighed and gently reiterated, "Please just start over again."

Dominique started again and explained the justification for their meeting. From what Dominique revealed, she and Dr. Haji started rather conflicted. William and Celise remained quiet and somewhat intimidated; at least, that was how they looked to Dominique.

Dr. Haji focused on the rules of the mission and the need to ration the supplies. On the other hand, Dominique took the approach that God has all the cattle on all the hills; therefore, all they must do was ask, and He would supply. The meeting was not heated, but there were differences of opinion on how to best move forward. Dominique told Dr. Haji that she would pray about the supplies and, while praying, remain faithful to the mission's goal.

Looking as if she had explained all she could, Dominique looked at Bella and said, "Do you believe that God has all the cattle on all the hills?"

Bella knew Dominique wanted her to affirm her contention that the supplies were not their concern but His. Just as Bella began to try to play both sides of the equation, the Holy Spirit gripped her soul. She heard Him say, "You just asked where your confidence is." Then, as clearly as if Bella just heard the voice of God, she said to God, *Thank You!* And to Dominique, she said, "Yes, I do believe God has all the cattle on all the hills."

Dominique grabbed both of Bella's hands and pulled her to her bed, saying, "Then, let's pray."

Unbeknownst to anyone, the next day, Dominique made a call home to speak with her dad. She explained the supplies situation and asked if there was anything he could think of to help get the needed supplies to the mission.

Thomas was not confused about the need as much as he was confused about why his daughter was calling him about the need. He stammered at first, as if he was not clear how he could help, and said, "Honey, doesn't the mission have a budget they have to work from?"

She told her dad that they did, but she added, "The budget is not sufficient to meet the needs…" She went on to tell her dad what she had experienced their first day and the awful poverty that held these dear people captive.

Thomas could sense he was talking to another daughter. This was not the unsure, fragile, manipulating person he used to know, and he said, "Darling, let me look into it."

Nearly squealing on the phone and so thankful for her dad, she said, "Oh, Dad, I know you can make this happen! Pray, Dad, pray…" And she finished by saying, "Love you so much! I gotta go."

As if he had been run over by a steamroller, Thomas just sat at his desk, contemplating what had just hit him. Realizing it was 1:00 a.m. in Africa and knowing that Dominique would have a very early morning, he was wondering what would have happened that kept her up so late. Unable to think, he bowed his head and prayed. Then, he walked slowly into the kitchen where Marie was making dinner; she turned and, seeing the tension in his face, said, "What?"

He responded, "I just got off the phone with our daughter."

After hearing the particulars of Dominique's request, Marie was not sure what to think. She thought, *Is Dominique asking us to fund her mission trip? How would we do that?* The rest of the evening, Thomas spent in his den, hearing repeatedly, "Oh, Dad, I know you can make this happen. Pray, Dad, pray…" So, he prayed.

Feeling guilty for her thoughts and torn, Marie conjured up again Dominique's request. For some reason, she felt they were being used, but at the same time, she also felt the pull to do the responsible thing, which she had no idea what it would be. With Thomas busy in his den, Marie went from room to room, trying to come to peace, but without remedy.

She stopped in the great room and looked out the large centerpiece window facing west. Staring helplessly and directly into the evening sunset, she had to raise her hand to shade her eyes. The brilliance of the light, exposing the subtleties of the entire chamber, left her on exhibit as well, and she felt small, but for some reason, not insignificant.

She turned away from the light and faced directly into the room, and nothing was left in the shadows. She contemplated that thought for a moment and then said to herself, "Marie, are you satisfied hiding in the shadows?"

Hearing that reproof from herself, she felt deep and hidden truths begin to pour into her heart and up into her mind. She stopped, as if for the first time, to contemplate where she really stood on all things right. Then, she bowed and said, "God, I do not like the idea of Dominique being in Africa; why would I want to support the mission that will keep her there?" Realizing that she just prayed what she was thinking, she opened her eyes and looked quickly up, gazing around the room.

Waiting for a response, she stood fearful and motionless. Then, a thought burst into her soul, and a verse, nearly audible, came to life: "Trust in the LORD with all your heart and lean not on your own understanding; in all your ways submit to him, and he will make your paths straight."[40] As if in a trance, Marie rushed for her phone, all the while thinking, *Oh my, I must call Colleen.* After getting off the phone with Marie, Colleen called Chloe, and they all committed to praying for Dominique and the mission.

CHAPTER 35

The next morning, after receiving Thomas's call, Hal Sealy sat at his office contemplating what they had just discussed. He remembered asking Thomas several times to clarify what he was proposing, but it still did not seem clear. He thought about calling Thomas back, but that did not seem the right response, so he prayed, as Thomas asked him to do.

Moments later, the same thing was happening with Dr. William James. He sat in his campus office, not sure what had just transpired. He, too, needed more information than Thomas was able to give. He was excited to hear of Dominique's adventure and was proud that one of his high school girls and his son were in the world making a difference, but he could not grasp how he could help.

He had a very busy day planned, and he was having difficulty prioritizing Thomas's situation into that schedule. Just before he moved on to the next thing, he remembered he told Thomas he would pray, so he did.

After praying and seeking God, Hal knew this was not a Thomas thing but a God thing, and he was impassioned. Wondering how to proceed, he jotted down some notes. Since Thomas left him a mission portfolio weeks ago, he decided his first move would be to contact them. After a straightforward conversation with the mission director, he realized they were extremely underfunded.

Coming out of prayer, Dr. James could not figure out why he was crying. Tears etched his face as he looked up from his desk and envisioned the picture that Thomas painted of the great need of these African people. Then, he saw William and Dominique, so young, trusting God with the mission and their lives. He could not remember the last time he was so moved; wonder began to build in his heart. He paused to gather his thoughts and made a call. He called the chairman of the school foundation.

Thomas, on the other hand, spent the morning talking with his many business acquaintances. Not sure how to sell Dominique's request, he prayed for wisdom and just let them hear her plea, in her words, then waited for their responses.

His most difficult call still had to be made. Since Dumas was half owner in their corporation, he could not move on funding a project without passing the idea first before his brother, and he thought, *Does my brother still want to talk to me?*

When Dumas answered the phone, Thomas had no direction to lead the conversation. Dumas was surprised to hear from his brother but was instantly excited. Then Dumas, too, started to sense the vast distance that still separated the two brothers.

Thomas cleared his throat and was surprised by the excitement stirring in him of having Dumas on the other end of the phone. Then, he prayed, *God help me.* He just opened his mouth, saying, "Dumas, please forgive me for keeping you out of our lives these last months. I have been foolish to allow bitterness to creep in between us. I am sorry for blaming you in any way for what happened to Dominique. Please forgive me."

Unable to believe what he was hearing, Dumas prayed and thanked God for answering his prayers. Then, he said, "There is nothing to forgive; we have both lost something so precious. How much now, more than ever, do we need each other to heal our losses? Thank you, Brother, for this call. It helps me trust God again."

They discussed many things, going way back when they lived as boys with their parents in Quebec, and they came to a consensus: God had not left them, but they had run away. Now, in His time, He was seeking them both out for this moment. Just before they ended the conversation, Thomas shared Dominique's request with his brother.

***

Not knowing how the meeting was fleshed out between Dr. Haji and Dominique, the team became uneasy. There was a funk that darkened the road that lay ahead of them. A week later, that same funk remained, and it was fracturing the team into two camps; it was mostly evident in how corporate team prayer lacked conviction or commitment.

Everyone was sensing the fragmenting, but no one knew what could be done to remedy the onslaught being perpetrated by the enemy on the mission's goal. Bella had been in constant prayer, not knowing what was happening but asking God's help. One day, after a lackluster team meeting, Bella stood up before the entire team and said, "Is it not just like the enemy of our souls to find a toehold where he can begin his plan to overthrow our Savior's will? We have allowed this."

Sheepishly, one by one, the entire team, including Dr. Haji, as if shame had overtaken them all, slowly bowed their heads, unable to make eye contact with one another. Bella continued, and she nearly yelled her next words, saying, "Look up at me."

The team was shocked to hear Bella's command, and every head popped quickly up. Now, with every eye on her, she looked around to each face, even Dominique, and firmly said, "I rebuke Satan in the name of Jesus Christ, and I exhort each of you to turn from this deception and renew your commitment to what we have been called to do."

At that point, Dr. Haji stepped forward and confessed her part in succumbing to this ploy. Dominique was just now beginning to understand by not following protocol, justified as she felt in helping the needy of Quadda, she had opened the door for attack.

She stood up and moved toward Dr. Haji, and Dr. Haji moved toward her. Surrounded by their befuddled teammates, they reached the middle of the room. Every eye was fixed on the two of them. Just then, Dominique reached out for Dr. Haji's hands and said, "Please forgive me; this is my fault. I have not been submissive to your God-given leadership, and I am sorry."

The room was silent, but the Holy Spirit was filling each heart, and a resounding change began to take place. Dr. Haji took Dominique by the shoulders, smiled, and, not taking her eyes from Dominique's gaze, said, "I don't believe you can claim the entirety of the blame for the dilemma we find ourselves in. I am supposed to lead, but right now, only half of the team is looking to me for direction. I have been foolish, and the lesson learned is: protocol does not take precedence over a sovereign God."

The two women continued to stare at each other; then, both began to smile a wry smile. As they did, they turned to their teammates and stared at them, smiling. The Holy Spirit confirmed the healing taking place, and every heart was keenly tuned into the center of the room. Just then, the entire team rushed in on the two women, and the two of them disappeared, enshrouded by the joyous huddle of praise.

* * *

It was hard for Bella and Dominique to sleep that night. They stayed up too late, but they were unable to stop praising God for His moving in their midst. Morning found the whole team exhausted but renewed in their commitment to God and each other.

Laying there, thinking about last night's happenings, Dominique wanted to talk to Bella about it, so she leaned over and pushed Bella with her foot. Bella, half snorted in the middle of a snore but sitting up quickly, startled by the abruptness of her awakening and nearly panicked, said to Dominique, "What?"

Dominique laughed at her wonderful roommate. They talked briefly, going over everything that took place. They both agreed that they had never spent a more powerful time in prayer. The team just went on and on, asking for forgiveness and seeking God for restoration and a new zeal for the people in this country.

As they made ready for another day, there came a knock on their door. It was Celise; she poked her head in and said, "Hey! In five minutes, the 'Doc' wants us all to gather in the cafeteria."

It was evident that last night, God had made the team anew. Each one was smiling and hugging each other, and smiles were everywhere. During that joy, everyone turned as they heard Dr. Haji say, "May I have your attention?"

As everyone began to gather around Dr. Haji, there was a sense in the group of something profound in her countenance; she beamed with joy. She looked over everyone, and with just a smile, she had the entire group smiling as well.

She paused, and as always, she made good eye contact with everyone. Then, most deliberately, she said, "Do we have an awesome and almighty God?"

In unison, the team shouted back, "Yes, we do!"

She looked at the team, and as if fire were pouring out of her eyes, she said it again, only more loudly, "Do we have an awesome and almighty God?"

The team, catching her inspiration, shouted more emphatically, "Yes, we do!"

She said it again, and the team looked at each other and went nuts, screaming, "*Yes, we do! Yes, we do! Yes, we do!*"

The worship was sweet to their souls and glorious to God. Then as if changing gears, Dr. Haji quieted the group and said, "It appears that Dominique has recently made a phone call, and it also appears that she is very well connected." The group was lost at where this was going, and as everyone stared at Dominique, she felt her face flush, and she fixed her eyes on Dr. Haji.

"Maybe I should say this differently," Dr. Haji hesitated. Then, she continued, "What really appears to have happened is God answers prayer by moving in the lives of people who can make a difference."

Dr. Haji could tell the anxiety was growing in the group, and she said, "I might as well just let it out; the call Dominique made has led God to prompt certain people to give to our mission. It is evident that God has all the cattle on all the hills, and He distributes His blessing on those who are faithful."

It was getting to the place where the team was about to shout, "What has happened?"

And with a glorious smile, Dr. Haji said, "As of today, our mission budget has been increased by seven million dollars, and several of the donors have requested seats on the mission board." Excited but not sure what this all really meant, the team started looking at each other, and then all eyes turned to Dominique.

Hoping to take the spotlight off Dominique, Dr. Haji said, "This means we will have the wherefore all, to profoundly expand, the outreach to these dear people, which God has called us to serve."

Cheers rang out from everyone, and though they knew it was God who provided their needs, the team rushed on Dominique and raised her up on several shoulders, shouting over and over, "Dominique!"

As they paraded Dominique around the room, her sheepish smile was not there because she was embarrassed, nor was it that she was proud; she was humbled and thankful. What went through her heart and into her mind was the thought of how her dad had heard God and God had worked the miraculous, impacting so many lives, and she prayed, *You have proved Yourself again, Lord; You will never leave us nor forsake us.*

* * *

With new vigor and ample funding, the team rose to God's challenge. It was not long before they had doubled their efforts in the hospital and in the community. Many new staff were coming to support the effort, and the effort was miraculously enhancing the lives of the community, not just physically but spiritually as well.

Converts to Christ were added daily, and with the added funds, buildings and discipling staff were added to meet those needs. The community was changing so quickly and wonderfully that government leadership teams began to seek visits to get feedback on how they could help facilitate the revival of body and soul that was taking place in their midst.

Due to the resounding evidence of renewal in his city, the mayor of Quadda asked for a personal meeting with Dr. Haji. His desire was to discuss a partnership to establish long-lasting solutions to the city's needs.

This partnership quickly transformed the physical makeup of the city proper. Working together, they identified problem areas on the streets and in the homes of the citizens. Some of the new funds were designated for the purpose of cleaning up certain run-down areas of the city.

Abandoned vehicles were removed from the streets, graffiti was painted over, broken windows were replaced, and even the jail system was given an overhaul. These improvements had instant positive results. The residents started to feel safe on the streets again, and the policing became less stressful as the outlaws had fewer trenches of terror to hold up in.

As the city continued to exude the new light of the Gospel message, and believers were added to the church daily, that transformation led to a new hope and boldness. Due to this new hope, the corporate citizenry began to seek a way to eradicate the criminal element, which still haunted them daily.

* * *

This overwhelming resurgence of good and right in Quadda and the surrounding areas was not a welcome change to one element of the city. Due to the mayor's clampdown on crime and a purging of the criminal element from within the police department, a righteous outcry rose from the homes and streets for a crackdown on crime.

Those entrusted with carrying out Sylvain's crime wave began to find themselves between a rock and a hard spot. Not only did they dare not cross their notorious leader, but now they had a police force that was not intimidated by their threats.

Many found the only alternative was to flee the area. Still, bolstered by his close associates and an undeterred passion for illicit income, rather than move on, Sylvain pulled all his resources together to exact a counterattack on those responsible for the upheaval that had maligned his prospects.

No one, at any time, really knew what Sylvain was thinking. Darkness was his dwelling place, and blindly, he called upon that dark entity to find his way. He was possessed with the thought of how to destroy his nemesis, and Dominique became the catalyst of his obsession.

He had spies constantly watch her movements. He would place himself in areas that he knew she would frequent. He would sit and observe her from a distance, taking in her every move, learning of her power over people.

His first attempt at disruption was to intimidate her, but she was rarely alone. One day, he had two of his strong-arm crew follow her and look for an opportunity to confront her. It just so happened that on this day, it was Bella and Dominique alone on the street, transporting new Bibles to the worship facility.

The entire team was in constant bliss as they saw God in their work daily. Unaware of the danger, laughing and singing joyously, they pulled the four-wheeled cart full of Bibles toward the new church facility.

The two assailants followed them closely; suddenly, the girls stopped to speak with one of the new converts from Bible study, and as they did, one of the men came up close and pretended to trip over the cart. He stumbled and fell.

Startled, Dominique reached out to help him and touched his hand, saying, "Are you okay?" He looked up to see her face, and he froze. He stared too long into her eyes, and fear started to overtake him; he stood up and pulled away. Dominique tried to apologize, and Bella was staring strangely at the man when, behind them, his partner came up and aggressively grabbed Dominique by the arm and swung her around.

He pulled her up close to his face, glared at her, and said, "Why don't you watch where you are going?"

As if, once again, she was reliving the nightmare of her past, fear started to grip her; then, something wonderful, something powerful happened: a peace filled her, and she said, "I am so sorry, please forgive us."

Aghast that this man had grabbed her dear friend, Bella began to pray, saying, "Oh, God, what is this?" And she stepped in next to Dominique.

A few people on the street were beginning to notice the man holding onto Dominique, and the crowd started moving her way. The angry man holding Dominique noticed the encroachment as well; just then, the other assailant, looking nervous, said, "Hey, let's get out of here." Still squeezing her arm, the attacker ruffly pulled her up again and said, "Next time, we will not be so gracious to you." And he pushed her toward Bella.

The two of them turned and moved quickly away, but the man whom Dominique had touched paused and looked back at her several times. His angry companion had to pull him away from the crowd, and he yelled at him, saying, "What is wrong with you?"

Watching from across the street, Sylvain was angered by the quick response of the crowd. He thought to himself, *This dark-haired prophetess is protected on the street*. He rose quickly and made his way across the street to where Bella and Dominique were being comforted by a police officer.

Sylvain stood back incognito, hoping to hear the conversation between Dominique and the officer. The officer asked the girls if they had ever seen those two men before, and they said, "No!" Bella explained the incident and how the one man had tripped over their cart, which appeared to anger his sidekick.

Bella continued to explain that Dominique apologized to the man who had fallen and tried to help him up, but the other man took great offense and ruffly grabbed Dominique by the arm, warning her of the "next time" they met.

Though somewhat shaken, Dominique told the officer that it was no big deal and that it was their fault since they had abruptly stopped the cart right in the middle of the walkway. Then she said, "We are probably not welcome here. Even though much good is being done, we are most likely misunderstood by some and seen as a disruption rather than a blessing."

Ensuring that the girls were all right, the officer told them he would file a report, but to identify the two intruders, he needed them to come to the police station and look at pictures.

Not wanting to hinder the outreach in the community and thinking that trying to identify the two men was an overexaggeration of the situation, Dominique told the officer that she did not feel that it was necessary to go to the station.

The officer disagreed and said, "There is an element in our midst that does not want to give up this territory to the good your team is doing. I must insist that if we are to clean up the streets, we need every hand on deck and every eye on the evil around us. You must come to the station."

CHAPTER 36

As he watched the officer lead the girls away, Sylvain realized that for the first time since he began reigning supreme on the streets of Quadda, there was opposition, and it was fierce.

Unsettled but determined, Sylvain turned and walked away. Heading back to his headquarters, he began plotting a plan. A plan that would plant fear into the lives of anyone who opposed his reign and reap the unconditional submission of the townspeople.

The whole episode that took place on the street had an amazing impact on Quadda. The people who gathered around Bella and Dominique realized they had power in numbers, and now that the police were allies, they felt empowered to share even more with the police the identities of the criminal element in their communities.

As the city and the police force rallied together to clean up their city of crime, more and more from Sylvain's army slithered off, hoping to inflict evil on their African brothers and sisters elsewhere.

After leaving the scene where Dominique was accosted, Brice, the man who faked tripping over the Bible cart and his partner, arrived back at Sylvain's headquarters. Sylvain congratulated them and told them to wait for further instructions; then, he dismissed them.

The entire time they stood before Sylvain, Brice feared his leader would detect the uneasiness he was feeling. Like his partner, he tried to put on a brave front for Sylvain, like he was ready and willing for his next assignment, but he was anything but ready.

On the way back to his room, Brice kept looking back over his shoulder as if someone was watching him. As he entered his room, he quickly locked the door and leaned against it.

Not knowing why he was so uneasy, Brice tried to make sense of his situation. He was well-known in the community. Before he left his wife and children, he was known in the community as a hard-working provider, a good husband, and a father.

He tried now to look back on his life before crime; nothing seemed to make sense. He remembered the day that Sylvain approached him to go to work in his organization. Knowing how dangerous Sylvain was, Brice was very wary, but Sylvain made sense. He told Brice, "Do you want to work hard or work easy for your money?"

Brice worked for his sister's husband as a mason. The work was hard, and he always felt his brother-in-law did not appreciate his expertise or work ethic. He could not help but complain to his wife, and she, in turn, would mention his complaint to her sister, who would, of course, say something to her husband, Brice's boss.

Due to his complaining, it was not long before Brice started getting the more difficult jobs on the work sites. Trying to understand his demotion, Brice asked his wife if she had mentioned anything to her sister, to which, of course, she said yes; she said she was just trying to help.

It was not just work; Brice was having difficulty with all facets of his life. It seemed that he and his bride were never on the same wavelengths of life. He loved his children but could never find time to be with them, to help them.

What finally broke the camel's back for Brice was that his wife gave her life to Jesus. As a Muslim, this was a dangerous thing to do. You could lose everything, even your life, by converting from Islam.

It had been two years since she first met with some of the people at the mission. The mission provided more than just spiritual guidance; it also addressed physical needs, such as food and medical assistance. She saw her need for a savior, confessed her sins, and was born again.

He could not see the need for himself, and Brice felt she was incessantly preaching at him that he, too, should give his life to Jesus. After about a year of constant battles in the home and the condemnation of his brother-in-law concerning his bride's conversion, without saying a word, one day, Brice quit his job and accepted Sylvain's offer for work and never returned home.

* * *

Afraid and not knowing why, he now found himself shrinking alone in his room. Going back over the recent days, Brice tried to assess what, or when, something happened that changed his perspective so drastically. He finally pinpointed a moment, and an incident that he remembered shook him loose of his moorings.

It was a normal day of strong-arming the local business owners into accepting safety for payment. He had just left a business and walked out into the sunshine feeling secure and happy with his life, the sun on his shoulders and a big smile on his face.

He looked across the street, and there was the dark-haired girl from the mission. She was surrounded by people; she was touching them and praying for them, and the more she reached out to the crowd, the more people came running to her. Soon, there were hundreds of the poorest people in the city packed in around this seemingly frail, very light-skinned, and dark-haired saint. Then, the rest of the mission team joined in, doing the same.

Deciding to see where this would all end up, Brice slipped across the street and lingered in close to the crowd. People were crying and asking for help, and this enchantress was praying for them and holding them. Then, Brice noticed that one of the other missionary staff reached out and grabbed the dark-haired girl and said something to her that Brice could not understand. To his surprise, he heard the dark-haired girl say, "We cannot leave these people without helping them; you must go and bring what you can." With that said, half of the mission team departed in their van, only to return moments later with food and water and medical supplies, which were distributed to the crowd.

Astonished by the compassion, Brice thought, *Why would they help such a band of deadbeats and losers?* He noticed that nearly everyone who showed up received help, whether spiritual or physical. After receiving the gifts, the crowd began to gather again around the dark-haired girl.

Paying very close attention, Brice focused on the same face that everyone else was staring at, and the scene became silent. He remembered she stood up and smiled, a smile that captured in such a way that all were mesmerized by the glow in her face.

What she said next is what Brice remembered most, and this, he thought to himself, was what had forced its way into his life and why he was hiding in his room.

The words came back to him, just like the day he heard her. She said, "What you have experienced today has not happened by the power of mere people but by the power of almighty God. He sees your suffering, and He cares. He cares so much that He sent His Son, Jesus, to die on the cross to take away your sins and offer you eternal life. He displayed His power by raising Him from the dead. Jesus now lives to intercede in your lives. Will you turn to Him and accept His gift of eternal life?"

Not able to move, Brice stood there frozen. He looked around at the crowd; they were still silent and staring. Then, one by one, people started coming forward and getting on their knees before the dark-haired girl. Before long, there were thirty or forty people on their knees, waiting for what was next.

Feeling like he needed to run but unable to move, Brice forced himself away. However, as he turned to leave, he looked back one more time, and there she was, the dark-haired girl staring directly into his eyes. She smiled, and that smile nearly tore him in two. Fear raced into his heart, and he had to turn away; he walked briskly down the street, not daring to look back again, but he felt her stare burning a hole in his soul, and he disappeared into the shadows of his life.

Back to his senses and in his room, he instantly went back to the scene after he tripped over the cart. He was held spellbound as he remembered that same smile from his first encounter with her and how she reached out and touched him, a touch and a smile he could never forget.

* * *

Though they were unable to identify the two men who accosted them, Dominique and Bella knew they would never forget their faces. Leaving the station and getting back to the distribution of the Bibles, Dominique seemed unfazed by the whole ordeal, but she stopped and looked at Bella, saying, "You know what? I have seen the man who tripped over the cart before. He was in the crowd, our first day here. We made eye contact, and he ran off."

Trying to take it all in, Bella mentally categorized that information, but she was on another plane. Though trusting God, she had come to some hard realizations. She looked at Dominique and said, "My dear friend…" The sound of her voice made Dominique stop, and she turned to Bella to hear her concern.

Bella continued, "We were in danger today. I know you want to make light of this, but we must be wise." As she always does when confronting subtle things, Dominique inquisitively wrinkled her nose and squinted at Bella. Her sparsely freckled nose seemed to stand out, and her dark eyes, peering bewildered, unconscious of today's plight, said, "Really?"

Trying to help Dominique see what transpired on the street today, Bella said, "Dominique, what did you think took place today?"

Dominique thought a minute and then said, "Other than the guy tripping over our cart and his friend being upset by our cart being in the way?" She paused again and said, "Why are you saying this was a planned event?"

Trying to keep calm and excited that Dominique was, at least, suggesting the idea of a plot, Bella said, "Yes, this could have been an attempt to intimidate us and our mission. The enemy of our souls and the enemy of this city does not want us here."

* * *

One day, after Bella and Dominique's event on the street, Dr. Haji called the team together to debrief the outcomes of their two months spent in Africa. She wanted the group to analyze the progress thus far and then break up into small groups and brainstorm for the future.

She started the meeting with a few statistical facts. She ran down a list she had compiled in her notebook. Dr. Haji shared that since they had arrived, over a hundred new converts were won for Christ, and they were being discipled to go out and multiply themselves in the community.

She told them that two indigenous pastors had accepted the challenge to come and serve in the new church at the warehouse. Hundreds of handout Bibles had been added to the church library. She paused to let that sink in, and she continued down her list.

"Also, our medical team has seen over 200 people each month, and thus far, thirteen major surgical procedures have been done. Thousands of meals have been served at the cafeteria, and hundreds of needy households are receiving weekly care packages, each filled with food and necessities."

She finished by sharing how the new budget allowed them to secure three new facilities. A building for the orphaned children, there were thousands of them, another building for the homeless adults, and a new storage warehouse to accommodate, doubling the number of supplies now being distributed.

Everyone cheered, and she led them in a thanksgiving prayer. Just before she dismissed them to their team brainstorming, she said, "There is a new directive for activities off our campus; teams leaving campus from now on must be comprised of at least three team members, and one of the threesomes must be a male.

Several weeks after Dominique's encounter with the two men, the local police chief stopped by to alert Dr. Haji and the team of the possible danger lurking in the community and to encourage them to take extra precautions.

CHAPTER 37

Everyone took turns leading team Bible studies. The next one, Dominique, was on the docket to lead. When she was not on the street ministering to the residents, brainstorming new adventures, and gaining new insight from God for the team's direction, Dominique was in God's Word.

Time in God's Word for Dominique was now essential; like eating was essential, God's Word sustained her. She knew that if she was taking in scripture, she would become more like Jesus, and then, naturally, prayer would become the exhalation of her soul. She was so changed she had little memory of the frightful, pathetic person she used to be.

Coalescing her thoughts around Bible study prep, she was led to one conclusion: she was unafraid. She was not fearful in the task of God's work. All her life, she had been so fearful, no more, and she rejoiced in her soul, thankful for the new her.

She paused to reflect, wondering how she could encourage the team. Her eyes left her desk and her Bible, and she looked around the room; she leaned her head back, closed her eyes, and said to God, "Oh, You… You are my life; lead me that I might lead others."

Then, a verse, one of her favorite verses, appeared inside her thoughts, and she repeated it out loud, saying, "Fear not, for I am with you; be not dismayed, for I am your God; I will strengthen you, I will help you, I will uphold you with my righteous right hand."[41]

She sat up and started writing, and that first thought flowed onto the paper. *What we do is dangerous*, she thought. But then, she clarified that thought, saying, "But fear is misplaced trust. Fear will force us to trust our own resources." Instantly, her mind went to Stephen, who was delivered up before the Sanhedrin; he had no way out but feared not, even unto death. In his last words, Stephen asked Jesus to forgive those who killed him.

Looking for a way to conclude her message, she remembered Jesus's words in Matthew 10:19–20. She wrote those verses in her notes, which say, "But when they arrest you, do not worry about what to say or how to say it. At that time you will be given what to say, for it will not be you speaking, but the Spirit of your Father speaking through you."[42] Satisfied with the content, she paused a moment to add a title. There was only one logical title, and she wrote it at the top of her notes: "Fear Not."

That night, before the team, Dominique boldly shared her thoughts. Sharing in a confidence beyond human, she spoke clearly and animated, praising God's name for this service to Him.

Everyone, including Dr. Haji, sat there wondering what just happened. It was so brief, only several minutes, but all were left pondering what they just heard and feeling sorrily inadequate.

In that unnerving moment, several people started looking around at each other, wondering if they were the only ones who felt inadequate. Then, Dominique asked, "Are there any thoughts or questions?" Most of the team remained silent, absorbing the deftness of her presentation but baffled by the application.

Looking up in a supportive posture, Bella looked directly into Dominique's eyes, moved her head slowly sideways, and then back and said, "Thank you, Dominique. That was a powerful message."

The silence was painful. Then, breaking in on the solemn moment, Dr. Haji, cleared her throat and said, "Well, as it relates to 'Fear Not,' it looks like we have some things to consider." She looked at Dominique and spoke, saying, "Thank you, Dominique, you have encouraged us." She stopped abruptly and reframed the statement, saying, "No, you have exhorted us to think boldly about our mission and God's perfect, sovereign plan for our lives; even in the danger, He has not called us to a life of fear."

Hoping to help solidify Dominique's exhortation, Bella said to Dominique, "Could you give us examples to help us glean from your perspective?"

Excited by the question, Dominique answered, "Yes, I do; I have been contemplating these thoughts for some time now." Then, she explained, saying, "Do you remember in Galatians 2:2, where Paul arrives in Jerusalem to meet the leaders there? He has spent the last fourteen years in ministry, dealing with one threat after the other. Knowing that the persecution of the church started in Jerusalem, he still goes there, and why? He says in verse 2, 'I went in response to a revelation.'[43] From there, Paul was sent on his missionary journey to the Gentiles."

Trying to fathom these new depths, the team paused in that thought, and continuing, Dominique said, "And remember in Acts 8:26–30, Phillip was visited by an angel who told him to go south to a road that ran from Jerusalem in Gaza. Phillip did not ask why he was being sent to the middle of nowhere; he just went. You know the story: he is sent to stand by a chariot where a eunuch is reading the book of Isaiah. The eunuch asks Phillip to get up into the chariot, and the eunuch is saved.

"The point of the two stories is a marvelous depiction of God's role in evangelism. The point of what I have learned is that we cannot fear, for if we do, we will not respond rightly when the Holy Spirit says go."

Just then, concluding that more than just head knowledge was necessary, Bella said, "Yes, what we have known about the danger of our calling mentally is naturally obscured due to not knowing it experientially."

Several heads began to nod in agreement, and she continued. "Like Stephen, we should not have a planned discourse with those who may deliver us up; rather, we can trust God to be faithful in our trials."

Smiling and enjoying the interaction, Dr. Haji said, "Who else would like to add to our conversation?" The medical staff remained silent, comfortable in what they were gleaning, but as if forced off his seat, William stood up. To the team, he looked like he landed awkwardly out in the middle of floor, not by choice, but unable to stay out of the fray, by God's leading, he stood there sheepishly smiling.

Still smiling, he said, "You know, to be honest, I believe most of my mission experience has been me doing what I think God wants me to do and having it all planned out in advance, asking God to make it go the way I want. What I am learning today, that is not a biblical perspective."

He looked down as if trying to measure his next words correctly; then, he looked up excitedly and spoke, "A passage my dad has on his wall, in his office, has always intrigued me: 2 Chronicles 16:9, and it says, 'For the eyes of the Lord range throughout the earth to strengthen those whose hearts are fully committed to him.'"[44] He paused again, then said, "I don't know which part of that verse is more challenging that my heart is not fully committed to Him, or the fact that I have pretty much made preaching the Gospel message something I do in my own strength."

Thinking that his comments were not rhetorical, Dr. Haji, started to ask others for their input, but William quickly interrupted and said, "Please let me continue." Dr. Haji nodded her approval, and he spoke again, saying, "We know that no one comes to the Father unless He calls them, right? Because that is undeniable, like Phillip, we are left waiting for God's instructions on where to go."

Peering around the room from face to face, he said, "What was it that Paul asked the Ephesians to do in chapter 6, verse 19? He said, 'Pray also for me, that whenever I speak, words may be given me so that I will fearlessly make known the mystery of the gospel.'[45] According to this verse, we mistakenly take God out of the Gospel equation when we have everything figured out in advance."

Seeing an opportunity to add to the mix, Bella said, "I agree; Paul in 2 Timothy 4:1–2 told his pupil,

> 'In the presence of God and of Christ Jesus, who will judge the living and the dead, and in view of his appearing and his kingdom, I give you this charge: Preach the word; be prepared in season and out of season; correct, rebuke, and encourage—with great patience and careful instruction.'"[46]

She held their attention for a moment and continued, "And then in verse 6, Paul said this: 'For I am already being poured out like a drink offering, and the time for my departure is near.'"

When Bella finished saying those last words, the entire team stopped to take in the ramifications. Having been silent for quite some time now, Dominique calmly interjected the bombshell thought of the devotion. She smiled just before she spoke again, but it was a different kind of smile, not a happy smile but a smile of confidence. The words just gently rolled off her tongue, and she said, "The difference between the Islamic suicide bomber and the Christian is that the suicide bomber seeks death; the Christian martyr suffers death."

Bringing her devotion to a close, she said, "Paul knew his time was near, and in verses 7 and 8 of the same chapter, he says, 'I have fought the good fight, I have finished the race, I have kept the faith. Now there is in store for me the crown of righteousness, which the Lord, the righteous Judge, will award to me on that day—and not only to me, but also to all who have longed for his appearing.'"[47]

She looked around the room, and perceiving the difficulty of hearing this message by her listeners, she said, "Until a year ago, I have lived my entire life in constant fear and mediocrity. It was not until I believed the word of the living God that I was able to see. It was not until I let go of my fear that power replaced it, and it wasn't until I was known by God that I had any idea there was an eternal purpose for my life; I have purpose, and the only thing that can hinder that truth is my fear. Is it too hard to believe that death is not the victor?"

What had started as a two-minute decree ended up being an intense discourse on the life and death realities of sharing the Gospel message and then culminating into soul peace, which comes from knowing the unfathomable power of God for those so-called.

Sensing it was time to bring the devotion to a close, Dr. Haji stepped into the middle of the group and said, "When we all entered this adventure, we already knew of the intense persecution that plagues this country, and we also know the enemy who solicits this evil. Our call comes with a two-phase command: 'Preach and fear not.' How it is possible, God only knows, but we have heard from the Lord tonight. Now, it is time to pray."

Prayer went on for another hour, and as the petitions were made, the Holy Spirit filled each heart with a new courage and a new commitment to go in whatever way God made available to bring forth the life-giving message of the Gospel of Christ.

***

Lounging back in their room, Bella and Dominique were both exhausted from the spiritual warfare that took place at devotions. Laying face down with her pillow over her head, Dominique realized she was just now starting to catch her breath. She lifted the pillow to say something to Bella, and there was Bella staring at her.

Embarrassed by Bella's stare, Dominique pulled her scattered hair back away from her face and sat up, saying, "Yes?"

Bella just continued staring, cocking her head from one side to the next. So, Dominique mimicked Bella's head movements and stared right back at her; for several seconds, they moved their heads in unison, staring at each other.

Unable to maintain this serious stare down, they simultaneously both burst into laughter and rolled over on Dominique's bed, facing each other. Now smiling genuinely at each other, Bella said, "I have a confession."

That surprised Dominique, and because she had no way of knowing where this was going, again, she said, "Yes?"

Starting slowly, Bella said, "I do not think I truly know who my best friend is. I used to think I knew who she was until you started mimicking me; that is why I was turning my head back and forth, looking at you from every angle, hoping to see you clearly, hoping to find you again."

Not knowing what to think, Dominique sat up abruptly, and she could not help but need an explanation, saying, "What are you talking about?"

Laughing and grabbing Dominique by the hands, Bella said, "I am just messing with you." She made sure that Dominique was laughing as well, and then she said, "But you are so different in the most wonderful way. You trust God in ways that I envy, and sometimes you frighten me in where you are willing to go for Jesus."

This conversation was a new twist in their relationship, and Dominique was truly at a loss, as if Bella was unhappy about her faith and commitment to Jesus. Not sure what to say, Dominique said, "You are the person most like Jesus that I know, your boldness at school, the power of your life, your willingness to confront evil, and most of all, your ardent love for me; I learned that all from you. You are my example."

Now, Bella was at a loss as she realized she had just put a damper on Dominique's zeal, and she said, "I heard clearly what you said tonight about the martyrs and that life is God's call for some, but I believe you are unaware sometimes of the danger you put yourself in. Maybe it is selfishness, but I do not want to see you harmed."

Touched by Bella's compassion, Dominique gripped her hands tightly and said, "You have protected me in so many ways; you have been my shield from the world's evil, but you are also the one who invited me on this mission. You are the one who made me aware of the dangers, and because of that warning, I nearly decided not to go, but after experiencing your deep commitment to Jesus and His call on my life, here I am—now, He is my shield. If He is for me, who could be against me?"

Knowing the truth of Dominique's claim seemed to enhance rather than relieve Bella's fears, and she slumped down in resignation, saying, "You are right." Still, she felt an ominous discomfort at what was playing out here in Africa.

* * *

Frustrated by the abrupt change in his empire, which the mission had wrought on his bottom line, Sylvain was spewing hateful maleficence toward the perpetrators, especially Dominique.

His closest cohorts looked on him as if he were possessed and bereft of common sense. They began to wonder about how safe they would be following what seemed like a madman.

Since the day Brice and his partner had accosted Dominique and Bella, Sylvain had ratcheted up his ire to an almost uncontrollable level, pouring out his wrath on the mission team and the local police.

All his forces were put at play. He built small teams of agitators and sent them out daily to wreak havoc on his enemies. Most of the time, they used just verbal attacks and some physical intimidation, like spilling supplies or pushing people aside, but after seeing little effect and the mission continuing to thrive, Sylvain upped the game.

Reports came into the mission that two police officers had been beaten, and one of them died in the hospital due to his injuries. At the same time, several of the small groups working out in the community were attacked physically and warned to stay off the streets or suffer the consequences.

In a two-week period, there were nine separate incidents where bodily harm was inflicted on the mission team and several police altercations as well. Due to the uptick in violence, the police chief petitioned the local government to add security in his district. He was denied the request and told there were no resources to send.

People on the street were being intimidated as well. They were told to stay away from the mission or else. Several people were beaten to send that message to the whole group. The battle plan was working out just the way Sylvain had envisioned, and the hospital and the mission team were forced to reevaluate their strategy.

As fear began to reign again in the community, the boldness of larger groups started to wane, as people were left to fend for themselves; Sylvain had gained a great victory.

* * *

Though the mission team was praying continually against this outpouring of hate and violence, nothing seemed to change. Less and less of the community felt safe coming to the hospital or accepting gifts from the small group teams dispersed to meet their needs.

Meeting with the authorities and her leadership team, Dr. Haji came up with a new plan of attack. She asked the authorities if they would supply the manpower to segregate specific areas in the community as safe places.

It took a while, but with the encouragement of the police and the mission, people started to come out to the safe places for supplies and treatment again. The police began to work with the community, saying, "We need your help to purge our city from these evil influences." The men of the community stepped up and formed militia teams of twelve men in each team, and they would patrol the safe spaces and be the eyes and ears for the police.

Along with the mission leaders, the church pastors and their congregations began a prayer vigil for God's help to overcome this attack on their lives. Though the church at the mission was being persecuted by Sylvain and his thugs, it grew. More and more people were coming to the Lord as they saw the courage and sacrifice of the mission team and the power of God moving in their lives.

It was difficult for the small groups to minister. Whenever they went out to serve, they were watched and intimidated. It became so bad that several of the medical team men suggested the teams be larger and that several of the men on the team carry weapons.

With Dr. Haji presiding over a brainstorming session, that suggestion was brought up before the entire team. Several of the men agreed, claiming, "Someone is going to die; do we wait till then?"

Silence held everyone captive as each member began to consider the suggestion. Shocked that this suggestion was being considered, Dominique stood up and spoke: "We know that many of the churches in the region call themselves Christian, and they are at war with the other religions, like the Muslim churches. They have justified the use of weapons to protect themselves and proselytize the other communities.

"Where in God's Word do we ever see Jesus suggesting that our weapons are anything but His Word impacting the world by the power of the Holy Spirit? We all know the verse I'm going to quote:

> 'The weapons we fight with are not the weapons of the world. On the contrary, they have divine power to demolish strongholds. We demolish arguments and every pretension that sets itself up against the knowledge of God, and we take captive every thought to make it obedient to Christ. And we will be ready to punish every act of disobedience, once your obedience is complete.'"[48]

She finished by saying, "God will not bless this idea."

She looked boldly around the room and said, "This battle is God's battle, and the enemy is the devil. How do we put out the fiery darts of the evil one? By putting on the full armor of God and taking up the shield of faith, that is God's provision, and nothing else will stand against our enemy."

Many at the meeting knew Dominique was correct, but Sylvain's continual bombardment left some wandering and wondering how they could continue.

CHAPTER 38

Having received several calls from Dominique, Aunt Colleen spent every day in prayer for her precious niece and the team. She also stayed in constant contact with Chloe, and they prayed together as well.

She could sense that Dominique was not divulging the entire scope of the mission challenges, but what she heard in Dominique's voice was a peace during those challenges.

One day, Colleen stepped outside to get some fresh air. She decided to gather the mail and walked slowly toward the mailbox. Receiving mail was just a routine; there was rarely anything in the mail of any significance.

Most of the time, her thoughts were on how Dominique was faring, and these same thoughts were on her mind as she pulled open the mailbox door. To her surprise, there was one large envelope inside, and she could see the writing on it. Her heart raced, as there was no doubt it was from Dominique.

Walking back to the house, Colleen turned the letter in her hand, looking at both sides. It was lightweight; she shook it in several directions to ascertain the contents. As she closed the door, her excitement became too much, and she ripped the envelope open.

Inside the envelope, Colleen found two items. One was a small note handwritten by Dominique, and it read: "Dear Aunt Colleen, I need your help." She continued, "I experienced something yesterday that has taken me apart. What seemed like what would be a routine practice evaluating the needs of the smaller villages outside of the city, we drove up upon a sight that broke my heart. The typed written note will describe what we saw. I had no other way to explain the sight, so I put it into words. Please read this and get back to me. P.S. This small village is a Muslim community, and they are the outcasts of this society."

The letter read:

Unable to stand any longer, he slowly squats to the bare, bleached, dry ground. A seemingly unbalanced and oversized head sets wobbly atop a disarrayed pile of unrecognizable bones. Skeletal remains covered with dry, leathery skin, no muscle, but alive.

From his sitting position, the collar, knee, shoulder, and elbow bones—all in the same proximity—are indistinguishable; which is which is not readily perceived. The irregular angles at which these fragments show protruding everywhere seem more like a spilled box of match sticks than a little boy; he is three years old.

Youth betrayed, the enemy is tireless, and a sadness in his eyes, far beyond horror, longs for the end. Yet, constantly, nervously, and always looking around, he does not understand. A noise behind him musters what strength he has, and he turns in hope, but hope is not there. It was just the shadow of a passerby that darkened for a moment his sunbaked existence. He strains to peer up, but not quick enough. He stares up into that ever-bright glare that has now replaced the shadow gone by; hope was not there.

Moments drag mercilessly on while he hopes for what will never appear. Except for the nervous glancing back and forth, he sits motionless, surrounded by so many but completely alone. His grotesque companions—all a mirror of himself—each a desperate reminder and nothing more.

No mother, how can she comfort when she can not bear to look upon his misery? No playmates; they have all matured beyond play. And no miracle, a truckload of food cannot mend this broken little body…

So, he stares, and that burdensome and oversized weight resting on his neck makes his head drop down, but with all his might, he pulls it back up, twisting as it rises, hoping to see help in another direction, only to find all the same.

This goes on until one moment, the culmination of agony upon agony, his head falls slowly down, and he is no longer able to lift that enormous weight. Now, his eyes focus only on the ground between his legs; he is unable to look for hope any longer.

There are no tears, just sadness, numb turmoil, then a letting go. No longer even seeing the ground, focusing on something childlike, entranced and enchanted, heavenly. Then, like so many before him, he closes his eyes and sleeps, crumbling there on the parched, angry ground, and except for the vultures surrounding him, he is silent and unnoticed…

Aunt Colleen, this is my experience… I cannot get this picture out of my mind; I am at a loss. Please help me to decipher what God is telling me.

Love,

Dominique

With the clear perspective of Dominique's vision, Colleen sat holding the letter; then, it dropped from her hand. Wanting to protect her niece from this carnage was out of her control.

She had no answer and definitely no quick fix, but she allowed herself to reflect on the character of God, and she began a letter to Dominique, saying:

I believe these poor little ones go directly into the arms of God. As far as understanding it, some things are beyond us. His ways are not our ways. We are not to know. These atrocities, in no way, malign the integrity of almighty God. Let us leave this where it is best understood: with God. If you can reach into those communities with Christ, there is a hope of change. Pray about that.

Love,

Aunt Colleen

Until this letter, each time they spoke, Colleen felt Dominique was growing in a discerning confidence, a confidence that made her proud but worried her as well. Knowing that the good times could not develop the maturity her niece was growing in, Colleen assumed Dominique was suffering for Christ; like it or not, she understood opposition comes with being in the enemy's territory. The horrifying contents of this letter put a new twist on what Dominique was living out.

Every time Dominique called home to Marie, Colleen could expect a call from her sister. Wanting reassurance, Marie would call Colleen and say, "Dominique sounds good, and she says things are going well, but what do you think? Thomas keeps telling me not to worry, but I cannot do that."

Each time Marie called, she was seeking a positive spin, which Colleen could not provide. One day, Colleen opened up to her sister, saying, "It is an amazing thing to hear her speak so boldly on the phone. This is not the girl we have known all of her life. This is a new Dominique, someone who is empowered beyond what parents and family can produce."

Not wanting to hear it but having to acknowledge the truth of her sister's insight, Marie replied, "You know the same thing that I do: our girl is in danger."

Quickly taking up the mantle again, Colleen reassured her sister, saying, "Wherever God has her, He has her back as well. God does not forsake His kids when they need Him the most; He would never leave her alone."

Unable to control what her heart was feeling, Marie cringed in her soul. Bereft to contain her inward agony, she whispered to her sister, saying, "What if we never see her again?"

Pausing to check if she was speaking too abruptly, Colleen measured her response. Knowing she had already wrestled with the exact same question that Marie just posited, she could barely believe what her heart was telling her to share with her sister. She tried to think of a misdirection tactic, but God would have none of it, and she just whispered calmly back to her sister, "Then, God needs her with Him more than we need her with us…"

* * *

The next several excursions that Dominique's team made out into the community had interesting dynamics. The community militia and the police worked hand in hand chaperoning them from one point to the next. Not that there were no attempts to intimidate, but the work was accomplished, and the team praised God for their success.

One day, as Dominique's team ventured out into the field of souls, a group of poor and needy people surrounded the girl with the long dark hair and began to touch her and even worship her.

This had happened several times before, and Dominique was unsure how to proceed, but today, sure that only God should be worshipped, she stood back and, in bold French, said, "No! I am just like you; you must not give praise to me but to the God who lives in me."

Several of the militia group and her team members helped settle the crowd and asked them to sit and listen to Dominique's plea. She allowed the Holy Spirit to tend to their hearts, and many gave their lives to Christ. They were taken to the church facility and baptized.

Unbeknownst to any of the team or the militia group, an ominous witness had observed the goings on with the crowd. Disguised and accompanied by bodyguards, Sylvian himself was only a few feet away, sitting at a table on the street.

Wonderfully distracted by God's movement amongst the people, the militia and the team were busy gathering up those going for baptism. Seeing an opportunity, Sylvian stood and walked up close to Dominique and said, "You are very brave, my dear, but you should be more careful."

He pushed his baseball cap back on his head, lifted his dark sunglasses up, and stared deeply into

Dominique's eyes, then smiled viciously at her and said, "See you soon." With the same intense glare, Dominique remained glued to his eyes.

Then, he looked down and pulled back his jacket. Dominique followed his eyes until she saw a pistol holstered on his belt. He smiled again, tipped his hat to her, and then, almost magically, he disappeared into the bustling crowd.

With all the excitement in the street, no one saw Sylvain approach or leave Dominique's side. She was left standing with the picture of Sylvain's face etched in her soul. Noticing her demeanor, William came up to her and said, "Are you all right?"

Still embracing the evil that had just been forced onto her sight, Dominique remained tense, looking in the direction where Sylvian had disappeared. William asked her again, "Dominique, what are you doing? We have people we need to get to the church."

Finally, she broke away from the query of the confrontation with Sylvain and said, "I am okay; let's get these people out of here."

* * *

Exiting speedily away from his rendezvous with Dominique, Sylvain could hardly contain how pleased he was with his plan and the encounter with the dark-haired girl. Arriving back at his headquarters, Sylvain intentionally began to belittle several of his comrades for fearing the little girl on the street. He maligned them, saying, "What you saw today, that is how you deal with the enemy. You do not allow them relevance or space in your world."

He stayed up late that night, planning how to execute the next step of his plot to overthrow the mission's agenda. He was still sure that getting the dark-haired girl out of the way would result in everyone else fleeing back to their own worlds. It thrilled Sylvain just to think about how devastating his next move would be and how the impact would result in returning him to rule this city.

Amused, nearly giddy, Sylvain moved over to his bed. He had planned his revenge, and exacting it would happen soon, he pulled his pillow up under his head and pondered the timing and actual confrontation of meeting once again with the dark-haired girl.

Just before he dosed off, he started feeling melancholy; that moment with the dark-haired girl was just too fleeting; he didn't want that moment to end, so he tried to interject himself back into the scene. Filled with excitement again, he lay there imagining himself glaring into her eyes.

Then, something happened; the smile on his face washed away, and he lay there uncomfortable. The eyes he so longed to glare into glared back at him, and he could not get those eyes out of his conscience.

He sat up quickly and shook his head, but to no avail; there, unrelenting, were those eyes again, so he moved quickly over to the bathroom and stared into the mirror. What he saw in the mirror unnerved him. The eyes he saw now were his own eyes, full of fear, darting back and forth, looking for an escape. Try as he may, he had no sleep that night.

When the sun finally came up, Sylvain was sitting at his table, still afraid to close his eyes. He looked down at his hand, and it was shaking. Then, he realized his whole body was shaking. Exhausted and trembling, he tried to make sense of what was happening to him, but he could not shake his bondage, for there, still before him, were those piercing eyes.

Trying to reason what was happening, he closed his eyes tightly, and for a brief minute, he felt relief. With his eyes still clutched tightly shut, he started to formulate in his mind why these eyes were so beguiling.

Then, with his logic coming back intact, he reasoned, saying to himself, "The dark-haired girl's eyes were not staring in hate like I was, but staring in compassion. Her eyes spoke to me, 'Do not fear; be at peace.'"

Though this revelation terrified him, he realized that the piercing content spoken from her eyes was not hate but love. All of a sudden, he quit shaking, which was a comfort, but he was appalled by the thought that it was her gaze that brought him peace.

CHAPTER 39

After arriving at the church and after the baptisms, Dominique pulled Bella and William aside and said, "I have something to tell you." Excited and still reeling over the glory of seeing God's power to save souls and knowing that God had used Dominique mightily, both William and Bella stared at her with broad smiles, waiting for her to speak.

The look on her face confused them; she didn't seem to be as excited as they were over the "Good News," which had prevailed in the lives of so many. Still looking straight into their eyes, Dominique did not move or begin to say anything, which caused Bella to ask, "What?"

Looking away for just a brief moment, she turned back to them and said, "During the busyness of rounding up converts for baptism today, a man approached me and said, 'You are very brave, my dear, but you should be more careful.'" In every detail, she shared the rest of the confrontation.

Confused by the news and remembering that she was surrounded by such an entourage, William said, "How could he even get close to you?" He looked at Dominique and said, "I never saw anyone." Then, he looked at Bella and said, "Did you see anyone?"

Before Bella could respond, Dominique grabbed William's arm and pulled him close, saying, "Trust me, he was there."

Having concluded that yes, she had been confronted, the three of them went to see Dr. Haji. Still praising God for the new converts, Dr. Haji said, "Isn't this just like Satan? We are used by God to rescue lost souls from his clutches, and he can't stand it." After intense prayer, Dr. Haji called the police to see how they wanted to proceed.

That night, Dominique tried to sleep but couldn't; she kept seeing before her the eerie stare of the man who threatened her. *The man's stare was angry, for sure*, she thought to herself, but she also saw in his stare a desperation with no remedy. She finally woke Bella up and asked her to pray for her thoughts and peace for this situation.

As Bella poured out her heart to God for her friend, it wasn't long before Dominique was transported from being anxious to being at peace and thankful. Back in bed, it was but a few moments before Bella's gentle snoring became the chime of comfort for her weary soul, and Dominique slept unhindered.

***

After the police left, Dr. Haji called the team together. She shared the police findings, saying, "There is a witness who saw the man who confronted Dominique yesterday. This witness is sure the man who did this is the leader of the crime element in the community. His name is Sylvain, and he is very dangerous. He is thought to be the mastermind behind all of the evil happening in this community, and he has murdered many people. He has a small army at his disposal and intimidates by spreading fear."

Trying to keep things in context, Dominique spoke up and said, "Kinda sounds like a turf war, doesn't it?"

Catching the drift of Dominique's audacity, Dr. Haji said, "Exactly. We have always known that we would be battling on a hallowed ground."

"So, what do we do now?" William chimed in.

The team was caught off guard and found themselves looking back and forth at each other. No less sure of God's plan for the mission, Bella spoke, "We take precautions and continue doing God's work. He will never leave us nor forsake us." Sure of that much, the team agreed, and they began to strategize for the future; they ended the meeting in prayer and went to work.

As brave as Bella's statement was, she had reservations of whether Dominique could be effective and safe at the same time. As they headed for the day's work, Dominique could tell Bella was sorely detached from the duties ahead. She reached out and touched Bella on the shoulder and said, "Hey, roomy."

Turning away, trying not to reveal the tears that had instantly flooded her eyes, Bella started to leave. Easing her hand down from Bella's shoulder, along her arm, and ending up holding her hand, Dominique pulled Bella back. Turned now toward each other, they stared as only the dearest of friends and sisters in Christ could do.

There were no words; Bella knew talking about her fears or more protection would have no impact on her dear friend. Staring as if really seeing her for the first time, Bella could see the confidence of Christ pouring out of Dominique and, accompanied by that confidence, her true joy and peace that comes only from Christ. Though they spoke nothing to each other, they were completely aware of God's providence; satisfied, they turned back to the duties of the day.

Moving forward, the hard part for Bella was not making small talk sound as if they were overlooking the obvious, and then she could relax in Dominique's faith. The balancing act was difficult. One day, Bella would be feeling up, and the next day, she would be feeling down. The rollercoaster-like ride of her emotions was taking its toll.

Another day, not sure who to confide in, Bella sought out William to bounce her feelings past. Having issues himself with the danger Dominique was in, William was pretty sure he knew what Bella was seeking.

After a few minutes of Bella rambling in her thoughts, William stopped her and said, "I know, I feel the same way. Can you explain why you are so distraught? Is there a trust factor that leads you to despair for our friend?"

Sheepishly, Bella let it out, saying, "Don't you feel like something terrible is about to happen to Dominique? She knows it too but seems unaffected by the inevitable."

Nodding his head, William spoke, "Yes, I sense it too, but can we pack her up and ship her back home? We are not her protection."

Looking empathetically at Bella, William spoke, "Considering what we have been called to do, demanding assurances that Dominique will be safe is unhealthy. Maybe this will help, or not, but C. S. Lewis once said, "God whispers to us in our pleasures, speaks in our conscience, but shouts in our pain: it is the megaphone to rouse a deaf world."

Continuing, William said, "You know that God always does what pleases Him, and what pleases Him is best, right? I know you do. It has been said, 'Where God puts a period, we cannot put a comma.'"

Moving close to Bella, William put his hand on her shoulder and said, "You are not alone; this scares me too."

For the first time in Bella's Christian walk, she had to admit her faith had never been tested at this level. She could remember being steadfast in so many cases, especially with Dominique; she lived believing there was nothing that God could not do. Now, she felt weak and reached out for William's hand and said, "Please pray God's strength for me."

Affirming her request, William said, "I will pray for both of us."

* * *

Several times since arriving in Africa, Dominique had contacted Mrs. Allard just to bounce things off her perspective. Mrs. Allard, not sure why she was calling this time, just felt led to reach out to Dominique.

Always ready for time with Dominique, Mrs. Allard listened carefully to Dominique share her life in Africa. She was excited by how, with each new conversation, it was evident that Dominique was growing exponentially in the knowledge and grace of God.

This day, in a strange twist, Dominique began to enquire of things on a deeper level. After some inconsequential chitchat, Dominique became silent and said nothing. Not wanting to rush things and still lingering on the other end of the conversation, Mrs. Allard waited patiently.

Not that her pausing to contemplate was new for Dominique; this was just part of the mental geometry of their comradery, but it wasn't long after Dominique's question that Mrs. Allard sensed a new level of inquiry.

Quiet, as if detached and far away from the presence of this conversation, nearly whispering, Dominique said, "How do you cope with missing Oliver?"

So many times in the past, Mrs. Allard could predict Dominique's question before she asked it. Today, however, it was Mrs. Allard who had to stop and evaluate what was just said.

Normally, it would be apropos for Mrs. Allard to say, "Why do you ask?" But today, asking a question after receiving a question was out of the question. So, now she had to stop and formulate an answer, and what surprised her was that she had no ready answer to Dominique's question.

On the other end of the line and still wistfully aware of where she was, Dominique was in no hurry for an answer. Knowing that the pause had been too long, but also under the stark surprise, Dominique's question had just plucked a heartstring, one that had not been plucked in some time. Mrs. Allard choked up and found herself tearful.

Almost defensively now, as if not wanting to delve into her emotion, Mrs. Allard really wanted to say, "Why do you ask?" but she relented and spoke what came first to her mind: "I cope by trusting that God has been taking the best care of him. Oliver is in the hands of the only one who knows all, and I know I will see Oliver again someday…"

Not having any real relevance to draw on, Dominique just said, "Oh…" Then, these thoughts crashed into her brain, and she quipped to herself, *The only people close to me who have died are Grandpa and Durand*. Then, she relayed the same thing she had just thought to herself verbally to Mrs. Allard.

That response sounded more like a question than a comment to Mrs. Allard, so now, she waited on Dominique to see where she wanted to go. Finally, she did speak, and she said, "There is a good chance I won't see Durand in heaven, and even though Aunt Colleen led my grandpa to Christ, I barely knew him." Then, whimsically, she said to Mrs. Allard, "Except for Jesus and my grandpa, I will know no one in heaven."

Realizing that Dominique had a point and that this topic was one they spent little time discussing, Mrs. Allard began planning how to fortify her young friend. She first tried putting herself in Dominique's shoes; she thought, *She is only just eighteen years old, too young to know this topic in depth. She grew up in a non-Christian environment, and she knows few Christians who have died.*

Since she was Dominique's mentor, Mrs. Allard started to feel guilty for not delving more into this topic. Just before heading into an extensive discourse on all the blessings of heaven, the Holy Spirit checked that, and Mrs. Allard felt it was time to ask Dominique a question, so she did, saying, "Darling, why these thoughts today?"

***

Heading out for an excursion with the team, Dominique was revitalized and ready to go. Reflecting on her talk with Mrs. Allard, she felt renewed, knowing now that heaven would be anything but boring; she was able to reopen her heart and found great joy in seeing these needy people from God's perspective. With her last thought before ending the conversation, Mrs. Allard said, "Have you forgotten, since being in Africa, all the souls God has allowed you the privilege of leading them to Him? They will be in heaven, and I am sure they will be looking you up."

Mrs. Allard had such a way of painting the nuances of life rightly, and Dominique had a fresh view of the mission and God's plan for her future. It renewed her confidence to know the comfort Mrs. Allard relied on each day to see, without seeing, God's care for Oliver's future.

It was also helpful to be reminded of all the people from scripture who would be in heaven and whom God was also managing their safekeeping. The best part of her last conversation with Mrs. Allard was her depiction of the new heaven and new earth and all that would be taking place in her welcome to her eternal home. It was invigorating for her to know now how much the Bible talked about heaven and how beautifully it was depicted so as to project a vision we could get a glimpse of from here on earth.

The clarity with which Mrs. Allard portrayed heaven helped Dominique to better understand a scripture, which had been confusing until now. She quoted it in her mind, saying, *"And God raised us up with Christ and seated us with him in the heavenly realms in Christ Jesus."*[49] She thought to herself, *Positionally, I am already in heaven, and knowing the truth of my future helps me to live now in anticipation of that reality.*

Pausing in that daunting awareness, she mused at her frailty and thought to herself, *How unhuman it is to remain undistracted while waiting on such a pristine moment. We scurry about, day to day, like ants in their domain, but we are never not under the watchful eyes of our precious Creator.* Her final thought was the best thought of all, and she said to herself, *The greatest thing about heaven is Jesus will be in heaven; I can only imagine what that will be like.*

That night, while trying to put into words her thoughts, Dominique wrote a poem; it went like this:

Satan's pomp, rejoice to destroy and see in me a shaken joy.

When peace would flood my constant scurry, his meager offer doubt and worry.

Oh run, oh run, reminds the race, and off I go, forgetting pace.

Terror nips as I go by, shadows grab, in fear, I cry.

And as I do, my Father hears, lifts, embraces, and dries my tears.

Oh, how wonderful snuggled close to Him my fear returns to joy again.

And when I wander around outside, and forget the love where You abide.

Help me remember Your love's reward, my precious, priceless, matchless Lord.

She found a tack and stuck the poem on the wall next to her bed. It was becoming clear that there was no human way around all the distractions racing at her soul, and she prayed, "Oh, Holy Spirit, my God. Since I am kept until that day, let me know Your strength for my minutes and days ahead, and let me not lean on my own understanding."

***

A few days later, after her discussion and prayer with William, Bella had a new confidence; she needed someone to talk to, a sounding board. Laying back on her bed, Bella sensed something was still undone. She confessed her lack of faith to God and knew she was forgiven, but she couldn't help but ask God, and she prayed, saying, "Dear God, please keep Dominique safe."

Not sure how to clearly verbalize her petition, Bella paused before God. It was as if, in her mind, she was staring at a large portrait, a tapestry of all the pieces of Dominique's life. Like a puzzle, all the pieces were in place except for the last one.

Fixed on the space that was the final piece, like a supernatural portal, it held her gaze; she could not look away, and she longed for a glimpse of the future for that last piece.

Suddenly, she came alert and knew she was no longer praying but analyzing the meaning of the vision in her mind. Then, as if hearing God speak, His word overwhelmed her human understanding, and she was held spellbound at His voice. This is what she heard:

"Bella, would I take one of My children up to the moment where I ask them to die for me and not supernaturally impose Myself into that moment? Dominique is as safe with Me now as she ever has been and ever will be; I will never leave her or forsake her."

Like being brought back from a deep dream, Bella struggled to come alert. Straining to see the one she had just heard, hoping for a glimpse of the one who spoke. She blinked her eyes several times and looked expectantly around the room, but she was alone.

She started to look down, hoping to reengage that voice, but then quickly, in hope, she looked up again, but there was no one there. Sure that she had just been in His presence, she slowly, humbly bowed her head and said, "Your will be done, not mine."

Excited and at genuine peace for her friend, she lifted herself up off the bed and started toward the door, but as she passed Dominique's bed, she noticed some kind of writing pinned to the wall. It wasn't clear enough to read from across Dominique's bed, so she placed her hands in the middle of Dominique's bed and leaned over to get a closer look.

She started reading out loud, saying, "Satan's pomp, rejoice to destroy. . ." Still reading out loud, she was just getting to the end of the poem when Dominique walked into the room.

Dominique could hear a voice as she came closer to her room, and just before she entered, she realized it was Bella's voice, but more than that, strangely, Bella was reading her poem on the wall out loud.

Startled by Dominique's sudden appearance, Bella jumped back off of Dominique's bed. Embarrassed by her encroachment into Dominique's domain and looking sheepishly, Bella smiled and said rather weakly, "Hey, roomy."

Since Bella was standing right next to Dominique's bed, Dominique moved over and sat down on Bella's bed. Bella sat down on Dominique's bed, and from there, they just sat, smiling at each other.

Not that she had to explain anything to Dominique, but still, Bella wanted to share with Dominique what she was doing, and she said, "I read your poem."

Still smiling, Dominique said, "Why were you reading it out loud? I heard you as I came in?"

Laughing, Bella said, "I don't know. Reading it out loud, it just seemed to flow better."

Laughing too, Dominique said, "So, what do you think?"

Trying to combine all that she had just heard from the Lord with now having read Dominique's poem, Bella found herself at real peace, and she said, "Along with what God has been teaching me, I think your poem solidifies the fact that I worry way too much about you being safe here."

Sensing this was a perfect time to share with Bella what she had been thinking for some time, Dominique nodded her head in approval. Then she looked deep into Bella's eyes and said, "You have not been yourself for some time now, and I believe your fear for my well-being has taken your joy and your courage. Where has my redheaded lioness gone?"

Knowing that Dominique was right, Bella paused for a second to organize her next thoughts. Having the clear direction of how to explain her actions, Bella said, "You are right, and I am sorry for being such a nag, more than that, a nag and a poor example of someone who lives by faith rather than sight."

What Dominique said next surprised Bella and confirmed her own conclusions concerning God's plan and protection for His kids. Jumping right in where God had just left off, Dominique spoke, "There is a newness in me now that goes far beyond who I used to be. God has affirmed His promise to me, and I know He will never leave me or forsake me."

Stopping as if to reflect in her soul, she stared down and just past Bella's feet to the floor. Then, like an explosion of joy, she looked up, and her countenance became bright, and she said, "Bella, I have come to the conclusion that if God requires that I die for Him, I will trust Him, for that would be a worthy life."

Straining to speak, hoping that her words would land rightly as God intended, Dominique stared into Bella's big green eyes and said, "I do not fear death, nor do I anguish over what words I should hope to say to my executioner, for words will be given me."

Finding it hard to believe her ears, Bella was balancing the difficulty of trying to hear Dominique clearly and, at the same time, factoring in the words that God, just minutes before, had spoken to her; she braced herself, holding tightly onto the bed.

Then, almost nonchalantly, Dominique capped her thoughts by saying, "If I am to die, would God leave me to fend for myself against the enemy of my soul? I think not. I don't foresee it, nor do I have a plan against it, but the Author and Finisher of my faith has bolstered my soul, and I know I will not be alone at the end of my days on earth. In fact, I will know as I am known, come what may; there is no fear in that fact."

Having heard the confirmation from her dear friend, Bella rejoiced in God's sovereign plan for their lives. Bound in God's ability to keep them, and as only like minds and like souls can, they reached for each other; squeezing Dominique's hand, Bella said, "Amen."

Poised over their commitment to God and recalling what Aunt Collen said "amen" meant, Dominique said, "So be it."

CHAPTER 40

Sensing God's hand in all their work, even with Dominique's threatening encounter, the mission team became renewed again. At the same time, Sylvian was becoming more emboldened. He, too, was discovering a new strength, a strength unknown to him before. A power emanating from within, but unbeknownst to him, was gaining complete control of his soul.

Even his evil minions were beginning to see an uncommon darkness permeating his countenance. Confiding among themselves, several of his lieutenants began to sense a foreboding element in Sylvain's schemes.

While contemplating the idea of following such a one, several of them were left unsure of their future. Afraid and unable to predict the outcome of possibly ending up on the wrong side of Sylvain's anger, some began to abandon their leader.

Knowing full well that double-crossing Sylvain was like putting a target on their back, still, rather than follow an unhinged tyrannical time bomb, his team began to dwindle daily until he had just a meager following.

It was more difficult with Brice. He owed Sylvain so much, more than just money. Sylvain had saved his life, and Sylvain never let him forget that. It was like he had become a slave to Sylvain.

It was a daily conundrum for Brice. He feared what Sylvain could do to him, but since coming into contact with the dark-haired girl, he had come face-to-face with a fear he had never known. He couldn't completely grasp why he feared her, but something was truly amiss; he feared the power displayed in the goodness that prevailed in all she did.

One day, several of Brice's closest comrades approached him. Knowing that Brice was Sylvain's right-hand man, they hoped to get him alone to get his perspective on what they felt was a foolish scheme; how could he kidnap the dark-haired girl? It appeared to them that Brice was leery of the plan as well.

They settled on a place just outside the city to meet. The two men arrived early and were waiting on Brice. As he came close, the bolder of the two men walked up briskly and shook Brice's hand. The other man came up close and stood warily, looking around as if they were being watched.

The bold one said to Brice, "Are you all in on this crazy plan that Sylvain has put into place? How can we kidnap the dark-haired girl without the entire city rising up and coming down around our heads?" The quiet man nodded his head, affirming his allegiance to the bold man.

Relieved to hear he was not alone and that he was not crazy for thinking this was the worst plan ever, Brice also started looking around nervously, fearful that they were being spied upon. Pulling his hat down until you could just barely see his eyes, he looked at the two men and said, "Now is not the time to discuss it. There are ears everywhere, and we are not safe."

Quickly ending the covert meeting, Brice hurried back to his home. All the way there, he kept thinking to himself, *What if Sylvain put these two guys up to have this meeting to test my loyalty?* He began to sense that there was no place left that he was safe. A snapshot of the impending doom framed like a portrait around his life, and his heart felt weak.

Feeling completely lost and all alone, Brice began to think about his wife and children. For so long, he had been just fine not having that burden to bear, but lately, he longed for the comfort he so fondly remembered in family life.

Being inside and just staring at the walls made him feel like he was locked in. Not knowing why or what he was doing, he left the house hurriedly and meandered around the neighborhood, but soon, he found himself staring at his children, playing in the street in front of his old house.

Busy as little ones are, they did not see him, but fearing they might, he moved to where he was sure he would not startle them. From there, entertained in their contagious interaction, replete with screams of joy and laughter, he found himself smiling. Then, something he had not done in over a year, he laughed, and when he laughed, his heart burst with joy, but it also burst with remorse; unable to control his response, as if in pain, he screamed loudly.

Startled by his outburst, he clutched his chest, and with tears streaming from his eyes, he turned to run, but he only made it several steps away when he was drawn helplessly back again to the scene of his anguish.

Turning slowly to face his fears and joys, there, awakened by his scream, were his three children staring at their dad. He froze, unable to do anything but cry, and then, what he thought could never happen again, simultaneously, all three of the children screamed at the top of their lungs, "Papa!"

Not hindered by the formalities of an estranged family dynamic, the youngest, his six-year-old daughter, screaming all the way, jumped toward her dad. Now that their sister had abandoned the established protocol, which released them from the brokered guidelines, the two older boys bolted in flight toward their dad as well.

Watching the threesome barreling his way, Brice was in bliss, but he also had to contemplate the outcome of this decision. He said to himself, *What have I done?* And then, as if an answer was given to him, he heard in his mind these words: *The right thing. You have done the right thing.*

He felt his knees buckle and found himself forced to the ground, and as he fell, all three children hit him at once, clamoring all over him, crying and hugging their dad. With six arms around his neck and eight eyes wetting his shirt, Brice felt alive; he felt new, and the truth of this moment, this time with his children, confirmed what was missing in his life. At that moment, he knew as long as he was estranged from his family, his heart could never be at ease.

Taken captive in this instance and at peace in his soul, he clung tightly to his children. Thankful, he closed his eyes and, looking up, said, "Thank you. I will never let them go again." Just then, he looked up, and there, standing in the middle of the street, stood his children's mother.

Startled, he took a deep breath and stood up. In doing so, the children turned to see what had his attention. The four of them could not look away and froze, staring directly into eyes of steel.

Stumbling to say something, Brice let out a sound, and as he did, his bride said, "Children, come here now." All three of them looked back and up into their father's face, longing to stay where they were, but knowing it could not be, pleading with their eyes, they looked back toward their mom. She didn't have to say it again; her countenance said it all, and they knew she meant now.

Fearing leaving their dad and, at the same time, fearing more not heeding their mother's command, one by one, they let go of the grip they had on their father and turned in obedience, walking slowly back to her side.

As the children moved toward her, she remained strategically focused directly into Brice's eyes. When the children drew close, she gathered them up like a hen with her chicks. Now huddled together, facing Brice, the four of them peered across the distance between them.

Still fixed on his bride's eyes, Brice started to take a step toward his family, but he checked that thought when he saw their mom react. Never taking her eyes off of him, she turned her head sideways as if to say, "How dare you?"

People on the street were beginning to take notice of the family dynamic, and they started to move closer. With the community alert to what was happening in the street, Brice was forced to look away from his family, and he nervously thought about turning to go.

Right in the middle of that thought, another thought raced into his mind, overriding his fear, and he bent down onto one knee, looked back into his bride's eyes, and said her name, "Alain." He hadn't said her name out loud in over a year; then he held out his hand and said it again, "Alain, please."

This was becoming quite a spectacle to all the onlookers, so Alain bent down, looked sternly at her children, and said, "Go into the house." And they did as their mother told them.

After dispatching the children to the house, Alain looked up slowly to see her husband, still on one knee, with his hand stretched out toward her. As she drew closer, she could see the tears pouring from his eyes, which she had never seen before in her proud husband.

Stopping a few feet away, she looked down at Brice and said, "What is it you want?"

Without hesitation, Brice pushed his hand out further toward Alain, and nearly sobbing, he said, "I want you."

Looking at Brice with disgust, Alain said, "Why now? What has changed?"

The onlooking crowd could hear the conversation, and they started talking to each other about what this all meant. One lady said to her neighbor, "I have never seen Brice bow to anything; he is so prideful." Another couple, knowing Brice's temper and attitude, moved closer to the pair should Alain need support.

Still on his knee and unconcerned with the audience of staring neighbors, Brice said, "You have no reason to believe me, and I do not deserve even this unorthodox audience with you, but if you hear me, I want you to know something."

Having heard so many excuses before, Alain found herself resistant to hearing more, but then she paused and thought, *This is my husband, and these are his children.* Her heart softened, and she prayed to herself, *Oh, God, what is this?* She was surprised when she heard herself say, "Go ahead, tell me what you want me to know."

He started by saying, "Alain, I am not the same person I used to be. You have no way of knowing that, but if you allow me to prove to you that this is the case, I will not let you down. I am so sorry for my behavior; please forgive me. I have been a terrible husband and father, but I want to be different; better for you and our children."

Having prayed this last year, long and hard for her wayward husband, Alain had given up on their marriage, but she had never seen Brice like this. A tear of hope gathered on the edge of her right eyelid, and for the first time, she looked down.

As she did, falling on both knees, Brice inched forward; he gently reached out for Alain's fingertips and brushed them with his hand. Bristling and pulling her hand back, she glared at him and said, "Why should I trust today that you are a different person? How can I accept that after what you have done? How do I know you are really sorry?"

As bold as he could ever remember being, Brice looked back into her eyes and said, "The Jesus I found so revolting in you has found me out. He has come to life for me through the life of the dark-haired missionary, and I am changed. Through the acts of kindness and dedication to our people, I have seen Him in her…"

CHAPTER 41

Though she received correspondence regularly from home folks, it was rare for Dominique to receive a package; this was a rather large package. Just as she began to excitedly tear into it, Bella walked into their room.

Looking up to see Bella, Dominique said, "Look what I got from home." Packages are not normal, and to receive one on the mission field is a rare treat. Excited too, and with wide-eyed expectation, Bella jumped onto the bed next to Dominique.

It was hard not to leap in and help, but Bella sat back patiently; then, to her joy, Dominique said, "Hey, help me out; I can't get into this thing." Together, they tore at the package until it bared the contents inside.

Turning the box upside down, Dominique poured everything that was contained within out on her bed. There before them, with the name of each person who sent it, were six smaller packages. Surprised, they looked up at each other with excitement. Still holding the box in the air and to ensure that all of the cargo was gone, Dominique peered back into the box, and there, taped in the bottom of the box, was a large envelope with Bella's name written on it.

Turning the box so Bella could see, Dominique said, "Whose name is on this one?" Just as Bella reached out for the box, Dominique pulled it away and said, "That must be a mistake; that is not my name on the envelope." Smiling shyly but strategically, Bella paused and, in a ploy, looked down. Then, suddenly, she dove and snatched the box from Dominique's hands.

As Bella worked on getting the envelope off the bottom of the box, Dominique was busy lifting and inspecting each of the six packages on her bed. She turned them all until the sender's name was on top, and then she lined them up in front of her.

Getting frustrated that she couldn't get the taped envelope off the bottom of the box, Bella looked up to complain to Dominique about who the jokester was that laminated the envelope to the box.

Just before starting to whine about it, Bella looked over at Dominique and saw all the packages lined up in front of her. She put the uncooperative box down and smiled. There, like a child at Christmas, Dominique sat, eyes wide open, hands pressed together in prayer fashion and held next to her chest; she looked ready to pounce. Just before she did, she sensed Bella's stare and looked up into her doting friend's eyes. She blushed, knowing that Bella had caught her in the ecstasy of this childlike state.

On the verge of laughing, Bella said, "Well, what are you waiting for? Get after it."

Before she could begin, she said to Bella, "Look who they are from. Everyone I love, and I know who loves me, is represented right now in this room." Knowing that she was so loved, the excitement of the gifts nearly turned into an emotional outburst.

With her eyes moist, she put her hand to her cheek, bowed toward Bella, and with a quivering smile, she said, "I am blessed." Bella acknowledged Dominique's blessing with a nod, and the two of them paused a moment in thankfulness.

Then, she sat up straight, looked at the packages, and back into Bella's eyes. She started to call out the names on the packages.

"This first one is from Mom and Dad, then Chase, after that is Chloe, and the next one is from Mrs. Martsen." She paused at this one to stare up into Bella's eyes as if to acknowledge what they both knew: Jesus had worked a miracle here. She continued down the packages, saying, "This funny wrapped one is from Mrs. Allard." She finished by putting her hand gently on the final package and said, "And this last one is from Aunt Colleen."

* * *

Having received letters from all the people who had sent Dominique a package, Bella reclined blissfully on her bed, enjoying the correspondence from home. Each letter was so encouraging. They were thankful that she was Dominique's best friend, and they promised they would never stop praying for the mission.

Chase sent several pictures of Dominique as a little girl, and Bella truly loved each one. She posted all of them on her wall next to her bed. There, she could see and get to know her best friend even better.

Trying not to make too much of it, Bella sensed there was a collaborative underlying theme in the letters. Though maybe not intentional, they came together to coordinate the same theme in each letter.

After analyzing this theme, which they shared together, it appeared to Bella that Dominique's loved ones were fearful for her safety. Though more overt, even Chase appealed to the question of her safety.

The first thing Bella gleaned from the letters, which concerned her, was that Dominique was not sharing with her family the dangerous encounters she had experienced here. This information put Bella between a rock and a hard spot. *How do I share, and possibly betray, a confidence that Dominique has not indulged to her family?*

In a sleepless night, wrestling and praying over this dilemma, Bella finally received a word from the Lord, and in her correspondence back to the inquirers, she made her case. She expressed the dangers that are a part of any mission endeavor; this was a fight for souls, but she confidently reassured everyone that God's plans for Dominique were perfect and should anyone want, due to fear, to change her circumstances, which God has ordained, they would be accusing God of not understanding His own will.

Knowing that Dominique would not want her loved ones to worry, Bella felt comfortable sending this message home, and the return letters were mailed. She did not mention this incident to Dominique.

* * *

Meanwhile, Dominique could not be happier. Each package was special in its own way. Some little treasure, revealing an intimacy she shared with those she loved. She placed them strategically around her room, where she could admire them at will, a constant reminder of her support team.

A short note accompanied the packages. Notes affirmed again and again how proud they were of her and how much she was loved by all, especially by Jesus. The note that was different from the rest came from Aunt Colleen. Though loving and encouraging, Aunt Colleen also shared a vision that God gave her concerning Dominique's future.

It was kind of spooky, and Dominique was not sure how to interpret it. The vision basically centered around Dominique's impact on the citizens of Quadda. In her letter, Aunt Colleen shared from her vision that the enemies of Christ were strong and motivated but that God would use Dominique to put an end to their reign of terror.

Ending the letter, Aunt Colleen shared a scripture from 1 Peter 2:23: "When they hurled their insults at him, he did not retaliate; when he suffered, he made no threats. Instead, he entrusted himself to him who judges justly."[50]

Understanding that the verse pertained to Jesus's suffering for mankind, therefore, going forward, Dominique purposed to dwell on it, trying to apply it to Aunt Colleen's vision for her.

Initially, her response to the verse was to apply it to sharing the Gospel with her new friends of Quadda. *Surely, that was it. These poor and lost people must know what Jesus is offering them.*

Then, another thought, a more serious unveiling. She paused to ponder the verse again. She thought to herself, *Maybe this vision and the verse were meant to better equip me for my own forthcoming struggles.* Either way, she was comforted because, as she contended for the faith, "entrusting herself to Him who judges justly," she was confident that the author of her faith would not be missing in the action surrounding her service for Him.

* * *

Bolstered in faith and in God's sovereign purposes for her life, Dominique committed to a constant prayerful excitement about what was coming next. Her commitment was like a contagion. As the rest of the team succumbed to the Dominique dynamic, a sustaining peace permeated the team and also the new converts who had been won to Christ in Quadda.

Sensing the renewal of the team, coupled with the overwhelming need in the city, Dr. Haji decided to double the outreach ministry to the underserved population, which the city government was unable to serve. Crippled by poverty and harassed by the criminal element, she built a coalition of the citizenry, police, and the mission team to reach into that element of the city on a daily basis.

Having secured the police and citizen militia for protection, she next called William, Bella, and Dominique to her office. Dr. Haji apprised them of the new directive and asked for input on how to accomplish this goal. Looking at each other expectantly, the three of them nodded their approval, then Dominique asked Dr. Haji if they could take some time to brainstorm a plan.

As Dr. Haji watched them leave her office, already brainstorming as they walked away, she was struck by how miraculous all that was taking place for Christ and His Kingdom. Having spent her life in the mission field, she was sure that nothing, to this extent had ever happened before; she paused and prayed, giving thanks for his power and goodness.

* * *

As the three missionaries planned the next phase of the ministry, they were keenly aware of a heightened need and the presence of the Holy Spirit moving them forward. It was becoming more and more evident that God had His sights on Quadda and its people. It was like He had taken this tiny hovel of broken humanity to be His pointer in time.

At the same time, Sylvain is now ready to move into the next phase of his plan to overthrow the spiritual upheaval, depleting his immoral domain. It didn't take long for him to see the battle lines being drawn. Each day now, as the mission team entered the impoverished avenue of shacks and shanties, the team was escorted by the militia and the police.

It was becoming nearly impossible to catch his nemesis alone. The dark-haired girl moved about without hindrance, and the people flocked to her; the entire city was beaming with the light of her God. Believing he could snatch her off the street was now out of the question. He put teams of his bandits out on the streets, trying to time her movements, but to no avail; she was untouchable as it stood.

One day, knowing that Sylvain was becoming impatient with his team, a lieutenant in his ranks came to him with an idea. Starting slowly, ensuring Sylvain that he had spent much time observing the dark-haired girl, he said, "She has a weakness."

Turning his head toward his ally, he leaned forward to hear more of this revelation. His confidant continued saying, "Her bodyguards know that she cares more for the suffering of these people than she cares for her own safety. Because of this, they are sworn to protect her every move." He paused and looked straight into Sylvain's eyes to see if Sylvain was tracking with him.

Seemingly stumped by the news, Sylvain said, "And what does that mean to me?"

Smiling, the lieutenant continued, "We must fabricate a dire situation where she is compelled to leave the compound in the middle of the night on her own."

Starting to smile, Sylvain said, "Go on."

His confidant continued, "I have observed her walking around the mission compound in the evening. She talks with others, but sometimes she is all alone. In those times, she is seeking solitude. She reads her Bible, stares up into the sky as if someone is watching her, and she bows her head to pray. At those times, because she is in the compound, her protectors are not as alert as on the streets. We just need a diversion to draw attention away from her and then present her with profound need. She is incapable of not going where a need is."

Loving the idea, Sylvain called his leadership team together to strategize the plan's workings. Surprised and wary of Brice's decision to move back home, Sylvain purposely left Brice out of the meeting.

Just as the team was gathering, Sylvain came up with a job he needed Brice to do. Unaware of the point of the meeting but well aware of the consequences of not following Sylvain's orders, Brice left the hideout feeling nervous.

Heading out in the dark, away from Sylvain, Brice glanced anxiously back, only to see Sylvain still standing at the back door, glaring menacingly at him. Brice looked back several times, but each time, it was the same. Enjoying this tactic, Sylvain finally stood up and then laughed out loud. As he did, he also took both arms and pushed them forward, motioning for Brice to be gone.

The last time Brice looked back, Sylvain had disappeared. Struggling with Sylvain's odd demeanor, Brice headed nervously into the dark. He could not help but sense that out before him, just around the next corner, an ominous fate laid in wait for him.

Unsure if this excursion was not Sylvain's plot to end his life, Brice looked in every direction, pulled his hat down tight on his head, and while confirming that his sidearm was in place, he set his sights and headed out into the dark and his destination.

Tonight, the evening seemed darker than Brice remembered. Vague lights from dimly lit dwellings fought to brighten his path, but he could not see anything clearly.

According to Sylvain's orders, he was to receive a package from a man who would meet him on a certain street at 10:00 p.m. As Brice stood on the corner of the meeting place, he began to sense he was being watched. As he tried to pierce the darkness before him, he found himself looking uneasily in every direction.

He was feeling so tense, he was ready to bolt, when out of the corner of his eye, just across the street from where he stood, there arose a pale red glow and a puff of smoke. In the presence of that eerie glow, the shadow of a person slowly emerged from the blackness and spoke to Brice, saying, "You look a little nervous tonight."

Not certain who this mystery person was or if he had made the proper contact, Brice clutched his side piece and said, "Sylvain sent me." Slowly, the ghostly apparition moved across the street and stood before Brice. This phantom figure took another drag from his cigarette, and as he did, his face was well lit up, and Brice recognized the man.

With the mood lightened, they chitchatted about the strained mood of the city and how much everything had changed since the dark-haired girl arrived, but soon, tiring of the doldrums and speculating on the viability of Sylvain's empire, the man reached from inside his coat and said, "Here is the package. Be very careful with this stuff." Then the man said, "Sylvain solicited me to procure this package, but I am warning you: remember, you never saw me or received anything from me. Got it?" Brice nodded his compliance, and with that, the man inexplicably vanished back into the cold dark night.

***

On the way back, Brice was somewhat relieved. The darkness was not so dark, but he could not stop but think, *Though I did not die at Sylvain's hands tonight, tomorrow is another day. I am foolish to think I can survive long working for this madman.*

Knowing that Sylvain did not trust him, Brice was forced to consider how to win Sylvain back. Entering the hideout with the package, Brice attempted to put a lift in his spirit and walked straight up to Sylvain and said, "Well, here is your package."

Appearing as if not to notice Brice, Sylvain continued to write on a notepad. Knowing better than to interrupt his boss, Brice remained silent but continued to hold out the package toward Sylvain.

Realizing they were at a stalemate, Sylvain slyly turned his head toward Brice and just stared at him. Not batting an eye, Brice continued to hold out the package. Slowly turning his chair toward Brice, Sylvain held out his hand and motioned Brice to come close with the package. Complying, Brice stepped within reach and placed the package into Sylvain's hands.

Looking down and into the package, a twisted smile etched onto Sylvain's face. Then, he looked up to Brice and said his first words, "Do you know what is in this package?"

It seemed strange at that point, but for some reason, Brice had never contemplated the contents of the package, so it was easy for him to say, without reservation, "I have no idea."

Looking Brice over, hoping he was lying, hoping to reveal the chink in his stoic retort, Sylvain said, "Are you sure?"

Shaking his head, Brice confidently affirmed his first answer and said, "Yes."

Assuming Brice was telling him the truth, Sylvain said, "Good, only those who are in need to know will know this secret."

This response from Sylvain was purposely humiliating and just another way to let Brice know he was no longer his boss's right-hand man and was on the outs. Hoping to change the subject, Brice said, "How did the meeting go?"

Almost juvenile in his response, Sylvain said, "Again, you will know when you need to know." At that, Sylvain looked hard into Brice's face and said, "Hey, there, family man, shouldn't you be getting on home to Momma?" With that, he dismissed Brice with his hand but smiled cruelly as if to say, "I am watching you."

* * *

Almost home, moving very slowly and in turmoil, Brice contemplated the predicament he found himself in. Scrutinizing his plight, he thought to himself, *Short of taking Sylvain out of the picture himself, I can see no way beyond this bondage to a lunatic.*

Brice did not know his bride was standing on the porch, and when he looked up from the depths of his darkness, he was startled, but then instantly, seeing her warm and smiling face, his sullen heart leaped for joy; only Alain could melt Brice's many burdens away.

Inside the house, he continued to hold her around the waist, and he turned her to him and said, "Oh, I am a blessed man; look at you." Then, out of nowhere, the thoughts of Sylvain crept into his bliss, and a frown nestled onto his forehead, displacing his peaceful smile.

Instantly noticing the change but careful to not overreact, Alain said, "Something on your mind?" Now that they were truly at peace in marriage, the only topic that could dampen this grace-filled revival was Sylvain's hold on their lives.

Looking up and trying to formulate a positive thought, Brice looked deep into Alain's eyes. Though the frown had left his countenance, the unbearable pain in his heart remained. Unable to conceal the deep sorrow, tears moistened his eyes. He stared at Alain, blinking several times, hoping to refrain from further emotion; humbled by the boldness of her spirit, Brice was forced to look away.

Gently placing her hands on Brice's cheeks, Alain caressed his face and tenderly elevated his head until he was looking straight into her eyes. The softness of her hands made his skin come alive, and he was shaking. Coupled with her loving touch, Brice found himself enraptured with the look on her face and the courage flowing from her soul.

Bound in this solemn moment and confident of their commitment to God and each other, Alain finally spoke, saying, "Do not fear, my darling; God will not be mocked. A man reaps what he sows." She bowed her head, and Brice followed. They prayed for God's protection and courage, trusting themselves to God's will.

CHAPTER 42

The entire region was being impacted through the grace of God and by the team God had specifically placed to serve Him there. Realizing God was doing more than they could ever think or imagine, Dr. Haji and the team were humbled and overwhelmed with all that lay before them.

Day by day, the numbers grew. These disadvantaged people did not need a sermon or a prayer meeting, but rather, the love of God pouring out into their midst and the flow of people pouring daily into the mission made manifest God's goodness.

In the family room just outside the dining hall, Dominique had placed a sign over the doorway leading out to where ministry began; it read, "In the same way, let your light shine before others, that they may see your good deeds and glorify your Father in heaven."[51]

Each morning before the ministry day unfolded, as they were leaving the family room, like a football team leaving the locker room, to begin God's work, all the team members, one by one, would jump up and slap the wall below the Scripture, saying loudly, "The day for you." It was like an army leaving for battle.

The team believed that with the local government and the militia groups now patrolling the mission area and the city streets, safety could be maintained. Still, Bella remained concerned that Dominique, being the main target, was vulnerable.

It did Bella no good to even bring the subject up to Dominique, so she, like the rest of the team, made it their priority to keep a careful eye on her; Dominique remained oblivious to anything except serving these people God put in their path.

It was apparent to everyone that God had singled out Dominique as his voice and instrument to bring his grace to this dreadfully needy people. As always, wherever she moved in the city or in the countryside, she was engulfed by crowds of these harassed and helpless people; they came from the furthest parts of the countryside to see this dark-haired girl who helped the lives of so many.

These everyday occurrences reminded Dominique of a scripture verse she had memorized, and as she saw the crowds surround her, the verse would materialize in her mind, playing to her senses, saying, "When he [Jesus] saw the crowds, he had compassion on them, because they were harassed and helpless, like sheep without a shepherd."[52]

The people could not get close enough to her, and they kept crowding in around her. Realizing the great need, Dominique thanked God, and then she put her hands up to get the crowd's attention. As she did, they became quiet and began settling in on the ground around her.

It was always a joy to see the people come at God's calling, but the team that traveled with Dominique, knowing the safety issues, had to be on alert. Having the crowd's attention, Dominique started the dialogue with what was always her first words, saying, in perfect French, "Why have you come today?"

Most of those in attendance were there because someone had shared with them the dark-haired girl and the good things the mission was doing to help the people. When she spoke, she said, "We are so glad you are here. God has sent us to help you." Hearing Dominique's voice, every eye became transfixed on her face. Then, as she always did, she would say, "God loves you," and with that, she would move from person to person, holding their hands, caressing their faces, and wiping the tears from their eyes.

This day started out like any other day in the ministry. With her touch and loving words, Dominique would soothe these hurting souls. In the meantime, the team would begin sharing all that the mission was able to do to help them, like meeting medical needs, supplying food and clothing, and providing daycare. When they had finished those details, the team would begin the process of moving those with the greatest need to the mission compound.

The Gospel message and discipling would be the natural outcome of the compassion the mission lavished on these needy people, which God had brought together by His sovereign hand.

Then, suddenly, Dominique heard someone calling her name, saying, "Dark-haired girl." This calling became louder and louder until Dominique stood up to see where the voice was coming from, and as this voice cried out again, Dominique turned to see a man holding his hand out to her while, at the same time, cradling his infant son with his other arm.

With tears pouring down his face, his eyes pleaded with Dominique to come to him. Due to the crowding of the people, he could come no closer to her. Looking around, Dominique realized she could not get to him either, but compelled to move, she focused her eyes on the man and started forward. Every eye was fixed on Dominique, and it became deafly silent.

With each step, the crowd began to make a way for her to move toward the man. Now, every eye was on the man, still holding out his hand, still pleading for her help. Never taking her eyes off the man, Dominique slowly closed the distance between them.

Then, she was there, and she reached out and took hold of the trembling hand held out to her. The crowds began to scramble so they could see what was taking place between Dominique and the man.

The man gripped Dominique's hand so tightly that it was painful, but what she felt was not her pain but the anguish of this desperate man. Taking her eyes off of the man's face, she looked down at the child and motioned him to hand his son to her.

The little boy, maybe two or three years old, was so thin, like holding fragile bones. With only a T-shirt covering his nakedness, Dominique took him into her arms. He was not conscious and so frail, but Dominique gently cradled him next to her heart; she could barely feel his heart beating, and she prayed, "Oh, sovereign God, see this little soul I am holding?" At that, she looked around and attempted to sit down. People had to move to make room for her to do that.

Once on the ground, she held him tighter and caressed the top of his head. She began to rock gently back and forth, and with tears streaming from her eyes, her mind took her back to the scene where she found the babies dying in the countryside, like black dots scattered on the bare ground. She said out loud in French, "Let the little children come to me, and do not hinder them, for the kingdom of heaven belongs to such as these."[53]

Staring down on to the needs of the one God placed in her arms, she prayed, "Oh, dear God, by Your divine plan, here and now, I hold this precious little one; take away his suffering." Knowing she was not the healer, she waited on the Lord.

Opening her eyes slowly, Dominique peered down on the gift wrapped in her arms, and as she did, the little boy blinked several times and opened his eyes, staring angelic up into her adoring gaze. He was not completely out of danger, but he was better, and an unspeakable joy tore its way into her heart, and the smile that only thanksgiving can generate broadened onto her face; that glorious joy was uncontainable, and the entire assembly began to cheer.

For those present, this scene was staggering. They had never seen this kind of compassion, this outpouring of love. No one could look away. The father of the boy just stood in silence. Then, Dominique stood up, taking the hand of the father and still holding dearly his son; she turned and began to walk toward the mission compound. Like the parting of the sea, the throng of people made way for Dominique and the man to pass through. This mass of bodies, not knowing where she was leading, fell in behind them and followed the dark-haired girl.

It was like a shepherd with their sheep; this large throng of broken mortals silently followed Dominique to the help that God had orchestrated for them to know. The rest of the team had nothing to say and walked silently as well. Occasionally, though, they would look up at each other, but all they could do was shake their heads and marvel at the will of their God happening before their eyes.

This kind of mass movement could not go unnoticed. In proximity, Sylvain sat in a chair next to a building. Seething at what he had just observed and troubled by the sway Dominique wielded over these people, he stood up in disgust.

It was less about jealousy and more about losing control of this very lucrative criminal venture he orchestrated. He watched as she led away what he considered his people. This only intensified his hatred for Dominique. His temper flared to the boiling point, and cursing loudly, he kicked his chair into the street, turned, and walked away, mumbling under his breath.

* * *

Realizing a lack of time was forcing his hand, Sylvain called all his minions together. The time had come to put an end to the one causing him such a financial drought. The plan had been accepted by Sylvain weeks ago. Except for Brice, the entire evil band was aware of their role: they were just waiting for the command to engage.

Because it was easy to observe the mission compound, especially at night, a sentinel was perched atop a hill, with a clear view of entire compound. Two other assailants were given the responsibility to place the explosives, which Brice had delivered to Sylvain, strategically in one of the buildings, which Dominique frequently walked by in her evening strolls around the compound.

Seeing the way clear, the sentinel gave the go-ahead to his accomplices. They snuck into the compound, crawling over a small brick wall, and delivered the device, cloaking it in the library. With the device in place, the plan could commence the next evening.

* * *

The next evening after a debrief of the day's ministry with Dr. Haji, the team members were encouraged to find solace and fellowship among themselves, a rest to recoup for the day ahead.

After lounging peacefully in the fellowship hall, the team usually broke up into smaller groups for closer fellowship. The common scenario for Dominique, Bella, and William was to head out to the lounge chairs scattered around the compound and take in the refreshing evening air.

Being very cognizant of how unaware Dominique was, not only her strength in ministry but also her inability to appreciate the danger she lived in daily, William and Bella made a pack to watch where she refused to look.

Though they all loved the ministry and what God was doing, small talk and laughing together was a welcome respite from the daily grind of serving others. It isn't left up to her, but Bella is a natural at keeping things light. It usually is not long, in their time outside together, that Dominique and William are busting up, laughing at their wonderful, funny friend.

After some refreshing gaiety, Bella stopped; her face took on a very ominous look. This caught William and Dominique's attention, and as they watched, wondering what she was thinking, her countenance slowly changed again, and a sly little smile replaced the other tenuous expression. She looked up at both of them and said, "I miss my mom."

That statement put a damper on the light comradery, and they all became solemn and silent. No one spoke for several minutes, and they did not look at each other but rather looked out into the dark evening, which at that time seemed to gobble them all up.

Finally, looking up and making eye contact, Dominique said, "I love you, guys; I don't know what I would do without you here with me." It didn't seem appropriate to respond, but both Bella and William smiled warmly at their friend as if to say, "Yeah, diddo."

Standing up and stretching while looking up at the evening sky, Dominique said, "I think I will take a short stroll around our little park here." Having said that, she added, "Good night." And she sauntered off into the pale night.

It would not be odd to see Dominique, on an evening stroll, unhurriedly moving around the compound. This was her ritual, the time she sought out her Lord and Savior. The compound is well-lit, and as she moved on her excursion with God, William and Bella could see her as she slowly passed under the bright lights, into the shadows, and then back into the light along her journey.

Watching Dominique walk so leisurely, so peacefully away, they didn't speak, but each marveling at the same time, the freedom with which this godly woman maneuvered life. Even at a distance, Dominique's radiance held their sway. From their elevated position on the back deck of the cafeteria, they were seeing with their own eyes God's grace and power manifest in the life of their dear friend.

Sometimes, she would stand for minutes in one place, evidently praying. The next moment, she would return from the shadows with her hands raised high over her head, praising God. Then, all alone with the master of her life, with her head tilted back, she would spin in circles and laugh out loud. There was no posturing in this soiree with the Lord, only the purity of their relationship. It was as if no one else existed.

Reaching the library and knowing that William and Bella never took their eyes off her, Dominique turned, and with a big smile, she waved at her watchmen of the night. Bella raised her hand to wave, and then they turned to look at each other. They were amazed at the sight before them; they smiled at each other.

Instantly and without warning, turning the dark night as bright as the day, the library exploded into a gigantic inferno.

The shock of the explosion rocked the chairs where William and Bella sat. Startled beyond reason, they could only turn away in terror. Shading his eyes from the brightness of the blast, William eventually turned to stare out to where Dominique just stood, but she had vanished into the heap of burning material that used to be the library.

Turning also in horror, Bella peered out to where her best friend had once been; she saw only the carnage of a thousand fires burning out of control. She took in a deep breath and let out an excruciating, eerie, and tortured scream, in which Dominique's name could be heard piercing into the now quieting foray of destruction.

Panicked and still screaming Dominique's name, Bella came alive, and her body sprang into action. Not even thinking of the danger, she sprinted to the place where she last saw her best friend. Right behind her and screaming Dominique's name as well, without losing sight of where he last saw her, William struggled to maneuver through the many fires that blocked his way to the spot where he last saw Dominique.

Both reached the spot where they had last seen Dominique standing, and there were only heaps of burning debris. Screaming her name and spinning in circles, they frantically looked in every direction but to no avail; she was not to be found.

Looking at each other, they both had the same expression on their faces as if to say, "Where did she go?" Just moments ago, they were smiling and laughing with their dear friend, but now only horror etched their faces, and they stared in disbelief. Just then, other team members began to arrive at their side; they all looked helpless and lost; they didn't know what to do.

Gaining some control of his senses, William tried to calm everyone down and said, "Listen to me, Dominique is missing. We last saw her standing right here before the blast. Let us spread out and comb every inch of this area until we find her." With that being said, they spread out, calling her name and looking under every pile of what used to be the library.

From the hilltop, the sentinel had a bird's eye view of the explosion. He was perplexed, as the goal of their mission was to capture her alive. With what he saw, he knew there was no way the dark-haired girl could have survived such an ordeal.

Worried about what to say to Sylvain, the sentinel raced back to the hideout. As he hurried back to his boss, he said to himself, *I would not want to be the person who detonated the bomb that killed that which should have been Sylvain's hostage.*

* * *

Awaking in severe pain, which emanated from most of her body, Dominique slowly sat up. She looked around and was at a loss; she had no idea what had happened to her; she could not hear due to her ears ringing intensely. Trying to rise, she felt a sharp pain in her abdomen and was forced to sit back down. Clearing her eyes to see, she looked down at her stomach, and embedded there was a large splinter oozing blood.

Afraid to pull the splinter out, she tried again to raise to her feet, and as she did, she reached up to rub her throbbing head. She was surprised to feel a large bald spot over half of the area she rubbed. Pulling her hand down from her head, she looked at her hand. There in her palm was only a frail pile of black ashes that used to be her hair; the hair that remained was mostly singed as well.

Finally on her feet, she tried to survey her damaged surroundings; she had no idea where she was. Everything looked the same, just piles of burning debris. The blast was so intense that it threw her a great distance from where she stood at impact. A large section of the library wall acted as a shield, which probably saved her life, carrying her to the back side of where the library used to sit.

Careful to keep her balance, she took a few small steps. The only light available emanated from the burning carnage, and in that dim light, she took stock of her physical condition. Half of her clothes were burnt off, and she could see and feel large burns on a great deal of her body.

Just as she was about to cry out for help, she heard a terrifying scream just outside the compound wall, which was now mostly destroyed. The scream happened again, and Dominique, though struggling to move, made an effort to seek out the distressed voice. She thought she could pinpoint the area where the scream came from, and she headed right for it. The scream happened again, and she knew she was getting close. She cried out as best she could, "I am coming to help you."

She was not dissuaded by her own suffering from the burns, but her heart burned for the one who cried out for help. Just as she thought she had to be right on the place where the screams occurred, two men jumped up from the tall grass and grabbed Dominique. They put a black bag over her head, picked her up under the arms and at her feet, and ran feverishly away from the compound.

From the pain pouring out from her broken body and the fear of being kidnapped by strange evil men, Dominique wanted to scream, but just as her voice rose up in her being, a peace came over her, and instead, she prayed, "Oh, my Father, You would never leave me or forsake me; please help me now."

When the kidnappers finally arrived at the getaway van, they hurriedly threw the van door open and roughly tossed their captive down onto the unyielding metal floor. Using a rope, they tied her hands behind her, and they put tape over her mouth. They both jumped into the van and sped away from the crime scene.

The captors were traveling so fast and on a very bumpy road that Dominique just bounced back and forth on the floor of the van. At one point, she became lodged between a heavy metal object that was traveling with her and the sidewall of the van.

Her head kept bouncing up and down, striking the metal object, and she thought she would pass out from the beating.

CHAPTER 43

Meanwhile, not fully understanding why Sylvain wanted him at his headquarters, Brice reluctantly stepped into the room. Mulling around the room, several other high-ranking henchmen were looking nervously at Sylvain; one man had Sylvain's attention, and they were whispering something to each other.

Not trying to bring attention to himself, Brice settled inconspicuously into one of the lounge chairs. When Sylvain and the man finished their conversation, Sylvain turned to survey the room. He and Brice instantly made eye contact. Walking over to Brice, Sylvain placed his hand on Brice's shoulder and said, "Now you will be in the loop."

Fearful of making any comment, Brice just stared up at Sylvain and remained silent. Walking confidently back to the center of the room, Sylvain said, "Without Brice, we would not have our captive tonight." Looking at Brice, Sylvain continued, "Yes, that package you retrieved for me has put the dark-haired girl in my clutches; thank you."

His mind began to swirl, and Brice could feel his heart rate rise. He looked again around the room, trying not to overreact, and just as he was ready to ask Sylvain what he meant by being thankful for his help, he heard a vehicle come skidding to a halt outside the headquarters.

Everyone rushed to the door to see the package delivered. The two captors aggressively pulled Dominique from the van, dragging her into the building; they threw her on the floor and slammed the door behind them.

Unable to move due to confinement and the searing pain, Dominique lost consciousness. She woke sometime later to the sound of voices in the room with her. One man seemed in charge as he questioned several other men. He continued to talk to his underlings as he walked close to Dominique. As he arrived next to her, he said, "Let us see what we have here." Then, lowering down, he pulled the bag off her head and the tape from her mouth.

He was shocked at first; instead of the tall and beautiful young woman he had sought for so long, there, before him, lay only a woeful-looking burnt and beaten wretch. Due to the brutal ride to Sylvain's headquarters, Dominique's face was completely bruised and bleeding in places. What wasn't burnt off her head, the rest of her long dark hair was severely singed.

Looking at her with pure disdain and gloating over his prize, he mocked her, saying, "Who is your God now?"

Dominique struggled to raise herself up on one elbow, and knowing God's comfort, she looked her antagonist straight in the eye. Unshaken, she said, "The same God who has always been with me is here with me now."

Hearing her response, Sylvain lost all control, and he spat on her, swearing at her with every word. Then, he stopped his ranting and glared at her for at least ten seconds. After that time, he turned to walk away but then spun back sharply and ferociously kicked Dominique squarely in her injured stomach.

With the splinter injury still throbbing, this assailing blow forced all the air out of her lungs, and she could not breathe. She began to panic, and as she did, memories of the Durand incident rushed back into her thoughts. The fear was about to overtake her, but then a peace that she could not really understand rested in her soul; she heard Jesus's very words: "Fear not, I am with you. It is Me; I will never leave you or forsake you."

Catching her breath and to Sylvain's amazement and chagrin, she calmly looked up at him and said, "My God is still here." At that, he ordered two of his lieutenants to secure her to a chair.

As they violently strapped her firmly to the chair in the most magnificent way, Dominique began to sense the Lord's presence; she looked up and thanked Him and remained staring up to heaven. Unable to withstand this scene, Sylvain raised his hand, ready to slap her in the face, but as he started that movement, Dominique looked down from God's presence and directly into Sylvain's eyes; he became frozen where he stood and began to shake.

His men in the room were shaken as well as they saw their austere leader falter before this fearless foe. Stepping back from Dominique, Sylvain reached for his sidearm and pointed it at her face. His hand was shaking so aggressively that he could not keep aim on his target.

Looking around at his men, who were watching this strange scene unfold, Sylvain began to feel unsure of their support, so he swore at them and said, "Do you want to see your boss truly in action? Do you want to see what I am capable of?"

With his hand still uncontrollable, he pointed the shaky sidearm again into Dominique's face. Leaning forward and narrowing the distance between the two of them, he scowled at Dominique and said, "Unless you renounce your allegiance to this God of yours, I am going to shoot you right in the face."

Not moving or showing any sign of fear, Dominique was tranquil, and she said, "No, I will not."

Screaming now at the top of his lungs, Sylvain said, "Don't you know that I have the power to let you live or let you die?"

Looking triumphantly at her assassin, she quoted Jesus before Pilate and said, "You would have no power over me if it were not given to you from above."[54]

Out of the corner of her eye, Dominique could see the other men in the room nervously shuffling around. She could clearly see Brice standing anxiously against the wall, and the man standing next to him seemed very familiar. Then, she remembered him. He was the one who was with Brice the day he tripped over their book cart. She recalled that he gruffly grabbed her arm and told her to be careful or something might happen to her.

This man began to move out and behind Sylvain. Having been called out by Dominique and unaware of the movement behind him, Sylvain raised the pistol again, but this time, his hand was stable, as if empowered by some unseen force.

Then, with a sly smile on his face, he looked insane to Dominique. Sylvain said, "Goodbye, darkhaired girl." As Sylvain was spewing his evil farewell, a brilliant white light illuminated the room. Brighter than any light ever shown, right in front of Dominique, there before her in the fullness of His eternal glory, stood Jesus holding out His arms, smiling. She could not look away from the acceptance of His smile, the only smile of infinite love, the beginning and ending of love. Then, the Creator and Sustainer of all love reached out to take her hand and said, "Well done, good and faithful servant… Come and share your master's happiness!"[55]

Finally, the discovery of all meaning, she knew as she was known. While Jesus was still speaking, Dominique began to slowly rise. Just then, a shot rang out. Instantaneously, a second shot was fired. In the midst of all this destruction, the restraints that held Dominique earthbound were released, and she was lifted straight into the embrace of her Savior's arms. They latched hold of each other. Weeping in the joy of His presence, she was finally holding that which she had hoped for. Then slowly, Jesus leaned back, and with His nail-scarred hand still embracing the back of her head, He looked at her as no other could and said, "Welcome home."

When the gun smoke cleared the air, a tragic and surreal depiction lay sprawled out before everyone. On the floor, dead, shot in the back by the other man Dominique identified earlier, lay Sylvain. The first shot struck Sylvain, but before he dropped to the floor, he was able to fire his weapon in Dominique's direction, striking her in the chest. With blood everywhere but no longer bound in the chair, Dominique leaned to the right, slouched over, dead.

Fear and trepidation held Brice frozen in his tracks; his logic reasoned this scene could not really be taking place, but overriding his fear, Brice quickly ran to Dominique and pulled her gently from the chair down onto the floor; there, he cradled her head in his lap.

Remaining calm, the man who shot Sylvain told the rest of Sylvain's gang to disperse. He told them to run because there would be a bounty on all their heads, and they should leave the area as soon as possible. With that said, they all rushed out and away from the memory of what had been Sylvain's tyranny.

With tears flowing down his cheeks, Brice was fixed on Dominique's face. Her eyes were still open, and she had a peaceful smile on her face. Wanting to scream for his friend to run for help, Brice knew there was no need; the dark-haired girl was no longer with them.

Clinging miserably to Dominique, not knowing what to do, Brice started to sway back and forth. He pulled his head up and back, and he let out a mournful cry for help, saying, "Dear Jesus, what have I done?"

Misery beat down on his soul as he contemplated his role in her death. Guilt and remorse plagued his thinking; he was forced to remember back when he first saw the dark-haired girl. He was on a mission for Sylvain to scare her away from her mission.

He continued to reminisce. He knew he could never be the same after he faked tripping over the book wagon. Truly caring about his stumble, he remembered the dark-haired girl taking hold of his hand to help him up. It was like yesterday, he remembered clearly. As he stood up from the fall, Brice looked directly into her eyes, and he was embarrassed; he could not let go of her hand nor look away from the compassion in her eyes.

Still remembering his first exposure to her, he was unable to turn away. Brice finally forced his hand free from hers and turned to leave. He was only about ten steps away when he was forced to look back at her again, and as he did, there she was, still smiling and looking right at him; she waved, and Brice turned to run away.

Brice was never the same following his first encounter with the dark-haired girl. It was not long after that day that he turned his life over to God and went home to his wife and children, but now, she lay dead in his arms, and he was to blame.

* * *

After hours of looking for her, under every pile of rubble, the mission team stood in the middle of the compound, dumbfounded; there was no trace of Dominique. As they were staring at each other in disbelief, heads slowly began to hang down as remorse overtook the team. They knew not what to do.

Unable to cope with this devastation, Bella screamed out, "No! No! She's here; keep looking; she has to be here!"

Just as she started to exhort the group to begin the search again, Dr. Haji reached over, taking Bella by the shoulders, and gently said, "Dominique is not here. This attack was formulated to keep us distracted while the fiends behind this evil made away with Dominique! She has been abducted."

Strained by the exhaustion and overwhelmed by Dr. Haji's cold finality, everything became harshly cold; unable to stand any longer, Bella slumped slowly to the now cold ground and wept woefully.

At this point, one by one, the entire team joined Bella, falling into the closest person's arms; they sobbed helplessly. With an intense anger welling up in William, he was unable to cry; he was furious, more furious than he had ever been before. Placing his hands on top of his head, he started to turn in circles. He could not get enough air to breathe; he began panting, gasping for relief. Finally, he was able to take in a deep breath, and with his lungs full, he leaned down, then raised his head again, and with a blood-curdling cry, he screamed to God, "Why, my God? Why!"

That plea, bouncing off the remaining compound structures, echoed throughout the entire compound, coming back again and again. Startled, every head turned toward the pain and stared motionless; then, there was complete silence.

CHAPTER 44

There were times since Dominique left on mission when Aunt Colleen would sense a deep foreboding for her precious niece's safety, but then, she would calm herself and give those feelings to God, chastising herself for lacking faith in God's protection.

She and Marie spoke daily to each other, wondering what Dominique was doing with her days. Even though they kept in the loop concerning how the mission was going, there was always a trepidation that comes with being a mother and an aunt.

One day, Marie would falter and need encouragement; the next day, it would be Colleen who needed buoying. Either way, the sisters were closer now than they had ever been. There was no news of furlough possibilities, so each day, they were called upon to pray together for the things their eyes could not see.

At the beginning of the mission excursion, Marie silently held Colleen responsible for Dominique's absence, an absence of prolonged misery. Slowly, due to Dominique's great faith, Marie began to understand that Dominique made her own decisions and there was no one to blame. Still, with Dominique being so young and distant, the grievous burden of motherhood left her doubting God's providence, and her prayers became more like bargaining with God than trusting him.

There was an extra burden on the sisters, and they felt it fruitless to seek support from Thomas and the boys. Like men, they all seemed unphased by the plethora of negative possibilities that could plague a young woman living in a very savage land.

During Marie's weakest times, Thomas would keep things light and upbeat. This was his way of encouraging his frail bride, but it also allowed him to lie to himself about his own uncertainty concerning Dominique's safety.

One day, after months of Dominique being in the mission field, Colleen was caught off guard by an anxiety; no matter how she prayed for release, it would would not dimmish. Afraid to confide in Thomas or Marie, Colleen sought out Chase to help reduce her lonely suffering.

Always the optimist, Chase encouraged his aunt to trust God and not to worry. For a time, Colleen was able to take Chase's advice as good news. Then, the anxiety returned with a vengeance. She didn't want to start over with Chase, so she kept these dreadful premonitions acutely to herself, which began to take a toll.

Again, the shared turmoil brought the sisters very close; it was hard for either of them to get something past the other. One day, after discerning an ongoing solemnness in her big sister, Marie decided to feel her out and get to the bottom of what seemed like a prolonged languishing.

Mornings around breakfast had become their special sister time. They would chat about all things, but inevitably, the things most important to the family and Dominique would dominate their thoughts.

The conversation slowed, and while taking a sip from her coffee, Marie looked across to Colleen. Seeming entranced, Colleen stared coldly at something on the floor. Slowly reaching across the table,

Marie lay hold of Colleen's hand and said, "Are you okay, dear?"

Realizing she was caught in this melancholy state, Colleen froze for a second. With this constant dread growing in her soul, she did not want to have this conversation with Marie. Then, with a thin smile on her face, she slowly turned to her little sister and said, "Oh, I have not been sleeping well; I am a little tired, that is all."

The look on her face did not tell the truth about what was going on inside her heart, and Marie sat up in her chair and said, "Come on, Sis, you have been like this for some time now; what is going on? Tell me."

Not expecting this kind of emotion to surface but needing someone to share her pain, Colleen was surprised. She put her hand over her mouth and looked deeply into her little sister's eyes. Tears dammed up, and she could not see clearly; then the dam was overwhelmed, and wet agony flooded down onto her reddening face.

Rarely seeing Colleen emotional, Marie did not know what to do or say. She gripped her sister's hand tightly and said, "Oh, darling, whatever is the matter?" Still unable to take her hand away from her mouth, Colleen reached for the dish towel on the table and began to swab the tears away.

It was scary to see her big sister this way; Marie was baffled and felt helpless to intervene. Turning again to Marie, Colleen shuddered and said, "Oh, my dear, I dare not tell you of my misery unless you become part of it." This caused Marie to sit back in her chair and shake her head as if to say, "Where are you going with this?"

Gaining some composure, Colleen leaned into her sister, hoping to close the space to which Marie had just escaped. Still holding hands, Colleen began saying, "I have not wanted to share these feelings with anyone, but they are just too unyielding. You have caught me, and I can hide no longer."

Looking away, processing how to share such news, Colleen took a deep breath and said, "Since the day God drew me to Himself, my fears always end up in His hands, where they belong, and peace has been the outcome. I have continued to leave my fears in God's hands, but for some reason, recently, they come back to me in chilling ferocity."

Aching for her sister, Marie leaned in again close, a show of support, but still confused, she thought, *This is my big sister; she does not get shaken*. Wanting to help, she feigned an understanding nod.

With thoughts rushing everywhere in her mind, Colleen turned slightly away from Marie and began again to stare coldly into the next room. She stayed there staring for what seemed like forever to Marie; then, she turned back. Sadness gripped her countenance, her lip quivered slightly, and she said to her sister, "My fears, my unsettledness have to do with Dominique."

At that moment, completely taken aback, without a hint of foreknowledge, Marie weakly said, "What?" The look on Marie's face became placid and expressionless; then, her eyes seemed to sink into their sockets. She lowered her head, and a darkness began to overshadow their morning get-together.

Hoping to calm Marie and the situation, Colleen said, "Please do not think I have any clarity on what has taken my joy, but I have prayed for God to take away these awful thoughts, and they are still with me. I trust that He will never leave us or forsake us, but I am still unable to shake these tremors."

Trying not to freak out and wanting to stabilize the fervor of what she just heard, Marie said,

"Okay, we know Dominique has chosen to trust God and follow His lead; therefore, Dominique is where God wants her, and remember you told me, 'If she could be in a better situation God would have her there.'"

Affirming her sister's critique, Colleen said, "That is true, and there is no doubt, but, to add to your rebuttal, still, I do not understand why I remain in constant turmoil."

Finally, coming to grips with the truth of her sister's plight, Marie said, "What exactly are you fearing? What are the details?"

Despairing to even think the words, Colleen let out a sigh and said, "I am sensing something has or is going to happen to Dominique, and I tremble before God, pleading His mercy."

CHAPTER 45

With the explosion knocking out the power, the only remaining light in the compound emanated from the still simmering embers, which used to be the library. In the fading red glow, the entire team remained frozen, startled, still focused on William. The final echoes of his excruciating shriek still filled the space around them.

The scene was otherworldly. Black smoke, covering the whole compound, billowed in huge plumes everywhere. As the wind lazily carried the black smog to and fro, the remaining buildings in the compound appeared as ghostly phantoms, lacking substance.

Due to the search through the rubble, most of the team, their skin and clothes, were mired with dark blotches of soot. With tears running down each face, looking as if they all had mascara tears, a motley collection of broken souls needed comfort. Once again, they began to reach out for each other.

Still sitting hapless on the scorched ground, Bella wiped her face; she was so broken she could not see. Slowly coming to her feet, she stumbled and fell into William. Not sure what was happening, but concerned about Bella's stability, William caught her and held her up straight.

As their eyes met, terror etched and outlined each of their expressions. Moving his head back and forth slowly, William was trying to keep his composure. Holding her with his hands, he could feel Bella begin to tremble. Trying to form words, Bella slowly opened her mouth to speak, but nothing came forth.

There was no realm for either of them where they could escape the aching, not only in their hearts but down to the depths of their souls; needing what they knew not, they quickly embraced and held tightly to each other.

While most of the team had been searching for Dominique, a small fire crew that worked on extinguishing the flames had most of the sizeable fires under control. This tidy but spent group finally was able to join the rest of the mourners; they could not help but discern that they had joined a steely assembly of suffering.

Overseeing the stark calamity laid out before her and not knowing what else to do, Dr. Haji prayed, saying, "Oh, God, You who hold all things together, what destruction You have allowed…" She paused, hoping to capture proper thoughts fitting for the King of the universe, but realized there were no words. Completely fragmented in her thinking, she lifted her head to heaven and screamed in her soul, "What do I say to the team?"

Looking back down, she realized she had screamed it out loud. So, there before her, every set of eyes focused strategically her way. At that point, she remembered what a good friend once told her about leadership. Those words came back overwhelmingly: "You know you are a leader; when you look behind you, someone is following."

Humbled by the situation, Dr. Haji looked mercifully at the flock and said, "I have no comforting words for you. I have no understanding of God's will here. I am bewildered and in shock, yet we all know the one who said, 'I will never leave you or forsake you.' He said, 'I am your strength and shield.' He has also said, 'Trust in the Lord with all your heart and lean not on your own understanding; in all your ways submit to him, and he will make your paths straight.'"[56]

Gazing over the throng before her, she waited and, for a full minute, said nothing. It became an excruciatingly long minute, then she lifted her chin and said, "Now, it is time for each of us, individually, to come to grips with what has happened; how you do that is up to you." Looking sternly at each person, she said, "It is nearly midnight; we will meet together again as a group at 2:00 a.m. in the cafeteria. This time is for you to be alone, and I do not want to see anyone in the cafeteria prior to 2:00 a.m. Is that understood?" She looked warily over the team and said, "See you then." Quickly turning, head down, she walked briskly away, disappearing into a smoking fog.

* * *

Continuing to hold Dominique, Brice tried to wipe the blood from her face with the sleeve of his shirt. To no avail, the red hews had become hardened. As stark as the blood mask was, it could not hide the terrible bruising all over her head.

Looking deep into her hollow gaze, Brice was lost as to how to fathom the pleasant smile and the peace that still etched her face. Knowing it had to be done, but not wanting to never see those eyes again, he reached slowly down and gently closed her eyelids.

Standing nervously next to Brice, Sylvain's assassin reached down and touched Brice's shoulder; Brice was unable to feel his presence. Then the man said, "Hey, she is dead, and we have got to get out of here." Not budging from where he sat, Brice began to rock back and forth, and he wept miserably. The man moved over in front of Brice and spoke harshly at him, saying, "You can not be here when the authorities arrive; please come with me."

Unnerved, Brice continued to rock gently. Giving up, the man said, "Have it your way; I am out of here." Unperceptive to anything except that he was holding the girl who had led him to Christ, which changed his life completely, saved his marriage, and made him finally whole. He thought to himself, *What do I do now? She is gone… How can I just leave her here?*

That thought stuck a nerve, and for the first time throughout this surreal and ghastly ordeal, Brice began to think. He said to himself, *I can do something.* And he scooped Dominique up into his arms and ran rapidly toward the mission compound.

He was surprised how little Dominique weighed; she was light, like a feather in his arms, and he ran with all the strength that God was now energizing in his soul. It was a trek to get back to the compound, but he did not feel safe carrying this precious cargo in a vehicle that the authorities might detain. There was very little light, but he ran unhindered, briskly, light of foot, down the tattered road to the only destination fit for God's "dark-haired girl."

There was no remorse; Brice remembered her brave smile through the pangs of torment, the peace on her face even in death. It was as if God was there with her, welcoming her home. This made him run faster, and he rejoiced in the life that she lived; he looked up and praised God for allowing him this moment with her.

As he came closer, Brice was surprised that the compound was not lit up; in fact, he could see no trace of it. Undeterred, still running as fast as he could, he lifted his head and prayed for God's help.

Then, he began to see what looked like candles all throughout the cafeteria, so he headed straight for it. He still could not see clearly the compound boundaries, so he slowed his pace to make sure he did not stumble with so dear a package.

The burning embers of the library remains helped him see a broken-down section of the compound wall, and he rushed through it. As Brice was moving along through the piles of debris, the awful truth dawned on him, and he said to himself, "This explosion is what injured the dark-haired girl."

Slowing to a walk, he could see many people sitting and talking throughout the cafeteria. It was still very dark. Not sure what to do, he carefully walked up to the glass double doors.

He stood there looking in; it was a busy scene inside: everyone was engaged, and they all appeared frantic and displaced. Then, one of the team turned to the entry, and there, seeing Brice cradling a collapsed person in his arms, they were forced to take a second look. The light coming from the many candles strewn around the room lit up like a canvas, their woeful presence in full view.

The team, unnerved by the stoic picture that stood in the dark, peered helplessly through the glass doors. The one who first saw the duo standing there screamed out, "Hey, look." And she pointed to the door.

Alarmed, everyone turned in the direction she pointed. Though they were brainstorming how God was going to bring their Dominique back, that quickly went on the back burner as many raced to the door to help the unfortunate person lying in this man's arms; this was the priority. This was why they came: to help these dear people.

Several of the medical staff arrived first and threw open the door. They did not know who Brice was, and asking no questions, they quickly sprang into action and relieved the injured person from Brice's hands.

At first, he did not want to let go, but this was why he came, and he lightly gave her into their arms. No one knew the injured person's status, so instantly, they began evaluating her condition.

Obviously, she was beaten and burnt beyond recognition, and there was no pulse. Coming to the situation a little later, Bella stared out the door at Brice, and he stared at her. "I know this man," she said to herself. Still staring, Bella watched the man's face twist slowly into a mask of despair, tears cascading down his face.

Due to the medical staff, Bella was unable to see the injured person. Neither the people helping nor the onlookers watching the medical staff could identify this battered soul, but after considering the sorrow etched on the face of the man standing at the door, Bella moved slowly toward the center of attraction. She peered over shoulders and arms until she could see the cold, pummeled face of this frayed soul.

Dr. Haji also came up close to see what she could do to help. She told all the onlookers to move back and give the team room to work. Except for Bella, the team moved back to give room.

Looking up from the body to Brice, Bella nearly retched. She held her trembling hand over her mouth; gloom filled every nook of her soul. A panic emitting from her thoughts worked its way down into her heart, and under the strain, her body convulsed; she could not breathe. Bending over slightly, she began to take air into her lungs, then at capacity, tearing through her vocal cords, a hoarse and mournful scream launched into the somber, still night air.

Startled by the outburst, every eye turned toward the sound. Riveted now on Bella's face, without understanding, the team stood motionless, awaiting what they could not comprehend. Terrorized by what her eyes had revealed and not wanting to, she could not help but peer down again at the tragedy lying on the floor before her, and Bella whispered, "Dominique…"

* * *

Hard to believe such a moment could exist; spiritual devastation bore its way into every crevasse of every soul. They were left to contemplate the grievous horror of God's perfect will for Dominique's life. Though they all knew God's ways are not their ways, only questions filled their nearly faithless intrigues; no one dared an attempt to explain away God's purposes.

Having nowhere to turn, not even God, Bella was dreadfully astray. Not wanting even to be in the presence of anyone, to make eye contact with anyone, to even open her eyes, she bolted from the scene and locked herself in her room, alone, life being beyond her willingness to fathom.

Unable to speak with Bella and without remedy, William found himself calm in the early morning, walking around outside. Taking in the obliteration he saw before him, uncertainty sought to estrange him from the point of his being; now, the mission seemed flawed and unsustainable.

Realizing he was alone, the only person outside, William felt a welling up of emotion, a sensation of complete loss. Looking down, he began to quicken his step. Though he did not have any direction to flee, he wanted to run out of the compound and into wherever the pain was not.

Just as he began to bolt, he looked up, and someone caught his eye; he focused and soon realized, sitting on top of the compound retaining wall, staring right at him, was Dr. Haji.

Looking for someone to blame for his turmoil but also hoping to eliminate any contact, William turned quickly aside. Several steps away, hearing Dr. Haji softly say his name, he stopped abruptly in his tracts.

With his back to Dr. Haji, he froze, stifled at his predicament. He had many thoughts, but paramount to all, flight overtook his senses. He had never been here before, so uncertain about what lay ahead and, at the same time, not caring about it, William took up a stoic stance.

Laid before him was a crossroads, and the broad way of flight seemed the best option. He pictured Dr. Haji peering out at him. Carefully, he began to allow his heart allegiance, and even as stubbornly as his pain held him, a crack in his protective armor forced him to turn toward the narrow road and his soft-spoken intruder.

CHAPTER 46

Weary with remorse, Dr. Haji shared with William the dreadful call home and the ensuing havoc that arose from so few dutiful words. Most answered the phone with little thought concerning the intention of the call. There is no predisposed hallowing of every call, that is, until the message of the call defiantly fractures what our hearing is capable of absorbing.

Unable to stand without support, still holding the phone at arm's length, Marie leaned against the pantry door. Numbness did not allow her to weep; fear and depression fogged her senses; hopelessness made her unable to concentrate, but boiling up from within, a defiance that forced its way to the surface of her being arose. She didn't feel weak any longer but strong in her complaint. Standing up straight, looking without seeing, her grip on the phone intensified, and with everything in her, she crashed the phone ferociously to the marble floor, breaking it into pieces.

Hearing the phone crash on the floor, Thomas hurried to the noise. The scene laid out before him was bizarre. There, standing over a demolished telephone, stood his bride; still looking at the destruction on the floor, she turned to see the intruder entering her world of despair.

Not knowing what to say, mystified by the look on Marie's face, Thomas lifted his hands and shrugged his shoulders, signaling, "What is going on here?" Staring pitifully at Thomas, shattered by the news just delivered to her, Marie lifted her hands and said the worst thing a mother could ever say and a father could ever hear. She said, "Dominique is gone." With that, Marie collapsed to the kitchen floor, sobbing terribly.

Unsure of what he just heard, Thomas sprang to the side of his disheveled mate. He lifted her up to hold her in his arms. Shaking uncontrollably, Marie allowed Thomas to embrace her tightly. Lifting her face up to make eye contact, Thomas looked deeply into Marie's frenzied and swelling face, saying, "What has happened?"

***

Trusting in the provision of God, the entire family remained grateful for the sustaining protection over Dominique's life on mission. That was until the fateful day of her death.

At the first news, no one could function. The grieving process took a heavy toll on any sanity, deluding even reason and scriptural perspectives from God's point of view. After struggling with the Lord for some time, Colleen became aware of a bitterness she had never known, not even when her husband left her for another woman.

This bitterness came to haunt her in her sleep and all her waking hours. Hopeful prayer became listless, vague words spoken to no one. This reminded her of those early days in Christ when she seemed to lose hope, and Chloe helped revive her faith.

Though this was different, Colleen knew that God could not be brought to account on any sovereign purposes for His people's lives; rather, this bitterness took hold because Colleen felt God did not sustain her broken heart; she could not help herself, let alone anyone else.

In this great moment of need, Colleen knew it was imperative for her to be there for Marie and Thomas—in fact, the entire family. This weight, though, became like a millstone hung around her neck; Colleen could not muster a positive thought for anyone.

One day, in the dismay of this major family dysfunction, Chase came to visit his aunt, Colleen. Still in school and struggling himself with balancing this loss and academics, Chase felt it was time to share with Aunt Colleen the peace he had come to concerning Dominique's death.

It had been so long since he looked into the amazing, spiritually tough eyes of his aunt, Colleen. He recalled the hope that she lived before a watching world, the hope that had raised many spiritually devastated souls searching for peace and also sustained him so often.

Opening the door, Colleen attempted to put on a good front, but Chase saw it for what it was, and Colleen knew he saw through it. Hugging him, she lingered, taking in love she so missed; she did not want to let go.

Always the optimist, Chase stared deep into his precious aunt's eyes and said, "You know, it has been too long since we have been at peace together." Taking a short step back, Chase had surprised her, and Colleen felt instantly uncomfortable.

Bowing her head slightly and looking up, she said, "What do you mean?"

Smiling softly but saying nothing, Chase continued to stare at his beloved aunt, which just intensified the uncomfortableness of the moment.

Looking down again, Colleen could not keep eye contact. It was a lot like being caught red-handed at something she knew was wrong but could not stop the doing. When she finally did look up, she knew she was found out, and her face was flushed, and tears welled up in her eyes.

Remaining still, looking lovingly at his aunt, Chase reached over and grabbed her hand. Rushed with emotion and finally letting go, Colleen softly said, "How do we do this?"

Gripping his aunt's hand even tighter, he finally spoke, saying, "By living your favorite verse. The verse you taught me to live by."

It was overwhelming and scary at the same time as Colleen let her favorite verse float through the recently vacant caverns of her mind. Then, slowly closing her eyes, she allowed the verse to roll down to her heart, and she said God's words in her mind: *I will never leave you or forsake you.* Instantly, alarms went off, and she felt the barrenness and the legitimate turmoil of feeling truly forsaken.

The peace Chase had just observed gracing his aunt's face quickly became a foreboding nightmare as an ugly frown coursed across her countenance. Undeterred, Chase raised his voice, and nearly screaming, he said, "Aunt Colleen, say it out loud!" At Chase's command, Colleen opened her eyes, and there, staring deep into her eyes, determined to win this battle, Chase said it again, "Say the verse out loud!"

As if her tongue would not work, Colleen just stared at Chase, and he gripped her hand even tighter and said, "Aunt Colleen, where was Jesus as Dominique was being tortured and murdered? She never knew a moment like that, and at that moment, Jesus was at His best for her." Putting his hand on Colleen's shoulder, Chase said, "Jesus was speaking to her, closer than we are now. Telling her, "Well done, good and faithful servant; come join in your master's joy. He never left her, and He will never leave us only to mourn."

With unbroken confidence, Chase continued to peer longingly into his aunt's eyes, then he said, "What do you think?"

A billion things rambled around in her mind, but she could not look away from her nephew. Colleen thought to herself, *Chase does not know how broken I am, how lost I am, how lonely I am…*

Then, while thinking, something happened: an awareness overtook her; the same awareness since becoming Christ's child had always sustained her, and she said to herself, *Jesus does know.*

Still staring at Chase, the frown on her face, dissipating quickly, was replaced by a shy and wistful smile. With her expression changing exponentially, she lifted her eyebrows. Then, Chase finally saw what he was waiting for: his aunt's steely, bright, and shining eyes—eyes of faith, eyes of wisdom. And in a very quiet and peaceful voice, she said to Chase, "He would never leave Dominique, and He will never leave us."

***

After Dominique's passing, many of the mission team, overwhelmed with grief and doubt, struggled with remaining faithful to the call. They would not have endured were it not for the daily comfort ministered to them by Dr. Haji. With her ability to see, despite their circumstances, God's hand in all that had taken place, they were renewed with a peace that passes understanding and a joy that rekindled their commitment to serve.

The mission did move on; in fact, it began to thrive like never before. With the criminal element eradicated and the testimony of Dominique's faith in God, a testimonial to her tender love and care, more young followers of Christ were inspired to join the ranks, and with God using the evidence of Dominique's faith, missions giving quadrupled.

The local community, along with the mission team, decided to have a memorial commissioned to honor Dominique. Leaders from many of the townships gathered to consider what to say about the dark-haired girl, words that would best express her God's gift to their families.

The mission itself, along with the Meuniers and Dr. James, came together to have a bust of Dominique sculptured. They planned on sending the bust to the mission, along with a large stone, where the inscriptions of the African people could be added below the sculpture.

The memorial was placed just as you enter the gates in the center of the compound. A round raised concrete platform with several steps was built to accommodate small groups to view the sculpture comfortably. The bust sitting on the inscription stone lifted to the height of a grown man so that when you looked at it, you were looking right into the eyes of an astonishing likeness of the dark-haired girl.

Along with a caption of a woman holding the hands of children, followed by a crowd, walking into the mission compound, a mason etched the eulogy in French, and it read:

Dominique (of the Lord)

If there is no enemy within, the enemy outside can do us no harm. She touched us with the fire of God and set us alight.

Thank you, our dark-haired girl.

Not just dreading traveling to the States for Dominique's memorial, Bella was more fearful of the invitation to stay with the Meuniers prior to her returning to the mission. Bound by the shackles of being the one who invited Dominique on mission, Bella felt small, fragile, a vagabond of faith, and fearful of Dominique's family ire.

All of what she knew about God's sovereign ways, which she had passed on to Dominique, became feeble as wisdom for her. Spending quality time with William, at first, bolstered both of their strength, but when alone, she fell back into consternation, remorse, and drudgery.

Pouring over all her memory verses and pleading with God for His peace, Bella still found no relief. Finally, it became scary; for the first time since receiving Jesus as her Savior, Bella experienced the pangs of being alone.

It was like in the book of Job when Satan came before God. God said to Satan, "Have you considered my servant Job?" God handed Job over to Satan and said, "Do what you will." She thought to herself, *Has God made a deal with the devil, saying, "Have you considered My servant Bella?"*

Going back over all the counseling sessions she had with hurting people, she thought she would find answers, but to no avail; she surmised, saying, "I am unable to counsel myself."

One day, befuddled and broken, Bella began to weep. Like a great storm gathering, finally reaching its preeminence, the vortex swirling overhead, she could hold up no longer; falling on her bed, she broke. She wept without meaning; she wept bitterly; she shook, sobbing violently, and could not stop.

That sorrowful cleansing continued for over an hour, not thinking, just raw emotion; then, with an easing and ebbing of fear, anger, and despair, she sat up in her bed. Looking around for anything that could be hope, she focused on a letter from Dominique pinned to the wall. The letter she had sent from home after her breakdown at school.

From her bed, the bold type was all she could make out, and it read: *"Bella, my dearest and best."* Oh, to hear her voice, Bella jumped up to the letter and pulled it off the wall. Taking the letter, she returned, sitting on the edge of her bed. She couldn't take her eyes off the words in bold: *"Bella, my dearest and best."*

She looked up as if to heaven and closed her eyes. Thinking she could have no more tears, still one more tear rolled down from her swollen eyes onto her cheek, and she reached up with her finger to gently feel the moisture and the memory of her dearest friend.

Pausing to cherish the moment, an inkling of peace peeked into a belligerent soul. Needing more, Bella looked down to study the letter; it read:

"Thank you for loving me. I was ready to die, to escape this world that had forsaken me. Jesus saved my life, but He used you, Bella, to bring me to Him and eternal life. I would have never known the love of God except for the love of Bella. I am more than saved, Bella; I am at peace for the first time in my life, and I am kept, and I know God will never leave me nor forsake me. Thank you, thank you, my dear. I love you."

It was like being together again, so Bella read again, quickly down through Dominique's love letter. Finishing the lines and longing for more, Bella turned the page over, but there was no more Dominique.

Holding the letter close and trying to relive the moment, Bella closed her eyes again and went back over the words in her mind. What stood out to her was surprising; it was not "Bella, my dearest and best" but the peace Dominique had, knowing God would never leave her or forsake her.

Still holding the letter, Bella felt a warming in her chest. What she had just read was a confirmation that God was working in Dominique's life through her. Then, she reasoned and said to herself, "But she is dead." Anger began to rise again, but the anger was short-lived, and she heard in her heart the only voice that made a difference: "My ways are not your ways."

At first, she wanted to answer back, saying, "Yes, and that is why I am angry," but she held that thought, only saying the word "yes." Hoping to hear more, Bella felt her countenance succumbed. In that pause, Bella realized she and her Lord were communicating; it had been so long.

Holding on to the word "yes," which she spoke, a holy fear was taking up in her, and she trembled, not just in fear but in awe. Staying quiet, Bella humbled herself and slowly came to her knees, leaning on the bed, and said, "Forgive me, Lord, I have sinned against You; speak, and I will listen."

Remaining silent, Bella strained to hear that still, small voice. Right at the end of straining, as if she could hear no deeper, she heard these words spoken softly: "I am able to do more than you think or imagine. Dominique is safe with Me and My child; I will never leave you nor forsake you."

All that truth, which could have moved a mountain, moved wonderfully into Bella's soul; it was like God speaking audibly His scripture into her heart. Unable to move from her knees, whispering, Bella said, "Thank You, Lord, even if for only a short time, for allowing Dominique into my life."

***

Among the immediate family, a small memorial service for Dominique was in the works, but there was no stamina or desire to make it happen. Several times, Chase tried to get the family grouped up for a session to plan, but there was little energy put forth. He expected as much from his big brothers; they were aloof and pagan. Dad was willing but lost as to how to help. Chase did not, however, expect apathy from Aunt Colleen and his mom. He concluded: sorrow had anesthetized their ability to move forward.

Sensing that taking off time from work would be the best thing he could do for his family, Thomas attempted to man up and lead his grief-stricken clan, but to his chagrin, he found his expansive home vacant and more like a mausoleum than a haven to heal.

Rarely finding someone to talk with, Thomas would walk from room to room and talk out loud to himself. The macabre, eerie echo would speak back only grief, not a comforting conversation.

One morning, while preparing a breakfast, which he knew no one would eat, Thomas looked up to see Chase walking toward him. Instantaneously, they both smiled; this bond was all that remained of civil cordiality, and they nurtured the connection.

Coming up behind his dad, Chase gave him a big hug, then backed away. That hug made his day; Thomas turned toward the comfort and said, "Good morning, Son." Having just retrieved the mail,

Chase smiled back at his dad and began to thumb through the correspondence.

He found one letter that caught his attention, and he said, "Hey, Dad, here is a letter from Dr. James." Excited to hear from his good friend, he took the letter from Chase and opened it. Looking up at Chase, Thomas said, "I wonder why he didn't just call."

The note was written on official William James letterhead. The note was brief, expressing Dr. James's desire to have a memorial for Dominique at the school. Not elaborating in great detail, Dr. James asked if Thomas would come to the school to brainstorm the service particulars.

Looking up at Chase, who was now chewing on the breakfast bacon, Thomas said, "Hey, do you want to go to William James with me? It appears that Dr. James wants to plan a memorial service for Dominique, and he needs our input."

CHAPTER 47

With the memorial just days away, Bella found herself trusting, once again, God's providence and protection. Having just arrived at the Meuniers' home and receiving a warm welcome, Bella still discerned a dark overshadowing of Dominique's family.

Even though they had received her warmly and always prodded Bella for stories of Dominique's mission adventures, they never came close to asking about that fateful day. After every gathering, except for Chase, the entire family would shuffle off to a room to be alone.

At first, Bella thought Chase was just putting up a good front, but after several days of conversation, she realized he was legit; he had come to peace with Dominique's death. With Chase being so forthright, Bella found spending time with him was a time of healing for her. Time with Chase, away from the house, was also refreshing, like a sabbatical. A departure from the more rigorous, needed grief management with the rest of Dominique's family.

This time with Chase helped Bella understand how very close he and Dominique were. Being just twenty-two years old, Chase was close enough to her age that they could be comfortable talking about anything.

One of the greatest intrigues for Bella was how spiritually mature Chase was. Everything, to him, was about God working out His sovereign will into the lives of His children. She was surprised but refreshed as well with his willingness to talk about God taking Dominique home.

At one conversation regarding Dominique, Chase said to Bella, "Do you know the best way to tell when God is completely embedded in a person's life?"

At first, Bella thought, *Maybe this is a quiz*. Turning her head slightly and then looking up briskly, she said to Chase, "Please tell me."

With that response, in that demeanor, Chase was caught off guard and thought to himself, *That question probably sounded arrogant and condescending*. Looking down and then back up, Chase could not help but focus on Bella's beautiful green eyes, eyes so pleasing that he nearly lost his train of thought.

Then, he caught himself and said, "What I mean is this: believers can walk right up on their own to the portal through which trials must be endured. Beyond that threshold is the unknown, that which is humanly impossible to grasp, but it is not until we cross that egress, and the bottom drops out from underneath our ability, no net to catch us, that we truly experience God and what His perfect will for our life is."

Contemplating the depth of his reply but embarrassed by Chase's steel stare, Bella carefully surveyed Chase's face, looking blankly back at him. With Chase still gazing at her, she was not sure if his stare was a subliminal continuation of the dialogue or something more intimate, but she could not look away.

Not fully aware of how much time had passed, just staring at each other, Chase finally bowed his head, looking down on the floor. Then, without making eye contact, he slowly raised his head, scanning the room as if remembering Dominique as a child; with him chasing her around the house, he said, "My sister knew God well."

Basically, Chase was describing Dominique's declaration of independence from the world's hold, which took place long before her death. Finally, it became clear to Bella. She let the warmth of her thoughts ramble wonderfully into the small, dark, light-yearning fissures of her soul.

Bella knew the truth; Dominique finally reached a place where her weakness was embraced rather than shunned. She understood that weakness tells us that we are unable, but that weakness, understood, propels us into supernatural strength. Bella's final summation became clear to her, and she said, "Scripture is faultless, and like the Apostle Paul, Dominique could experientially say, 'When I am weak, then I am strong.'"[57]

Remaining silent, with both Bella and Chase looking vacantly in different directions, summarizing together what just happened between them, Chase turned his head toward Bella, and at the same time, Bella turned to face Chase.

Continuing to peer into Bella's eyes, Chase's stern countenance began to melt away. He looked at Bella as if seeing her for the first time. This emotional exchange, with Dominique as the focal point, had amended their connection. Unable to control it, a shy, gentle smile formed on his lips, and at the same time, he reached out, touching Bella's hand, saying, "Thank you for being my sister's friend."

Looking at Chase's hand covering hers and not sure how to decipher this pleasant diversion from what they had just experienced, Bella sensed a mini-invasion of her space and instinctively started to pull her hand back.

Looking quickly down and feeling the warmth of the two hands gently touching, Bella fought the impulse of flight. Feeling who knows what, she left her hand motionless, covered by Chase's hand. Uncomfortable and comfortable at the same time, Bella's mind raced through all of the scenarios of what this could mean, and she looked back up again into Chase's pleasing image.

Time stood still, but then, bodily nearness, coupled with their trance-like stare-down, Chase and Bella simultaneously jumped as if they had just awoken, startled by the moment.

Embarrassed, Bella pulled her hand back and looked swiftly down into her lap. You could cut the air with a knife, and they both knew something had just happened. Ever the gentleman and encourager, Chase tenderly touched Bella's shoulder and said, "I have really enjoyed this time together; you bring such calm to the violence of our shared suffering."

*　*　*

With the memorial taking place the next day, the entire family, Bella included, all sought solace alone and a time of reflection. Still angered with God, Marie remained held up in her room. Realizing the futility of an attempt at consoling Marie, both Thomas and Chase retreated to their own contemplations of grief.

Like any mother grieving the loss of their child, Marie went in and out of despair and reason. The devastation of guilt-wracked her soul. She thought to herself, *If I had only been able to dissuade her from going on mission, she would be here with me today.*

Being beyond crying, Marie felt anger was all that sustained her. Sensing she was all alone, her suffering forged into a deep darkness, which allowed no light to enter. Going over and over in her mind, all the cherished memories of Dominique's life did not help. In fact, those memories now unyieldingly stalked her mind, leaving her despondent of life and hopeless.

Finally, dread-consumed, exhausted, Marie could no longer keep her eyes open, but just before she left being awake, she lingered, pondering all these things in her heart, and she said out loud, "God, someday, I hope I can forgive You for being who You are."

* * *

The encounter with Chase left Bella confused but aware that something took place within the brief connection that they had just shared. She also felt Chase gave her a new confidence, a new boldness to talk about the one they both loved so dearly. She was no longer anxious about sharing her thoughts of Dominique. In fact, she was excited and ready to share her dear friend with whoever would listen.

Being scheduled last to speak can be unsettling. Having just a moment of fear, Bella wondered if she would have anything new to offer after all the praise that would be leveled on Dominique. Sure that no one knew Dominique as she did, she relented of her fear.

The William James auditorium is a splendid venue for any special gathering, especially a celebration of life. Dr. James knows excellence, and that was his commitment to Dominique and her family.

After a brief opening statement, praising Dominique for her exceptional life and the enduring honor of her attending this school, Dr. James raised up a plaque over his head and said, "As an example of a life well lived for Christ, this plaque will hang in the halls of this school for our posterity."

Turning to read the plaque, he pointed to the inscription and said, "The only inscription on this plaque will be 'Dominique.' This is being done purposefully for the day when someone asks, 'Who is this plaque honoring?' Then, those who know will have opportunity, once again, to honor God's humble servant."

In a very emotional few minutes, Mrs. Martsen gave her testimony of how Dominique had changed her life. How she had opened her eyes to see what really loving students meant. Looking up to heaven, she said, "Thank you, Dominique," and she left the stage, weeping.

Next was Mrs. Allard. She had much to say in the way of praise, but the thought that caught everyone's heart was her final statement. She ended by saying, "Is it so strange to believe that Dominique lived as if God exists?"

Standing in front of a very large crowd of students, friends, and loved ones, Bella took a deep breath and began her eulogy: "I did not think it possible for a human to be so Christ-like. It is humbling and amazing to have lived with such a one."

Looking out over the audience, Bella stood tall and lifted her voice, saying, "Without having been there to observe it, there is no way you could understand the humble life she lived before God. How God spoke through her and how God moved through her, how people clamored to be near her. There is no other way to explain it: God was magnificently exposed through her life.

"Most of us here can still remember a young girl who walked the halls of this campus when not so magnificent. She came here selfish and broken, a miserable soul and angry at the world. She did not want to be here. She did not know what she wanted. What she did know was how to inflame with strife every relationship in her life. Being her roommate allowed me a privileged, first-hand exposure to a woeful but wonderful girl named Dominique…"

These memories caused Bella to pause; holding back the tears, she looked down. Collecting her composure and her thoughts, she looked up again, and while scanning her audience, a big smile broadened across her face, and she said, "How could we forget Dominique's first day back at school? Do you remember? She and I had just been feuding in our room. While I left for the cafeteria, she was still in bed and had ten minutes to not be late for breakfast. She arrived for breakfast, completely disheveled. Her shoes were untied; her long black hair was everywhere on top of her head. Her uniform shirt was untucked, and when she burst through the doors into the cafeteria, there we all were, staring in disbelief."

Finishing that statement, Bella smiled again and said, "Do you remember?" Perusing the audience again, she slowly peered back and forth, attempting to catch every eye; she said again, "Do you remember?"

Getting back to her story of Dominique's arrival at the cafeteria, Bella continued, "When Dominique came through the doors, there we all were, every eye on her and, for the most part, fixed in disdain."

For effect, Bella paused again. Then she went on, saying, "Of course, shocked by her reception, Dominique stepped back and leaned against the wall next to the door. She was horrified as she surveyed the searing eyes of her peers. It was evident she was not well, and she bowed at the waist, staying in that position for some time. Faithful as always to the need, Mrs. Allard came up carefully to Dominique and took her by the arm, slowly walking her to her table to sit down."

With a bewildered look on her face, Bella said, "Why have I shared this story with you today?" Using another pause for effect, Bella finished her thoughts, saying, "That was the day when all who truly understand the mercy of God realized God had brought Dominique to our school to love and protect.

"The results of that love and protection worked its way out to the mission field and into the lives of thousands of lost and needy souls. Our school and the relationships forged here were an integral piece in God's plan for Dominique's grand purpose. What was her purpose? 'For her, to live was Christ, and to die was gain.'[58] She believed what God said in Revelation 2:10: 'You will suffer persecution, be faithful even to the point of death, and I will give you life as your victor's crown.'[59] She was faithful to the point of death and received her victor's crown.

"You are asking yourself, 'How did she do that? How could I ever do that?'" Bella looked out sharply, back and forth at her listeners; her green eyes turned dark, and she leaned forward and then paused. You could hear a mouse running down the aisle. The gathered were silent, frozen in anticipation of what was next, and then Bella whispered the word, "Fearless." Those who had ears to hear turned to look at each other, unsure of what they just heard. Bella paused to let that hushed utterance sink in. It was only a whisper, but the message thundered, echoing back and forth throughout the auditorium. For effect, she said it again, "Fearless… She knew no fear. Dominique believed God when He said, 'I will never leave you or forsake you.' Because Dominique did not fear, in God's army, she was a force to be reckoned with, and she had the victor's crown…" Bella ended with this verse: "The Spirit you received does not make you slaves, so that you live in fear again; rather, the Spirit you received brought about your adoption to sonship. And by him we cry, 'Abba, Father.'"[60]

***

Leaving the stage, Bella felt awkward, burdened by how impossible it was to be tasked with explaining the life and circumstances of someone so distinct as Dominique. She paused to look back on the audience, now exiting the auditorium. Saddened, she said to herself, "How many heard today? How many are capable of faithfully walking in relationship the way Dominique did with her Savior? She is an elite child of God."

Entering into the foyer, Bella felt disconnected. She was not part of the family, and an eerie loneliness crept in and over her. She checked her thoughts and decided she was just melancholy; besides, she really did not feel hospitable at the moment.

Considering the throng before her, Bella focused on the least uncomplicated exit and maneuvered her way toward the outdoors. Finally reaching her goal, she stepped out into the warm sunshine, paused to appreciate God's goodness, and then turned left to walk down the sidewalk that ran alongside the auditorium.

Not sure of anything except God's goodness and His purposes for her, Bella picked up her pace and braced herself for what was ahead.

To her right, she could see many people still meandering around the auditorium. It felt good to be alone in this transitory moment of time. She looked down, then looked to her right again. The crowd was dwindling away. Then, in the shadows of the building next to the auditorium, about a hundred feet in the distance, she saw a solitary figure walking in the same direction and at the same pace as she was.

She stopped to get a better look at the person shadowing her. When she stopped, this phantom person stopped as well. Due to the shadows that covered the sidewalk, Bella was unable to make out her escort.

Turning to walk again, Bella started off, but this time, she remained staring at the phantom across the way. As she started to walk again, the apparition began to walk as well. Becoming somewhat alarmed by her companion's action, Bella stopped, raised her hand, and yelled across the distance, saying, "Hey, is there something I can do for you?"

Still riveted on the person in the shadows, Bella raised her other hand as if to ask, "What do you want?" At that, the silhouette of her shadow person raised their hand and started to walk out into the sunlight.

As the ghostly image became exposed by the light, Bella shook her head and dropped both hands. There, standing with a wry grin on his face, stood Chase. He raised his hand again and called out, saying, "Just wondered if you needed a lift back to my house for the reception."

Never looking away, they both began to move slowly toward each other. Happy that this stocker was everything but dangerous, Bella smiled boldly and said, "I was hoping to see you. Why were you hiding?"

As they came within about ten feet of each other, they both stopped, and Chase said, "I was not sure you wanted to be disturbed. I watched you leave the building; it appeared you were distracted."

Lowering her gaze, Bella attempted to get hold of her emotions. She looked up again, but before she could speak, Chase said, "You spoke so wonderfully today; thank you for taking the time to get to know my little sister so well. Our family will be forever in your debt."

Not sure if any response was humble enough or if the whole family truly did appreciate her friendship with Dominique, Bella just stared at Chase. As she did, she began to fancy the likeness of Dominique in his face. His dark eyes and hair, his almost alabaster skin. She had not noticed this before; it was uncanny.

The silence between them became awkward. Chase had nothing to say, and Bella was without words herself. Knowing they were more than just acquaintances running into each other at a memorial, Bella finally mustered the courage and said, "What now? I am just a mournful missionary adrift in eternity, and what about you? What is next?"

Coming to grips with the significance of Bella's question, Chase answered, saying, "Interesting." He paused, then said, "Missions are very important to me. My sister was a missionary as well; in fact, my dad is on the board of directors of that same mission. I have prayed for that mission since my sister began considering the mission."

Not sure Chase understood the significance of her question, Bella considered stating the same thing another way. As the words began to coalesce in her mind, Chase began closing the distance between them. He came closer until he was standing right in front of her.

With Chase being in such close proximity, Bella became tense, and the thoughts she had prepared to clarify her earlier question quickly evaporated from her mind. They were so close; all Chase could do was stare; he was fixed on the most beautiful green eyes he had ever seen.

Lost in his mind, Chase rambled as he thought to himself, *Bella's eyes are not just eerie green but nearly translucent green, aided by the tiny freckles outlining her sculpted nose.* Chase was mesmerized. It finally occurred to him he had been holding his breath; embarrassed, he let out a rush of air.

On the other hand, Bella was trapped gazing into Chase's dark black eyes. She was familiar with these eyes, reminding her of a love lost. This memory settled in, and her countenance began to change; she asked herself, *What are you doing?* Unable to hold eye contact any longer, Bella started to look away, but while commencing to look away, Chase's eyes moistened, and Bella's gaze locked again.

Thoughts were bursting everywhere, and Bella felt her skin start to tingle. Finally, aware of where he was and who he was with, Chase reached with his left hand for Bella's right hand. He guided his fingertips gently to caress only the tips of Bella's fingers.

Overwhelmed by emotion, Bella's eyes started to blink. This fragile blinking was so adorable for Chase; a broad smile overtook his stoic stare, and he said, "I have been made aware that you have some very strict rules for dating."

ABOUT THE AUTHOR

When my phone rings, it says, "The best dad ever." My name is Stacey, and I am his daughter. Robert Holliday is my dad; let me tell you about him.

My dad served in the army for two years. After that, he married my mom, and they are soon to celebrate their fiftieth anniversary. I am their only child, and they spoil me. In the early seventies, he performed in a Christian light rock band. They made an album in 1977.

After failing miserably as a business owner (do not worry, he agrees with me), he fulfilled his lifelong dream, enrolling at Multnomah Bible College, where he received his bachelor's degree in Christian education with a pastoral minor.

Loving children of all ages, thrilled to be a teacher and a principal, he began a nearly twenty-year career in Christian education. His final occupation was the most difficult for me. As a hospice chaplain, hundreds of his patients would pass yearly, but he loved ministering to the elderly. His day was filled with praying and singing songs to these most needy people. Now, he leads worship at our small North Idaho church.

Life is hard, but God is good. Recently, my dad was diagnosed with stage four prostate cancer. We rejoice that he is in remission, and he believes God just slowed him down a little to give him more time for writing.

Finally, my dad loves hunting and the outdoors. His health is limiting him in that exercise; he has replaced that passion with another, loving my grandson. Their excursions make him tired but overjoyed, but most of all, my dad loves Jesus, my mom, and me.

ENDNOTES

1. Hebrews 13:5 (NIV)
2. Luke 1:13a (NIV)
3. Luke 9:57–62 (NIV)
4. John 14:6 (NIV)
5. John 3:16 (NIV)
6. Hebrews 11:6 (NIV)
7. Romans 3:23 (NIV)
8. Romans 6:23 (NIV)
9. Matthew 4:17 (ESV)
10. Luke 13:3 (ESV)
11. Luke 9:59b (NIV)
12. Hebrews 13:5b (ESV)
13. 2 Corinthians 10:4–5 (KJV)
14. 1 Peter 3:15b (NIV; paraphrased)
15. Luke 9:22–24 (NIV; brackets added for clarity)
16. James 1:2–4 (NIV)
17. Hebrews 11:1 (KJV)
18. Genesis 1:1 (NIV)
19. Psalm 19:1–2 (NIV)
20. Romans 1:20 (ESV)
21. Psalm 14:1 (NIV)
22. Philippians 2:13 (NIV)
23. Acts 17:26 (NIV)
24. 2 Corinthians 10:4–5 (NIV)
25. Galatians 5:17 (NIV)
26. Romans 7:20 (NIV)
27. Romans 7:23 (NIV)
28. Romans 7:24b–25 (NIV)
29. 1 John 1:9–10 (NIV)
30. Psalm 23:1–4 (NIV)
31. Luke 18:29–30 (NIV)
32. Luke 9:57–62 (NIV)
33. 2 Corinthians 5:17 (NIV)
34. Matthew 11:28 (NIV)
35. Philippians 1:21 (NIV)
36. 1 John 1:9 (NIV; paraphrased)
37. Psalm 96:1–3 (NIV)
38. Philippians 2:17 (NIV)
39. 1 Corinthians 9:24–45 (NIV)
40. Proverbs 3:5–6 (NIV)
41. Isaiah 41:10 (ESV)
42. Matthew 10:19–20 (NIV)
43. Galatians 2:2a (NIV)
44. 2 Chronicles 16:9a (NIV)

45	Ephesians 6:19 (NIV)
46	2 Timothy 4:1–2, 6 (NIV)
47	2 Timothy 4:7–8 (NIV)
48	2 Corinthians 10:4–6 (NIV)
49	Ephesians 2:6 (NIV)
50	1 Peter 2:23 (NIV)
51	Matthew 5:16 (NIV)
52	Matthew 9:36 (NIV)
53	Matthew 19:14 (NIV)
54	John 19:11a (NIV)
55	Matthew 25:23 (NIV)
56	Proverbs 3:5–6 (NIV)
57	2 Corinthians 12:10b (NIV)
58	Philippians 1:21 (NIV; paraphrased)
59	Revelation 2:10b (NIV; paraphrased)
60	Romans 8:15 (NIV)

Printed in the USA
CPSIA information can be obtained
at www.ICGtesting.com
LVHW081407071224
798534LV00016B/69